Praise for

THE DAMNATION GAME

"WILL FRY YOUR EYES OFF! Keep the lights on."

—Larry King

"A DELICIOUSLY SCARY TALE. . . . Barker's brilliantly literary work has raised horror to a level of excellence it has rarely reached before."   —Whitley Streiber

"ORIGINAL AND MEMORABLE . . . engrossing . . . disturbing. . . . Horror mavens who enjoy violence and harrowing imagery will find plenty of both here. But there is more to *The Damnation Game* than gore. This story of a supernaturally powerful man who can resurrect the dead probes the many varieties of corruption."   —*Publishers Weekly*

"A MASTERLY NOVEL . . . a thrill a minute."

—*Chicago Sun-Times*

"A TOUR DE FORCE of gruesome supernatural horror . . . startling, hard-hitting, graphic . . . brilliantly executed."

—Fantasy Review

"WILL HOLD YOU IN ITS SPELL. Barker has a keen knack for ripping the skin off every detail and exposing the horrors lurking just below the surface. . . . Captivating and original."

—*South Herald Tribune*

"A WRITER OF STUNNING IMAGINATION. . . . With his artist's eye for detail, Barker instills a mythic quality into his vision of hell."   —*The Atlanta Journal & Constitution*

BOOKS BY CLIVE BARKER

NOVELS

THE DAMNATION GAME

WEAVEWORLD

THE GREAT AND SECRET SHOW

THE HELLBOUND HEART

IMAJICA

EVERVILLE

SACRAMENT

GALILEE

COLDHEART CANYON

MISTER B. GONE

THE SCARLET GOSPELS

SHORT STORIES

BOOKS OF BLOOD, VOLUMES ONE TO THREE

IN THE FLESH

THE INHUMAN CONDITION

CABAL

FOR CHILDREN

THE THIEF OF ALWAYS

ABARAT

ABARAT: DAYS OF MAGIC, NIGHTS OF WAR

ABARAT: ABSOLUTE MIDNIGHT

ARTWORK

IMAGINER, VOLUMES ONE TO EIGHT

AUTHOR WEBSITE: WWW.CLIVEBARKER.INFO

THE
DAMNATION
GAME

CLIVE BARKER

BERKLEY
NEW YORK

BERKLEY
An imprint of Penguin Random House LLC
penguinrandomhouse.com

Copyright © 1985 by Clive Barker
"Introduction" copyright © 2002 by Clive Barker
Excerpt from "Perseus in the Wind" by Freya Stark,
reprinted by permission of John Murray Ltd.
Excerpt from *The Hour Glass* by W. B. Yeats, reprinted by
permission of Macmillan Publishing Co.
Penguin Random House supports copyright. Copyright fuels creativity,
encourages diverse voices, promotes free speech, and creates a vibrant culture.
Thank you for buying an authorized edition of this book and for complying with
copyright laws by not reproducing, scanning, or distributing any part of it in any
form without permission. You are supporting writers and allowing Penguin
Random House to continue to publish books for every reader.

BERKLEY and the BERKLEY & B colophon are registered trademarks of
Penguin Random House LLC.

ISBN: 9780593334973

Sphere Books edition / 1985
Ace/Putnam hardcover edition / May 1987
Charter edition / July 1988
Berkley mass-market edition / November 1990
Berkley trade paperback edition / May 2021

Printed in the United States of America
1st Printing

Book design by George Towne

To
J. R. G.

ACKNOWLEDGMENTS

My thanks to Mary Roscoe, who worked tirelessly to type this manuscript and still found time to offer a host of articulate criticisms along the way: also to David T. Cunningham, who typed up a number of later additions. Amongst the readers whose enthusiasm and insights were invaluable I must thank Julie Blake, John Gregson and Vernon Conway. I am also grateful to Douglas Bennett, who engineered an unforgettable prison tour for me, and to Alasdair Cameron, who commissioned two plays to keep me in spaghetti while I worked on the book. Last—though far from least—my thanks to Nann du Sautoy, and also to Barbara Boote at Sphere Books.

CONTENTS

Nor yet exempt, though ruling them like slaves,
From chance, and death, and mutability.

—SHELLEY, *Prometheus Unbound*

INTRODUCTION

The year was 1983, and there were new horror novels on the shelves every couple of weeks, or so it seemed; many with covers and titles and ideas that directly echoed covers, titles and ideas from the man who had lately changed the way horror novels were written, auctioned, marketed, and read: Stephen King. Luckily (entirely by chance; I can claim no great visionary skill in this) I had started my writing career with three linked volumes of short stories, the *Books of Blood*, thus separating myself out somewhat from the pack of eager pretenders to King's throne. However, though the *Books of Blood* had been very well received—not least by Mr. King himself, who had been career-makingly kind about them—they had sold slowly, and there was no doubt in either my mind or that of my editor that if I was going to make a more substantial mark on the literary world, and earn myself more substantial remuneration in the process, then I was going to have to turn my hand to a novel.

Twenty years ago a horror novel was a *long* work of fiction. The models for bestsellers in the market (with a few exceptions, such as *Carrie*) were substantial works of storytelling: four hundred, five hundred, six hundred pages long. I, therefore, knew from the outset that I would not be penning a slim little volume. This would need to be a weighty tome if it was to compete with the leaders in the field. That was about the only point of similarity. I wanted the tome and style of my book to feel completely unlike the mighty American novels that dominated the marketplace.

I began with a treatment. It was called *Out of the Empty Quarter*, and, if I remember correctly, I was quite the peacock about it. Unfortunately my then editor, Barbara Boote, did not share my enthusiasm. She very politely said no. In hindsight, I think she was probably correct in her judgment. In my hunger to be unlike any of the other novelists on the shelves I had pushed the envelope too far. *Out of the Empty Quarter* did not really resemble a horror novel, which was, after all, what I had been engaged to write.

Little in a writer's life goes to waste however. A few years later, as I put together my first *fantasy* novel *Weaveworld*, I went back to the material that I had developed for *Out of the Empty Quarter* and folded it into the new book. It fit beautifully. Barbara had done me a great kindness, dissuading me from using the Empty Quarter prematurely.

A short aside. My fascination with the Empty Quarter (which is a vast area of the Sahara Desert renowned for being one of the most barren wastelands on Earth) came through the work of the first non-Bedu to cross it. His name is Wilfred Thesinger, and he was one of the most ambitious explorers in history. He had also written a number of books about his explorations, accompanied by wonderfully loving photographs of his desert comrades, but by the time I came to write *Weaveworld* his books had slipped out of print, and I had to dig hard through all the secondhand bookstores in London to find them.

One day, however, visiting my new editor at what was then Harper and Row, I passed an office in which an old and weather-beaten man was sitting alone at a table piled high with large format books, meticulously signing them. I stopped; studied the man; moved on, thought better of my fearfulness, and went back to the office. I knocked on the door. He waved me in. "Are you, by any chance Wilfred Thesinger?" I asked him. The weathered face was illuminated by a handsome smile. Yes, he was *indeed* Wilfred Thesinger. He was signing a new Harper and Row edition of his works, though I doubt most of the folks in the offices around even knew who he was, much less knew he was there. I was uncharacteristically tongue-tied. I do remember trying to explain that I had been inspired by his adventures to create a work of fantasy, but he was probably wholly unfamiliar with the *genre*. His experiences of the Empty Quarter were quite fantastic enough. So I thanked him and went about my business. It was one of the most magical encounters of my life. If I didn't still have a signed copy of his book, signed for me on that day, I would half think I'd dreamed the meeting.

Anyway . . .

Having been rejected once by Barbara I was careful going into my second treatment to be sure there was plenty of horror on the plate. The novel was initially planned to be called *Mamoulian's Game*, and the treatment bears a reasonable likeness to the novel that follows this introduction. I have since become notorious for allowing the material I pitch to my editor to transform itself into something vaster and often stranger than I originally proposed. But back then I was more conservative. Having agreed on the outline of the book, I kept reasonably close to what was on the page.

Inevitably I learned a good deal as I researched the novel. Two particular visits come to mind, situated at either end of the British social spectrum. One was a visit to Pentonville Prison, which took place over a couple of days. Nothing, let me tell you, has put me in such a God-loving, law-abiding mood as that time sealed up with the doleful occupants of Pentonville. Happily, they took kindly to me. I was a writer, and they all had tales to tell. One or two even proposed that I put away whatever I was working on and turn to fictionalizing their stories. In fact nothing they told me found its way into the book, but the stench of desperation, rage, and waste that permeated the prison *is* there in *The Damnation Game*'s pages, I think.

The complementary visit to that time in prison was a trip to a very exclusive casino, where I researched the gambling scenes from the book. This was vital stuff; I had to get it right. The hero of the novel is addicted to the dice and the wheel, and it's an addiction I don't share, so it was very important to me that I watched the gambling elite at play. My host was a famous Wall Street man who was interested in my company (ah, youth!) for more than gambling purposes, and by way of seduction gave me enough money to play on the big table three times. If I remember correctly the minimum bet was one thousand pounds and I lost all three bets in about as many seconds as it takes to write this down. The rest of the time I did as I had intended and *watched*.

A few years later my host that night fell from financial glory, his subsequent downfall—such as I understood it from the business pages of the *Times*—directly relevant to the subject of this book. As the quote that opens this novel suggests, nobody—however rich, however mighty—is ever really safe.

> *. . . nor yet exempt, though ruling them like slaves,*
> *From chance, and death, and mutability . . .*
> —SHELLEY: *Prometheus Unbound*

So, with my research done, I began to write. I had known from the beginning what the meat of the book was to be. At the heart of the novel is the story of Faust. This tale—the story of a great and powerful man who does a deal with dark forces so as to access knowledge and power that he can reach no other way, then pays a terrible price for his deal making—is one of the great root narratives of our culture. Why does it work so well? Because it is so *human*. As a species we have an enduring fascination with the challenge of tricking our way past the guardians in whom God put divine knowledge to play with things humankind was not meant to know. Perhaps in our hearts it's a desire to play the Devil's game—*the damnation game*—to be a fallen angel for a while and know what it's like in his lovely, lonely pit, just as long as the price to be paid for the deal is put at some distance.

That, of course, is the essence of the Faustian pact: *The price must be far off.* Only then will Faust's seducer, Mephistopheles, be able to persuade his victim to sign on the dotted line.

There are a number of great retellings of Faust. The German

literary titan Goethe wrote a *Faust* in 1808 and there are musical pieces based on the subject by such diverse talents as Berlioz, Liszt, and Schumann. But my favorite version was written around 1592 by Christopher Marlowe. It is called *The Tragical History of Doctor Faustus*. Here's what I wrote about it in 1988:

> *Goethe's treatment may be more philosophically complex, and arguably contains characters more sensitively drawn; it is certainly the more humane of the two interpretations. But Marlowe's variation values theatricality and poetic dazzle over moral texture, and the kid I was when I first read it liked the choice. He still does. Maybe in my dotage I'll be more profoundly moved by Goethe's brilliantly argued case for the redeemability of the human spirit (indeed, I may need its reassurances), but I'm still too close to Marlowe in age and temper to relinquish my first love.*

As you can imagine these observations make very interesting reading a decade and a half later. As I write this piece I am in my fiftieth year. I've seen a lot of sad, distressing sights since I penned my observations above. But my point-of-view remains unchanged. I still have sufficient hunger for sheer theatricality to fall on Marlowe's side if asked to pick between the versions. There's certainly no doubt in my mind that it makes the better, inspiring force to a horror novelist, especially one with an appetite for *grand guignol* spectacle. Goethe, in the luminosity of his humanism, forgives his Faust the crimes of curiosity and commends him to the bosom of his love. But Marlowe (whose own life was a blood-and-thunder tragedy that ended with his brutal murder in his twenty-ninth year) tells the Young Turk's version of the doctor's final hours. It's all din and grue: pure theatre. There's no forgiveness. No heavenly choir. Only the bloody price paid.

One final aside. My Shakespeare lecturer at University—who I rather distrusted for her oft-pronounced objection to modem fantasy—taught me much, often when the chat slid away from the main subject under discussion. I once remember her telling me about a production of Marlowe's *Tragical History of Doctor Faustus*, which she had seen at The Royal Shakespeare Company in Stratford-upon-Avon.

The production had been so powerful, she said, that two-thirds of the way through the performance it passed through her mind that *just this once* Marlowe's great, doomed philosopher would be saved from the infernal flames.

What was her lesson? Just this, I think: Perhaps the true merit of a tale is not its originality (what tale could ever be truly without precedent?) but in the intensity of its retelling, which may momentarily unseat all expectations.

I hope, in the pages that follow, to do a *little* of that myself. To carry you a little distance away from the familiar territory of a horror novel, into some *terra incognita*.

Will you allow me, by way of preparation, a moment of theatricality?

The house lights dim. The conversation of the audience is reduced to a whisper, then fades completely as

THE CURTAIN RISES

And another tale of Faust begins.

                              Clive Barker
                              Los Angeles—May 17, 2002

PART ONE

TERRA INCOGNITA

Hell is the place of those who have denied;
They find there what they planted and what dug,
A Lake of Spaces, and a Wood of Nothing,
And wander there and drift, and never cease
Wailing for substance.

—W. B. YEATS, *THE HOUR GLASS*

1

The air was electric the day the thief crossed the city, certain that tonight, after so many weeks of frustration, he would finally locate the card-player. It was not an easy journey. Eighty-five percent of Warsaw had been leveled, either by the months of mortar bombardment that had preceded the Russian liberation of the city, or by the program of demolition the Nazis had undertaken before their retreat. Several sectors were virtually impassable by vehicle. Mountains of rubble—still nurturing the dead like bulbs ready to sprout as the spring weather warmed—clogged the streets. Even in the more accessible districts the once-elegant façades swooned dangerously, their foundations growling.

But after almost three months of plying his trade here, the thief had become used to navigating this urban wilderness. Indeed, he took pleasure in its desolate splendor: its perspectives tinged lilac by the dust that still settled from the stratosphere, its squares and parkways so unnaturally silent; the sense he had, trespassing here, that this was what the end of the world would be like. By day there were even a few landmarks remaining—forlorn signposts that would be dismantled in time—by which the traveler could chart his route. The gas works beside the Poniatowski Bridge was still recognizable, as was the zoo on the other side of the river; the clock-tower of Central Station showed its head, though the clock had long since disappeared; these and a handful of other pockmarked tributes to Warsaw's civic beauty survived, their trembling presence poignant, even to the thief.

This wasn't his home. He had no home, nor had for a decade. He was a nomad and a scavenger, and for a short space Warsaw offered sufficient pickings to keep him here. Soon, when he'd recovered energies depleted in his recent wanderings, it would be time to move on. But while the first signs of spring murmured in the air he lingered here, enjoying the freedom of the city.

There were hazards certainly, but then where were there not for a man of his profession? And the war years had polished his powers of self-preservation to such brilliance that little intimidated him. He was safer here than the true citizens of Warsaw, the few bewildered survivors of the holocaust who were gradually beginning to filter back into the city, looking for lost homes, lost faces. They scrabbled in the wreckage or stood on street corners listening to the dirge of the river, and waited for the Russians to round them up in the name of Karl Marx. New barricades were being established every day. The military were slowly but systematically reclaiming some order from the confusion, dividing and subdividing the city as they would, in time, the entire country. The curfews and the checkpoints did little to hobble the thief, however. In the lining of his well-cut coat he kept identification papers of every kind—some forged, most stolen—one of which would be suitable for whatever situation arose. What they lacked in credibility he made up for with repartee and cigarettes, both of which he possessed in abundance. They were all a man needed—in that city, in that year—to feel like the lord of creation.

And such creation! No need here for either appetite or curiosity to go unsatisfied. The profoundest secrets of body and spirit were available to anyone with the itch to see. Games were made of them. Only the previous week the thief had heard tell of a young man who played the ancient game of cups and ball (now you see it, now you don't) but substituted, with insanity's wit, three buckets and a baby's head.

That was the least of it; the infant was dead, and the dead don't suffer. There were, however, other pastimes available for hire in the city, delights that used the living as their raw material. For those with the craving and the price of entry, a traffic in human flesh had begun. The occupying army, no longer distracted by battle, had discovered sex again, and there was profit in it. Half a loaf of bread could purchase one of the refugee girls—many so young they scarcely had breasts to knead—to be used and re-used in the covering darkness, their complaints unheard or silenced by a bayonet when they lost their charm. Such casual homicide was overlooked in a city where tens of thousands had died. For a few weeks—between one regime and the next—anything was possible: no act found culpable, no depravity taboo.

A boys' brothel had been opened in the Zoliborz District. Here, in an underground salon hung with salvaged paintings, one could choose from chicks of six or seven up, all fetchingly slimmed by malnutrition and tight as any connoisseur could wish. It was very popular with the officer class, but too expensive, the thief had heard it muttered, for the noncommissioned ranks. Lenin's tenets of equal choice for all did not stretch, it seemed, to pederasty.

Sport, of a kind, was more cheaply available. Dogfights were a particularly popular attraction that season. Homeless curs, returning to the city to pick at the meat of their masters, were trapped, fed to fighting strength and then pitted against each other to the death. It was an appalling spectacle, but a love of betting took the thief to the fights again and again. He'd made a tidy profit one night by putting his money on a runty but cunning terrier who'd bested a dog three times its size by chewing off its opponent's testicles.

And if, after a time, your taste for dogs or boys or women palled, there were more esoteric entertainments available.

In a crude amphitheater dug from the debris of the Bastion of Holy Mary the thief had seen an anonymous actor singlehandedly perform Goethe's *Faust*, Parts One and Two. Though the thief's German was far from perfect, the performance had made a lasting impression. The story was familiar enough for him to follow the action—the pact with Mephisto, the debates, the conjuring tricks, and then, as the promised damnation approached, despair and terrors. Much of the argument was indecipherable, but the actor's possession by his twin roles—one moment Tempter, the next Tempted—was so impressive the thief left with his belly churning.

Two days later he had gone back to see the play again, or at least to speak to the actor. But there were to be no encores. The performer's enthusiasm for Goethe had been interpreted as pro-Nazi propaganda; the thief found him hanging, joy decayed, from a telegraph pole. He was naked. His bare feet had been eaten at and his eyes taken out by birds; his torso was riddled with bullet holes. The sight pacified the thief. He saw it as proof that the confused feelings the actor had aroused were iniquitous; if this was the state to which his art had brought him the man had clearly been a scoundrel and a sham. His mouth gaped, but the birds had taken his tongue as well as his eyes. No loss.

Besides, there were far more rewarding diversions. The women the thief could take or leave, and the boys were not to his taste, but the gambling he loved, and always had. So it was back to the dogfights to chance his fortunes on a mongrel. If not there, then to some barrack-room dice game, or—in desperation—betting with a bored sentry on the speed of a passing cloud. The method and the circumstance scarcely concerned him: he cared only to gamble. Since his adolescence it had been his one true vice; it was the indulgence he had become a thief to fund. Before the war he'd played in casinos across Europe; chemin de fer was his game, though he was not averse to roulette. Now he looked back at those years through the veil war had drawn across them, and remembered the contests as he remembered dreams on waking: as something irretrievable, and slipping further away with every breath.

That sense of loss changed, however, when he heard about the card-player—Mamoulian, they called him—who, it was said, never lost a game, and who came and went in this deceitful city like a creature who was not, perhaps, even real.

But then, after Mamoulian, everything changed.

2

So much was rumor; and so much of that rumor not even rooted
in truth. Simply lies told by bored soldiers. The military mind,
the thief had discovered, was capable of inventions more baroque
than a poet's, and more lethal.

So when he heard tell of a master cardsharp who appeared out
of nowhere, and challenged every would-be gambler to a game
and unfailingly won, he suspected the story to be just that: a
story. But something about the way this apocryphal tale lingered
confounded expectation. It didn't fade away to be replaced by
some yet more ludicrous romance. It appeared repeatedly—in the
conversation of the men at the dogfights; in gossip, in graffiti.
What was more, though the names changed the salient facts were
the same from one account to the next. The thief began to suspect
there was truth in the story after all. Perhaps there *was* a brilliant
gambler operating somewhere in the city. Not perfectly invulnerable,
of course; no one was that. But the man, if he existed, was certainly
something special. Talk of him was always conducted with a
caution that was like reverence; soldiers who claimed to have seen
him play spoke of his elegance, his almost hypnotic calm. When
they talked of Mamoulian they were peasants speaking of nobility,
and the thief—never one to concede the superiority of any man—
added a zeal to unseat this king to his reasons for seeking the card-
player out.

But beyond the general picture he garnered from the grapevine,
there were few specifics. He knew that he would have to find and
interrogate a man who had actually faced this paragon across a

gaming table before he could really begin to separate truth from speculation.

It took two weeks to find such a man. His name was Konstantin Vasiliev, a second lieutenant, who, it was said, had lost everything he had playing against Mamoulian. The Russian was broad as a bull; the thief felt dwarfed by him. But while some big men nurture spirits expansive enough to fill their anatomies, Vasiliev seemed almost empty. If he had ever possessed such virility, it was now gone. Left in the husk was a frail and fidgety child.

It took an hour of coaxing, the best part of a bottle of black-market vodka and half a pack of cigarettes to get Vasiliev to answer with more than a monosyllable, but when the disclosures came they came gushingly, the confessions of a man on the verge of total breakdown. There was self-pity in his talk, and anger too; but mostly there was the stench of dread. Vasiliev was a man in mortal terror. The thief was mightily impressed: not by the tears or the desperation, but by the fact that Mamoulian, this faceless card-player, had broken the giant sitting across the floor from him. Under the guise of consolation and friendly advice he proceeded to pump the Russian for every sliver of information he could provide, looking all the time for some significant detail to make flesh and blood of the chimera he was investigating.

"You say he wins without fail?"

"Always."

"So what's his method? How does he cheat?"

Vasiliev looked up from his contemplation of the bare boards of the floor.

"Cheat?" he said, incredulously. "He doesn't cheat. I've played cards all my life, with the best and the worst. I've seen every trick a man can pull. And I tell you now, he was clean."

"The luckiest player gets defeated once in a while. The laws of chance—"

A look of innocent amusement crossed Vasiliev's face, and for a moment the thief glimpsed the man who'd occupied this fortress before his fall from sanity.

"The laws of chance are nothing to him. Don't you see? He isn't like you or me. How could a man always win without having some power over the cards?"

"You believe that?"

Vasiliev shrugged, and slumped again. "To him," he said, almost contemplative in his utter dismay, "winning is beauty. It is like life itself."

The vacant eyes returned to tracing the rough grain of the floorboards as the thief somersaulted the words over in his head: "*Winning is beauty. It is like life itself.*" It was strange talk, and made him uneasy. Before he could work his way into its meaning, however, Vasiliev was leaning closer to him, his breath fearful, his vast hand catching hold of the thief's sleeve as he spoke.

"I've put in for a transfer, did they tell you that? I'll be away from here in a few days, and nobody'll be any the wiser. I'm getting medals when I get home. That's why they're transferring me: because I'm a hero, and heroes get what they ask for. Then I'll be gone, and he'll never find me."

"Why would he want to?"

The hand on the sleeve fisted; Vasiliev pulled the thief in toward him. "I owe him the shirt off my back," he said. "If I stay, he'll have me killed. He's killed others, him and his comrades."

"He's not alone?" said the thief. He had pictured the card-player as being a man without associates; made him, in fact, in his own image.

Vasiliev blew his nose into his hand, and leaned back in the chair. It creaked under his bulk.

"Who knows what's true or false in this place, eh?" he said, eyes swimming. "I mean, if I told you he had dead men with him, would you believe me?" He answered his own question with a shake of his head. "No. You'd think I was mad . . ."

Once, the thief thought, this man had been capable of certainty; of action; perhaps even of heroism. Now all that noble stuff had been siphoned off: the champion was reduced to a sniveling rag, blabbering nonsense. He inwardly applauded the brilliance of Mamoulian's victory. He had always hated heroes.

"One last question—" he began.

"You want to know where you can find him."

"Yes."

The Russian stared at the ball of his thumb, sighing deeply. This was all so wearisome.

"What do you gain if you play him?" he asked, and again returned his own answer. "Only humiliation. Perhaps death."

The thief stood up. "Then you don't know where he is?" he said, making to pocket the half-empty packet of cigarettes that lay on the table between them.

"Wait." Vasiliev reached for the pack before it slid out of sight. "Wait."

The thief placed the cigarettes back on the table, and Vasiliev covered them with one proprietorial hand. He looked up at his interrogator as he spoke.

"The last time I heard, he was north of here. Up by Muranowski Square. You know it?"

The thief nodded. It was not a region he relished visiting, but he knew it. "And how do I find him, once I get there?" he asked.

The Russian looked perplexed by the question.

"I don't even know what he looks like," the thief said, trying to make Vasiliev understand.

"You won't need to find him," Vasiliev replied, understanding all too well. "If he wants you to play, he'll find you."

3

The next night, the first of many such nights, the thief had gone looking for the card-player. Though it was by now April, the weather was still bitter that year. He'd come back to his room in the partially demolished hotel he occupied numb with cold, frustration and—though he scarcely admitted it even to himself— fear. The region around Muranowski Square was a hell within a hell. Many of the bomb craters here let on to the sewers; the stench out of them was unmistakable. Others, used as fire pits to cremate executed citizens, still flared intermittently when a flame found a belly swollen with gas, or a pool of human fat. Every step taken in this new-found land was an adventure, even to the thief. Death, its forms multitudinous, waited everywhere. Sitting on the edge of a crater, warming its feet in the flames; standing, lunatic, amongst the refuse; at laughing play in a garden of bone and shrapnel.

Fear notwithstanding, he'd returned to the district on several occasions; but the card-player eluded him. And with every failed attempt, with every journey that ended in defeat, the thief became more preoccupied with the pursuit. In his mind this faceless gambler began to take on something of the force of legend. Just to see the man in the flesh, to verify his physical existence in the same world that he, the thief, occupied, became an article of faith. A means, God help him, by which he could ratify his own existence.

After a week and a half of fruitless searching, he went back to find Vasiliev. The Russian was dead. His body, throat slit from ear to ear, had been found the previous day, floating facedown in one of the sewers the Army was clearing in Wola. He was not alone. There had been three other bodies with him, all slaughtered in a similar fashion, all set alight and burning like fire ships as they drifted down the tunnel on a river of excrement. One of the soldiers who had been in the sewer when the flotilla appeared told the thief that the bodies had seemed to float in the darkness. For a breathless moment it had been like the steady approach of angels.

Then, of course, the horror. Extinguishing the burning corpses, their hair, their backs; then turning them over, and the face of Vasiliev, caught in the beam of a flashlight, carrying a look of wonder, like a child in awe of some lethal conjuror.

His transfer papers had arrived that same afternoon.

In fact the papers seemed to have been the cause of an administrative error that had closed Vasiliev's tragedy on a comic note. The bodies, once identified, had been buried in Warsaw, except for Second Lieutenant Vasiliev, whose war record demanded less cursory treatment. Plans were afoot to transport the body back to Mother Russia, where he would be buried with state honors in his hometown. But somebody, alighting upon the transfer papers, had taken them to apply to Vasiliev dead, not Vasiliev living. Mysteriously, the body disappeared. Nobody would admit responsibility: the corpse had simply been shipped out to some new posting.

Vasiliev's death merely served to intensify the thief's curiosity. Mamoulian's arrogance fascinated him. Here was a scavenger, a man who made a living off the weakness of others, who had yet grown so insolent with success that he dared to murder—or have murdered on his behalf—those who crossed him. The thief became jittery with anticipation. In his dreams, when he was able to sleep, he wandered in Muranowski Square. It was filled with a fog like a living thing, which promised at any moment to divide and reveal the card-player. He was like a man in love.

4

Tonight, the ceiling of squalid cloud above Europe had broken: blue, albeit pale, had spread over his head, wider and wider. Now, toward evening, the sky was absolutely clear above him. In the southwest vast cumulus, their cauliflower heads tinted ocher and gold, were fattening with thunder, but the thought of their anger only excited him. Tonight, the air was electric, and he would find the card-player, he was sure. He had been sure since he woke that morning.

As evening began to fall he went north toward the square, scarcely thinking of where he was going, the route was so familiar to him. He walked through two checkpoints without being challenged, the confidence in his step password enough. Tonight he was inevitable. His place here, breathing the scented, lilac air, stars glimmering at his zenith, was unassailable. He felt static run in the hairs on the back of his hand, and smiled. He saw a man, something unrecognizable in his arms, screaming at a window, and smiled. Not far away, the Vistula, gross with rain and melt-water, roared toward the sea. He was no less irresistible.

The gold went out of the cumulus; the lucid blue darkened toward night.

As he was about to come into Muranowski Square something flickered in front of him, a twist of wind scooted past him, and the air was suddenly full of white confetti. Impossible, surely, that there was a wedding taking place here? One of the whirling fragments lodged on his eyelash, and he plucked it off. It wasn't confetti at all: it was a petal. He pressed it between thumb and forefinger. Its scented oil spilled from the fractured tissue.

In search of the source, he walked on a little way, and rounding the corner into the square itself discovered the ghost of a tree, prodigious with blossom, hanging in the air. It seemed unrooted, its snow-head lit by starlight, its trunk shadowy. He held his breath, shocked by this beauty, and walked toward it as he might have approached a wild animal, cautious in case it took fright. Something turned his stomach over. It wasn't awe of the blossom, or even the remnants of the joy he'd felt walking here. That was slipping away. A different sensation gripped him here in the square.

He was a man so used to atrocities that he had long counted himself unblanchable. So why did he stand now a few feet away from the tree, his fingernails, meticulously kept, pressed into his palms with anxiety, defying the umbrella of flowers to unveil its worst? There was nothing to fear here. Just petals in the air, shadow on the ground. And still he breathed shallowly, hoping against hope that his fright was baseless.

Come on, he thought, if you've got something to show me, I'm waiting.

At his silent invitation two things happened. Behind him a guttural voice asked: "Who are you?" in Polish. Distracted for the merest heartbeat by surprise, his eyes lost focus on the tree, and in that instant a figure dislodged itself from beneath the blossom-weighed branches and slouched, momentarily, into the starlight. In the cheating murk the thief wasn't certain what he saw: a discarded face looking blankly in his direction perhaps, hair seared off. A scabby carcass, wide as a bull's. Vasiliev's vast hands.

All or nothing of this; and already the figure was retiring into hiding beyond the tree, its wounded head brushing the branches as it went. A drizzle of petals fluttered onto its charcoal shoulders.

"Did you hear me?" said the voice at his back. The thief didn't turn. He went on staring at the tree, narrowing his eyes, attempting to separate substance from illusion. But the man, whoever he was, had gone. It could not have been the Russian, of course; reason proclaimed against it. Vasiliev was dead, found with his face down in the filth of a sewer. His body was probably already on its way to some far-flung outpost of the Russian empire. He wasn't here; he couldn't *be* here. But the thief felt an urgent need to pursue the stranger nevertheless, just to tap his shoulder, to have him turn round, to look into his face and verify that it was not Konstantin. Too late already; the questioner behind him had taken fierce hold of his arm, and was demanding an answer. The branches of the tree had stopped shaking, the petals had stopped falling, the man was away.

Sighing, the thief turned to his interrogator.

The figure in front of him was smiling a welcome. It was a woman, despite the rasp of the voice, dressed in oversized trousers, tied with a rope, but otherwise naked. Her head was shaved; her toenails lacquered. All this he took in with senses heightened from the shock of the tree, and from the pleasure of her nudity. The sheened globes of her breasts were perfect. He felt his fists opening, the palms tingling to touch them. But perhaps his appraisal of the body was too frank. He glanced back up at her face to see if she was still smiling. She was; but his gaze lingered on her face this time, and he realized that what he'd taken to be a smile was a permanent fixture. Her lips had been sliced off, exposing gums and teeth. There were ghastly scars on her cheeks, the remains of wounds that had severed the tendons and induced a rictus that teased her mouth open. Her look appalled him.

"You want . . . ?" she began.

Want? he thought, his eyes flicking back to the breasts. Her casual nudity aroused him, despite the mutilation of her face. He was disgusted with the idea of taking her—to kiss that lipless mouth was more than orgasm was worth—and yet if she offered he'd accept, and damn the disgust.

"You want . . . ?" she began again, in that slurred hybrid of a voice, neither male nor female. It was difficult for her to shape and expel words without the aid of lips. She got the rest of the question out, however. "You want the cards?"

He'd missed the point entirely. She had no interest in him, sexual or otherwise. She was simply a messenger. *Mamoulian was here*. Within spitting distance, probably. Perhaps watching him even now.

But the confusion of emotions in him blurred the elation he should have felt at this moment. Instead of triumph, he grappled with a headful of contrary images: blossom, breasts, darkness; the burned man's face, turning too briefly toward him; lust, fear; a single star appearing from a flank of cloud. Hardly thinking of what he was saying, he replied:

"Yes. I want the cards."

She nodded, turned away from him, and started past the tree, its branches still rocking where the man who was not Vasiliev had touched them, and crossed the square. He followed. It was possible to forget this go-between's face while looking at the grace of her barefooted steps. She didn't seem to care what she trod on. Not once did she falter, despite the glass, brick and shrapnel underfoot.

She led him across to the remains of a large house on the opposite side of the square. Its ravaged exterior, once impressive, still stood; there was even a doorway in it, though no door. Through it, the light of a bonfire flickered. Rubble from the interior spilled through the doorway and blocked the lower half, obliging both woman and thief to duck down and scramble up into the house itself. In the gloom the sleeve of his coat snagged on something; the cloth tore. She didn't turn to see if he was hurt, though he cursed audibly. She simply led on over the mounds of brick and fallen roof timbers while he stumbled after her, feeling ridiculously clumsy. By the light of the bonfire he could see the size of the interior; this had once been a fine house. There was little time for study, however. The woman was past the fire now, and climbing toward a staircase. He followed, sweating. The fire spat; he glanced around at it, and glimpsed somebody on the far side, keeping out of sight behind the flames. Even as he watched, the fire keeper threw more tinder down, and a constellation of livid specks was thrown up against the sky.

The woman was climbing the stairs. He hurried after her, his shadow—thrown by the fire—huge on the wall. She was at the top of the stairs when he was halfway up, and now she was slipping through a second doorway and gone. He followed on as quickly as he could, and turned through the doorway after her.

The firelight only found its way fitfully into the room he'd stepped into, and he could scarcely make anything out at first.

"Close the door," somebody asked. It took him a few beats to realize that the request was being made of him. He half-turned, fumbled for the handle, found that there was none, and pushed the door closed on aching hinges.

That done, he looked back into the room. The woman was standing two or three yards in front of him, her perpetually amused face looking at him, the smile a gray sickle.

"Your coat," she said, and stretched out her hands to help him shoulder it off. Once done, she stepped out of his eyeline, and the object of his long search came into view.

It was not Mamoulian, however, that took his eye at first. It was the carved wooden altar piece set against the wall behind him, a Gothic masterwork which blazed, even in the gloom, with gold and scarlet and blue. Spoils of war, the thief thought; so that's what the bastard does with his fortune. Now he looked at the figure in front of the triptych. A single wick, immersed in oil, guttered smokily on the table at which he sat. The illumination it threw up on to the card-player's face was bright but unstable.

"So, Pilgrim," the man said, "you found me. Finally."

"You found *me*, surely," the thief replied; it had been as Vasiliev had predicted.

"You fancy a game or two, I hear. Is that right?"

"Why not?" He tried to sound as nonchalant as possible, though his heart was beating a double tattoo in his chest. Coming into the card-player's presence, he felt pitifully unprepared. Sweat glued his hair to his forehead; there was brick dust on his hands and muck under his nails: I must look, he squirmed, like the thief I am.

By contrast, Mamoulian was a picture of propriety. There was nothing in the sober clothes—the black tie, the gray suit—that suggested a profiteer: he appeared, this legend, like a stockbroker. His face, like his dress, was unrepentantly plain, its taut and finely etched skin waxen by the charmless oil flame. He looked sixty or thereabouts, cheeks slightly hollowed, nose large, aristocratic; brow wide and high. His hair had receded to the back of his skull; what remained was feathery and white. But there was neither frailty nor fatigue in his posture. He sat upright in his chair, and his agile hands fanned and gathered a pack of cards with loving familiarity. Only his eyes belonged to the thief's dream of him. No stockbroker ever had such naked eyes. Such glacial, unforgiving eyes.

"I hoped you'd come, Pilgrim. Sooner or later," he said. His English was without inflection.

"Am I late?" the thief asked, half-joking.

Mamoulian laid the cards down. He seemed to take the inquiry quite seriously. "We'll see." He paused before saying, "You know, of course, that I play for very high stakes."

"I heard."

"If you wish to withdraw now, before we go any further, I would perfectly understand." The little speech was made without a trace of irony.

"Don't you want me to play?"

Mamoulian pressed his thin, dry lips together and frowned. "On the contrary," he said, "I very much want you to play."

There was a flicker—was there not?—of pathos there. The thief wasn't sure if it was a slip of the tongue, or the subtlest of theatrics. "But I am not sympathetic . . ." he went on, "to those who do not pay their debts."

"You mean the lieutenant," the thief chanced.

Mamoulian stared at him. "I know no lieutenant," he said flatly. "I know only gamblers, like myself. A few are good, most are not. They all come here to test their mettle, as you have."

He had picked up the pack again, and it was moving in his hands as if the cards were alive. Fifty-two moths fluttering in the queasy light, each one marked a little differently from the last.

They were almost indecently beautiful; their glossy faces the most unflawed thing the thief had set eyes on in months.

"I want to play," he said, defying the hypnotic passage of cards.

"Then sit down, Pilgrim," Mamoulian said, as though the question had never been at issue.

Almost soundlessly the woman had set a chair behind him. As he sat down, the thief met Mamoulian's gaze. Was there anything in those joyless eyes that intended him harm? No, nothing. There was nothing there to fear.

Murmuring his thanks for the invitation, he unbuttoned the cuffs of his shirt and folded the sleeves back in preparation for play.

After a time, the game began.

PART TWO

ASYLUM

The Devil is by no means the worst that there is; I would rather have dealings with him than with many a human being. He honours his agreements much more promptly than many a swindler on Earth. To be true, when payment is due he comes on the dot; just as twelve strikes, fetches his soul and goes off home to Hell like a good Devil. He's just a businessman as is right and proper.

—J. N. NESTROY, *HOLLENANGST*

I. PROVIDENCE

5

After serving six years of his sentence at Wandsworth, Marty Strauss was used to waiting. He waited to wash and shave himself every morning; he waited to eat, he waited to defecate; he waited for freedom. So much waiting. It was all part of the punishment, of course; as was the interview he'd been summoned to this dreary afternoon. But while the waiting had come to seem easy, the interviews never had. He loathed the bureaucratic spotlight: the Parole File bulging with the Discipline Reports, the Home Circumstance Reports, the Psychiatric Evaluations; the way every few months you stood stripped in front of some uncivil servant while he told you what a foul thing you were. It hurt him so much he knew he'd never be healed of it; never forget the hot rooms filled with insinuation and dashed hopes. He'd dream them forever.

"Come in, Strauss."

The room hadn't changed since he'd last been here; only become staler. The man on the opposite side of the table hadn't changed either. His name was Somervale, and there were any number of prisoners in Wandsworth who nightly said prayers for his pulverization. Today he was not alone behind the plastic-topped table.

"Sit down, Strauss."

Marty glanced across at Somervale's associate. He was no prison officer. His suit was too tasteful, his fingernails too well-manicured. He looked to be in late middle-age, solidly built, and his nose was slightly crooked, as if it had once been broken and then imperfectly reset. Somervale offered the introduction:

"Strauss. This is Mr. Toy . . ."

"Hello," Marty said.

The tanned face returned his gaze; it was a look of frank appraisal.

"I'm pleased to meet you," Toy said.

His scrutiny was more than casual curiosity, though what— thought Marty—was there to see? A man with time on his hands, and on his face; a body grown sluggish with too much bad food and too little exercise; an ineptly trimmed mustache; a pair of eyes glazed with boredom. Marty knew every dull detail of his own appearance. He wasn't worth a second glance any longer. And yet the bright blue eyes stared on, apparently fascinated.

"I think we should get down to business," Toy said to Somervale. He put his hands palm down on the tabletop. "How much have you told Mr. Strauss?"

Mr. Strauss. The prefix was an almost forgotten courtesy.

"I've told him nothing," Somervale replied.

"Then we should begin at the beginning," Toy said. He leaned back in his chair, hands still on the table.

"As you like," said Somervale, clearly gearing himself up for a substantial speech. "Mr. Toy—" he began.

But he got no further before his guest broke in.

"If I may?" said Toy, "perhaps I can best summarize the situation."

"Whatever suits," said Somervale. He fumbled in his jacket pocket for a cigarette, barely masking his chagrin. Toy ignored him. The off-center face continued to look across at Marty.

"My employer—" Toy began "—is a man by the name of Joseph Whitehead. I don't know if that means anything to you?" He didn't wait for a reply, but went on. "If you haven't heard of him, you're doubtless familiar with the Whitehead Corporation, which he founded. It's one of the largest pharmaceutical empires in Europe—"

The name rang a faint bell in Marty's head, and it had some

scandalous association. But it was tantalizingly vague, and he had no time to puzzle it through, because Toy was in full flight.

"—Although Mr. Whitehead is now in his late sixties, he still keeps control of the corporation. He's a self-made man, you understand, and he's dedicated his life to its creation. He chooses, however, not to be as *visible* as he once was—"

A front-page photograph suddenly developed in Strauss' head. A man with his hand up against the glare of a flashbulb; a private moment snatched by some lurking paparazzo for public consumption.

"—He shuns publicity almost completely, and since his wife's death he has little taste for the social arena—"

Sharing the unwelcome attention Strauss remembered a woman whose beauty astonished, even by the unflattering light. The wife of whom Toy spoke, perhaps.

"—Instead he chooses to mastermind his corporation out of the spotlight, concerning himself in his leisure hours with social issues. Among them, overcrowding in prisons, and the deterioration of the prison service generally."

The last remark was undoubtedly barbed, and found Somervale with deadly accuracy. He ground out his half-smoked cigarette in the tinfoil ashtray, throwing the other man a sour glance.

"When the time came to engage a new personal bodyguard—" Toy continued, "—it was Mr. Whitehead's decision to seek a suitable candidate amongst men coming up for parole rather than going through the usual agencies."

He can't mean me, Strauss thought. The idea was too fine to tease himself with, and too ludicrous. And yet if that wasn't it, why was Toy here, why all the palaver?

"He's looking for a man who is nearing the end of his sentence. One who deserves, in both his and my own estimation, to have an opportunity to be reintroduced into society with a job behind him, and some self-esteem to go with it. Your case was drawn to my attention, Martin. I may call you Martin?"

"Usually it's Marty."

"Fine. Marty it is. Frankly, I don't want to raise your hopes. I'm interviewing several other candidates in addition to yourself, and of course at the end of the day I may find that none are suitable. At this juncture I simply want to ascertain whether you would be interested in such an option were it to be made available to you."

Marty began to smile. Not outwardly, but inside, where Somervale couldn't get at it.

"Do you understand what I'm asking?"

"Yes. I understand."

"Joe . . . Mr. Whitehead . . . needs somebody who will be completely devoted to his well-being; who would indeed be prepared to put his life at risk rather than have harm come to his employer. Now I realize that's a lot to ask."

Marty's brow furrowed. It *was* a lot, especially after the six-and-a-half-year lesson in self-reliance he'd had at Wandsworth. Toy was swift to sense Marty's hesitation.

"That bothers you," he said.

Marty shrugged gently. "Yes and no. I mean, I've never been asked to do that before. I don't want to give you some shit about me being really keen to get killed for somebody, because I'm not. I'd be lying through my teeth if I said I was."

Toy's nods encouraged Marty to go on.

"That's it really," he said.

"Are you married?" Toy asked.

"Separated."

"May I ask; are there divorce proceedings in the offing?"

Marty grimaced. He loathed talking about this. It was *his* wound; his to tend and fret over. No fellow prisoner had ever wrung the story out of him, even in those three-in-the-morning confessionals that he'd endured with his previous cellmate, before Feaver, who never talked of anything but food and paper women, had arrived. But he would have to say something now. They surely had the details filed away somehow anyway. Toy probably knew more about what Charmaine was doing, and with whom, than he did.

"Charmaine and me . . ." He tried to summon words for this knot of feelings, but nothing emerged but a blunt statement. "I don't think there's much chance of us getting back together, if that's what you're after."

Toy sensed the raw edge in Marty's voice; so did Somervale. For the first time since Toy had entered the arena the officer began to show some interest in the exchange. He wants to watch me talk my way out of a job, Marty thought; he could see the anticipation written all over Somervale's face. Well, damn him, he wasn't going to have the satisfaction.

"It's not a problem—" Marty said flatly. "Or if it is, it's mine. I'm still getting used to the fact that she won't be there when I get out. That's all it is, really."

Toy was smiling now, an amiable smile.

"Really, Marty—" he said, "—I don't want to pry. I'm only concerned that we understand the full facts of the situation. Were you to be employed by Mr. Whitehead, you would be required to live on his estate with him, and it would be a necessary condition of your employment that you could not leave without the express permission of either Mr. Whitehead or myself. In other words you would not be stepping into unconditional freedom. Far from it. You might wish to consider the estate as a sort of open prison. It's important for me to know of any ties you have that might make such constraints temptingly easy to break."

"Yes, I see."

"Furthermore, if for any reason your relationship with Mr. Whitehead was not satisfactory; if you or he felt that the job was not suitable, then I'm afraid—"

"—I'd be back here to finish my sentence."

"Yes."

There was an awkward pause, in which Toy sighed quietly. It took him only a moment to recover his equilibrium, then he took off in a new direction.

"There's just a few more questions I'd like to ask. You've done some boxing, am I right?"

"Some. A while back—"

Toy looked disappointed. "You gave it up?"

"Yes," Marty replied. "I kept on with the weight training for a while."

"Do you have any self-defense training of any kind? Judo? Karate?"

Marty contemplated lying, but what would be the use of that? All Toy had to do was consult the screws at Wandsworth. "No," he said.

"Pity."

Marty's belly shrank. "I'm healthy though," he said. "And strong. I can learn." He was aware that an unwelcome tremor had slipped into his voice from somewhere.

"We don't want a learner, I'm afraid," Somervale pointed out, barely able to suppress the triumph in his tone.

Marty leaned forward across the table, trying to blot out Somervale's leechlike presence.

"I can do this job, Mr. Toy," he insisted, "I *know* I can do this job. Just give me a chance—"

The tremor was growing; his belly was an acrobat. Better stop now, before he said or did something he regretted. But the words and the feelings just kept on coming.

"Give me an opportunity to prove I can do it. That's not much to ask, is it? And if I fuck it up it's *my fault*, see? Just a chance, that's all I'm asking."

Toy looked up at him with something like condolence in his face. Was it all over then? Had he made up his mind already—one wrong answer and the whole thing goes sour—was he already mentally packing up his briefcase and returning the *Strauss, M.* file into Somervale's clammy hands to be slotted back between one forgotten con and another?

Marty bit his tongue, and sat back in the uncomfortable chair, fixing his gaze on his trembling hands. He couldn't bear to look at the bruised elegance of Toy's face, not now that he'd opened himself up so wide. Toy would see in, oh yes, to all the hurt and the wanting, and he couldn't bear that.

"At your trial . . ." Toy said.

What now? Why was he prolonging the agony? All Marty wanted was to go to his cell, where Feaver would be sitting on the bunk and playing with his dolls, where there was a familiar dullness that he could take refuge in. But Toy wasn't finished; he wanted the truth, the whole truth and nothing but.

"At your trial you testified that your prime motivation for involvement in the robbery was to pay off substantial gambling debts. Am I correct?"

Marty had moved his attention from his hands to his shoes. The laces were undone, and though they were long enough to be double-knotted he never had the patience to work at complicated knots. He liked a simple bow. When you needed to untie a bow you pulled and behold—like magic—it was gone.

"Is that right?" Toy asked again.

"Yes; that's right," Marty told him. He'd got so far; why not finish the story? "There were four of us. And two guns. We tried to take a security van. Things got out of hand." He glanced up from his shoes; Toy was watching intently. "The driver was shot in the stomach. He died later. It's all in the file, isn't it?" Toy nodded. "And about the van? Is that in the file too?" Toy didn't reply. "*It was empty*," Marty said. "We had it wrong from the beginning. The fucking thing was empty."

"And the debts?"

"Huh?"

"Your debts to Macnamara. They're still outstanding?"

The man was really beginning to get on Marty's nerves. What did Toy care if he owed a few grand here and there? This was just sympathetic camouflage, so that he could make a dignified exit.

"Answer Mr. Toy, Strauss," Somervale said.

"What's it to you?"

"Interest," said Toy, frankly.

"I see."

Sod his interest, Marty thought, he could choke on it. They'd had as much of a confessional as they were going to get.

"Can I go now?" he said.

He looked up. Not at Toy but at Somervale, who was smirking behind his cigarette smoke, well satisfied that the interview had been a disaster.

"I think so, Strauss," he said. "As long as Mr. Toy doesn't have any more questions."

"No," said Toy, the voice dead. "No; I'm well satisfied."

Marty stood up, still avoiding Toy's eyes. The small room was full of ugly sounds. The chair's heels scraping on the floor, the rasp of Somervale's smoker's cough. Toy was shunting away his notes. It was all over.

Somervale said: "You can go."

"I've enjoyed meeting you, Mr. Strauss," Toy said to Marty's back as he reached the door, and Marty turned around without thinking to see the other man smiling at him, his hand extended to be shaken. I've enjoyed meeting you, Mr. Strauss.

Marty nodded and shook hands.

"Thank you for your time," Toy said.

Marty closed the door behind him and made his way back to his cell, escorted by Priestley, the landing officer. They said nothing.

Marty watched the birds swooping in the roof of the building, alighting on the landing rails for tidbits. They came and they went when it suited them, finding niches to nest in, taking their sovereignty for granted. He envied them nothing. Or if he did, now wasn't the time to admit to it.

6

Thirteen days passed, and there was no further word from either Toy or Somervale. Not that Marty was truly expecting any. The chance had been lost; he'd almost stage-managed its final moments with his refusal to talk about Macnamara. That way he had expected to nip any trial by hope in the bud. In that, he'd failed. No matter how he tried to forget the interview with Toy, he couldn't. The encounter had thrown him badly off-balance, and his instability was as distressing as its cause. He thought he had learned the art of indifference by now, the same way that children learned that hot water scalds: by painful experience.

He'd had plenty of that. During the first twelve months of his sentence he'd fought against everything and everyone he'd encountered. He'd made no friends that year, nor the least impression on the system; all he'd earned for his troubles were bruises and bad times. In the second year, chastened by defeat, he'd gone underground with his private war; he'd taken up weight training and boxing, and concentrated on the challenge of building and maintaining a body that would serve him when the time for retribution came round. But in the middle of the third year, loneliness had intervened: an ache that no amount of self-inflicted punishment (muscles driven to the pain threshold and beyond, day after day) could disguise. He made a truce that year, with himself and his incarceration. It was an uneasy peace, but things began to improve from then on. He even began to feel at home in the echoing corridors, and in his cell, and in the shrinking enclave of his head, where most pleasurable experience was now a distant memory.

The fourth year had brought new terrors. He was twenty-nine that year; thirty loomed, and he remembered all too accurately how his younger self, with time to burn, had dismissed men his age as spent. It was a painful realization, and the old claustrophobia (trapped not behind bars, but behind his life) returned more forcibly than ever, and with it a new foolhardiness. He'd gained his tattoos that year: a scarlet and blue lightning bolt on his upper left arm, and "USA" on his right forearm. Just before Christmas Charmaine had written to him to suggest that a divorce might be best, and he'd thought nothing of it. What was the use? Indifference was the best remedy. Once you conceded defeat, life was a feather bed. In the light of that wisdom, the fifth year was a breeze. He had access to dope; he had the clout that came with being an experienced con; he had every damned thing but his freedom, and that he could wait for.

And then Toy had come along, and try as hard as he could to forget he'd ever heard the man's name, he found himself turning the half-hour of the interview over and over in his head, examining every exchange in the minutest detail as though he might turn up a nugget of prophecy. It was a fruitless exercise, of course, but it didn't stop the rehearsals going on, and the process became almost comforting in its way. He told nobody; not even Feaver. It was his secret: the room; Toy; Somervale's defeat.

On the second Sunday after the meeting with Toy, Charmaine came to visit. The interview was the usual mess; like a transatlantic telephone call—all the timing spoiled by the second delay between question and response. It wasn't the babble of other conversations in the room that soured things, things were simply sour. No avoiding that fact now. His early attempts at salvage had long since been abandoned. After the cool inquiries about the health of relatives and friends it was down to the nitty-gritty of dissolution.

He'd written to her in the early letters: *You're beautiful, Charmaine. I think of you at night, I dream about you all the time.*

But then her looks had seemed to lose their edge—and anyway

his dreams of her face and body under him had stopped—and though he kept up the pretense in the letters for a while his loving sentences had begun to sound patently fake, and he'd stopped writing about such intimacies. It felt adolescent, to tell her he thought of her face; what would she imagine him doing but sweating in the dark and playing with himself like a twelve-year-old? He didn't want her thinking that.

Maybe, on reflection, that had been a mistake. Perhaps the deterioration of their marriage had begun there, with him feeling ridiculous, and giving up writing love letters. But hadn't she changed too? Her eyes looked at him even now with such naked suspicion.

"Flynn sends his regards."

"Oh. Good. You see him, do you?"

"Once in a while."

"How's he doing?"

She'd taken to looking at the clock, rather than at him, which he was glad of. It gave him a chance to study her without feeling intrusive. When she allowed her features to relax, he still found her attractive. But he had, he believed, perfect control over his response to her now. He could look at her—at the translucent lobes of her ears, at the sweep of her neck—and view her quite dispassionately. That, at least, prison had taught him: not to want what he could not have.

"Oh, he's fine—" she replied.

It took him a moment to reorientate himself; who was she talking about? Oh, yes: Flynn. There was a man who'd never got his fingers dirty. Flynn the wise; Flynn the flash.

"He sends his best," she said.

"You told me," he reminded her.

Another pause; the conversation was more crucifying every time she came. Not for him so much as for her. She seemed to go through a trauma every time she spat a single word out.

"I went to see the solicitors again."

"Oh, yes."

"It's all going ahead, apparently. They said the papers would be through next month."

"What do I do, just sign them?"

"Well . . . he said we needed to talk about the house, and all the stuff we've got together."

"You have it."

"But it's ours, isn't it? I mean, it belongs to both of us. And when you come out you're going to need somewhere to live, and furniture and everything."

"Do you want to sell the house?"

Another wretched pause, as though she was trembling on the edge of saying something far more important than the banalities that would surely surface.

"I'm sorry, Marty," she said.

"What for?"

She shook her head, a tiny shake. Her hair shimmered.

"Don't know," she said.

"This isn't your fault. None of this is your fault."

"I can't help—"

She stopped and looked up at him, suddenly more alive in the urgency of her fright—was that what it was, *fright?*—than she'd been in a dozen other wooden exchanges they'd endured in one chilling room or another. Her eyes were liquefying, swelling up with tears.

"What's wrong?"

She stared at him: the tears brimmed.

"Char . . . what's wrong?"

"It's all over, Marty," she said, as though this fact had hit her for the first time; over, finished, fare thee well.

He nodded; "Yes."

"I don't want you . . ." She stopped, paused, then tried again. "You mustn't blame me."

"I don't blame you. I've never blamed you. Christ, you've been here, haven't you? All this time. I hate seeing you in this place, you know. But you came; when I needed you, you were there."

"I thought it would be all right," she said, talking on as though he'd not even spoken, "I really did. I thought you'd be coming out soon—and maybe we'd make it work, you know. We still had the house and all. But these last couple of years, everything just started falling apart."

He watched her suffering, thinking: I'll never be able to forget this, because I caused it, and I'm the most miserable shit on God's earth because look what I did. There'd been tears at the beginning, of course, and letters from her full of hurt and half-buried accusations, but this wracking distress she was showing now went so much deeper. It wasn't from a twenty-two-year-old, for one thing, it was coming from a grown woman; and it shamed him deeply to think he'd caused it, shamed him in a way he thought he'd put behind him.

She blew her nose on a tissue teased from a packet.

"Everything's a mess," she said.

"Yes."

"I just want to sort it out."

She gave a cursory glance at her watch, too fast to register the time, and stood up.

"I'd better go, Marty."

"Appointment?"

"No . . ." she replied, a transparent lie which she made no real effort to carry off, "might do some shopping later on. Always makes me feel better. You know me."

No, he thought. No I don't know you. If I once did, and I'm not even sure of that, it was a different you, and God I miss her. He stopped himself. This was not the way to part with her; he knew that from past encounters. The trick was to be cold, to finish on a note of formality, so that he could go back to his cell and forget her until the next time.

"I wanted you to understand," she said. "But I don't think I explained it very well. It's just such a bloody mess."

She didn't say goodbye: tears were beginning again, and he was certain that she was frightened, under the talk of solicitors, that she would recant at the last moment—out of weakness, or love, or both—and by walking out without turning around she was keeping the possibility at bay.

Defeated, he went back to the cell. Feaver was asleep. He'd stuck a vulva torn from one of his magazines onto his forehead with spit, a favorite routine of his. It gaped—a third eye—above his closed lids, staring and staring without hope of sleep.

7

S trauss?"
Priestley was at the open door, staring into the cell. Beside him, on the wall some wit had scrawled: "*If you feel horny, kick the door. A cunt will appear.*" It was a familiar joke—he'd seen the same gag or similar on a number of cell walls—but now, looking at Priestley's thick face, the association of ideas—the enemy and a woman's sex—struck him as obscene.

"Strauss?"

"Yes, sir."

"Mr. Somervale wants to see you. About three-fifteen. I'll come and collect you. Be ready at ten past."

"Yes, sir."

Priestley turned to go.

"Can you tell me what it's about, sir?"

"How the fuck should I know?"

S omervale was waiting in the Interview Room at three-fifteen. Marty's file was on the table in front of him, its drawstrings still knotted. Beside it, a buff envelope, unmarked. Somervale himself was standing by the reinforced glass window, smoking.

"Come in," he said. There was no invitation to sit down; nor did he turn from the window.

Marty closed the door behind him, and waited. Somervale exhaled smoke through his nostrils noisily.

"What do you suppose, Strauss?" he said.

"I beg your pardon, sir?"

"I said: what do you suppose, eh? Imagine."

Marty followed none of this so far, and wondered if the confusion was his or Somervale's. After an age, Somervale said: "My wife died."

Marty wondered what he was expected to say. As it was, Somervale didn't give him time to formulate a response. He followed the first three words with five more:

"They're letting you out, Strauss!"

He placed the bald facts side by side as if they belonged together; as if the entire world was in collusion against him.

"Am I going with Mr. Toy?" Marty asked.

"He and the board believe you are a suitable candidate for the job at Whitehead's estate," Somervale said. "Imagine." He made a low sound in his throat, which could have been laughter. "You'll be under close scrutiny, of course. Not by me, but by whoever follows me. And if you once step out of line . . ."

"I understand."

"I wonder if you do." Somervale drew on his cigarette, still not turning around. "I wonder if you understand just what kind of freedom you've chosen—"

Marty wasn't about to let this kind of talk spoil his escalating euphoria. Somervale was defeated; let him talk.

"Joseph Whitehead may be one of the richest men in Europe but he's also one of the most eccentric, I hear. God knows what you're letting yourself in for, but I tell you, I think you may find life in here a good deal more palatable."

Somervale's words evaporated; his sour grapes fell on deaf ears. Either through exhaustion, or because he sensed that he'd lost his audience, he gave up his disparaging monologue almost as soon as it began, and turned from the window to finish this distasteful business as expeditiously as he could. Marty was shocked to see the change in the man. In the weeks since they'd last met, Somervale had aged years; he looked as though he'd survived the intervening time on cigarettes and grief. His skin was like stale bread.

"Mr. Toy will pick you up from the gates next Friday afternoon. That's February thirteenth. Are you superstitious?"

"No."

Somervale handed the envelope across to Marty.

"All the details are in there. In the next couple of days you'll have a medical, and somebody will be here to go through your position vis-à-vis the parole board. Rules are being bent on your behalf, Strauss. God knows why. There's a dozen more worthy candidates in your wing alone."

Marty opened the envelope, quickly scanned the tightly typed pages, and pocketed them.

"You won't be seeing me again," Somervale was saying, "for which I'm sure you're suitably grateful."

Marty let not a flicker of response cross his face. His feigned indifference seemed to ignite a pocket of unused loathing in Somervale's fatigued frame. His bad teeth showed as he said: "If I were you, I'd thank God, Strauss. I'd thank God from the bottom of my heart."

"What for . . . sir?"

"But then I don't suppose you've got much room for God, have you?"

The words contained pain and contempt in equal measure. Marty couldn't help thinking of Somervale alone in a double bed; a husband without a wife, and without the faith to believe in seeing her again; incapable of tears. And another thought came fast upon the first: that Somervale's stone heart, which had been broken at one terrible stroke, was not so dissimilar from his own. Both hard men, both keeping the world at bay while they waged private wars in their guts. Both ending up with the very weapons they'd forged to defeat their enemies turned on themselves. It was a vile realization, and had Marty not been buoyant with the news of his release he might not have dared think it. But there it was. He and Somervale, like two lizards lying in the same stinking mud, suddenly seemed very like twins.

"What are you thinking, Strauss?" Somervale asked.

Marty shrugged.

"Nothing," he said.

"Liar," said the other. Picking up the file, he walked out of the Interview Room, leaving the door open behind him.

Marty telephoned Charmaine the following day, and told her what had happened. She seemed pleased, which was gratifying. When he came off the phone he was shaking, but he felt good.

He lived the last few days at Wandsworth with stolen eyes, or that's how it seemed. Everything about prison life that he had become so used to—the casual cruelty, the endless jeering, the power games, the sex games—all seemed new to him again, as they had been six years before.

They were wasted years, of course. Nothing could bring them back, nothing could fill them up with useful experience. The thought depressed him. He had so little to go out into the world with. Two tattoos, a body that had seen better days, memories of anger and despair. In the journey ahead he was going to be traveling light.

8

The night before he left Wandsworth he had a dream. His nightlife had not been much to shout about during the years of his sentence. Wet dreams about Charmaine had soon stopped, as had his more exotic flights of fancy, as though his subconscious, sympathetic to confinement, wanted to avoid taunting him with dreams of freedom. Once in a while he'd wake in the middle of the night with his head swimming in glories, but most of his dreams were as pointless and as repetitive as his waking life. But this was a different experience altogether.

He dreamed a cathedral of sorts, an unfinished, perhaps unfinishable, masterpiece of towers and spires and soaring buttresses, too vast to exist in the physical world—gravity denied it—but here, in his head, an awesome reality. It was night as he walked toward it, the gravel crunching underfoot, the air smelling of honeysuckle, and from inside he could hear singing. Ecstatic voices, a boys' choir he thought, rising and falling wordlessly. There were no people visible in the silken darkness around him: no fellow tourists to gape at this wonder. Just him, and the voices.

And then, miraculously, he flew.

He was weightless, and the wind had him, and he was ascending the steep side of the cathedral with breath-snatching velocity. He flew, it seemed, not like a bird, but, paradoxically, like some airborne fish. Like a dolphin—yes, that's what he was— his arms close by his side sometimes, sometimes plowing the blue air as he rose, a smooth, naked thing that skimmed the slates and looped the spires, fingertips grazing the dew on the stonework, flicking raindrops off the gutter pipes. If he'd ever dreamed anything so sweet, he couldn't remember it. The intensity of his joy was almost too much, and it startled him awake.

He was back, wide-eyed, in the forced heat of the cell, with Feaver on the bunk below, masturbating. The bunk rocked rhythmically, speed increasing, and Feaver climaxed with a stifled grunt. Marty tried to block reality, and concentrate on recapturing his dream. He closed his eyes again, willing the image back to him, saying *come on, come on* to the dark. For one shattering moment, the dream returned: only this time it wasn't triumph, it was terror, and he was pitching out of the sky from a hundred miles high, and the cathedral was rushing toward him, its spires sharpening themselves on the wind in preparation for his arrival—

He shook himself awake, canceling the plunge before it could be finished, and lay the rest of the night staring at the ceiling until a wretched gloom, the first light of dawn, spilled through the window to announce the day.

9

No profligate sky greeted his release. Just a commonplace Friday afternoon, with business as usual on Trinity Road.

Toy had been waiting for him in the reception wing when Marty was brought down from his landing. He had longer yet to wait, while the officers went through a dozen bureaucratic rituals; belongings to be checked and returned, release papers to be signed and countersigned. It took almost an hour of such formalities before they unlocked the doors and let them both out into the open air.

With little more than a handshake of welcome Toy led him across the forecourt of the prison to where a dark red Daimler was parked, the driver's seat occupied.

"Come on, Marty," he said, opening the door, "too cold to linger."

It *was* cold: the wind was vicious. But the chill couldn't freeze his joy. He was a free man, for God's sake; free within carefully prescribed limits perhaps, but it was a beginning. He was at least putting behind him all the paraphernalia of prison: the bucket in the corner of the cell, the keys, the numbers. Now he had to be the equal of the choices and opportunities that would lead from here.

Toy had already taken refuge in the back of the car.

"Marty," he summoned again, his suede-gloved hand beckoning. "We should hurry, or we'll get snarled up getting out of the city."

"Yes. I'm here—"

Marty got in. The interior of the car smelled of polish, stale cigar smoke and leather; luxuriant scents.

"Should I put the case in the boot?" Marty said.

The driver turned from the wheel.

"You got room back there," he said. A West Indian, dressed not in chauffeur's livery but in a battered leather flying jacket, looked Marty up and down. He offered no welcoming smile.

"Luther," said Toy, "this is Marty."

"Put the case over the front seat," the driver replied; he leaned across and opened the front passenger door. Marty got out and slid his case and plastic bag of belongings onto the front seat beside a litter of newspapers and a thumbed copy of *Playboy*, then got into the back with Toy and slammed the door.

"No need to slam," said Luther, but Marty scarcely heard the remark. Not many cons get picked up from the gates of Wandsworth in a Daimler, he was thinking: maybe this time I've fallen on my feet.

The car purred away from the gates and made a left onto Trinity Road.

"Luther's been with the estate for two years," Toy said.

"Three," the other man corrected him.

"Is it?" Toy replied. "Three then. He drives me around; takes Mr. Whitehead when he goes down to London."

"Don't do that no more."

Marty caught the driver's eye in the mirror.

"You been in that shit-house long?" the man asked, pouncing without a flicker of hesitation.

"Long enough," Marty replied. He wasn't going to try to hide anything; there was no sense in that. He waited for the next inevitable question: what were you in for? But it didn't come. Luther turned his attention back to the business of the road, apparently satisfied. Marty was happy to let the conversation drop. All he wanted to do was watch this brave new world go by, and drink it all in. The people, the shopfronts, the advertisements, he had a hunger for all the details, no matter how trivial. He glued his eyes to the window. There was so much to see, and yet he had the distinct impression that it was all artificial, as though the people in the street, in the other cars, were actors, all cast to type and playing their parts immaculately. His mind, struggling to accommodate the welter of information—on every side a new vista, at every corner a different parade passing—simply rejected their reality. It was all stage-managed, his brain told him, all a fiction. Because look, these people behaved as though they'd lived without him, as though the world had gone on while he'd been locked away, and some childlike part of him—the part that, hiding its eyes, believes itself hidden—could not conceive of a life for anyone without him to see it.

His common sense told him otherwise, of course. Whatever his confused senses might suspect, the world was older, and more weary probably, since he and it had last met. He would have to renew his acquaintance with it: learn how its nature had changed; learn again its etiquette, its touchiness, its potential for pleasure.

They crossed the river via the Wandsworth Bridge and drove through Earl's Court and Shepherd's Bush onto Westway. It was the middle of a Friday afternoon, and the traffic was heavy; commuters eager to be home for the weekend. He stared blatantly at the faces of the drivers in the cars they overtook, guessing occupations, or trying to catch the eyes of the women.

Mile by mile, the strangeness he'd felt initially began to wear off, and by the time they reached the M40 he was starting to tire of the spectacle. Toy had nodded off in his corner of the back seat, his hands in his lap. Luther was occupied with leapfrogging down the highway.

Only one event slowed their progress. Twenty miles short of Oxford blue lights flashed on the road up ahead, and the sound of a siren speeding toward them from behind announced an accident. The procession of cars slowed, like a line of mourners pausing to glance into a coffin.

A car had slewed across the eastbound lanes, crossed the divide, and met, head-on, a van coming in the opposite direction. All of the westbound lanes were blocked, either by wreckage or by police cars, and the travelers were obliged to use the shoulder to skirt the scattered wreckage. "What's happened; can you see?" Luther asked, his attention too occupied by navigating past the signaling policeman for him to see for himself. Marty described the scene as best he could.

A man, with blood streaming down his face as if somebody had cracked a blood-yolked egg on his head, was standing in the middle of the chaos, hypnotized by shock. Behind him a group—police and rescued passengers alike—gathered around the concertinaed front section of the car to speak to somebody trapped in the driver's seat. The figure was slumped, motionless. As they crept past, one of these comforters, her coat soaked either with her own blood or that of the driver, turned away from the vehicle and began to applaud. At least that was how Marty interpreted the slapping together of her hands: as applause. It was as if she were suffering the same delusion he'd tasted so recently—that this was all some meticulous but distasteful illusion—and at any moment it would all come to a welcome end. He wanted to lean out of the car window and tell her that she was wrong; that this was the real world—long-legged women, crystal sky and all. But she'd know that tomorrow, wouldn't she? Plenty of time for grief then. But for now she clapped, and she was still clapping when the accident slid out of sight behind them.

II. THE FOX

10

Asylum, Whitehead knew, was a traitorous word. In one breath it meant a sanctuary, a place of refuge, of safety. In another, its meaning twisted on itself: asylum came to mean a madhouse, a hole for broken minds to bury themselves in. It was, he reminded himself, a semantic trick, no more. Why then did the ambiguity run in his head so often?

He sat in that too-comfortable chair beside the window where he had sat now for a season of evenings watching the night begin to skulk across the lawn and thinking, without much shape to his ruminations, about how one thing became another; about how difficult it was to hold on to anything. Life was a random business. Whitehead had learned that lesson years ago, at the hands of a master, and he had never forgotten it. Whether you were rewarded for your good works or skinned alive, it was all down to chance. No use to cleave to some system of numbers or divinities; they all crumbled in the end. Fortune belonged to the man who was willing to risk everything on a single throw.

He'd done that. Not once, but many times at the beginning of his career, when he was still laying the foundations of his empire. And thanks to that extraordinary sixth sense he possessed, the ability to preempt the roll of the dice, the risks had almost always paid off. Other corporations had their virtuosi: computers that calculated the odds to the tenth place, advisers who kept their ears pressed to the stock markets of Tokyo, London and New York, but they were all overshadowed by Whitehead's instinct. When it came to knowing the *moment*, for sensing the collision of time and opportunity that made a good decision into a great one, a commonplace takeover into a coup, nobody was Old Man Whitehead's superior, and all the smart young men in the corporation's boardrooms knew that. Joe's oracular advice still had to be sought before any significant expansion was undertaken or contract signed.

He guessed this authority, which remained absolute, was resented in some circles. No doubt there were those who thought he should let go his hold completely and leave the university men and their computers to get on with business. But Whitehead had won these skills, these unique powers of second-guessing, at some hazard; foolish then that they lie forgotten when they could be used to lay a finger on the wheel. Besides, the old man had an argument the young turks could never gainsay: his methods worked. He'd never been properly schooled; his life before fame was—much to the journalists' dismay—a blank, but he had made the Whitehead Corporation out of nothing. Its fate, for better or worse, was still his passionate concern.

There was no room for passion tonight, however, sitting in that chair (a chair to die in, he'd sometimes thought) beside the window. Tonight there was only unease: that old man's complaint.

How he loathed age! It was hardly bearable to be so *reduced*. Not that he was infirm; just that a dozen minor ailments conspired against his comfort so that seldom a day passed without some irritation—an ulcerous mouth, or a chafing between the buttocks that itched furiously—fixing his attentions in the body when the urge to self-preservation called them elsewhere. The curse of age, he'd decided, was distraction, and he couldn't afford the luxury of negligent thinking. There was danger in contemplating itch and ulcer. As soon as his mind was turned, something would take out his throat. That was what the unease was telling him. *Don't look away for a moment; don't think you're safe because, old man, I've a message for you: the worst is yet to come.*

Toy knocked once before entering the study.

"Bill . . ."

Whitehead momentarily forgot the lawn and the advancing darkness as he turned to face his friend.

". . . you got here."

"Of course we got here, Joe. Are we late?"

"No, no. No problems?"

"Things are fine."

"Good."

"Strauss is downstairs."

In the diminishing light Whitehead crossed to the table and poured himself a sparing glass of vodka. He had been holding off from drinking until now; a shot to celebrate Toy's safe arrival.

"You want one?"

It was a ritual question, with a ritual response: "No thanks."

"You're going back to town, then?"

"When you've seen Strauss."

"It's too late for the theater. Why don't you stay, Bill? Go back tomorrow morning when it's light."

"I've got business," Toy said, allowing himself the gentlest of smiles on the final word. This was another ritual, one of many between the two men. Toy's business in London, which the old man knew had nothing to do with the corporation, went unquestioned; it always had.

"And what's your impression?"

"Of Strauss? Much as I thought at the interview. I think he'll be fine. And if he isn't, there's plenty more where he came from."

"I need someone who isn't going to scare easily. Things could get very unpleasant."

Toy offered a noncommittal grunt and hoped that the talk on this matter wouldn't go any further. He was tired after a day of waiting and traveling, and he wanted to look forward to the evening; this was no time to talk over that business again.

Whitehead had put down his drained glass on the tray and gone back to the window. It was darkening in the room quite rapidly now, and when the old man stood with his back to Toy he was welded by shadow into something monolithic. After thirty years in Whitehead's employ—three decades with scarcely a cross word spoken between them—Toy was still as much in awe of Whitehead as of some potentate with the power of life and death over him. He still took a pause to find his equilibrium before entering into Whitehead's presence; he still found traces of the stammer he'd had when they'd met returning on occasion. It was a legitimate response, he felt. The man was *power*: more power than he could ever hope, or indeed would ever want, to possess: and it sat with deceptive lightness on Joe Whitehead's substantial shoulders. In all their years of association, in conference or boardroom, he had never seen Whitehead want for the appropriate gesture or remark. He was simply the most confident man Toy had ever met: certain to his marrow of his own supreme worth, his skills honed to such an edge that a man could be undone by a word, gutted for life, his self-esteem drained and his career tattered. Toy had seen it done countless times, and often to men he considered his betters. Which begged the question (he asked it even now, staring at Whitehead's back): why did the great man pass the time of day with him? Perhaps it was simply history. Was that it? History and sentiment.

"I'm thinking of filling in the outdoor pool."

Toy thanked God Whitehead had changed the subject. No talk of the past, for tonight at least.

"—I don't swim out there any longer, even in the summer."

"Put some fishes in."

Whitehead turned his head slightly to see if there was a smile on Toy's face. He never signaled a joke in the tone of his voice, and it was easy, Whitehead knew, to offend the man's sensibilities if one laughed when no joke was intended, or the other way about. Toy wasn't smiling.

"Fishes?" said Whitehead.

"Ornamental carp, perhaps. Aren't they called koi? Exquisite things."

Toy liked the pool. At night it was lit from below, and the

surface moved in mesmerizing eddies, the turquoise enchanting. If there was a chill in the air the heated water gave off a wispy breath that melted away six inches from the surface. In fact, though he'd hated swimming, the pool was a favorite place of his. He wasn't certain if Whitehead knew this: he probably did. Papa knew most things, he'd found, whether they'd been voiced or not.

"You like the pool," Whitehead stated.

There: proof.

"Yes. I do."

"Then we'll keep it."

"Well not just—"

Whitehead raised his hand to ward off further debate, pleased to be giving this gift.

"We'll keep it," he said. "And you can fill it with koi."

He sat back down in the chair.

"Shall I put the lawn lights on?" Toy asked.

"No," said Whitehead. The dying light from the window cast his head in bronze, a latter-day Medici perhaps, with his weary-lidded, pit-set eyes, the white beard and mustache cropped nickingly close to his skin, the whole construction seemingly too weighty for the column supporting it. Aware that his eyes were boring into the old man's back, and that Joe would surely sense it, Toy sloughed off the lethargy of the room and pressed himself back into action.

"Well . . . shall I fetch Strauss, Joe? Do you want to see him or not?"

The words took an age to cross the room in the thickening darkness. For several heartbeats Toy wasn't even certain that Whitehead had heard him.

Then the oracle spoke. Not a prophecy, but a question.

"Will we survive, Bill?"

The words were spoken so quietly they only just carried, hooked on motes of dust and wafted from his lips. Toy's heart sank. It was the old theme again: the same paranoid song.

"I hear more and more rumors, Bill. They can't all be groundless."

He was still looking out the window. Rooks circled above the wood half a mile or so across the lawn. Was he watching them? Toy doubted it. He'd seen Whitehead like this often of late, sunk down into himself, scanning the past with his mind's eye. It wasn't a vision Toy had access to, but he could guess at Joe's present fears—he'd been there, after all, in the early days—and he knew too that however much he loved the old man there were some burdens he would never be capable, or willing, to share. He wasn't strong enough; he was at heart still the boxer Whitehead had employed as a bodyguard three decades before. Now, of course, he wore a four-hundred-pound suit, and his nails were as immaculately kept as his manners. But his mind was the same as ever, superstitious and fragile. The dreams the great dreamed were not for him. Nor were their nightmares.

Again, Whitehead posed the haunted question:

"Will we survive?"

This time Toy felt obliged to reply.

"Everything's fine, Joe. You know it is. Profits up in most sectors . . ."

But evasion wasn't what the old man wanted and Toy knew it. He let the words falter, leaving a silence, after the faltering, more wretched than ever. Toy's stare, now fixed on Whitehead again, was unblinking, and at the corners of his eyes the murk that had taken over the room began to flicker and crawl. He dropped his lids: they almost grated across his eyeballs. Patterns danced in his head (wheels, stars and windows) and when he opened his eyes again the night finally had a stranglehold on the interior.

The bronze head remained unmoved. But it spoke, and the words seemed to come from Whitehead's bowels, dirtied with fear.

"I'm afraid, Willy," he said. "All my life I've never been as frightened as I am now."

He spoke slowly, without the least emphasis, as if he despised the melodrama of his words and was refusing to magnify it further.

"All these years, living without fear; I'd forgotten what it was like. How crippling it is. How it drains your willpower. I just sit here, day in, day out. Locked up in this place, with the alarms, the fences, the dogs. I watch the lawn and the trees—"

He *was* watching.

"—and sooner or later, the light begins to fade."

He paused: a long, deep hush, except for the distant crows.

"I can bear the night itself. It's not pleasant, but it's unambiguous. It's twilight I can't deal with. That's when the bad sweats come over me. When the light's going, and nothing's quite real anymore, quite solid. Just forms. Things that once had shapes . . ."

It had been a winter of such evenings: colorless drizzles that eroded distance and killed sound; weeks on end of uncertain light, when troubled dawn became troubled dusk with no day intervening. There had been too few hard-frosted days like today; just one discouraging month upon another.

"I sit here every evening now," the old man was saying. "It's a test I set myself. Just to sit and watch everything eroded. *Defying* it all."

Toy could taste the profundity of Papa's despair. He hadn't been like this ever before; not even after Evangeline's death.

It was almost completely dark outside and in; without the lawn lights on, the grounds were pitch. But Whitehead still sat, facing the black window, watching.

"It's all there, of course," he said.

"What is?"

"The trees, the lawn. When dawn comes tomorrow they'll be waiting."

"Yes, of course."

"You know, as a child I thought somebody came and took the world away in the night and then came back and unrolled it all again the following morning."

He stirred in his seat; his hand moved to his head. Impossible to see what he was doing.

"The things we believe as children: they never leave us, do they? They're just waiting for time to roll around, and us to start believing in them all over again. It's the same old patch, Bill. You know? I mean, we think we move on, we get stronger, we get wiser, but all the time we're standing on the same patch."

He sighed, and looked around at Toy. Light from the hallway fawned through the door, which Toy had left slightly ajar. By it, even across the room, Whitehead's eyes and cheeks glittered with tears.

"You'd better put on the light, Bill," he said.

"Yes."

"And bring up Strauss."

There was no sign of his distress apparent in his voice. But then Joe was an expert at disguising his feelings; Toy knew that of old. He could close down the hoods of his eyes and seal up his mouth, and not even a mind-reader could work out what he was thinking. It was a skill he'd used to devastating effect in the boardroom: nobody ever knew which way the old fox would jump. He'd learned the technique playing cards, presumably. That, and how to wait.

11

They had driven through the electric gates of Whitehead's estate and into another world. Lawns laid out immaculately on either side of the sepia-graveled driveway; a distant aspect of woodland off to the right, which disappeared behind a line of cypresses as they bore around toward the house itself. It was late afternoon by the time they arrived, but the mellowing light only enhanced the charm of the place, its formality offset by a rising mist that blurred the scalpel edge of grass and tree.

The main building was less spectacular than Marty had anticipated; just a large, Georgian country house, solid but plain, with modern extensions sprawling away from the main structure. They drove past the front door, with its white pillared porch, to a side entrance, and Toy invited him through into the kitchen.

"Put your bags down and help yourself to some coffee," he said. "I'm just going up to see the boss man. Make yourself comfortable."

Alone for the first time since leaving Wandsworth Marty felt uncomfortable. The door was open at his back; there were no locks on the windows, no officers patrolling the corridors beyond the kitchen. It was paradoxical, but he felt unprotected, almost vulnerable. After a few minutes he got up from the table, switched on the fluorescent light (night was falling quickly, and there were no automatic switches here) and poured himself a mug of black coffee from the percolator. It was heavy and slightly bitter, brewed and rebrewed he guessed, not like the insipid stuff he was used to.

It was twenty-five minutes before Toy came back in, apologized for the delay, and told him that Mr. Whitehead would see him now.

"Leave your bags," he said. "Luther will see to them."

Toy led the way from the kitchen, which was part of the extension, into the main house. The corridors were gloomy, but everywhere Marty's eye was amazed. The building was a museum. Paintings covered the walls from floor to ceiling; on the tables and shelves were vases and ceramic figurines whose enamels gleamed. There was no time to linger, however. They wove through the maze of halls, Marty's sense of direction more confounded with every turn, until they reached the study. Toy knocked, opened the door, and ushered Marty in.

With little but a badly remembered photograph of Whitehead to build upon, Marty's portrait of his new employer had been chiefly invention—and totally wrong. Where he'd imagined frailty, he found robustness. Where he'd expected the eccentricity of a recluse he found a furrowed, subtle face that scanned him, even as he entered the study, with efficiency and humor.

"Mr. Strauss," said Whitehead, "welcome."

Behind Whitehead, the curtains were still open, and through the window the floodlights suddenly came on, illuminating the piercing green of the lawns for a good two hundred yards. It was like a conjurer's trick, the sudden appearance of this sward, but Whitehead ignored it. He walked toward Marty. Though he was a large man, and much of his bulk had turned to fat, the weight sat on his frame quite easily. There was no sense of awkwardness. The grace of his gait, the almost oiled smoothness of his arm as he extended it to Marty, the suppleness of the proffered fingers, all suggested a man at peace with his physique.

They shook hands. Either Marty was hot, or the other man cold: Marty immediately took the error to be his. A man like Whitehead was surely never too hot or too cold; he controlled his temperature with the same ease he controlled his finances. Hadn't Toy dropped into their few exchanges in the car the fact that Whitehead had never been seriously ill in his life? Now Marty was face-to-face with the paragon he could believe it. Not a whisper of flatulence would dare this man's bowels.

"I'm Joseph Whitehead," he said. "Welcome to the Sanctuary."

"Thank you."

"You'll have a drink? Celebrate."

"Yes, please."

"What will it be?"

Marty's mind suddenly went blank, and he found himself gaping like a stranded fish. It was Toy, God save him, who suggested:

"Scotch?"

"That'd be fine."

"The usual for me," said Whitehead. "Come and sit down, Mr. Strauss."

They sat. The chairs were comfortable; not antiques, like the tables in the corridors, but functional, modern pieces. The entire room shared this style: it was a working environment, not a museum. The few pictures on the dark blue walls looked, to Marty's uneducated eye, as recent as the furniture; they were large and slapdash. The most prominently placed, and the most representational, was signed *Matisse*, and pictured a bilious pink woman sprawled on a bilious yellow chaise longue.

"Your whisky."

Marty accepted the glass Toy was offering.

"We had Luther buy you a selection of new clothes; they're up in your room," Whitehead was telling Marty. "Just a couple of suits, shirts and so on, to start with. Later on, we'll maybe send you out shopping for yourself." He drained his glass of neat vodka before continuing. "Do they still issue suits to prisoners, or did they discontinue that? Smacks of the poorhouse, I suppose. Wouldn't be too tactful in these enlightened times. People might begin to think you were criminals by necessity—"

Marty wasn't at all sure about this line of chat: was Whitehead making fun of him? The monologue went on, its tenor quite friendly, while Marty tried to sort out irony from straightforward opinion. It was difficult. He was reminded, in the space of a few minutes listening to Whitehead talk, of how much subtler things were on the outside. By comparison with this man's shifting, richly inflected talk the cleverest conversationalist in Wandsworth was an amateur. Toy slipped a second large whisky into Marty's hand, but he scarcely noticed. Whitehead's voice was hypnotic; and strangely soothing.

"Toy has explained your duties to you, has he?"

"Yes, I think so."

"I want you to make this house your home, Strauss. Become familiar with it. There are one or two places that will be out-of-bounds to you; Toy will tell you where. Please observe those constraints. The rest of the place is at your disposal."

Marty nodded, and downed his whisky; it ran down his gullet like quicksilver.

"Tomorrow . . ."

Whitehead stood up, the thought unfinished, and returned to the window. The grass shone as though freshly painted.

". . . we'll take a walk around the place, you and I."

"Fine."

"See what's to be seen. Introduce you to Bella, and the others."

There was more staff? Toy hadn't mentioned them; but inevitably there would be others here: guards, cooks, gardeners. The place probably swarmed with functionaries.

"Come talk to me tomorrow, eh?"

Marty drained the rest of his scotch and Toy gestured that he should stand up. Whitehead seemed suddenly to have lost interest in them both. His assessment was over, at least for today; his thoughts were already elsewhere, his stare directed out of the window at the gleaming lawn.

"Yes, sir. Tomorrow."

"But before you come—" Whitehead said, glancing around at Marty.

"Yes, sir."

"Shave off your mustache. Anybody would think you'd got something to hide."

12

Toy gave Marty a perfunctory tour of the house before taking him upstairs, promising a more thorough walkabout when time wasn't so pressing. Then he delivered Marty to a long, airy room on the top story, and at the side of the house.

"This is yours," he said. Luther had left the suitcase and the plastic bag on the bed; their tattiness looked out of place in the

sleek utility of the room. It had, like the study, contemporary
fittings.

"It's a bit bare at the moment," said Toy. "So do whatever you
want with it. If you've got photographs—"

"Not really."

"Well, we ought to get something on the walls. There are some
books"—he nodded to the far end of the room, where several
shelves groaned under a weight of volumes—"but the library
downstairs is at your disposal. I'll show you the layout sometime
next week, when you've settled in. There's a video up here, too,
and another downstairs. Again, Joe doesn't really have much
interest in it, so help yourself." "Sounds good."

"There's a small dressing room through to the left. As Joe
said, you'll find some fresh clothes in there. Your bathroom is
through the other door. Shower and so on. And I think that's it.
I hope it's adequate."

"It's fine," Marty said. Toy glanced at his watch and turned to
leave.

"Just before you go . . ."

"Problem?"

"No problem," Marty said. "Jesus, no problem at all. I just
want you to know I'm grateful—"

"No need."

"But I am," Marty insisted; he'd been trying to find a cue for
this speech since Trinity Road. "I'm *very* grateful. I don't know
how or why you chose me—but I appreciate it."

Toy was mildly discomforted by this show of feeling, but
Marty was glad to have it said.

"Believe me, Marty. I wouldn't have chosen you if I didn't
think you could do the job. You're here now. It's up to you to
make the best of it. I'm going to be around, of course, but after
this you're more or less your own man."

"Yes. I realize that."

"I'll leave you then. See you at the beginning of the week.
Pearl's left food out for you in the kitchen, by the way. Goodnight."

"Goodnight."

Toy left him alone. He sat down on the bed and opened his suitcase. The badly packed clothes smelled of prison detergent, and he didn't want to take them out. Instead he dug down to the bottom of the case until his hands found his razor and shaving foam. Then he undressed, slung his stale clothes on the floor, and went into the bathroom.

It was spacious, mirrored, and seductively lit. Freshly laundered towels hung on a heated rack. There was a shower as well as a bath and a bidet: an embarrassment of waterworks. Whatever else happened to him here, he'd be clean. He switched on the mirror light and set the shaving implements down on the glass shelf above the sink. He needn't have bothered with his search. Toy, or perhaps Luther, had laid a complete shaving kit out for him; razor, preshave, foam, cologne. All unopened, pristine: waiting for him. He looked at himself in the mirror—that intimate self-scrutiny which was expected of women but which men seldom practiced except in locked bathrooms. The anxieties of the day showed on his face: his skin was anemic, and the bags under his eyes full. Like a man searching for some treasure, he plundered his face for clues. Was his past written here, he wondered, in all its grubby detail; etched, perhaps, too deeply to be erased?

He needed some sun, no doubt of that, and decent exercise out in the open air. From tomorrow, he thought, a new regime. He'd run every day till he was so fit he was unrecognizable. Get himself to a proper dentist too. His gums bled worryingly often, and in one or two places they were receding from the tooth. He was proud of his teeth: they were even and strong, like his mother's. He tried his smile on the mirror, but it had lost some of its former sparkle. He'd have to exercise that too. He was in the big wide world again; and maybe in time there'd be women to woo with that smile.

His surveillance shifted from face to body. A wedge of fat was sitting on the muscle of his abdomen: he was easily a stone overweight. He'd have to work at that. Watch his diet, and keep

the exercise up until he was back to the twelve stone three he'd
been when he first went to Wandsworth. The extra weight apart,
he felt quite good about himself. Maybe the warm light flattered
him, but prison didn't seem to have changed him radically. He
still had all his hair; he wasn't scarred—except for the tattoos,
and a small crescent to the left of his mouth; he wasn't doped up
to the eyeballs. Maybe he *was* a survivor after all.

His hand had crept to his groin as he perused himself, and he'd
idly teased himself semierect. He hadn't been thinking of
Charmaine. If there was any lust in his arousal it was narcissistic.
Many of the cons he'd lived with had found it easy to slake their
sexual thirst with their cellmates, but Marty had never been
comfortable with the idea. Not simply out of distaste for the acts—
though he felt that acutely—but because that unnaturalness was
forced upon him. It was just another way that prison humiliated a
man. Instead, he'd locked his sexuality away, and used his cock for
pissing and little else. Now, toying with it like a vain adolescent, he
wondered if he could still use the damn thing.

He ran the shower lukewarm and stepped in, slicking himself
down from head to foot with lemon-scented soap. In a day of
pleasures this was perhaps the best. The water was stimulating,
like standing in a spring rain. His body began to wake. Yes, that
was it, he thought: I've been dead, and I'm coming back to life.
He'd been buried in the asshole of the world, a hole so deep he
thought he'd never scramble out of it, but he *had*, damn it. He was
out. He rinsed, and then indulged himself with a repeat of the
ritual, this time running the water considerably hotter and harder.
The bathroom filled with steam and the slap of the water on the
shower tiles.

When he stepped out and turned the flow off, his head buzzed
with heat, whisky and fatigue. He moved to the mirror and cleared
an oval in the condensation with the ball of his fist. The water
had brought new color to his cheeks. His hair was plastered to his
head like a brown-blond skullcap. He'd let it grow, he thought, as
long as Whitehead didn't object; get it styled perhaps. But there was

more pressing business now; the removal of the condemned mustache. He wasn't particularly hirsute. The mustache had taken him several weeks to grow, and he'd had to tolerate the usual run of witless remarks while he was doing it. But if the boss man wanted him barefaced, who was he to argue? Whitehead's opinion on the matter had sounded more like an order than a suggestion.

Despite the well-supplied cabinet in the bathroom (everything from aspirin to crab-killing preparations), there were no scissors, and he had to soap the hairs thoroughly to soften them and then go at them directly with the razor. The blade protested, and so did his skin, but stroke by stroke his upper lip came back into view, the hard-earned mustache hitting the sink in a slop of suds, only to be sucked away down the drain. It took him half an hour to do the job to his satisfaction. He nicked himself in two or three places, and sealed the cuts as best he could with spit.

By the time he'd finished the steam had cleared from the bathroom, and only patches of mist marred his reflection. He looked at his face in the mirror. His naked upper lip was pink and vulnerable, and the groove at its center curiously over-perfect in its formation, but his sudden nudity wasn't such a bad sight.

Content, he sluiced the remains of his mustache from the sides of the sink, wrapped a towel about his middle and sauntered back into the bedroom. In the centrally heated warmth of the house, he was practically dry: no need for toweling. Weariness and hunger fought in him as he sat on the edge of the bed. There was food downstairs for him, or so Toy had said. Well, maybe he'd just lie back on his virginal sheet, head on the scented pillow, and close his eyes for half an hour, then get up and wander down to eat supper. He slung off the towel and lay on the bed, half-pulling the duvet over him, and in the act of doing so, fell asleep. There were no dreams; or if there were he slept too securely to remember them.

It was morning in moments.

13

If he had forgotten the geography of the house from his brief tour the previous night, it took only a sense of smell to lead him back to the kitchen. Bacon was frying, fresh coffee was being perked. At the stove stood a red-haired woman. She turned from her work and nodded.

"You must be Martin," she said; her voice carried a faint Irish inflection. "You're up late."

He looked at the clock on the wall. It was a few minutes past seven.

"You've got a fine morning to start."

The back door was open; he crossed the expanse of the kitchen to survey the day. It *was* fine; another clear sky. Frost sugared the lawn. In the misted distance he could see what looked like tennis courts, and beyond them, a stand of trees.

"I'm Pearl, by the way," the woman announced. "I cook for Mr. Whitehead. Hungry, are you?"

"I am now I'm down here."

"We believe in breakfast here. Something to set you up for the day." She was busy transferring bacon from the frying pan on the stove to the oven. The work surface beside the hob was littered with food: tomatoes, sausages, slices of black pudding. "There's coffee on the side there. Help yourself."

The percolator burped and fizzed as he poured himself a mug of coffee, the same dark but fragrant roast he'd tasted the night before.

"You'll have to get used to using the kitchen when I'm not here. I don't live in. I just come and go."

"Who cooks for Mr. Whitehead when you're away?"

"He likes to do it himself on occasion. But you'll have to put in a hand."

"I can scarcely boil water."

"You'll learn."

She turned to look at him, egg in hand. She was older than he'd at first thought: maybe fifty.

"Don't fret yourself about it," she said. "How hungry?"

"Ravenous."

"I left a cold spread out last night."

"I fell asleep."

She broke one egg into the frying pan, and then a second, as she said, "Mr. Whitehead doesn't have fancy tastes, except for his strawberries. He won't be expecting soufflés, don't worry. Most of the stuff's in the freezer next door: all you have to do is unwrap it and put it in the microwave."

Marty scanned the kitchen, taking in all the equipment: food processor, microwave oven, electric carving knife. Behind him, mounted on the wall, was a row of television screens. He hadn't noticed them last night. Before he could inquire about them, however, Pearl was offering further gastronomic details. "He often gets hungry in the middle of the night, or so Nick used to say. He keeps such funny hours, you see."

"Who's Nick?"

"Your predecessor. He left just before Christmas. I quite liked him; but Bill said he got a little light-fingered."

"I see."

She shrugged. "Still, you can't tell, can you? I mean, he—" She halted in midsentence, quietly cursing her tongue, and covered her embarrassment by coaxing the eggs out of the pan and onto the plate to join the food she'd already assembled there. Marty finished her thought out loud for her.

"He didn't look like a thief; is that what you were going to say?"

"I didn't mean it like that," she insisted, transferring the plate from stove to table. "Careful, the plate's hot." Her face had gone the color of her hair.

"It's all right," Marty told her.

"I liked Nick," she reiterated. "Really I did. I've broken one of the eggs. I'm sorry."

Marty looked down at the full plate. One of the yolks had indeed broken and was pooling around a fried tomato.

"Looks fine to me," he said with genuine appetite, and set to eating. Pearl refilled his mug, found a cup for herself, filled that, and sat down with him.

"Bill speaks very highly of you," she said.

"I wasn't sure he'd taken to me at first."

"Oh, yes," she said, "very much. Partly because of your boxing, of course. He used to be a professional boxer himself."

"Really?"

"I thought he'd have told you. This is thirty years ago. Before he worked for Mr. Whitehead. You want some toast?"

"If there's some going."

She got up and cut two slices of white bread, then slipped them into the toaster. She hesitated a moment before returning to the table. "I really am sorry," she said.

"About the egg?"

"About mentioning Nick and thieving—"

"I asked," Marty replied. "Besides, you've every right to be cautious. I'm an ex-con. Not even ex, really. I could go back if I put a foot wrong"—he loathed saying this, as if the mere speaking of the words made the possibility more real—"but I'm not going to let Mr. Toy down. Or myself. OK?"

She nodded, clearly relieved that nothing had been soured between them, and sat down again to finish her coffee. "You're not like Nick," she said, "I can tell that already."

"Was he odd?" Marty said. "Glass eye or something?"

"Well, he wasn't—" She seemed to regret this fresh line of

conversation before it was begun. "It's no matter," she said, dismissing it.

"No. Go on."

"Well, for what it's worth, I think he had debts."

Marty tried not to register anything but the mildest interest. But something must have showed in his eyes, a flicker of panic perhaps. Pearl frowned.

"What sort of debts?" he asked, lightly.

The toast popped up, claiming Pearl's attention. She crossed to fetch the slices and brought them back to the table. "Excuse fingers," she said.

"Thanks."

"I don't know how much he owed."

"No, I don't mean how big, I meant . . . where did they come from?"

Was he making this sound like an idle inquiry, he wondered, or was she able to see from the way he clutched his fork, or his sudden loss of appetite, that this was a significant question? He had to ask it, however it might seem to her. She thought for a moment before answering. When she did, there was something of the street-corner gossip in her slightly lowered voice; whatever came next was to be a secret between them.

"He used to come down here at all times of the day and make telephone calls. He told me he was calling people in the business— he was a stuntman, you see, or had been—but I soon cottoned on that he was making bets. It's my guess that's where the debts came from. Gambling."

Somehow Marty had known the answer before it came. It begged, of course, another question: was it just coincidence that Whitehead had employed two bodyguards, both, at some point in their lives, gamblers? Both—it now appeared—*thieves* for their hobby? Toy had never shown much interest in that aspect of Marty's life. But then maybe all the salient facts were in the file that Somervale had always carried: the psychologist's reports, the trial transcripts, everything Toy would ever need to know about the compulsion that had driven Marty to theft. He tried to shrug off the discomfort he felt about all this. What the hell did it matter? It was old news; he was healthy now.

"You finished with your plate?"

"Yes, thanks."

"More coffee?"

"I'll get it."

Pearl took the plate from in front of Marty, scraped the uneaten food onto a second plate—"For the birds," she said—and started to load plates, cutlery and pans alike into the dishwasher. Marty refilled his mug and watched her at work. She was an attractive woman; middle-age suited her.

"How many staff does Whitehead have altogether?"

"*Mr.* Whitehead," she said, gently correcting him. "Staff? Well, there's me. I come and go like I said. And there's Mr. Toy, of course."

"He doesn't live here either, right?"

"He stays overnight when they have conferences here."

"Is that regular?"

"Oh, yes. There's a lot of meetings go on in the house. People in and out all the time. That's why Mr. Whitehead's so security conscious."

"Does he ever go down to London?"

"Not now," she said. "He used to jet around quite a bit. Off to New York or Hamburg or some such place. But not now. Now he just stays here all year round and makes the rest of the world come to him. Where was I?"

"Staff."

"Oh, yes. The place used to swarm with people. Security staff; servants; upstairs maids. But then he went through a very suspicious patch. Thought one of them might poison him or murder him in his bath. So he sacked them all: just like that. Said he was happier with just a few of us: the ones he trusted. That way he wasn't surrounded by people he didn't know."

"He doesn't know me."

"Maybe not yet. But he's canny: like nobody I've ever met."

The telephone rang. She picked it up. He knew it must be Whitehead on the other end. Pearl looked caught in the act.

"Oh . . . yes. It's my fault. I kept him talking. Right away." The receiver was quickly replaced. "Mr. Whitehead's waiting for you. You'd better hurry. He's with the dogs."

14

The kennels were located behind a group of outhouses—once stables, perhaps—two hundred yards to the back of the main house. A sprawling collection of breeze-block sheds and wire-mesh enclosures, they had been built simply to fulfill their function, with no thought for architectural felicities; they were an eyesore.

It was chilly out in the open air, and crossing the crusty grass toward the kennels Marty had rapidly regretted his shirtsleeves. But there'd been an urgency in Pearl's voice as she sent him on his way, and he didn't want to leave Whitehead—no, he must learn to think of the man as *Mr.* Whitehead—waiting longer than he already had. As it was, the great man seemed unruffled by his late arrival.

"I thought we'd take a look at the dogs this morning. Then maybe we'll make a tour of the grounds, yes?"

"Yes, sir."

He was dressed in a heavy black coat, the thick fur collar of which cradled his head.

"You like dogs?"

"You asking me honestly, sir?"

"Of course."

"Not much."

"Was your mother bitten, or were you?" There was a twitch of a smile in the bloodshot eyes.

"Neither of us that I can remember, sir."

Whitehead grunted. "Well you're about to meet the tribe, Strauss, whether you like them or not. It's important they get to recognize you. They're trained to tear intruders apart. We don't want them making any mistakes."

A figure had emerged from one of the larger sheds, carrying a choke-chain. It took two glances for Marty to work out whether the newcomer was male or female. The cropped hair, the shabby anorak and the boots all suggested masculinity; but there was something in the molding of the face that betrayed the illusion.

"This is Lillian. She looks after the dogs."

The woman nodded a greeting without even glancing at Marty.

At her appearance several dogs—large, shaggy Alsatians— had emerged from the kennels into the concrete run, and were sniffing at her through the wire, whining a welcome. She shushed them unsuccessfully; the welcome escalated into barks, and now one or two were standing on their hind legs, man-height against the mesh, their tails wagging furiously. The din worsened.

"Be quiet," she snapped across to them, and almost all were chastened into silence. One male, however, larger than the rest, still stood against the wire, demanding attention, until Lillian drew off her leather glove and put her fingers through the mesh to scratch his deep-furred throat.

"Martin here has taken over in Nick's stead," said Whitehead. "He'll be here all the time from now on. I thought he should meet the dogs, and have the dogs meet him."

"Makes sense," Lillian replied, without enthusiasm.

"How many are there?" Marty inquired.

"Fully grown? Nine. Five males, four females. This is Saul," she said, speaking of the dog she was still stroking. "He's the oldest, and the biggest. The male over in the corner is Job. He's one of Saul's sons. He's not too well at the moment."

Job had half-lain down in the corner of the enclosure and was licking his testicles with some enthusiasm. He seemed to know he had become the center of conversation, because he looked up from his toilet for a moment. In the look he gave them there was everything Marty hated about the species: the threat, the shiftiness, the barely subdued resentment of its masters.

"The bitches are over there—"

There were two dogs trotting up and down the length of the enclosure.

"—the lighter one's Dido, and the darker's Zoe."

It was odd to hear these brutes called by such names; it seemed wholly inappropriate. And surely they resented the woman's christenings; mocked her, probably, behind her back.

"Come over here," Lillian said, summoning Marty as she might one of her pack. Like them, he came.

"Saul," she said to the animal behind the wire, "this is a friend. Come closer," she told Marty, "he can't smell you from over there."

The dog had dropped down onto all fours. Marty approached the wire cautiously.

"Don't be afraid. Go right up to him. Let him get a good sniff of you."

"They don't like fear," said Whitehead. "Isn't that right, Lillian?"

"That's right. If they smell it on you, they know they've got you. Then they're merciless. You have to stand up to them."

Marty approached the dog. It looked up at him testily: he stared back.

"Don't try and outstare him," Lillian advised. "It makes the dog aggressive. Just let him get your scent, so he knows you."

Saul sniffed at Marty's legs and crotch through the mesh, much to Marty's discomfort. Then, apparently satisfied, he wandered away.

"Good enough," said Lillian. "Next time, no wire. And in a while, you'll be handling him." She was taking some pleasure in Marty's unease, he was sure of it. But he said nothing; just let her lead the way into the largest of the sheds.

"Now you must meet Bella," she said.

Inside the kennels the smell of disinfectant, stale urine and dogs was overpowering. Lillian's entrance was greeted with another sustained round of barking and wire-pawing. The shed had a walkway down the center, with cages off to the right and left. Two of these held a single dog, both bitches, one considerably smaller than the other. Lillian rolled off the details as they passed each cage—the dogs' names, and their place on the incestuous family tree. Marty attended to all she was saying, and immediately forgot it again. His mind was otherwise occupied. It wasn't just the intimate presence of the dogs that unnerved him, but the suffocating familiarity of this interior. The walkway; the cells with their concrete floors, their blankets, their bare bulbs: it was like home from home. And now he began to see the dogs in a new light; saw another meaning in Job's baleful glance as he looked up from his ablutions; understood, better than Lillian or Whitehead ever could, how these prisoners must view him and his species.

He stopped to look into one of the cages: not out of any particular interest, but to focus on something other than the anxiety he felt in this claustrophobic hut.

"What's this one called?" he asked.

The dog in the cage was at the door; another sizable male, though not on the scale of Saul.

"That's Laurousse," Lillian replied.

The dog looked friendlier than the others, and Marty overcame his nerves and went down on his haunches in the narrow corridor, extending a tentative hand toward the cage.

"He'll be fine with you," she said.

Marty put his fingers to the mesh. Laurousse sniffed them inquisitively; his nose was damp and cold.

"Good dog," Marty said. "Laurousse."

The dog began to wag its tail, happy to be named by this sweating stranger.

"Good dog."

Down here, closer to the blankets and the straw, the smell of excrement and fur was even stronger. But the dog was delighted that Marty had come down to its level, and was attempting to lick his fingers through the wire. Marty felt the fear in him dispelled by the dog's enthusiasm: far from meaning him harm, it showed unalloyed pleasure.

Only now did he become aware of Whitehead's scrutiny. The old man was standing a few feet off to his left, his bulk entirely blocking the narrow passage between the cages, watching intently. Marty stood up self-consciously, leaving the dog to whine and wag below him, and followed Lillian further down the line of cages. The dog-keeper was singing the praises of another member of the tribe. Marty tuned in to her conversation:

"—and this is Bella," she announced. Her voice had softened; there was a dreamy quality in it that he hadn't caught before. When Marty reached the cage into which she was pointing, he saw why.

Bella half-lay and half-sat in the mesh shadows at the end of her cage, arranged like a black-snouted Madonna on a bed of blankets and straw, with blind pups suckling at her teats. Setting eyes on her, Marty's reservations about the dogs evaporated.

"Six pups," Lillian announced as proudly as if they were her own, "all strong and healthy."

More than strong and healthy, they were beautiful; fat balls of contentment nestling against each other in the luxury of their mother's lap. It seemed inconceivable that creatures so vulnerable could grow into iron-gray lords like Saul, or suspicious rebels like Job.

Bella, sensing a newcomer among her congregation, pricked up her ears. Her head was superbly proportioned, tones of sable and gold mingling in her coat to glamorous effect, her brown eyes vigilant but soft in the half-light. She was so *finished*; so completely

CLIVE BARKER

herself. The only response to her presence—and one that Marty willingly granted—was awe.

Lillian peered through the wire, introducing Marty to this mother of mothers.

"This is Mr. Strauss, Bella," she said. "You'll see him now and again; he's a friend."

There was no baby-talk condescension in Lillian's voice. She spoke to the dog as to an equal, and despite Marty's initial uncertainty about the woman, he found himself warming to her. Love wasn't an easy thing to come by, he knew that to his cost. Whatever shape it came in, it made sense to respect it. Lillian loved this dog—her grace, her dignity. It was a love he could approve of, if not entirely understand.

Bella sniffed the air, and seemed satisfied that she had the measure of Marty. Lillian reluctantly turned from the cage to Strauss.

"She might even take to you, given time. She's a great seductress, you know. A great seductress."

Behind them, Whitehead grunted at this sentimental nonsense.

"Shall we look over the grounds?" he suggested impatiently. "I think we're done here."

"Come back when you've settled in," Lillian said; her manner had defrosted noticeably since Marty had shown some appreciation of her charges, "and I'll put them through their paces for you."

"Thanks. I will."

I wanted you to see the dogs," Whitehead said as they left the enclosures behind, and started at a brisk pace across the lawn to the perimeter fence. That was only part of the reason for the visit, though; Marty knew that damn well. Whitehead had intended the experience as a salutary reminder of what Marty had left behind him. There, but for the grace of Joseph Whitehead, he would go again. Well, the lesson was learned. He'd jump through hoops of fire for the old man rather than go back into the custody of corridors and cells. There wasn't even a Bella there; no sublime and secret mother locked away in the heart of Wandsworth. Just lost men like himself.

The day was warming: the sun was up, a pale lemon balloon drifting above the rookery, and the frost was melting from the lawns. For the first time Marty began to get some sense of the scale of the estate. Distances opened up to either side of them: he could see water, a lake, or river perhaps, shining beyond a bank of trees. On the west side of the house there were rows of cypresses, suggesting walkways, fountains perhaps; to the other side, a banked garden surrounded by a low stone wall. It would take him weeks to get the layout of the place.

They had reached the double fence that ran right around the estate. A good ten feet high, both fences were topped by sharpened steel struts that curved out toward the would-be intruder. These were in turn crowned with spirals of barbed wire. The whole construction hummed, almost imperceptibly, with an electric charge. Whitehead regarded it with evident satisfaction.

"Impressive, eh?"

Marty nodded. Again, the sight woke echoes.

"It offers a measure of security," Whitehead said.

He turned left at the fence, and began to walk its length, the conversation—if that it could be called—coming from him in the form of a series of non sequiturs, as if he were too impatient with the elliptical structure of normal exchanges to bear with it. He simply threw statements, or clusters of remarks, down, and expected Marty to make whatever sense he could of them.

"It's not a perfect system: fences, dogs, cameras. You saw the screens in the kitchen?"

"Yes."

"I've got the same upstairs. The cameras offer total surveillance day and night." He jerked a thumb up at one of the camera's floodlights mounted beside them. There was one set on every tenth upright. They swiveled back and forth slowly, like the heads of mechanical birds.

"Luther'll show you how to run through them in sequence.

Cost a small fortune to install, and I'm not sure it's more than cosmetic. These people aren't fools."

"You've had break-ins?"

"Not here. At the London house it used to happen all the time. Of course, that was when I was more *visible*. The unrepentant tycoon. Evangeline and me in every scandal sheet. The open sewer of Fleet Street; it never fails to appall me."

"I thought you owned a newspaper?"

"Been reading up on me?"

"Not exactly; I—"

"Don't believe the biographies, or the gossip columns, or even *Who's Who*. They lie. I lie"—he finished the declension, entertained by his own cynicism—"he, she, or it lies. Scribblers. Dirt peddlers. Contemptible, the lot of them."

Was that what he was keeping out with these lethal fences: dirt peddlers? A fortress against a tide of scandal and shit? If so, it was an elaborate way to go about it. Marty wondered if this wasn't simply monstrous egotism. Was the hemisphere that interested in the private life of Joseph Whitehead?

"What are you thinking, Mr. Strauss?"

"About the fences," Marty lied, proving Whitehead's earlier point.

"No, Strauss," Whitehead corrected him. "You're thinking: what have I got myself into, locked up with a lunatic?"

Marty sensed any further denial would sound like guilt. He said nothing.

"Isn't that the conventional wisdom where I'm concerned? The failing plutocrat, festering in solitude. Don't they say that about me?"

"Something like that," Marty finally replied.

"And still you came."

"Yes."

"Of course you came. You thought that however offbeat I am, nothing could be as bad as another stretch behind locked doors, isn't that right? And you wanted *out*. At any cost. You were desperate."

"Of course I wanted out. Anybody would."

"I'm glad you admit to that. Because your wanting gives me considerable power over you, don't you think? You daren't cheat me. You must cleave to me the way the dogs cleave to Lillian, not because she represents their next meal but because she's their world. You must make me *your world*, Mr. Strauss; my preservation, my sanity, my smallest comfort must be uppermost in your mind every waking moment. If it is, I promise you freedoms you never dreamed of experiencing. The kind of freedoms that are only in the gift of very wealthy men. If not, I will put you back in prison with your record book irredeemably spoiled. Understand me?"

"I understand."

Whitehead nodded.

"Come then," he said. "Walk beside me."

He turned and walked on. The fence swung around behind the back of the woods at this point, and rather than plunging into the undergrowth Whitehead suggested they truncate their journey by heading toward the pool. "One tree looks much like the next to me," he commented. "You can come here and trudge around to your heart's content later on." They skirted the edge of the woods long enough for Marty to get an impression of their density, however. The trees hadn't been systematically planted; this was no regimented Forestry Commission reserve. They stood close to each other, their limbs intertwined, a mixture of deciduous varieties and pines all fighting for growing space. Only occasionally, where an oak or a lime stood bare-branched this early in the year, did light bless the undergrowth. He promised himself a return here before spring prettified it.

Whitehead summoned Marty's thoughts back into focus.

"From now on I expect you to be within summoning distance most of the time. I don't want you with me every moment of the day . . . just need you in the vicinity. On occasion, and only with my permission, you'll be permitted to leave on your own. You can drive?"

"Yes."

"Well, there's no shortage of cars, so we'll sort something out for you. This isn't strictly within the guidelines set out by the parole board. Their recommendation was that you remain, as it were, in custody here for six probationary months. But I frankly see no reason to prevent you visiting your loved ones—at least when there are other people around to look after my welfare."

"Thank you. I appreciate it."

"I'm afraid I can't allow you any time just at the moment. Your presence *here* is vital."

"Problems?"

"My life is constantly threatened, Strauss. I, or rather my offices, receive hate mail all the time. The difficulty is in separating the crank who spends his time writing filth to public figures from the genuine assassin."

"Why should anyone want to assassinate you?"

"I'm one of the wealthiest men outside America. I own companies that employ tens of thousands of people; I own tracts of land so large I could not walk them in the years remaining to me if I began now; I own ships, art, horseflesh. It's easy to make an icon of me. To think that if I and my life were brought down there'd be peace on earth and goodwill to men."

"I see."

"Sweet dreams," he said bitterly.

The pace of their march had begun to slow. The great man's breath was rather shorter now than it had been half an hour before. Listening to him talk it was easy to forget his advanced years. His opinions had all the absolutism of youth. No room here for the mellowness of advancing years; for ambiguity or doubt.

"I think it's time we headed back," he said.

The monologue had finally lapsed, and Marty had no taste for further talk. No energy either. Whitehead's style—with its unsignaled swerves and bends—had exhausted him. He'd have to get used to the pose of the attentive listener: find a face to use when these lectures began, and put it on. Learn to nod knowingly in the right places, to murmur platitudes at the appropriate breaks in the flow. It would take a while, but he'd get the trick of handling Whitehead in time.

"This is my fortress, Mr. Strauss," the old man announced as they approached the house. It didn't look particularly garrisoned: the brick was too warm to be stern. "Its sole function is to keep me from harm."

"Like me."

"Like you, Mr. Strauss."

Behind the house, one of the dogs had started barking. The solo rapidly became a chorus.

"Feeding time," Whitehead said.

15

It took several weeks' living on the estate for Marty to understand fully the rhythm of the Whitehead household. Like the benign dictatorship it was, the shape of each day was defined absolutely by Whitehead's plans and whims. As the old man had told Marty that first day, the house was a shrine to him; his worshipers came daily to touch the hem of his opinion. Some of their faces he recognized: captains of industry; two or three government ministers (one of whom had recently left office in disgrace; was he coming here, Marty wondered, asking for forgiveness or retribution?); pundits, guardians of public morality—many people Marty knew by sight but couldn't name, even more he didn't know at all. He was introduced to none of them.

Once or twice a week he might be asked to remain in the room while the meetings were held, but more often than not he was required only to be within hailing distance. Wherever he was, he was invisible as far as most of the guests were concerned: ignored, treated at best as part of the furniture. At first it was irritating; everyone in the house had a name but him, it seemed. As time passed, however, he grew to be glad of his anonymity. He wasn't required to give an opinion on everything, so he could let his mind drift with no danger of being called into the conversation. It was good too to be dislocated from the concerns of these almighty people: their lives seemed, he thought, fraught and artificial. He saw in many of their faces looks he recognized from his years in Wandsworth: the constant fretting over minor gibes, over their place in the hierarchy. The rules might be more civil in this circle than in Wandsworth; but the struggles, he began to understand, were fundamentally the same. All power games of one kind or another. He was pleased to have no part in them.

Besides, his mind had more important issues to mull over. For one thing, there was Charmaine. More out of curiosity than passion, perhaps, he had begun to think about her a good deal. He found himself wondering how her body looked seven years on. Did she still shave the thin line of hair that ran down from her navel to her pubes; did her fresh sweat still smell so pungent? He wondered too if she still loved love the way she had. She had shown more unreserved appetite for the physical act than any woman he'd known; it was one of the reasons he'd married her. Was it still so? And if it was, with whom did she slake her thirst? He turned these and a dozen other questions about her over and over in his head, and promised himself that at the first opportunity he'd go and see her.

The weeks saw his physique improve. The strict regime of exercise he'd set for himself that first night began as a torment, but after a few days of punished and complaining muscles the exertion began to bear fruit. He got up at five-thirty each morning and took an hourlong run around the grounds. After a week of following the same circuit he altered the route, which allowed him to explore the estate at the same time as exercising. There was a great deal to see. Spring hadn't arrived in force yet, but there were stirrings. Crocuses were beginning to show themselves, as were the spears of daffodils. On the trees, fat buds were starting to split; leaves were unfurling. It had taken him almost a week to cover the estate fully, and to work out the relation of one part of it to another; now he more or less had a grasp of the arrangement. He knew the lake, the dovecote, the swimming pool, the tennis courts, the kennels, the woods and the gardens. One morning, when the sky was exceptionally clear, he had circuited the entire grounds, hugging the fence all the way around the estate even when it threaded its way along the back of the woods. He now reckoned he had as thorough a knowledge of the place as anyone, including its owner.

It was a joy; not just the exploration, and the freedom of running miles without someone looking over your shoulder all the time, but the reacquaintance with a dozen natural spectacles. He loved being up to watch the sun rise, and it was almost as though he was running to meet it, as though dawn was for him and him alone, a promise of light and warmth and life to come.

He soon lost the ring of flab around his middle; the divide of his abdominals showed again: the washboard stomach he'd always been so proud of as a younger man, and thought he'd lost forever. Muscles he'd forgotten he had came back into play, at first to make their presence felt in aching, then to simply live a glowing, ruddy life. He was sweating out years of frustration and showering it away, and he was lighter for it. He was aware, once more, of his body as a system, its parts correspondents, its health dependent on balance and respectful usage.

If Whitehead noted any change in his manner or physique, no comment was made. But Toy, on one of his trips up to the house from London, immediately registered the change in him. Marty noted an alteration in Toy too, but for the worse. It wasn't plausible to comment on how weary he looked; Marty felt their relationship wouldn't yet allow for such familiarity. He just hoped

Toy wasn't suffering from something serious. The sudden wasting of his wide face suggested a devouring somewhere in the man's innards. The nimbleness in his step, which Marty put down to Toy's years in the ring, had also gone.

There were other mysteries here, besides Toy's decline. For one thing, there was the collection: the works of the great masters that lined the corridors of the sanctuary. They were neglected. Nobody had dusted their surfaces in months, perhaps years, and in addition to the yellowing varnish that dimmed their fineness they were further spoiled by a layer of grime. Marty had never had much taste for art, but given time to look at these pictures, he found his appetite for it good. Many of them, the portraits and the religious works, he didn't really like: they weren't of people he knew or events he understood. But in a small hallway on the first floor that led to the extension that had been Evangeline's suite, and was now the sauna and solarium, he found two paintings that caught his imagination. They were both landscapes, by the same anonymous hand, and to judge by their poky location they were not great works. But their curious amalgam of real scenery—trees and winding roads under blue and yellow skies—with totally fanciful details—a dragon with speckled wings devouring a man on that road; a flight of women levitating above the forest; a distant city, burning—this marriage of real and unreal was so persuasively painted that Marty found himself going back and back again to these two haunted canvases, finding more fantastical detail hidden in thicket or heat-haze each time he went.

The paintings weren't the only things that whetted his curiosity. The upper floor of the main house, where Whitehead had a suite of rooms, was entirely out-of-bounds to him, and he was more than once tempted to slip up when he knew the old man was otherwise engaged, to nose around the forbidden territory. He suspected Whitehead used the top story as a vantage point from which to spy on his acolytes' comings and goings. That went some way to explaining the other mystery: the sense, he had, running his circuits, that he was being watched. But he resisted the temptation to investigate. It was perhaps more than his job was worth.

When he wasn't working he spent much of his time in the library. There, if he felt curious about the outside world, were current issues of *Time* magazine, *The Washington Post*, *The Times*, and several other journals—*Le Monde*, *Frankfurter Algemeine Zeitung*, *The New York Times*, which Luther brought in. He would flick through them looking for tidbits, sometimes taking them down to the sauna and reading them there. When he tired of newspapers, there were thousands of books to choose from, not, to his delight, all intimidating tomes. There *were* plenty of those, the assembled classics of world literature, but beside them on the shelves were tattered, well-thumbed paperback editions of science fiction books, their covers lurid, the copy on them paradigms of excess. Marty began to read them, picking those with the most suggestive covers first. There was also the video. Toy had supplied him with a dozen tapes of boxing highlights, which Marty was systematically viewing, rerunning favorite victories to his heart's content. He could sit all evening watching the matches, awed by the economy and the grace of the great fighters. Toy, ever thoughtful, had also supplied a couple of pornographic tapes, handing them across to Marty with a conspiratorial smile and some comment about not eating them all at once. The tapes were copies of storyless loops, anonymous couples and trios who threw off their clothes in the first thirty seconds and got down to the nitty-gritty inside a minute. Nothing sophisticated: but they served a useful purpose, and, as Toy had obviously guessed, good air, exercise and optimism were doing wonders for Marty's libido. There was going to come a time when self-abuse in front of a video screen was not going to be satisfaction enough. Increasingly, Marty dreamed of Charmaine: unambiguous dreams set in the bedroom of Number Twenty-six. Frustration gave him courage, and the next time he saw Toy he asked to be allowed to go and see her.

Toy promised to ask the boss about it, but nothing had come of it. In the meanwhile he had to be content with tapes and their stage-managed gasps and grunts.

Systematically he began to put names to the faces that appeared most regularly at the house; Whitehead's most trusted advisers. Toy, of course, was regularly in evidence. There was also a lawyer called Ottaway, a thin, well-dressed man of forty or so, whom Marty took a dislike to when he first overheard the man's conversation. Ottaway spoke with that air of the legal fan-dancer, all tease and cover-ups, that Marty had experienced firsthand. It brought back sour memories.

There was another, called Curtsinger, a sober-suited individual with an excruciating taste in ties and a worse one in colognes, who, though often in Ottaway's company, seemed far more benign. He was one of the few who actually acknowledged Marty's presence in a room—usually with a small, sharp nod. On one occasion, celebrating some deal that had just been made, Curtsinger had slipped a large cigar into the pocket of Marty's jacket; after that, Marty would have forgiven him anything.

The third face that seemed to be in regular attendance at Whitehead's side was the most enigmatic of the three: a swarthy troll of a man called Dwoskin. Here was a Cassius to Toy's Brutus. His immaculate, pale gray suits, his meticulously folded handkerchiefs, the precision of his every gesture—all spoke of an obsessive whose rituals of tidiness were designed to counter the excess of his physicality. But there was more: an undercurrent of danger about the man that Marty's years in Wandsworth had taught him to be alive to. In fact, it was there in the others too. Beneath Ottoway's frigid exterior and Curtsinger's sugar coating there were men who were not—it was Somervale's phrase—entirely savory.

At first Marty dismissed the feeling as lower-class prejudice; a nobody mistrusting the rich and influential on principle. But the more meetings he sat in on, the more heated debates he was peripheral to, the more certain he became that there was in their dealings a scarcely concealed subtext of deceit, even of criminality. Much of their talk he scarcely understood—the subtleties of the stock market were a closed book to him—but the civilized vocabulary could not completely sanitize the essential drift. They were interested in the mechanics of deception: how to manipulate the law and the market alike. Their exchanges were littered with talk of tax avoidance, of selling between subsidiaries to inflate prices artificially, of packaging placebos as panaceas. There was no apology implicit in their stance; on the contrary the talk of illicit maneuvers, of political allegiances bought and sold, were positively applauded. And among these manipulators, Whitehead was the kingpin. In his presence they were reverential. Out of it, as they jockeyed for position closest to his feet, they were ruthless. He could, and did, silence them with a half-lifted hand. His every word was venerated, as if it fell from the lips of a Messiah. The charade amused Marty mightily: but applying the rule of thumb he had learned in prison he knew that in order to earn such devotion Whitehead must have sinned more deeply than his admirers. In cunning, he didn't doubt Whitehead's skills: he'd experienced his powers of persuasion already. But as time went by the other question burned more brightly: was he also a thief? And if not that, what *was* his crime?

16

Ease, she came to understand as she watched the runner from her window, is all; if not all, it was the best part of what she delighted in, watching him. She didn't know his name, though she could have inquired. It pleased her more to have him anonymous, an angel dressed in a gray track suit, his breath a flux of mist at his lips as he ran. She'd heard Pearl talk of the new bodyguard, and presumed this was he. Did it really matter what his name was? Such details could only weigh down her mythmaking.

It was a bad time for her, for many reasons, and on those defeated mornings, sitting at her window having scarcely slept the night before, the sight of the angel running across the lawn or flickering between the cypress trees was a sign she clung to, a portent of better times to come. The regularity of his appearance was something she came to count on, and when sleep was good and she missed him in the morning, she felt an undeniable sense of loss for the rest of the day, and would make a special point of keeping her rendezvous with him the next morning.

But she couldn't bring herself to leave the sunshine island, to cross so many dangerous reefs to get to where he was. Even to signal her existence in the house to him risked too much. She wondered if he was much of a detective. If he was, perhaps he had discovered her presence in the house by some witty means: seen her cigarette stubs in the kitchen sink, or smelled the scent of her in a room she had left scant minutes before. Or perhaps angels, being divinities, needed no such devices. Perhaps he simply *knew*, without the clues, that she was there, standing behind the sky at a window, or pressed behind a locked door when he went whistling down the corridor.

There was no use in reaching for him though, even if she could have found the courage. What would she have to say to him? Nothing. And when, inevitably, he sighed his irritation with her and turned his back, she would be lost in a no-man's-land, isolated from the one place she felt secure, that sunshine island that came to her out of a pure white cloud, that place that poppies bled to give her.

"You've eaten nothing today," Pearl chided. It was a familiar complaint. "You'll waste away."

"Leave me be, will you?"

"I'll have to tell him, you know."

"No, Pearl." Carys gave Pearl a pleading look. "Don't say

anything. Please. You know how he gets. I'll hate you if you say anything."

Pearl stood at the door with the tray, disapproval on her face. She wasn't about to crumble at the appeal or at the blackmail. "Are you trying to starve yourself again?" she asked unsympathetically.

"No. I just don't have much appetite, that's all."

Pearl shrugged.

"I don't understand you," she said. "Half the time you look suicidal. Today—"

Carys smiled radiantly.

"It's *your* life," the woman said.

"Before you go, Pearl . . ."

"What?"

"Tell me about the runner."

Pearl looked bemused: it wasn't like the girl to show any interest in goings-on in the house. She stayed up here behind locked doors and dreamed. But today she was insistent:

"The one who races himself every morning. In the track suit. Who is he?"

Where was the harm in telling her? Curiosity was a sign of health, and she had too little of either.

"His name's Marty."

Marty. Carys tried the name in her head, and it fitted him fine. The angel's name was Marty.

"Marty what?"

"I can't remember."

Carys stood up. The smile had gone. She had that hard look that she got when she really wanted something; the corners of her mouth pulled down. It was a look she shared with Mr. Whitehead, and it intimidated Pearl. Carys knew that.

"You know my memory," Pearl said, apologetically. "I don't remember his surname."

"Well, who is he?"

"Your father's bodyguard; he's taken over from Nick," Pearl replied. "He's an ex-prisoner, apparently. Robbery with violence."

"Really?"

"And rather lacking in social graces."

"Marty."

"Strauss," Pearl said, with a note of triumph. "Martin Strauss; that's it."

There: he was named, Carys thought. There was a primitive power in naming someone. It gave you a handle on a person. Martin Strauss.

"Thank you," she said, genuinely pleased.

"Why do you want to know?"

"Just wondered who he was. People come and go."

"Well I think he's staying," Pearl said, and left the room. As she closed the door Carys said:

"Does he have a middle name?"

But Pearl didn't hear.

It was strange, to think the runner had been a prisoner; still *was* a prisoner in a way, racing around and around the grounds, breathing in clear air, breathing out clouds, frowning as he ran. Perhaps he'd understand, more than the old man or Toy or Pearl, what it felt like to be on the sunshine island, and not know how to get off. Or worse, to know how, but never to dare it, for fear of never getting back to safety.

Now that she knew his name and his crimes, the romance of his morning run wasn't spoiled by the information. He still trailed glory; but now she saw the weight in his body when previously she'd seen only the lightness of his step.

She decided, after an age of indecision, that watching was not going to be enough.

As Marty became fitter, so he demanded more of himself during his morning run. The circuit he made grew bigger, though by now he was covering the larger distance in the same time as he had the shorter. Sometimes, to add spice to the exercise, he'd plunge into the woods, careless of the undergrowth and the low branches, his even stride degenerating into an *ad hoc* collection of leaps and dashes. On the other side of the wood was the weir, and here, if he was in the mood, he might halt for a few minutes. There were herons here; three that he'd seen. It would soon be nesting time and they would presumably pair off. He wondered what would happen to the third bird then? Would it fly off in search of its own mate, or linger, thinking adulterous thoughts? The weeks ahead would tell.

Some days, fascinated by the way Whitehead watched him from the top of the house, he'd slow as he passed by, hoping to catch his face. But the watcher was too careful to be caught.

And then one morning she was waiting at the dovecote for him as he made the long curve back toward the house, and he knew at once that he'd been wrong about it being the old man who'd been spying. *This* was the cautious observer at the upper window. It was barely a quarter to seven in the morning, and still chilly. She'd been waiting a while to judge by the flush on her cheeks and nose. Her eyes were shining with cold.

He stopped, puffing out steam like a traction engine.

"Hello, Marty," she said.

"Hello."

"You don't know me."

"No."

She hugged her duffle coat more tightly around her. She was skinny, and looked twenty at the most. Her eyes, so dark a brown they looked black at three paces, were in him like claws. The ruddy face was wide, and without makeup. She looked, he thought, hungry. He looked, she thought, ravenous.

"You're the one from upstairs," he ventured.

"Yes. You didn't mind me spying, did you?" she inquired, guilelessly.

"Why should I?"

She extended a slim, gloveless hand to the stone of the dovecote.

"It's beautiful, isn't it?" she said.

The building had never struck Marty as even interesting before, simply as a landmark by which to pace his run.

"It's one of the biggest dovecotes in England," she said. "Did you know that?"

"No."

"Ever been in?"

He shook his head.

"It's a bizarre place," she said, and led the way around the barrel-shaped building to the door. She had some difficulty pushing it open; the damp weather had swelled the wood. Marty had to double up to follow her inside. It was even chillier there than out, and he shivered, the sweat on his brow and sternum cooling now he'd stopped running. But it was, as she had promised, bizarre: just a single round room with a hole in the roof to allow the birds access and egress. The walls were lined with square holes, nesting niches presumably, set in perfect rows—like tenement windows—from floor to roof. All were empty. Judging by the absence of excrement or feathers on the floor, the building had not been used in many years. Its forsakenness gave it a melancholy air; its unique architecture rendered it useless for any function but that for which it had been built. The girl had crossed the impacted earth floor and was counting the nesting niches around from the door.

"Seventeen, eighteen—"

He watched her back. Her hair was unevenly cropped at the nape of her neck. The coat she wore was too big for her: it wasn't even hers, he guessed. Who was she? Pearl's daughter?

She'd stopped counting. Now she put her hand into one of the holes, making a little noise of discovery as her fingers located something. It was a hiding place, he realized. She was about to trust him with a secret. She turned, and showed him her treasure.

"I'd forgotten till I came back in," she said, "what I used to hide here."

It was a fossil, or rather the fragment of one, a spiral shell that had lain at the bottom of some pre-Cambrian sea, before the world was green. In its flutes, which she was stroking, motes of dust gathered. It crossed Marty's mind, watching the intensity of her involvement with this piece of stone, that the girl was not entirely sane. But the thought vanished when she looked up at him; her eyes were too clear and too willful. If she had any insanity in her it was invited, a streak of lunacy she was pleased to entertain. She grinned at him as if she'd known what he was thinking: cunning and charm were mixed in her face in equal parts.

"Are there no doves, then?" he said.

"No, there haven't been, as long as I've been here."

"Not even a few?"

"If you just have a few they die in winter. If you keep a full dovecote they all keep each other warm. But when there's only a handful they don't generate enough heat, and they freeze to death."

He nodded. It seemed regrettable to leave the building empty. "They should fill it up again."

"I don't know," she said. "I like it like this."

She slipped the fossil back into her hidey-hole.

"Now you know my special place," she said, and the cunning had gone; it was all charm. He was entranced.

"I don't know your name."

"Carys," she said, then after a moment, added: "It's Welsh."

"Oh."

He couldn't help staring at her. She suddenly seemed embarrassed, and she went back to the door quickly, ducking out into the open air. It had begun to rain, a soft, mid-March drizzle. She put up the hood of her duffle coat; he put up his track-suit hood.

"Maybe you'll show me the rest of the grounds?" he said, not certain that this was the appropriate question, but more certain that he didn't want this conversation to end here without some possibility of them meeting again. She made a noncommittal noise by way of reply. The corners of her mouth were tucked down.

"Tomorrow?" he said.

This time she didn't answer at all. Instead, she started to walk toward the house. He tagged along, knowing their exchange would falter entirely if he didn't find some way to keep it alive.

"It's strange being in the house with no one to talk to," he said.

That seemed to strike a chord.

"It's Papa's house," she said simply. "We just live in it."

Papa. So, she was his daughter. Now he recognized the old man's mouth on her, those pinched-down corners that on him seemed so stoical, and on her, simply sad.

"Don't tell anyone," she said.

He presumed she meant about their meeting, but he didn't press her. There were more important questions to ask, if she didn't race away. He wanted to signal his interest in her. But he could think of nothing to say. The sudden change in her tempo, from gentle, elliptical conversation to this staccato, confounded him.

"Are you all right?" he asked.

She looked around at him, and beneath her hood she seemed almost to be in mourning.

"I have to hurry," she said. "I'm wanted."

She picked up the pace of her step, signaling only in the hunch of her shoulders a desire to leave him behind. He obliged and slowed, leaving her to go back to the house without a glance or a wave.

Rather than return to the kitchen, where he'd have to endure Pearl's banter while he breakfasted, he started back across the field, giving the dovecote a wide berth, until he reached the perimeter fence, and punished himself with another complete circuit. When he ran into the woods he found himself involuntarily scanning the ground underfoot, looking for fossils.

17

Two days later, about eleven-thirty at night, he got a summons from Whitehead.

"I'm in the study," he said on the phone. "I'd like a word with you."

The study, though it boasted half a dozen lamps, was almost in darkness. Only the crane-necked lamp on the desk burned, and that threw its light onto a heap of papers rather than into the room. Whitehead was sitting in the leather chair beside the window. On the table beside him was a bottle of vodka and an almost empty glass. He didn't turn when Marty knocked and entered, but simply addressed Marty from his vantage point in front of the floodlit lawn.

"I think it's time I gave you more leash, Strauss," he said. "You've done a fine job so far. I'm pleased."

"Thank you, sir."

"Bill Toy will be up here overnight tomorrow, and so will Luther, so this might be an opportunity for you to go down to London."

It was eight weeks, almost to the day, since he'd arrived at the estate: and here, at last, was a tentative signal that his place was secure.

"I've had Luther sort out a vehicle for you. Speak to him about it when he arrives. And there's some money on the desk for you—"

Marty glanced across at the desk-top; there was indeed a pile of notes there.

"Go on, take it."

Marty's fingers fairly itched, but he kept control of his enthusiasm.

"It'll cover petrol and a night in the city."

Marty didn't count the notes; simply folded them and pocketed them.

"Thank you, sir."

"There's an address there too."

"Yes, sir."

"Take it. The shop belongs to a man called Halifax. He supplies me with strawberries, out of season. Will you pick up my order, please?"

"Of course."

"That's the only errand I want you to run. As long as you're back by midmorning Saturday, the rest of the time's your own."

"Thank you."

Whitehead's hand reached out for the glass of vodka, and Marty thought he was going to turn and look at him; he didn't. This interview was apparently over.

"Is that all, sir?"

"All? Yes, I think so. Don't you?"

It was many months since Whitehead had gone to bed sober. He'd started to use vodka as a soporific when the night terrors began; at first just a glass or two to dull the edge of his fear, then gradually increasing the dosage as, with time, his body became immune to it. He took no pleasure in drunkenness. He loathed putting his spinning head down on the pillow and hearing his thoughts whine in his ears. But he feared the fear more.

Now, as he sat watching the lawn, a fox stepped across the threshold of the floodlights, blanched by the brilliant illumination, and stared at the house. Its stillness lent it perfection; its eyes, catching the light, gleamed in its pricked head. It waited a moment only. Suddenly it seemed to sense danger—the dogs perhaps—and it turned tail and was gone. Whitehead still watched the spot it had disappeared from long after it had loped away, hoping against hope that it would come back and share his solitude for a space. But it had other business in the night.

There was a time when he'd been a fox: thin and sharp; a night wanderer. But things had changed. Providence had been bountiful, dreams had come true; and the fox, always a shape-changer, had grown fat and easy. The world had changed too: it had become a geography of profit and loss. Distances had shrunk to the length of his command. He had forgotten, with time, his previous life.

But of late he remembered it more and more. It came back in brilliant but reproachful detail, when the events of the day before were a fog. But he knew in his heart of hearts there was no way back to that blessed state.

And forward from here? That was a journey into a hopeless place, where no signpost would point him right or left—all directions being equal there—nor would there be hill or tree or habitation to mark the way. Such a place. Such a terrible place.

But he wouldn't be alone there. In that nowhere he would have a companion.

And when, in the fullness of time, he set his eyes on that land and its tenant he would wish, oh *Christ* how he would wish, that he had stayed a fox.

III. THE LAST EUROPEAN

18

Anthony Breer, the Razor-Eater, returned to his tiny flat in the late afternoon, made himself instant coffee in his favorite cup, then sat at the table in the failing light and started to tie himself a noose. He'd known from early morning that today was the day. No need to go down to the library; if, in time, they noticed his absence and wrote to him demanding to know where he was, he wouldn't be answering. Besides, the sky had looked as grubby as his sheets at dawn, and being a rational man he'd thought: why bother to wash the sheets when the world's so dirty, and I'm so dirty, and there's no chance of ever getting any of it clean? The best thing is to put an end to this squalid existence once and for all.

He'd seen hanged people aplenty. Only photographs, of course, in a book he'd stolen from work about war crimes, marked *"Not for the open shelves. To be issued only on request."* The warning had really got his imagination working: here was a book people weren't really meant to see. He'd slipped it into his bag unopened, knowing from the very title—*Soviet Documents on Nazi Atrocities*—that this was a volume almost as sweet in the anticipation as in the reading. But in that he'd been wrong. Mouth-watering as that day had been, knowing that his bag contained this taboo treasure, that delight was nothing compared to the revelations of the book itself. There were pictures of the burned-out ruins of Chekhov's cottage in Istra, and others of the desecration of the Tchaikovsky residence. But mostly—and more importantly—there were photographs of the dead. Some of them heaped in piles, others lying in bloody snow, frozen solid. Children with their skulls broken open, people lying in trenches, shot in the face, others with swastikas carved into their chests and buttocks. But to the Razor-Eater's greedy eyes, the best photographs were of people being hanged. There was one Breer looked at very often. It pictured a handsome young man being strung up from a makeshift gallows. The photographer had caught him in his last moments, staring directly at the camera, a wan and beatific smile on his face.

That was the look Breer wanted them to find on *his* face when they broke down the door of this very room and found him suspended up here, pirouetting in the breeze from the hallway. He thought about how they would stare at him, coo at him, shake their heads in wonder at his pale white feet and his courage in doing this tremendous thing. And while he thought, he knotted and unknotted the noose, determined to make as professional a job of it as he possibly could.

His only anxiety was the confession. Despite his working with books day in, day out, words weren't his strongest point: they slipped away for him, like beauty from his fat hands. But he wanted to say something about the children, just so they'd know, the people who found him and photographed him, that this wasn't a nobody they were staring at, but a man who'd done the worst things in the world for the best possible reasons. That was vital: that they knew who he was, because maybe in time they'd make sense of him in a way that he'd never been able to.

They had methods of interrogation, he knew, even with dead people. They'd lay him in an ice room and examine him minutely, and when they'd studied him from the outside they'd start looking at his inside, and oh! what things they'd find. They'd saw off the top of his skull and take out his brain; examine it for tumors, slice it thinly like expensive ham, probe at it in a hundred ways to find out the why and how of him. But that wouldn't work, would it? He, of all people, should know that. You cut up a thing that's alive and beautiful to find out *how* it's alive and *why* it's beautiful and before you know it, it's neither of those things, and you're standing there with blood on your face and tears in your sight and only the terrible ache of guilt to show for it. No, they'd get nothing from his brain, they'd have to look further than that. They'd have to unzip him from neck to pubis, snip his ribs and fold them back. Only then could they unravel his guts, and rummage in his stomach, and juggle his liver and lights. There, oh yes, there, they'd find plenty to feast their eyes on.

Maybe that was the best confession then, he mused as he retied the noose one final time. No use to try to find the right words, because what were words anyway? Trash, useless for the hot heart of things. No, they'd find all they needed to know if they just looked inside him. Find the story of the lost children, find the glory of his martyrdom. And they'd know, once and for all, that he was of the Tribe of the Razor-Eaters.

He finished the noose, made himself a second cup of coffee, and started work on getting the rope secure. First he removed the lamp that hung from the middle of the ceiling, then he tied the noose up there in its place. It was strong. He swung from it for a few moments to make certain of it, and though the beams grunted a little, and there was a patter of plaster on his head, it bore his weight.

By now it was early evening, and he was tired, the fatigue making him more clumsy than usual. He shunted around the room tidying it up, his pig-fat body wracked with sighs as he bundled up the stained sheets and tucked them out of sight, rinsed his coffee cup, and carefully poured away the milk so that it wouldn't curdle before they came. He turned on the radio as he worked; it would help to cover the sound of the chair being kicked over when the time came: there were others in the house and he didn't want any last-minute reprieve. The usual banalities filled from the radio station filled the room: songs of love and loss and love found again. Vicious and painful lies, all of them.

There was little strength left in the day once he'd finished preparing the room. He heard feet in the hallway and doors being opened elsewhere in the house as the occupants of the other rooms came home from work. They, like him, lived alone. He knew none of them by name; none of them, seeing him taken out escorted by police, would know his.

He undressed completely and washed himself at the sink, his testicles small as walnuts, tight to his body, his belly flab—the fat of his breasts and upper arms—quivering as the cold convulsed him. Once satisfied with his cleanliness, he sat on the mattress edge and cut his toenails. Then he dressed in freshly laundered clothes: the blue shirt, the gray trousers. He wore no shoes or socks. Of the physique that shamed him, his feet were his only pride.

It was almost dark by the time he finished, and the night was black and rainy. Time to go, he thought.

He positioned the chair carefully, stepped up onto it, and reached for the rope. The noose was, if anything, an inch or two too high, and he had to go on tiptoe to fit it snugly around his neck, but he fitted it securely with a little maneuvering. Once he had the knot pulled tight against his skin he said his prayers and kicked the chair over.

Panic began immediately, and his hands, which he'd always trusted, betrayed him at this vital juncture, springing up from his sides and tearing at the rope as it tightened. The initial drop had not broken his neck, but his spine felt like a vast centipede sewn into his back, writhing now every way it could, causing his legs to spasm. The pain was the least of it: the real anguish came from being out of control, smelling his bowels giving out into his clean trousers without his say-so, his penis stiffening without a lustful thought in his popping head, his heels digging the air looking for purchase, fingers still scrabbling at the rope. All suddenly not his own, all too hot for their own preservation to hold still and die.

But their efforts were in vain. He'd planned this too carefully for it to go awry. The rope was tightening still, the cavortings of the centipede weakening. Life, this unwelcome visitor, would leave very soon. There was a lot of noise in his head, almost as though he was underground, and hearing all the sounds of the earth. Rushing noises, the roar of great hidden weirs, the bubbling of molten stone. Breer, the great Razor-Eater, knew the earth very well. He'd buried dead beauties in it all too often, and filled his mouth with soil as penitence for the intrusion, chewing on it as he covered over their pastel bodies. Now the earth noises had blotted out everything—his gasps, the music from the radio, and the traffic outside the window. Sight was going too; lace darkness crept over the room, its patterns pulsing. He knew he was turning—there was the bed, now the wardrobe, now the sink— but the forms he fitfully saw were decaying.

His body had given up the good fight. His tongue flapped perhaps, or maybe he imagined the motion, just as surely as he imagined the sound of somebody calling his name.

Quite abruptly, sight went out completely, and death was on him. No flood of regrets attended the ending, no lightning regurgitation of a life history encrusted with guilt. Just a dark, and a deeper dark, and now a dark so deep night was luminous by comparison with it. And it was over, easily.

No; not over.

Not quite over. A cluster of unwelcome sensations swarmed over him, intruding on the privacy of his death. A breeze warmed his face, assaulting his nerve endings. An ungracious breath choked him, pressing into his flaccid lungs without the least invitation.

He fought the resurrection, but his Savior was insistent. The room began to reassemble itself around him. First light, then form. Now color, albeit drained and grimy. The noises—fiery rivers and liquid stone alike—were gone. He was hearing himself cough, and smelling his own vomit. Despair mocked him. Could he not even kill himself successfully?

Somebody said his name. He shook his head, but the voice came again, and this time his upturned eyes found a face.

And *oh* it was not over: far from it. He had not been delivered into Heaven or Hell. Neither would dare boast the face he was now staring up into.

"I thought I'd lost you, Anthony," said the Last European.

19

He had righted the chair Breer had used to stand on for his suicide attempt, and was sitting on it, looking as unsullied as ever. Breer tried to say something, but his tongue felt too fat for his mouth, and when he felt it his fingers came back bloody.

"You bit your tongue in your enthusiasm," said the European. "You won't be able to eat or speak too well for a while. But it'll heal, Anthony. Everything heals given time."

Breer had no energy to get up off the floor; all he could do was lie there, the noose still tight around his neck, staring up at the severed rope that still depended from the light fixture. The European had obviously just cut him down and let him fall. His body had begun to shake; his teeth were chattering like a mad monkey's.

"You're in shock," said the European. "You lie there . . . I'll make some tea, shall I? Sweet tea is just the thing."

It took some effort, but Breer managed to haul himself off the floor and onto the bed. His trousers were soiled, front and back: he felt disgusting. But the European didn't mind. He forgave all, Breer knew that. No other man Breer had ever met was quite so capable of forgiveness; it humbled him to be in the company and the care of such easy humanity. Here was a man who knew the secret heart of his corruption, and never once spoke a word of censure.

Propped up on the bed, feeling the signs of life reappearing in his wracked body, Breer watched the European making the tea. They were very different people. Breer had always felt awed by this man. Yet hadn't the European told him once: "*I am the last of my tribe, Anthony, just as you are the last of yours. We are in so many ways the same*"? Breer hadn't understood the significance of the remark when he'd first heard it, but he'd come to understand in time. "*I am the last true European; you are the last of the Razor-Eaters. We should try to help each other.*" And the European had gone on to do just that, keeping Breer from capture on two or three occasions, celebrating his trespasses, teaching him that to be a Razor-Eater was a worthy estate. In return for this education he'd asked scarcely anything: a few minor services, no more. But Breer wasn't so trusting that he didn't suspect a time would come when the Last European—please call me Mr. Mamoulian, he used to say, but Breer had never really got his tongue around that comical name—when this strange companion would ask for help in his turn. It wouldn't be an odd job or two he'd ask either; it would be something terrible. Breer knew that, and feared it.

In dying he had hoped to escape the debt ever being called in. The longer he'd been away from Mr. Mamoulian—and it was six years since they'd last met—the more the memory of the man had come to frighten Breer. The European's image had not faded with time: quite the contrary. His eyes, his hands, the caress of his voice had stayed crystal-clear when yesterday's events had become a blur. It was as if Mamoulian had never *quite* gone, as though he'd left a sliver of himself in Breer's head to polish up his picture when time dirtied it; to keep a watch on his servant's every deed.

No surprise then, that the man had come in when he had, interrupting the death scene before it could be played out. No surprise either that he was talking to Breer now as though they'd never been parted, as though he was the loving husband to Breer's devoted wife, and the years had never intervened. Breer watched Mamoulian move from sink to table as he prepared the tea, locating the pot, setting out the cups, performing each domestic act with hypnotic economy. The debt would have to be paid, he knew that now. There would be no darkness until it *was* paid. At the thought, Breer began to sob quietly.

"Don't cry," said Mamoulian, not turning from the sink.

"I wanted to die," Breer murmured. The words came out as though through a mouthful of pebbles.

"You can't perish yet, Anthony. You owe me a little time. Surely you must see that?"

"I wanted to die," was all Breer could repeat in response. He was trying not to hate the European, because the man would know. He'd feel it for certain, and maybe lose his temper. But it was so difficult: resentment bubbled up through the sobbing.

"Has life been treating you badly?" the European asked.

Breer sniffed. He didn't want a father confessor, he wanted the dark. Couldn't Mamoulian understand that he was past explanations, past healing? He was shit on the shoe of a mongol, the most worthless, irredeemable thing in creation. The image of himself as a Razor-Eater, as the last representative of a once-terrible tribe, had kept his self-esteem intact for a few perilous years, but the fantasy had long since lost its power to sanctify his vileness. There was no possibility of working the same trick twice. And it *was* a trick, just a trick, Breer knew that, and hated Mamoulian all the more for his manipulations. I want to be dead, was all he could think.

Did he say the words out loud? He hadn't heard himself speak, but Mamoulian answered him as though he had.

"Of course you do. I understand, I really do. You think it's all an illusion: tribes, and dreams of salvation. But take it from me, it isn't. There's purpose in the world yet. For both of us."

Breer drew the back of his hand across his swollen eyes, and tried to control his sobs. His teeth no longer chattered; that was something.

"Have the years been so cruel?" the European inquired.

"Yes," Breer said sullenly.

The other nodded, looking across at the Razor-Eater with compassion in his eyes; or at least an adequate impersonation of same.

"At least they didn't lock you away," he said. "You've been careful."

"You taught me how," Breer conceded.

"I showed you only what you already knew, but were too confused by other people to see. If you've forgotten, I can show you again."

Breer looked down at the cup of sweet, milkless tea the European had set on the bedside table.

"—or do you no longer trust me?"

"Things have changed," Breer mumbled with his thick mouth.

Now it was Mamoulian's turn to sigh. He sat on the chair again, and sipped at his own tea before replying.

"Yes, I'm afraid you're right. There's less and less place for us here. But does that mean we should throw up our hands and die?"

Looking at the sober, aristocratic face, at the haunted hollows of his eyes, Breer began to remember why he'd trusted this man. The fear he'd felt was dwindling, the anger too. There was a calm in the air, and it was seeping into Breer's system.

"Drink your tea, Anthony."

"Thank you."

"Then I think you should change your trousers."

Breer blushed; he couldn't help himself.

"Your body responded quite naturally, there's nothing to be ashamed of. Semen and shit make the world go round."

The European laughed, softly, into his teacup, and Breer, not feeling the joke to be at his expense, joined in.

"I never forgot you," Mamoulian said. "I told you I'd come back for you and I meant what I said."

Breer nursed his cup in hands that still trembled, and met Mamoulian's gaze. The look was as unfathomable as he'd remembered, but he felt warm toward the man. As the European said, he hadn't forgotten, he hadn't gone away never to return. Maybe he had his own reasons for being here now, maybe he'd come to squeeze payment out of a long-standing debtor, but that was better, wasn't it, than being forgotten entirely?

"Why come back now?" he asked, putting down his cup.

"I have business," Mamoulian replied.

"And you need my help?"

"That's right."

Breer nodded. The tears had stopped entirely. The tea had done him good: he felt strong enough to ask an insolent question or two.

"What about me?" came the reply.

The European frowned at the inquiry. The lamp beside the bed flickered, as though the bulb was at crisis point, and about to go out.

"What *about* you?" he asked.

Breer was aware that he was on tricky ground, but he was determined not to be weak. If Mamoulian wanted help, then he should be prepared to deliver something in exchange.

"What's in it for me?" he asked.

"You can be with me again," the European said.

Breer grunted. The offer was less than tempting.

"Is that not enough?" Mamoulian wanted to know. The lamplight was more fitful by the moment, and Breer had suddenly lost his taste for impertinence.

"*Answer me, Anthony*," the European insisted. "If you've got an objection, voice it."

The flickering was worsening, and Breer knew he'd made an error, pressing Mamoulian for a covenant. Why hadn't he remembered that the European loathed bargains and bargainers alike? Instinctively he fingered the noose groove around his neck. It was deep, and permanent.

"I'm sorry . . ." he said, rather lamely.

Just before the lamp bulb gave out completely, he saw Mamoulian shake his head. A tiny shake, like a tick. Then the room was drowned in darkness.

"Are you with me, Anthony?" the Last European murmured. The voice, normally so even, was twisted out of true.

"Yes . . ." Breer replied. His lazy eyes weren't becoming accustomed to the dark with their usual speed. He squinted, trying to sort out the European's form in the surrounding gloom.

He needn't have troubled himself. Scant seconds later something across the room from him seemed to ignite, and suddenly, awesomely, the European was providing his own illumination.

Now, with this lurid lantern show to set his sanity reeling, tea and apologies were forgotten. The dark, life itself, were forgotten; and there was only time, in a room turned inside out with terrors and petals, to stare and stare and maybe, if one had a sense of the ridiculous, to say a little prayer.

20

Alone in Breer's sordid one-room flat the Last European sat himself down and played solitaire with his favorite pack of cards. The Razor-Eater had dressed himself up and gone out to taste the night. If he concentrated, Mamoulian could find the parasite with his mind, and taste vicariously whatever experiences the other man was enjoying. But he had no appetite for such games. Besides, he knew all too well what the Razor-Eater would be doing, and it frankly revolted him. All pursuits of the flesh, whether conventional or perverse, appalled him, and as he grew older the disgust deepened. On some days he could barely stand to look at the human animal without the roving gloss of its eye or the pinkness of its tongue awaking nausea in him. But Breer would be useful in the struggle to come; and his bizarre desires gave him an insight, albeit crude, into Mamoulian's tragedy, an insight that made him a more compliant attendant than the usual companions the European had tolerated in his long, long life.

Most of the men and women in whom Mamoulian had placed his trust had betrayed him. The pattern had repeated itself so often down the decades that he was sure he would one day become hardened to the pain such betrayals caused. But he never achieved such precious indifference. The cruelty of other people—their callous usage of him—never failed to wound him, and though he had extended his charitable hand to all manner of crippled psyches, such ingratitude was unforgivable. Perhaps, he mused, when this endgame was all over and done with—when he'd collected his debts in blood, dread and night—then maybe he'd lose the terrible itch that tormented him day and night, that drove him on without hope of peace to new ambitions and new betrayals. Maybe when all this was over he would be able to lie down and die.

The pack in his hand was pornographic. He played with it only when he was feeling strong, and only then alone. Handling the images of extreme sensuality was a test he set himself, one that if he failed, he would fail in private. Today the filth on the cards was, after all, just human depravity; he could turn the designs over and not be distressed by them. He even appreciated their wit: the way each of the suits detailed a different area of sexual activity, the spots incorporated into each intricately rendered picture. Hearts represented male/female congress, though by no means limited to the missionary position. Spades were oralist, depicting simple fellatio and its more elaborate variations. Clubs were analist: the spot cards portraying homosexual and heterosexual buggery, the court cards, anal sex with animals. Diamonds, the most exquisitely drawn of the suits, were sadomasochistic, and here the artist's imagination had known no bounds. On these cards men and women suffered all manner of humiliation, their wracked bodies bearing diamond-shaped wounds to designate each card.

But the grossest image in the pack was that of the Joker. He was a coprophiliac, and sat down before a plateful of steaming excrement, his eyes vast with greed, while a scabby monkey, its bald face horribly human, bared its puckered backside to the viewer.

Mamoulian picked up the card and studied the picture. The leering face of the shit-eating fool brought the bitterest of smiles to his bloodless lips. This was surely the definitive human portrait.

The other pictures on the cards, with their pretensions to love and physical pleasure, only hid this terrible truth away for a while. Sooner or later, however ripe the body, however glorious the face, whatever wealth or power or faith could promise, a man was escorted to a table groaning under the weight of his own excrement and obliged, even though his instincts might revolt, to eat.

That was what he was here for. To make a man eat shit.

He dropped the card onto the table, and spat a barking laugh from his throat. There would be such torment soon; such terrible scenes.

No pit is deep enough, he promised the room; the cards and cups; the whole dirty world.

No pit is deep enough.

IV. SKELETON DANCE

21

The man in the underground train was naming constellations. "Andromeda . . . Ursa, the Bear . . . Cygnus, the Swan . . ." His monologue was for the most part ignored, though when a couple of young men told him to shut his trap he replied, barely altering the rhythm of his naming, with a smile and a "You'll die for that," slipped between one star and the next. The reply silenced the heckler, and the lunatic went back to his sky-watching.

Toy took it as a good sign. He was much preoccupied by signs these days, though he'd never really thought of himself as a superstitious man. Perhaps it was his mother's Catholicism, which he'd rejected at an early age, at last finding an outlet. In place of the myths of Virgin birth and transubstantiation he was finding significance in small coincidences—avoiding standing ladders and performing half-remembered rituals with spilled salt. All this was quite recent—only the last year or two—and it had started with the woman he was even now going to meet: Yvonne. It wasn't that she was a God-fearing woman. She wasn't. But the consolation she'd brought into his life brought with it the danger of its disappearance. That was what made him cautious with ladders and respectful to salt: the fear of losing her. With Yvonne in his life he had new reason to keep the fates friendly.

He had met her six years ago. She'd been a secretary then, working with the UK Branch of a German chemical corporation. A sprightly, good-looking woman in her middle thirties, whose formality, he'd guessed, disguised humor and warmth in abundance. He'd been attracted to her from the beginning, but his natural hesitancy in such matters, and the considerable difference in their ages, kept him from making any overtures. Eventually it was Yvonne who broke the ice between them, commenting on small things about his appearance—a recent haircut, a new tie—and so making her interest in him perfectly plain. Once the signal had been given, Toy had proposed dinner, and she'd accepted. It had been the beginning of the most rewarding months of Toy's life.

He was not an overly emotional man. The very lack of extremes in his nature had made him a useful part of Whitehead's entourage, and he had nurtured his reserve as the salable commodity it was until, by the time he met Yvonne, he'd almost come to believe his own publicity. She it was who first called him a cold fish; she who taught him (difficult lesson that it was) the importance of showing weakness, if not to the world at large at least to intimates. It had taken him time. He was fifty-three when they met, and this new way of thinking went against the grain. But she persisted, and slowly, the melt began. Once it did, he wondered how he had ever lived the life he had for the previous twenty years; a life of servitude to a man whose compassion was negligible, and ego, monstrous. He saw, through Yvonne's eyes, the cruelty in Whitehead, the arrogance, the mythmaking; and though he showed, he hoped, no change in his superficial attitudes to his employer, beneath the conciliation and the humility there increasingly simmered a resentment that approached hatred. Only now, after six years, could Toy contemplate his own contradictory feelings about the old man, and even now he found himself forgetting the worst, at least when he was out of Yvonne's sphere of influence. It was so difficult when he was in the house, subject to Whitehead's whim, to keep the perspective she'd given him, to see the sacred monster for what he was: monstrous, but far from sacred.

After twelve months Toy had moved Yvonne into the house Whitehead had purchased for him in Pimlico; a retreat from the world of the Whitehead Corporation that the old man never inquired about, a place where he and Yvonne could talk—or be silent—together; where he could indulge his passion for Schubert, and she could write letters to her family, which was spread across half the globe.

That night, when he got back, he told her about the man on the train, the constellation namer. She found the whole story pointless; couldn't see the romance of it at all.

"I just thought it was strange," he said.

"I suppose it is," she replied, unimpressed, and went back to her dinner preparations. A few words on, she stopped.

"What's wrong, Billy?"

"Why should something be wrong?"

"Everything's fine?"

"Yes."

"Really?"

She was always quick to ferret out his secrets. He gave up before she really began on him; it wasn't worth the effort of deception. He stroked the ridge of his broken nose, a familiar trick when he was nervous. Then he said, "It's all going to come down. Everything." His voice trembled and fell away. When it was clear he wasn't going to elaborate she put down the dinner plates and crossed to his chair. He looked up, almost startled, when she touched his ear.

"What are you thinking about?" she asked, more gently than before.

He took hold of her hand.

"There might come a time . . . not so far away . . . when I'd ask you to leave with mc," he said.

"Leave?"

"Just up and go."

"Where?"

"I haven't thought that through yet. We'd just go." He halted, and looked at her fingers, which were now dovetailed with his. "Would you come with me?" he asked at last.

"Of course."

"Ask no questions?"

"What is this, Billy?"

"I said: ask no questions."

"Just go?"

"Just go."

She looked long and hard at him: he was washed out, poor love. Too much of that wretched old fart in Oxford. How she hated Whitehead, though she'd never met him.

"Yes, of course I'd go," she replied.

He nodded. She thought he might cry.

"When?" she said.

"I don't know." He tried to smile, but it looked misbegotten. "Perhaps it won't even be necessary. But I think it's all going to come down, and when it does I don't want us to be there."

"You make it sound like the end of the world."

He didn't reply. She didn't feel able to chisel at him for answers: he was too delicate.

"Just one question?" she ventured. "It's important to me."

"One."

"Did you do something, Billy? I mean, something illegal? Is that what it is?"

His Adam's apple bobbed as he swallowed his grief. There was so much more she had to teach him yet; about allowing those feelings out. He wanted to: she could see so much bubbling away behind his eyes. But there, for now, it would stay. She knew better than to press him. He'd only withdraw. And he needed her undemanding presence more than she needed answers.

"It's all right," she said, "there's no need to tell me if you don't want to."

His hand was gripping hers so tightly she thought they'd never unknot them.

"Oh, Billy. Nothing's *that* terrible," she murmured.

Again, he made no reply.

22

The old haunts were much the same as Marty had remembered them, but he felt like a ghost there. Along the rubbish-strewn back alleys where he'd fought and run as a boy there were new combatants, and, he suspected, far more serious games. They were glue sniffers, these grubby ten-year-olds, according to the pages of the Sunday tabloids. They would grow up, disenfranchised, into needle freaks and pill pushers; they cared for nothing and nobody, least of all themselves.

He'd been an adolescent criminal, of course. Theft was a rite of passage here. But it had usually been that lazy, almost passive form of thieving: sidling up to something and walking, or driving, away with it. If the theft looked too problematic, forget it. Plenty of other shiny things to be fingered. It wasn't *crime* in the way he'd come to understand the word later. It was the magpie instinct at work, taking whatever opportunity offered, never intending much harm by it, or working up a sweat if things didn't quite fall your way.

But these kids—there was a group of them lounging on the corner of Knox Street—they looked like a more lethal breed altogether. Though they'd grown up in the same lusterless environment, he and they, with its few wretched attempts at tree planting, its barbed wire and glass-topped walls, its relentless concrete—though they shared all that, he knew they'd have nothing to say to one another. Their desperation and their lassitude intimidated him: he felt nothing was beyond them. Not a place to grow up in, this street, or any of them, along the row. In a way he was glad his mother had died before the worst of the changes disfigured the neighborhood.

He got to Number Twenty-six. It had been repainted. On one of her visits Charmaine had told him Terry, one of her brothers-in-law, had done it for her a couple of years back, but Marty had forgotten, and the change of color, after so many years of imagining it green and white, was a slap in the face. It was a bad job, purely cosmetic, and the paint on the windowsills was lifting and peeling already. Through the window the lace curtains that he'd always loathed so much had been replaced with a blind, which was down. On the window ledge inside a collection of porcelain figures, wedding presents, gathered dust, trapped in the forsaken space between blind and glass.

He still had his keys, but he couldn't bring himself to use them. Besides, she'd probably changed the lock. Instead, he pressed the bell. It didn't ring in the house, and he knew it was audible from the street, so it clearly no longer worked. He rapped his knuckles on the door.

For half a minute there was no sound from inside. Then, eventually, he heard dragging footsteps (she'd be wearing open-backed sandals, he guessed, and they made her walk ragged), and Charmaine opened the door. Her face was not made-up, and its nakedness made even plainer response to his standing there. She was unpleasantly surprised.

"Marty," was all she managed to say. No welcoming smile, no tears.

"I came on the off-chance," he said, attempting nonchalance. But it was obvious that he'd made a tactical error from the moment she sighted him.

"I thought you weren't allowed out—" she said, then corrected herself, "—I mean, you know, I thought you weren't allowed off the estate."

"I asked for special dispensation," he said. "Can I come in, or do we talk on the doorstep?"

"Oh . . . oh, yes. Of course."

He stepped inside, and she closed the door behind him. There was an uncomfortable moment in the narrow hallway. Their proximity seemed to demand an embrace, yet he felt unable, and she unwilling, to make the gesture. She compromised with a patently artificial smile, followed by a light kiss on the cheek.

"I'm sorry," she said, apologizing for nothing in particular. She led him down the hallway to the kitchen. "I just didn't expect you, that's all. Come on in. The place is in chaos, I'm afraid."

The house smelled stale; as though it needed a good airing. Washing, drying on the radiators, made the atmosphere muggy, like the sauna back at the Sanctuary.

"Take a seat," she said, lifting a bag of unsorted groceries off one of the kitchen chairs, "I'll just finish here." There was a second load of dirty washing on the kitchen table—hygienic as ever—which she began to load into the washing machine, her chatter nervous, her eyes never meeting his as she concentrated on the matter in hand; the towels, the underwear, the blouses. He recognized none of the clothes, and found himself ferreting through the soiled items looking for something he had seen her in before. If not six years before, then in visits to the prison. But it was all new stuff.

"—I just didn't expect you—" she was saying, closing the machine and loading powder into it. "I was sure you'd call first. And look at me; I look like a wet rag. God, it would be today, I've got so much to do—" She finished with the machine, pushed the sleeves of her sweater back up, said: "Coffee?" and turned to the kettle to make some without waiting for an answer. "You look well, Marty, you really do."

How did she know? She'd scarcely taken two glances at him in her whirlwind of activity. Whereas he, he couldn't take his eyes off her. He sat watching her at the sink, wringing out a cloth to swab down the counter, and nothing had changed in six years— not really—just a few lines on their faces. He had a feeling in him that was like panic; something to be held down for fear it make a fool of him.

She made him coffee; talked about the way the neighborhood had changed; about Terry and the saga of choosing the paint for the front of the house; about how much it cost on the subway from Mile End to Wandsworth; about how well he looked—"You really do, Marty, I'm not just saying that"—she talked about everything but something. It wasn't Charmaine talking, and that hurt. Hurt her too, he knew. She was marking time with him, that was all it was, filling the minutes with vacuous chat until he gave up in despair and left.

"Look," she said. "I really must change."

"Going out?"

"Yes."

"Oh."

"—if you'd said, Marty, I would have cleared a space. Why didn't you ring me?"

"Maybe we could go out for a meal sometime?" he suggested.

"Maybe."

She was viciously noncommittal.

"—things are a bit hectic just at the moment."

"I'd like a chance to talk. You know, properly."

She was getting edgy: he knew the signs well, and she was aware of his scrutiny. She picked up the coffee mugs and took them to the sink.

"I really must dash," she said. "Make yourself some more coffee if you want. Stuff's in the—well, you know where it is. There's a lot of things of yours here, you know. Motorcycle magazines and stuff. I'll sort them out for you. Excuse me. I have to change."

She hurried—positively raced, he thought—into the hallway, and went upstairs. He heard her moving about heavily; she was never light-footed. Water was running in the bathroom. The toilet flushed. He wandered through from the kitchen into the back room. It smelled of old cigarettes, and the ashtray balanced on the arm of the new sofa was brimming. He stood in the doorway and stared at the objects in the room rather as he had at the dirty washing, searching for something familiar. There was very little. The clock on the wall was a wedding present, and still in the same place. The stereo in the corner was new, a flashy model that Terry had probably acquired for her. Judging by the dust on the lid it was seldom used, and the collection of records haphazardly stacked alongside was as small as ever. Among those records was there still a copy of Buddy Holly singing "True Love Ways"? They'd played that so often it must have been worn thin; they'd danced to it together in this very room—not danced exactly, but used the music as an excuse to hold each other, as if excuses were needed. It was one of those love songs that made him feel romantic and unhappy simultaneously—as though every phrase of it was charged with loss of the very love it celebrated. Those were the best kind of love songs, and the truest.

Unable to bear the room any longer, he went upstairs.

She was still in the bathroom. There was no lock on the door; she'd been locked in a bathroom as a small child, and had such a terror of the same thing happening again she'd always insisted there be no locks on any of the internal doors in the house. You had to whistle on the toilet if you wanted to stop people walking in on you. He pushed the door open. She was dressed only in her panties; arm raised, shaving her armpit. She caught his eye in the mirror, then went back to what she was doing.

"I didn't want any more coffee," he said lamely.

"Got used to the expensive stuff, have you?" she said.

Her body was a few feet from him, and he felt the pull of it. He knew every mole on her back, knew the places a touch would make her laugh. Such familiarity was a kind of ownership, he felt; she owned him for the same reasons, if she would just exercise her right. He crossed to her and put his fingertips on her lower back, and ran them up her spine.

"Charmaine."

She looked at him in the mirror again—the first unswerving look she'd granted him since he'd arrived at the house—and he knew that any hope of physicality between them was a lost cause.

"I'm not available, Marty," she said plainly.

"We're still married."

"I don't want you to stay. I'm sorry."

That's how she'd begun this meeting: with "I'm sorry." Now

she wanted to finish it in the same way; no genuine apology intended, just a polite brush-off.

"I've thought about this so often," he said.

"So have I," she replied. "But I stopped thinking about it five years ago. It won't do any good; you know that as well as I do."

His fingers were now on her shoulder. He was sure there was a charge in their contact, a buzz of excitement exchanged between her flesh and his. Her nipples had hardened; perhaps the draft from the landing, perhaps his touch.

"I'd like you to go," she said very quietly, looking down into the sink. There was a tremor in her voice that could easily become tears. He wanted tears from her, shameful as it was. If she wept he'd kiss her to console her, and his consolation would harden as she softened, and they'd finish up in bed; he knew it. That was why she was fighting so hard to show nothing, knowing the scenario as well as he did, and determined not to leave herself open to his affection.

"Please," she said again, with indisputable finality. His hand dropped from her shoulder. There was no spark between them; it was all in his mind. All ancient history.

"Maybe some other time." He muttered the cliché as if it were poisoned.

"Yes," she said, pleased to sound a note of conciliation, however lame. "Ring me first though."

"I'll let myself out."

23

He wandered around for an hour, dodging hordes of school-children returning home, picking fights and noses as they went. There were signs of spring, even here. Nature could scarcely be bountiful in such restraining circumstances, but it did its best. In tiny front gardens, and in window boxes, flowers blossomed; the few saplings that had survived vandalism showed sweet green leaves. If they survived a few more seasons of frost and malice they might grow large enough for birds to nest in. Nothing exotic: brawling starlings at best, probably. But they'd offer shade in high summer, and places for the moon to sit if you looked out your bedroom window one night. He found himself full of such inappropriate thoughts—moon and starlings—like an adolescent first in love. Coming back here had been a mistake; it had been a self-inflicted cruelty that had hurt Charmaine too. Useless to go back and apologize, that would only make matters messier. He'd ring her, as she'd suggested, and ask her out to one farewell dinner. Then he'd tell her, whether it was true or not, that he was ready for them to part permanently, and he hoped he'd see her once in a while, and they'd say goodbye in a civilized fashion, without enmity, and she'd go back to whatever life she was making for herself, and he'd go to his. To Whitehead, to Carys. Yes, to Carys.

And suddenly tears were on him like a fury, tearing him to pieces, and he was standing in the middle of some street he didn't recognize, blinded by them. Schoolchildren buffeted him as they ran past, some turning, some seeing his anguish and yelling obscenities at him as they went. This is ridiculous, he told himself, but no amount of name-calling would halt the flow. So he wandered, hand to face, into an alley, and stayed there till the bout passed. Part of him felt quite removed from this burst of emotion. It looked down, this untouched part, on his sobbing self, and shook its head in contempt for his weakness and confusion. He hated to see men cry, it embarrassed him; but there was no gainsaying it. He was lost; that was all there was to it, lost and afraid. That was worth crying for.

When the flow stopped he felt better, but shaky. He wiped his face, and stayed in the backwater of the alley until he'd regained his composure.

It was four-forty. He'd already been to Holborn and picked up

the strawberries; that was his first duty when he drove into town.
Now, with that done, and Charmaine seen, the rest of the night
sprawled in front of him, waiting to be pleasured. But he'd lost a
lot of his enthusiasm for a night of adventure. In a while the pubs
would open, and he could get a couple of whiskies inside him.
That would help rid him of the twitches in his stomach. Maybe it
would also whet his appetite again, but he doubted it.

To occupy the time before opening, he wandered down to the
shopping precinct. It had been opened two years before he was
put inside, a soulless warren of white tiles, plastic palms, and
flashy, up-market shops. Now, almost a decade after it was built,
it looked about ready for demolition. It was scarred with graffiti,
its tunnels and stairways filthy, many of its shops closed up, others
so bereft of charm or custom surely the only option open to the
owners was to fire them one of these nights, collect the insurance,
and run for the hills. He found a small newsstand manned by a
forlorn Pakistani, bought a packet of cigarettes and retraced his
steps to The Eclipse.

It was just past opening time, and the pub was almost deserted.
A couple of skinheads were playing darts; in the lounge bar
somebody was celebrating: an off-key chorus of "Happy Birthday,
Dear Maureen," drifted through. The television had been turned
up for the early-evening news, but he couldn't catch much of it
over the noise of the celebrants, and wasn't that interested anyway.
Collecting a whisky from the bar he went to sit down, and began
to smoke his way through the pack of cigarettes he'd bought. He
felt drained. The liquor, instead of putting some spark into him,
only made his limbs more leaden.

His thoughts drifted. Free association of ideas brought images
into peculiar communion. Carys, and him, and Buddy Holly.
That song, "True Love Ways," playing in the dovecote, while he
danced with the girl in the chilly air.

When he shook the pictures from his head there were new
customers at the bar; a group of young men making enough noise,
braying laughter mostly, to blank out both the sound of the

television and the birthday party. One of them was clearly the hub of the entertainment, a lanky, rubber-jointed individual with a smile wide enough to play Chopin on. It took Marty several seconds to register that he knew this clown: it was Flynn. Of all the people he'd thought he might run into on this turf, Flynn was just about the last. Marty half-stood, as Flynn's glance—an almost magical coincidence—roved the room and fell on him. Marty froze, like an actor who'd forgotten his next move, unable to advance or retreat. He wasn't sure he was ready for a dose of Flynn. Then the comedian's face lit up with recognition, and it was too late for retreat.

"Jesus fucking Christ," said Flynn. The grin faded, to be replaced, momentarily, with a look of total bewilderment, before returning—more radiant than ever. "Look who's here, will you?" and now he was coming toward Marty, arms outspread in welcome, the loudest shirt man had ever created revealed beneath the well-cut jacket.

"Fucking hell. *Marty! Marty!*"

They half-embraced, half-shook hands. It was a difficult reunion, but Flynn blustered over the cracks with a salesman's efficiency.

"What do you know? Of all people. Of *all* people!"

"Hello, Flynn."

Marty felt like a dowdy cousin in front of this instant joy machine, all quips and color. Flynn's smile was immovably in place now, and he was escorting Marty across to the bar, introducing the circle of his audience (Marty caught half of the names, and could put faces to none of them), then it was a double brandy for everyone to celebrate Marty's homecoming.

"Didn't know you were out so soon," Flynn said, toasting his victim. "Here's to time off for good behavior."

The rest of the party made no attempt to interrupt the master's flow, and took instead to talking among themselves, leaving Marty at Flynn's mercy. He'd changed very little. The style of the clothes, of course, that was different: he was dressed, as ever, as last year's fashions demanded; he was losing hair too, receding at quite a rate; but apart from that he was the same wisecracking faker he'd always been, laying out a sparkling collection of fabrications for Marty to inspect. His involvement with the music business, his contacts in L.A., his plans to open a recording studio in the neighborhood. "Done a lot of thinking about you," he said. "Wondered how you were getting on. Meant to visit; but I didn't think you'd thank me for it." He was right. "Besides, I'm never here, you know? So tell me, old son, what are you doing back?"

"I came to see Charmaine."

"Oh." He seemed almost to have forgotten who she was. "She OK?"

"So-so. *You* sound as if you're doing well."

"I've had my hassles, you know, but then who hasn't? I'm all right though, you know." He lowered his voice to the barely audible. "The big money's in dope these days. Not grass, the hard stuff. I handle cocaine mostly; occasionally the big H. I don't like to touch it . . . but I've got expensive tastes." He pulled a "what a world this is" face, turned to the bar to order more drinks, then talked on, a seamless train of self-inflation and off-color remarks. After some initial resistance Marty found himself succumbing to him. His tide of invention was as irresistible as ever. Only occasionally did he pause to ask a question of his audience, which was fine by Marty. He had little he wanted to tell. It had always been that way. Flynn the rude boy, fast and smooth; Marty the quiet one, the one with all the doubts. Like alter egos. Simply being with Flynn again Marty could feel himself flung into sharper relief.

The evening passed very quickly. People joined Flynn, drank with him, and wandered off again, having been entertained by the court jester for a while. There were some individuals Marty knew among the traffic of drinkers, and a few uncomfortable encounters, but it was all easier than he'd expected, smoothed on its way by Flynn's bonhomie. About ten-fifteen he ducked out for a quarter of an hour—"Just got to sort out a little business"—and came back with a wad of money in his inside pocket, which he immediately began to spend.

"What you need," he told Marty when they were both awash with drink, "what you need is a good woman. No—" he giggled, "—no, no, no. What you need is a *bad* woman."

Marty nodded; his head felt unstable on his neck. "You got it in one," he said.

"Let's go find us a lady, eh? Shall we do that?"

"Suits me."

"I mean, you need company, man, and so do I. And I do a bit of that on the side, you know? I've got a few ladies available. I'll see you all right."

Marty was too drunk to argue. Besides the thought of a woman—bought or seduced, what the hell did it matter?—was the best idea he'd heard in a long while. Flynn went away, made a telephone call, and came back leering.

"No trouble," he said. "No trouble at all. One more drink, then we'll hit the road."

Lamblike, Marty followed his lead. They had one more drink together, then staggered out of The Eclipse and around the corner to Flynn's car, a Volvo that had seen better days. They drove for five minutes to a house on the estate. The door was opened by a good-looking black woman.

"Ursula, this is my friend Marty. Marty, say hello to Ursula."

"Hello, Ursula."

"Where's the glasses, honey? Daddy bought a bottle."

They drank some more together, and then went upstairs; it was only then that Marty realized Flynn wasn't going to leave. This was intended to be *ménage à trois*, like the old days. His initial disquiet vanished when the girl began to undress for them. The drink had taken the edge off his inhibitions, and he sat on the bed encouraging her in her strip, dimly aware that Flynn was probably as much entertained by his evident craving as he was by the girl. Let him watch, Marty thought, it's his party.

In the small, badly lit bedroom Ursula's body looked sculpted from black butter. In between her full breasts a small gold cross lay, glistening. Her skin glistened too; each pore was marked with a pinprick of sweat. Flynn had started to undress as well, and Marty followed suit, stumbling as he pulled off his jeans, unwilling to relinquish the sight of the girl as she sat up on the bed and put her hands to her groin.

What followed was a swift reeducation in the craft of sex. Like a swimmer who returns to water after years of absence, he soon remembered the strokes. In the next two hours he gathered fistfuls of memories to take back with him: looking around from Ursula's amused face to see Flynn kneeling at the bottom of the bed sucking her toes; Ursula cooing like a black dove over his erection before devouring it to the root; Flynn licking his hands and grinning, and licking and grinning. And finally the two of them sharing Ursula, Flynn buried in her backside, making true what, as an eleven-year-old, he had claimed you did with women.

Afterward, they dozed together. Sometime in the middle of the night Marty stirred to see Flynn dressing, and shrinking away. Home presumably; wherever home was these days and nights.

24

He woke just before dawn, disoriented for several seconds until he heard Ursula's steady exhalations at his side. He said goodbye to her as she dozed, and found a cab to take him back to his car. He was back at the Sanctuary by eight-thirty. Exhaustion would hit him eventually, and a hangover too, but he knew his body clock well. There'd be a few hours' grace before the debt had to be paid.

Pearl was in the kitchen tidying up after breakfast. They

exchanged a few pleasantries, and he sat down to drink three cups of black coffee, one after the other. His mouth tasted foul, and Ursula's perfume, which had smelled ambrosial the previous night, was oversweet this morning. It lingered on his hands and in his hair.

"Good night?" Pearl asked. He nodded without answering. "You'd better get a good breakfast inside you; I won't be able to get you any lunch today."

"Why not?"

"Too busy with the dinner party."

"What dinner party?"

"Bill will tell you. He wants to see you. He's in the library."

Toy looked weary, but not as ill as he had when last they'd met. Maybe he'd seen a doctor in the interim, or taken a holiday.

"You wanted to speak to me?"

"Yes, Marty, yes. You enjoy your night on the town?"

"Very much. Thank you for making it possible."

"It wasn't my doing; it was Joe. You're well liked, Marty. Lillian tells me even the dogs have taken to you."

Toy crossed to the table, opened the cigarette box, and selected a cigarette. Marty had not seen him smoke before.

"You won't be seeing Mr. Whitehead today; there's going to be a little get-together tonight—"

"Yes, Pearl told me."

"It's nothing special. Mr. Whitehead has dinners for a select few every now and then. The point is, he likes them to be private gatherings, so you won't be required."

This pleased Marty. At least he could go lie down, catch up on some sleep.

"Obviously we'd like you to be in the house, should you be needed for any reason, but I think it's unlikely."

"Thank you, sir."

"I think you can call me Bill in private, Marty; I don't see any need for formality any longer."

"OK."

"I mean . . ." He stopped to light the cigarette. ". . . we're all servants here, aren't we? In one way or another."

By the time he'd showered, thought about a run and discounted the idea as masochistic, then lain down to doze, the first signs of the inevitable hangover were on the way. There was no cure that he knew of. The only option was to sleep it off.

He didn't wake until the middle of the afternoon, and only then roused by hunger. There was no sound in the house. Downstairs the kitchen was empty, only the buzz of a fly at the window—the first Marty had seen this season—interrupted the glacial calm. Pearl had obviously finished whatever preparations were required for this evening's dinner party, and gone, perhaps to come back later. He went to the refrigerator and rifled it for something to quieten his growling belly. The sandwich he constructed looked like an unmade bed, with sheets of ham tumbling out from its bread blankets, but it did the job. He put on the coffee percolator and went in search of company.

It was as though everyone had gone from the face of the earth. Wandering through the deserted house the pit of the afternoon swallowed him. The stillness, and the remains of his headache, conspired to make him jittery. He found himself glancing behind him like a man on an ill-lit street. Upstairs was even quieter than down; his footsteps on the carpeted landing were so hushed he might not have had weight at all. Even so, he found himself creeping.

Halfway along the landing—Whitehead's landing—came the cutoff point beyond which he had been instructed not to go. The old man's private suite was this end of the house, as was Carys' bedroom. Which room was it most likely to be? He tried to recreate the outside of the house, to locate the room by a process of elimination, but he lacked the imaginative skill to correlate the exterior with the closed doors of the corridor ahead.

Not all were closed. The third along on his right was slightly ajar: and from inside, now his ears were attuned to the lowest level of audibility, he could hear the sound of movement. Surely it was her. He crossed the invisible threshold into forbidden territory, not thinking of what the punishment for trespass might be, too eager to see her face, maybe to speak to her. He reached the door, and peered through.

Carys was there. She was semirecumbent on the bed, staring into middle distance. Marty was just about to step in to speak to her when somebody else moved in the room, hidden from him by the door. He didn't have to wait for the voice to know that it was Whitehead.

"Why do you treat me so badly?" he was asking her, his voice hushed. "You know how it hurts me when you're like this."

She said nothing: if she even heard him she made no sign of it.

"I don't ask so much of you, do I?" he appealed. Her eyes flickered in his direction. "Well, do I?"

Eventually, she deigned to reply. When she did her voice was so quiet Marty could barely catch the words. "Aren't you ashamed?" she asked him.

"There are worse things, Carys, than having somebody need you; believe me."

"I know," she replied, taking her eyes off him. There was such pain, and such submission in the face of that pain, in those two words: *I know*. It made Marty suddenly sick with longing for her; to touch her, to try to heal the anonymous hurt. Whitehead crossed the room and came to sit beside her on the edge of the bed. Marty stepped back from the door, fearful of being spotted, but Whitehead's attention was concentrated on the enigma in front of him.

"*What* do you know?" he asked her. The former gentility had suddenly evaporated. "Are you keeping something from me?"

"Just dreams," she replied. "More and more."

"Of what?"

"You know. The same."

"Your mother?"

Carys nodded, almost invisibly. "And others," she said.
"Who?"
"They never show themselves."
The old man sighed, and looked away from her. "And in the dreams?" he asked. "What happens?"
"She tries to speak to me. She tries to tell me something."
Whitehead didn't inquire further: he seemed to be out of questions. His shoulders had slumped. Carys looked at him, sensing his defeat.
"Where is she, Papa?" she asked him, leaning forward for the first time and putting an arm around his neck. It was a blatantly manipulative gesture; she offered this intimacy only to get what she wanted from him. How much had she offered, or he taken, in their time together? Her face came close to his; the late-afternoon light enchanted it. "Tell me, Papa," she asked again, "where do you think she is?" and this time Marty grasped the taunt that lay beneath the apparently innocent question. What it signified, he didn't know. What this whole scene, with its talk of coldness and shame, meant, was far from clear. He was glad, in a way, not to know. But this question, that she asked him so mock-lovingly, had been asked—and he *had* to wait a moment longer, until the old man had answered it. "Where is she, Papa?"
"In dreams," he replied, his face averted from her. "Just in dreams."
She dropped her arm from his shoulder.
"Never lie to me," she charged him icily.
"It's all I can tell you," he replied; his tone was almost pitiable. "If you know more than I do—" He turned and looked at her, his voice urgent. "*Do* you know something?"
"Oh, Papa," she murmured reproachfully, "more conspiracies?" How many feints and counterfeints were there in this exchange? Marty puzzled. "You don't suspect *me* now, surely?"
Whitehead frowned. "No, never you, darling," he said. "Never you."

He raised his hand to her face and leaned forward to put his dry lips to hers. Before they touched, Marty left the door and slipped away.

There were some things he couldn't bring himself to watch.

25

C ars began to arrive at the house in the early evening. There were voices Marty recognized in the hallway. It would be the usual crowd, he guessed; among them the Fan-Dancer and his comrades; Ottaway, Curtsinger and Dwoskin. He heard women's voices too. They'd brought their wives, or their mistresses. He wondered what kind of women they were. Once beautiful, now sour and lovelorn. Bored with their husbands, no doubt, who thought more of moneymaking than of them. He caught whiffs of their laughter, and later, of their perfume, in the hallway. He'd always had a good sense of smell. Saul would be proud of him.

About eight-fifteen he went into the kitchen and heated up the plate of ravioli Pearl had left for him, then retired into the library to watch a few boxing videos. The events of the afternoon still niggled him. Try as he might he couldn't remove Carys from his head, and his emotional state, over which he had so little control, irritated him. Why couldn't he be like Flynn, who bought a woman for the night, then walked away the next morning? Why did his feelings always become blurred, so that he couldn't sort one from the other? On the television set the match was getting bloodier, but he scarcely registered the punishment or the victory. His mind was conjuring Carys' sealed face as she lay on the bed, probing it, looking for explanations.

Leaving the fight commentator to babble on, he went through to the kitchen to fetch another couple of beers from the refrigerator. At this end of the house there was not even a hint of noise from the party-goers. Besides, such a civilized gathering would be hushed, wouldn't it? Just the clink of cut glass, and talk of rich men's pleasures.

Well, fuck them all, he thought. Whitehead and Carys and all of them. It wasn't his world and he wanted no part of it, or them, or her. He could get all the women he wanted anytime—just pick up the phone and call Flynn. No trouble. Let them play their damn-fool games: he wasn't interested. He drained the first can of beer standing in the kitchen, then got out two more cans and took them through to the lounge. He was going to get really blind tonight. Oh, yes. He was going to get so drunk nothing would matter. Especially not her. Because he didn't care. *He didn't care*.

The tape had finished, and the screen had gone blank. It buzzed with a squirming pattern of dots. White noise. Wasn't that what they called it? It was a portrait of chaos, that hissing, those writhing dots; the universe humming to itself. Empty airwaves were never really empty.

He turned the set off. He didn't want to watch any more matches. His head buzzed like the box; white noise in there too.

He slumped down in the chair and downed the second can of beer in two throatfuls. The image of Carys with Whitehead swam into focus again. "Go away," he told it, aloud; but it lingered. Did he *want* her, was that it? Would this unease be pacified if he took her to the dovecote one of these afternoons and humped her till she begged him never to stop? The wretched thought only disgusted him; he couldn't defuse these ambiguities with pornography.

As he opened the third beer he found his hands were sweating, a clammy sweat he associated with sickness, like the first signs of flu. He wiped his palms on his jeans and put the beer down. There was more than infatuation fueling his nervousness. Something was wrong. He got up and went to the lounge window. He was staring into the pitch darkness beyond the glass, when it struck him what the wrongness might be. The lights on the lawn and perimeter fence had not been put on tonight. He would have to do it. For the first time since he'd arrived at the house it was real night outside, a night more black than any he'd experienced in many years. In Wandsworth there was always light; floods on the walls burned from twilight to dawn. But here, without streetlamps, there was just night outside.

Night; and white noise.

26

Though Marty had imagined otherwise, Carys wasn't at the dinner party. There were very few freedoms left to her; refusing her father's invitations to dinner was one of them. She had endured an afternoon of his sudden tears, his just as sudden accusations. She was weary of his kisses and his doubts. So tonight she'd given herself a larger fix than usual, greedy for forgetfulness. Now all she wanted to do was lie down and bask in not being.

Even as she lay her head on the pillow, something, or someone, touched her. She came around again, startled. The bedroom was empty. The lamps were on and the curtains drawn. There was nobody there: it was a trick of the senses, no more. Yet she could still feel the nerve endings at the nape of her neck tingle where the touch had seemed to come, responding, anemonelike, to the intrusion. She put her fingers there and massaged the place. The jolt had snatched lethargy away for a while. There was no chance of putting her head back down until her heart had stopped hammering.

Sitting up, she wondered where her runner was. Probably at

the dinner party with the rest of Papa's court. They'd like that: to have him among them to condescend to. She didn't think of him as an angel any longer. After all he had a name now, and a history (Toy had told her everything he knew). He'd long lost his divinity. He was who he was—Martin Francis Strauss—a man with green-gray eyes; with a scar on his cheek and hands that were eloquent, like an actor's hands, except that she didn't think he'd be very good at professional deceit: his eyes betrayed him too easily.

Then the touch came again, and this time she distinctly felt fingers catching her nape, as though the bone of her spine had been pinched, so, so lightly, between somebody's forefinger and thumb. It was absurd illusion, but too persuasive to be dismissed.

She sat down at her dressing table and felt tremors moving out through her body from her jittering stomach. Was this just the result of a bad fix? She'd never had any problems before: the H that Luther bought from his Stratford suppliers was always of the highest quality: Papa could afford it.

Go back and lie down, she told herself. Even if you can't sleep, lie down. But the bed, as she stood and turned to walk back to it, receded from her, all the contents of the room withdrawing into a corner as though they were painted on linen and had been plucked away from her by some hidden hand.

Then the fingers seemed to be back on her neck again, more insistent this time, as if working their way into her. She reached around and rubbed the back of her neck vigorously, cursing Luther loudly for bringing her bad stuff. He was probably buying cut heroin instead of the pure, and pocketing the difference. Her anger cleansed her head for a few moments, or so it seemed, for nothing else happened. She walked steadily across to the bed, orientating herself by putting her hand on the flower-patterned wall as she went. Things began to right themselves; the room found its proper perspective again. Sighing with relief she lay down without pulling back the covers, and closed her eyes. Something danced on the inside of her lids. Shapes formed, dispersed and re-formed. None of them made the least sense: they were splashes and sprawls, a lunatic's graffiti. She watched them with her mind's eye, mesmerized by their fluent transformations, scarcely aware in her fascination that the invisible fingers had found her neck again and were insinuating themselves into her substance with all the subtle efficiency of a good masseur.

And then sleep.

She didn't hear the dogs begin to bark: Marty did. At first just a solitary barking, somewhere off to the southeast of the house, but the alarm call was almost immediately taken up by a volley of other voices.

He got up boozily from in front of the dead television and went back to the window.

A wind had got up. It had probably blown some dead branch down, which had disturbed the dogs. He'd noticed several dead elms that needed felling in the corner of the estate; probably one of those was the culprit. Still, he'd better look. He went through to the kitchen, and turned on the video screens, flicking from camera to camera along the perimeter fence. There was nothing to see. As he flipped to the cameras just east of the woods, however, the pictures disappeared. White noise replaced the sight of floodlit grass. Three cameras were out of action in all.

"Shit," he said. If a tree were down, and that became a likelier option than ever if the cameras weren't working, he'd have a clearing-up job on his hands. It was odd that the alarms hadn't started, though. Any fall that had incapacitated three cameras must have breached the fence's systems: yet no bells rang, no sirens wailed. He took his anorak off the hook beside the back door, picked up a flashlight, and went outside.

The fence lights glimmered at the periphery of his vision; scanning them quickly he could see none that were out. He set off toward the racket of dogs. It was a balmy night, despite the wind: the first confident warmth of spring. He was glad to be going on a walkabout, even if it was a fool's errand. It might not even be a tree at all; simply an electrical fault. Nothing was infallible. The house fell away behind him, the lit windows diminished. Now, all around him, darkness. He was isolated for two hundred yards between the lights of the fence and those of the house, a strip of no-man's-land over which he stumbled, flashlight inefficiently lighting the turf a few strides ahead of him. In the woods, the wind found an occasional voice; otherwise there was silence.

Eventually he reached the fence where he approximated the noise of the dogs to have come from. All the lights in either direction were working: there was no visible sign of disturbance. Despite the reassuring correctness of the scene, something about it, about the night and the balmy wind, felt odd. Maybe the dark wasn't so benign after all, the warmth in the air not entirely natural for the season. A tick had begun in his stomach, and his bladder was heavy with beer. It was vexing that there were no dogs to be seen or heard. Either he'd made an error of judgment in approximating their position or they'd moved from the spot, pursuing. Or, the absurd thought came, *pursued*.

The lamps in the uprights of the fence rocked their hooded heads in a fresh gust of wind; the scene danced giddily in the pitching light. He decided he could go no further without relieving his aching bladder. He turned off the flashlight, pocketed it, and unzipped, back to the fence and the light. It was a great relief to piss into the grass; the physical satisfaction made him whoop.

Halfway through, the lights behind him flickered. At first he thought it was simply a trick of the wind. But no, they were actually dimming. Even as they faded, along the perimeter to his right the dogs began again, anger and panic in their voices.

He couldn't stop pissing once he'd started, and for valuable seconds he cursed his lack of bladder control. When he was done he zipped up and started to run in the direction of the din. As he went, the lights came back on again, falteringly, their circuits buzzing as they did so. But they were set too infrequently along the line of the fence to offer much reassurance. Between them, patches of darkness sprawled, so that for one pace out of every ten all was clarity, for the other nine, night. Despite the fear clutching at his gut he ran all-out, the fence flickering past him. Light, darkness, light, darkness—

Ahead, a tableau resolved itself. An intruder was standing on the far side of a light pool thrown down by one of the lamps. The dogs were everywhere, at his heels, at his chest, snapping and tearing at him. The man was still standing upright, legs apart, while they milled around him.

Marty now realized how close he was to witnessing a massacre. The dogs were berserk, tearing at the intruder with all the fury they could muster. Curiously, despite the venom in their attack, their tails were between their legs, and their low growls, as they circled looking for another opening, were unmistakably fearful. Job, he saw, was not even attempting to pounce: he slunk around, his eyes closed to slits, watching the heroics of the rest.

Marty started calling them off by name, using the strong, simple commands Lillian had taught him.

"Stand! Saul! Stand! Dido!"

The dogs were immaculately tutored: he'd seen them put through these exercises a dozen times. Now, despite the intensity of their anger, they relinquished their victim when they heard the command. Reluctantly they fell back, ears flattened, teeth exposed, eyes clamped on the man.

Marty started to walk steadily toward the intruder, who was left standing in a ring of watchful dogs, reeling and bloody. He carried no visible weapon; indeed he looked more like a derelict than a would-be assassin. His plain dark jacket was torn in a dozen places by the attack, and where his skin was exposed blood shone.

"Keep them . . . off me," he said, his voice wounded. There were bites all over his body. In some places, particularly his legs, pieces of his flesh had been ripped away. The middle finger of his left hand had been bitten through at the second joint, and was depending by a thread of sinew. Blood splashed on the grass. It amazed Marty that the man was even standing upright.

The dogs still circled him, ready to renew the assault if and when the order were granted; one or two of them glanced at Marty impatiently. They were itching to finish their wounded victim off. But the derelict wouldn't grant them a sign of his fear. He only had eyes for Marty, and those eyes were pinpricks in livid white.

"Don't move," Marty said, "if you want to remain alive. If you try to run they'll bring you down. Do you understand? I haven't got that much control over them."

The other said nothing; simply stared. His agony, Marty knew, must be acute. He wasn't even a young man. His uneven growth of stubble showed more gray than black. The skull behind the lax and waxen flesh was severe, the features set on it used and weary: tragic even. His suffering was only apparent in the greasy sheen of his skin, and the fixedness of his facial muscles. His stare had the stillness of a hurricane's eye, and its menace.

"How did you get in?" Marty asked.

"Get them away," the man said. He spoke as if he expected to be obeyed.

"Come back to the house with me."

The other shook his head, unwilling even to debate the possibility.

"Get them *away*," he said again.

Marty conceded to the other's authority, though not certain why. He called the dogs to him by name. They came to heel with rebuking looks, unhappy to surrender their prize.

"*Now* come back to the house," Marty said.

"No need."

"You'll bleed to death, for God's sake."

"I loathe dogs," the man said, still not taking his eyes off Marty. "We both do."

Marty hadn't time to think clearly about what the man was saying; he just wanted to stop the situation from escalating again. Blood loss had surely weakened the man. If he fell down Marty wasn't certain he could prevent the dogs from going in for the kill.

They were around his legs, glancing up at him irritably; their breath was hot on him.

"If you don't come on your own accord, I'll take you."

"No." The intruder raised his injured hand to chest height and glanced down at it. "I don't need your kindnesses, thank you," he said.

He bit down on the sinew of the mutilated finger, as a seamstress might through a thread. The discarded joints fell to the grass. Then he clenched his seeping hand into a fist, and thrust it into his ravaged jacket.

Marty said: "Christ Almighty." Suddenly the lights along the fence were flickering again. Only this time they went out altogether. In the sudden pitch, Saul whined. Marty knew the dog's voice, and shared his apprehension.

"What's happening, boy?" he asked the dog, wishing to God it could reply. And then the dark broke; something lit the scene that was neither electricity nor starlight. The intruder was the source. He'd begun to burn with a faint luminescence. Light was dripping from his fingertips and oozing from the bloody holes in his coat. It enveloped his head in a flickering gray halo that consumed neither flesh nor bone, the light licking out of mouth and eyes and nostrils. Now it began to take on shapes, or seemed to. It was all *seems*. Phantoms sprang from the flux of light. Marty glimpsed dogs, then a woman, then a face; all, and yet perhaps none of these, a flurry of apparitions that transformed before they congealed. And in the center of these momentary phenomena the intruder's eyes stared on at Marty: clear and cold.

Then, without a comprehensible cue, the entertainment took on a different tone altogether. A look of anguish slid across the fabricator's face; a drool of bloody darkness spilled from his eyes, extinguishing whatever played in the vapor, leaving only bright worms of fire to trace his skull. Then they too went out, and just as suddenly as the illusions had appeared, they were gone, and there was just a torn man standing beside the humming fence.

The lights were coming back on again, their illumination so

flat it drained any last vestige of magic. Marty looked at the bland
flesh, the empty eyes, the sheer drabness of the figure in front of
him and believed none of it—

"Tell Joseph," said the intruder.

—it had all been trickery of some kind—

"Tell him what?"

"That I was here."

—but if it was just trickery, why didn't he step forward and
apprehend the man?

"Who are you?" he asked.

"*Just tell him.*"

Marty nodded; he had no courage left in him.

"Then, go home."

"Home?"

"Away from here," the intruder said. "Out of harm's way."

He turned from Marty and the dogs, and as he did so the
lights faltered and failed for several dozen yards in either direction.

When they came back on again, the magician had gone.

27

Is that all he said?"

As ever, Whitehead had his back to Marty as he spoke, and
it was impossible to gauge his response to the account of the
night's events. Marty had offered a carefully doctored description
of what had actually happened. He'd told Whitehead about his
hearing the dogs and about the chase and the brief conversation
he'd had with the intruder. What he'd left out was the part that he
couldn't explain: the images the man had seemingly conjured
from his body. That he made no attempt to describe, or even

report. He'd simply told the old man that the lights along the fence had failed and that under the cover of darkness the intruder had made off. It made a lame finale to the encounter but he had no powers to improve on his story. His mind, still juggling the visions of the previous night, was too uncertain of objective truth to contemplate a more elaborate lie.

He hadn't slept for over twenty-four hours now. He'd spent the bulk of the night checking the perimeter, scouring the fence for the place the intruder had breached. There was no break in the wire, however. Either the man had slipped into the grounds when the gates were opened for one of the guests' cars, which was plausible; or else he had scaled the fence, disregarding an electric charge that would have struck most men dead. Having seen the tricks the man was capable of Marty was not about to discount this second scenario. After all, this same man had rendered the alarms inoperative—*and* somehow drained the lights of power along the stretch of fence. How he'd achieved these feats was anybody's guess. Certainly scant minutes after the man's disappearance the entire system was fully operational again: the alarms working and the cameras functioning all around the boundary.

Once he'd checked the fences thoroughly, he'd gone back into the house and sat in the kitchen to reconstruct every detail of what he'd just experienced. About four in the morning he'd heard the dinner party break up: laughter, the slamming of car doors. He'd made no move to report the break-in then and there. There was, he reasoned, no use in souring Whitehead's evening. He just sat and listened to the noise of people at the other end of the house. Their voices were incoherent smears; as if he were underground, and they above. And while he listened, drained after his adrenaline high, memories of the man at the fence flickered in front of him.

He told none of this to Whitehead. Just the plainest outline of events, and those few words: "*Tell him that I was here.*" It was enough.

"Was he badly hurt?" Whitehead said, not turning from the window.

"He lost a finger, as I said. And he was bleeding pretty badly."

"In pain, would you say?"

Marty hesitated before replying. Pain was not the word he wanted to employ; not pain as he understood it. But if he used some other word, like anguish—something that hinted at the gulfs behind the glacial eyes—he risked trespass into areas he was not prepared to go; especially not with Whitehead. He was certain that if he once let the old man sense any ambivalence, the knives would be out. So he replied:

"Yes. He was in pain."

"And you say he bit the finger off?"

"Yes."

"Maybe you'd look for it later."

"I have. I think one of the dogs must have taken it."

Did Whitehead chuckle to himself? It sounded so.

"Don't you believe me?" Marty said, taking the laughter to be at his expense.

"Of course I believe you. It was only a matter of time before he came."

"You know who he is?"

"Yes."

"Then you can have him arrested."

The private amusement had stopped. The words that followed were colorless.

"This is no conventional trespasser, Strauss, as I'm sure you're aware. The man is a professional assassin of the first rank. He came here with the express purpose of killing me. With your intervention, and that of the dogs, he was prevented. But he will try again—"

"All the more reason to have him found, sir."

"No police force in Europe could locate him."

"—if he's a known assassin—" Marty said, pressing the point. His refusal to let this bone go until he had the marrow from it had begun to irritate the old man. He growled his reply.

"He's known to *me*. Perhaps to a few others who have encountered him down the years . . . but that's all."

Whitehead crossed from the window to his desk, unlocked it, and brought out something wrapped in cloth. He laid it on the polished desk-top and unwrapped it. It was a gun.

"You'll carry this with you at all times in future," he told Marty. "Pick it up. It won't bite."

Marty took the gun from the desk. It was cold and heavy.

"Have no hesitation, Strauss. This man is lethal."

Marty passed the gun from hand to hand; it felt ugly.

"Problem?" Whitehead inquired.

Marty chewed on his words before speaking them. "It's only . . . well, I'm on parole, sir. I'm supposed to be obeying the letter of the law. Now you give me a gun, and tell me to shoot on sight. I mean, I'm sure you're right about him being an assassin, but I don't think he was even armed."

Whitehead's expression, hitherto impartial, changed as Marty spoke. His teeth showed yellow as he snapped his reply.

"You're my property, Strauss. You concern yourself with *me*, or you get the Hell out of here tomorrow morning. *Me!*" He jabbed a finger at his own chest. "Not yourself. *Forget yourself.*"

Marty swallowed a throatful of possible retorts: none were polite.

"You want to go back to Wandsworth?" the old man said. All signs of anger had disappeared; the yellow teeth were sheathed. "Do you?"

"No. Of course not."

"You can go if you want. Just say the word."

"I said no! . . . sir."

"Then you listen," the old man said. "The man you met last night means me harm. He came here to kill me. If he comes again—*and he will*—I want you to return the compliment. Then we'll see, won't we, boy?"—the teeth showed again, a fox's smile. "Oh, yes . . . we'll see."

Carys woke feeling seedy. At first she remembered nothing of the previous night, but she gradually began to recall the bad trip that she'd undergone: the room like a living thing, the phantom fingertips that had plucked—oh, so gently—at the hairs on the nape of her neck.

She couldn't remember what had happened when the fingers had delved too deep. Had she lain down, was that it? Yes, now she remembered, she *had* lain down. It was only then, when her head hit the pillow and sleep claimed her, that the bad times had really begun.

Not dreams: at least not like she'd had before. There'd been no theatrics, no symbols, no fugitive memories weaving between the horrors. There had been nothing at all: and that had been (still was) the terror. She had been delivered into a void.

"Void."

It was just a dead word when she spoke it aloud: it didn't begin to describe the place she'd discovered; its emptiness more immaculate, the terrors it awoke more atrocious, the hope of salvation in its deeps more fragile than in any place she had ever guessed at. It was a legendary Nowhere, beside which every other dark was blindingly bright, every other despair she had endured a mere flirtation with the pit, not the pit itself.

Its architect had been there too. She remembered something of his mild physiognomy, which had convinced her not a jot. See how extraordinary this emptiness is, he had boasted; how pure, how absolute? A world of marvels can't compare, can never *hope* to compare, with such sublime nothingness.

And when she awoke the boasts remained. It was as if the vision were true, while the reality she now occupied was a fiction. As if color and shape and substance were pretty distractions designed to paste over the fact of this emptiness he had shown her. Now she waited, scarcely aware of time passing, occasionally stroking the sheet or feeling the weave of the carpet under her bare feet, waiting in despair for the moment it all peeled back and the void appeared again to devour her.

Well, she thought, I'll go to the sunshine island. If ever she deserved to play there awhile, she deserved it now, having suffered so much. But something soured the thought. Wasn't the island a fiction too? If she went there now, wasn't she weaker next time the architect came, void in hand? Her heart started to beat very loudly in her ears. Who was there to help her? Nobody who understood. Just Pearl, with her accusing eyes and her sly contempt; and Whitehead, content to feed her H as long as it kept her compliant; and Marty, her runner, sweet in his way, but so naively pragmatic she could never begin to explain the complexities of the dimensions she lived in. He was a one-world man; he would look at her bewildered, trying to understand, and failing.

No; she had no guides, no signposts. It would be better if she went back the way she knew. Back to the island.

It was a chemical lie, and it killed with time; but life killed in time, didn't it? And if dying was all there was, didn't it make sense to go to it happy rather than fester in a dirty hole of a world where the void whispered at every corner? So when Pearl came upstairs with her H, she took it, thanked her politely, and went to the island, dancing.

28

Fear could make the world go round if its wheels were efficiently oiled. Marty had seen the system in practice at Wandsworth: a hierarchy built upon fear. It was violent, unstable and unjust, but perfectly workable.

Seeing Whitehead, the calm, still center of his universe, so changed by fear, so sweaty, so full of panic, had come as an unwelcome shock. Marty had no personal feelings for the old man—or none that he was aware of—but he'd seen Whitehead's species of integrity at work, and had profited by it. Now, he felt, the stability he had come to enjoy was threatened with extinction. Already the old man was clearly withholding information—perhaps pivotal to Marty's understanding of the situation—about the intruder and his motives. In place of Whitehead's previous plain talking, there was innuendo and threats. That was his prerogative, of course. But it left Marty with a guessing game on his hands.

One point was unarguable: whatever Whitehead claimed, the man at the fence had been no conventional hired killer. Several inexplicable things had happened at the fence. The lights had waxed and waned as if on cue; the cameras had mysteriously failed when the man had appeared. The dogs had registered this riddle too. Why else had they shown such a confusion of anger and apprehension? And there remained the illusions—those air-burning pictures. No sleight of hand, however elaborate, could explain them satisfactorily. If Whitehead knew this "assassin" as well as he claimed, then he must know the man's skills too: he was simply too afraid to talk about them.

Marty spent the day asking the discreetest of questions around the house but it rapidly became apparent that Whitehead had said nothing of the events to Pearl, Lillian or Luther. This was odd. Surely now was the very time to make everyone more vigilant? The only person to suggest he had any knowledge of the night's events was Bill Toy, but when Marty raised the subject he was evasive.

"I realize you've been put in a difficult situation, Marty, but so are we all at the moment."

"I just feel I could do the job better—"

"—if you knew the facts."

"Yes."

"Well, I think you have to concede that Joe knows best." He made a rueful face. "We should all have that tattooed on our hands, don't you think? *Joe Knows Best*. I wish I could tell more.

I wish I *knew* more. I think it's probably easiest for all concerned if you let the matter drop."

"He gave me a gun, Bill."

"I know."

"And he told me to use it."

Toy nodded; he looked pained by all of this, even regretful.

"These are bad times, Marty. We're all . . . all having to do a lot of things we don't want to, believe me."

Marty did believe him; he trusted Toy sufficiently to know that if there'd been anything he *could* say on the subject, it would have been said. It was entirely possible that Toy didn't even know who had broken the seal on the Sanctuary. If it was some private confrontation between Whitehead and the stranger, then maybe a full explanation could only come from the old man himself, and that would clearly not be forthcoming.

Marty had one final interviewee. Carys.

He hadn't seen her since he'd trespassed on the upper landing the day before. What he'd seen between Carys and her father had unsettled him, and there was, he knew, a childish urge in him to punish her by withholding his company. Now he felt obliged to seek her out, however uncomfortable the meeting might prove.

He found her that afternoon, loitering in the vicinity of the dovecote. She was wrapped up in a fur coat that looked as if it had been bought at a thrift shop; it was several sizes too big for her, and moth-eaten. As it was, she seemed overdressed. The weather was warm even if the wind was gusty, and the clouds that passed across a Wedgwood-blue sky carried little threat: too small, too white. They were April clouds, containing at worst a light shower.

"Carys."

She fixed him with eyes so ringed with tiredness his first thought was that they were bruised. In her hand she had a bundle, rather than a bunch, of flowers, many still buds.

"Smell," she said, proffering them.

He sniffed at them. They were practically scentless: they just smelled of eagerness and earth.

"Can't smell much."

"Good," she said. "I thought I was losing my senses."

She let the bundle drop to the ground, impatient with them.

"You don't mind if I interrupt, do you?"

She shook her head. "Interrupt all you like," she replied. The strangeness of her manner struck him more forcibly than ever; she always spoke as though she had some private joke on her mind. He longed to join in the game, to learn her secret language, but she seemed so sealed up, an anchorite behind a wall of sly smiles.

"I suppose you heard the dogs last night," he said.

"I don't remember," she replied, frowning. "Maybe."

"Did anybody say anything to you about it?"

"Why should they?"

"I don't know. I just thought—"

She put him out of his discomfort with a fierce little nod of her head.

"Yes, if you want to know. Pearl told me there's been an intruder. And you scared him off, is that right? You and the dogs."

"Me and the dogs."

"And which of you bit off his finger?"

Had Pearl told her about the finger too, or was it the old man who'd vouchsafed that vicious detail? Had they been together today, in her room? He canceled the scene before it flared up in his head.

"Did Pearl tell you that?" he said.

"I haven't seen the old man," she replied, "if that's what you're driving at."

His thought encapsulated; it was eerie. She even used his phraseology. "The old man," she called him, not "Papa."

"Shall we walk down to the lake?" she suggested, not really seeming to care one way or the other.

"Sure."

"You were right about the dovecote, you know," she said. "It's ugly when it's empty like this. I never thought of it like that before." The image of the deserted dovecote genuinely seemed to unnerve her. She shivered, even in the thick coat.

"Did you run today?" she asked.

"No. I was too tired."

"Was it that bad?"

"Was *what* that bad?"

"Last night."

He didn't know how to begin to answer. Yes, of course, it had been bad, but even if he trusted her enough to describe the illusion he'd seen—and he was by no means sure he did—his vocabulary was woefully inadequate.

Carys paused as they came in sight of the lake. Small white flowers starred the grass beneath their feet, Marty didn't know their names. She studied them as she said:

"Is it just another prison, Marty?"

"What?"

"Being here."

She had her father's skill with non sequiturs. He hadn't anticipated the question at all, and it threw him. Nobody had really asked him how he'd felt since arriving. Certainly not beyond a superficial inquiry as to his comfort. Perhaps consequently he hadn't really bothered to ask himself. His answer—when it came—came haltingly.

"Yes . . . I suppose it's still a prison, I hadn't really thought . . . I mean, I can't just up and leave anytime I want to, can I? But it doesn't compare . . . with Wandsworth"—again, his vocabulary failed him—"this is just another world."

He wanted to say he loved the trees, the size of the sky, the white florets they stepped through as they walked, but he knew such utterances would sound leaden out of his mouth. He hadn't got the knack of that kind of talk: not like Flynn, who could babble instant poetry as though it were a second tongue. Irish blood, he used to claim, to explain this loquacity. All Marty could say was:

"I can run here."

She murmured something he failed to catch; perhaps just assent. Whatever, his answer seemed to satisfy her, and he could feel the anger he'd started out with, the resentment at her clever talk and her secret life with Papa, dissolving.

"Do you play tennis?" she asked, again out of nowhere.

"No; I never have."

"Like to learn?" she suggested, half-looking around at him and grinning. "I could teach you. When the weather gets warmer."

She looked too frail for any strenuous exercise; living on the edge all the time seemed to weary her, though on the edge of *what* he didn't know.

"You teach me: I'll play," he said, happy with the bargain.

"That's a deal?" she asked.

"A deal."

—and her eyes, he thought, are so dark; ambiguous eyes that dodge and skim sometimes, and sometimes, when you least expect it, look at you with such directness you're sure she's stripping your soul.

—and he isn't handsome, she thought; he's too used to be that, and he runs to keep himself fit because if he stopped he'd get flabby. He's probably a narcissist: I bet he stands in front of the mirror every night and looks at himself and wishes he was still a pretty-boy instead of being solid and somber.

She caught a thought from him, her mind reaching up, easily up, above her head (this was the way she pictured it, at least) and snatching it out of the air. She did it all the time—to Pearl, to her father—often forgetting that other people lacked the skill to pry with such casualness.

The thought she had snatched was: *I would have to learn to be gentle*; that, or something like it. He was afraid she'd bruise, for Christ's sake. That was why he was all dammed up when he was with her, so circuitous in his dealings.

"I'm not going to break," she said, and a patch of skin at his neck blushed.

"I'm sorry," he answered. She wasn't sure if he was conceding his error or simply hadn't understood her observation.

"There's no need to handle me with kid gloves. I don't want that from you. I get it all the time."

He threw her a disconsolate glance. Why didn't he believe what she told him? She waited, hoping for some clue, but none was offered, however tentative.

They'd come to the weir that fed the lake. It was high, and fast. People had drowned in it, she'd been told, as recently as a couple of decades ago, just before Papa had bought the estate. She started to explain all this, and about a coach and horses that had been driven into the lake during a storm, telling him without listening to herself, working out how to get past his courtesy and his machismo to the part of him that might be of use to her.

"And the coach is still in there?" he asked, staring into the threshing water.

"Presumably," she said. The story had lost its charm already.

"Why don't you trust me?" she asked him straight out.

He didn't reply; but he was clearly struggling with something. The frown of puzzlement he displayed deepened to dismay. Damn, she thought, I've really spoiled things somehow. But it was done. She'd asked him outright, and she was ready to take the bad news, whatever it was.

Almost without planning the theft, she stole another thought from him, and it was shockingly clear: like living it. Through his eyes she saw the door of her bedroom, and her lying on the bed beyond it, glassy-eyed, with Papa sitting close by. When was this? she wondered. Yesterday? The day before? Had he heard them talking about it; was that what woke such distaste in him? He'd played the detective, and he hadn't liked what he'd discovered.

"I'm not very good with people," he said, answering her question about trust. "I never have been."

How he squirmed rather than tell the truth. He was being obscenely polite with her. She wanted to wring his neck.

"You spied on us," she said with brutal plainness. "That's all it is, isn't it? You saw Papa and me together—"

She tried to frame the remark as if it were a wild guess. It didn't quite convince as such, and she knew it. But what the hell? It was said now, and he would have to invent his own reasons as to how she'd reached that conclusion.

"What did you overhear?" she demanded, but got no response. It wasn't anger that tongue-tied him, but shame for his peeping. The blushing had infected his face from ear to ear.

"He treats you like he owns you," he murmured, not taking his eyes off the roiling water.

"He does, in a way."

"Why?"

"I'm all he's got. He's alone . . ."

"Yes."

". . . and afraid."

"Does he ever let you leave the Sanctuary?"

"I've got no desire to go," she said. "I've got all I want here."

He wanted to ask her what she did for bed companions, but he'd embarrassed himself enough as it was. She found the thought anyway, and fast upon the thought, the image of Whitehead leaning forward to kiss her. Perhaps it was more than a fatherly kiss. Though she tried not to think of that possibility too often, she could not avoid its presence. Marty was more acute than she'd given him credit for; he'd caught that subtext, subtle as it was.

"I don't trust him," he said. He took his gaze off the water to look around at her. His bewilderment was perfectly apparent.

"I know how to handle him," she replied. "I've made a bargain with him. He understands bargains. He gets me to stay with him, and I get what I want."

"Which is?"

Now *she* looked away. The spume off the whipping water was a grubby brown. "A little sunshine," she finally replied.

"I thought that came free," Marty said, puzzled.

"Not the way I like it," she answered. What did he want from her? Apologies? If so, he'd be disappointed.

"I should get back to the house," he said.

Suddenly, she said: "Don't hate me, Marty."

"I don't," he came back.

"There's a lot of us the same."

"The same?"

"Belonging to him."

Another ugly truth. She was positively brimful of them today.

"You could get the hell out of here if you really wanted to, couldn't you?" he said, peevishly.

She nodded. "I suppose I could. But where?"

The question made no sense to him. There was an entire world outside the fences, and she surely didn't lack the finances to explore it, not Joseph Whitehead's daughter. Did she really find the prospect so stale? They made such a strange pair. He with his experience so unnaturally abbreviated—years of his life wasted—and now anxious to make up for lost time. She, so apathetic, fatigued by the very thought of escape from her self-defined prison.

"You could go *anywhere*," he said.

"That's as good as nowhere," she replied flatly; it was a destination that remained much on her mind. She glanced across at him, hoping some light would have dawned, but he didn't show a glimmer of comprehension.

"Never mind," she said.

"Are you coming?"

"No, I think I'll stay here for a while."

"Don't throw yourself in."

"Can't swim, eh?" she replied, testily. He frowned, not understanding. "Doesn't matter. I never took you for a hero."

He left her standing inches from the edge of the bank, watching the water. What he'd told her was true; he *wasn't* good with people. But with women, he was even worse. He should have taken the cloth, the way his mother had always wanted him to.

That would have solved the problem; except that he had no grasp of religion either, and never had. Maybe that was part of the problem between him and the girl: they neither of them believed a damn thing. There was nothing to say, there were no issues to debate. He glanced around. Carys had walked a short way along the bank from the spot where he'd left her. The sun glared off the skin of the water and burned into her outline. It was almost as if she wasn't real at all.

PART THREE
DEUCE

deuce[1] n. The two at dice or cards;
(Tennis) state of score (40 all, games all)
at which either party must gain two consecutive
points or games to win.

deuce[2] n. Plague, mischief; the Devil.

V. SUPERSTITION

29

Less than a week after the talk at the weir, the first hairline cracks began to appear in the pillars of the Whitehead Empire. They rapidly widened. Spontaneous selling began on the world's stock markets, a sudden failure of faith in the Empire's credibility. Crippling losses in share values soon mounted. The selling fever, once contracted, appeared well-nigh incurable. In the space of a day there were more visitors to the estate than Marty had ever seen before. Among them, of course, the familiar faces. But this time there were dozens of others, financial analysts, he presumed. Japanese and European visitors mingled with the English, until the place rang with more accents than the United Nations.

The kitchen, much to Pearl's irritation, became an impromptu meeting place for those not immediately required at the great man's hand. They gathered around the large table, demanding coffee in endless supply, to debate the strategies they had congregated here to formulate. Much of their debating, as ever, was lost on Marty, but it was clear from the snippets he overheard that the corporation was facing no explicable emergency. There were falls of staggering proportions happening everywhere; talk of government intervention to prevent imminent collapse in Germany and Sweden; talk too of the sabotage that had instigated this catastrophe. It seemed to be the conventional wisdom among these prophets that only an elaborate plan—one that had been in preparation for several years—could have damaged the fortunes of the corporation so fundamentally. There were murmurs of secret government interference; of a conspiracy of the competition. The paranoia in the house knew no bounds.

There was something about the way these men fretted and fought, hands carving up the air in their efforts to contradict the previous speaker's remarks, that struck Marty as absurd. After all, they never saw the billions they lost and gained, or the people whose lives they so casually rearranged. It was all an abstraction; numbers in their heads. Marty couldn't see the use of it. To have power over notional fortunes was just a dream of power, not power itself.

On the third day, with everyone drained of gambits, and praying now for a resurrection that showed no sign of coming, Marty encountered Bill Toy, engaged in a heated debate with Dwoskin. To his surprise Toy, seeing Marty passing by, called him across, cutting the conversation short. Dwoskin hurried away scowling, leaving Toy and Marty to talk.

"Well, stranger," said Toy, "and how are you doing?"

"I'm OK," Marty said. Toy looked as if he hadn't slept in a long while. "And you?"

"I'll survive."

"Any idea of what's going on?"

Toy offered a wry smile. "Not really," he said, "I've never been a money-man. Hate the breed. Weasels."

"Everyone's saying it's a disaster."

"Oh, yes," he said with equanimity, "I think it probably is."

Marty's face fell. He'd been hoping for some words of reassurance. Toy caught his discomfort, and its origins. "Nothing terrible's going to happen," he said, "as long as we stay levelheaded. You'll still be in a job, if that's what you're worried about."

"It did cross my mind."

"Don't let it." Toy put his hand on Marty's shoulder. "If I thought things looked that bad, I'd tell you."

"I know. I just get jittery."

"Who doesn't?" Toy tightened his grip on Marty. "What say the two of us go on the town when the worst of this is over?"

"I'd like to."

"Ever been to the Academy Casino?"

"Never had the money."

"I'll take you. We'll lose some of Joe's fortune for him, eh?"

"Sounds good to me."

The anxiety still lingered on Marty's face.

"Look," said Toy, "it's not your fight. You understand me? Whatever happens from now on, it won't be your fault. We've made some mistakes along the way, and now we've got to pay for them."

"Mistakes?"

"Sometimes people don't forgive, Marty."

"All this"—Marty spread a hand to take in the whole circus— "because people don't forgive?"

"Take it from me. It's the best reason in the world."

It struck Marty that Toy had become an outsider of late; that he wasn't the pivotal figure in the old man's worldview that he had been. Did that explain the sour look that had crept across his weary face?

"Do you know who's responsible?" Marty asked.

"What do boxers know?" Toy said with an unmistakable trace of irony; and Marty was suddenly certain the man knew everything.

The panic days stretched into a week without any sign of letup. The faces of the advisers changed, but the smart suits and the smart talk remained the same. Despite the influx of new people, Whitehead had become increasingly laxer with his security arrangements. Marty was required to be with the old man less and less; the crisis seemed to have put all thoughts of assassination out of Papa's head.

The period was not without its surprises. On the first Sunday Curtsinger took Marty aside and undertook a labored seduction speech that began with boxing, moved laterally to the pleasures of intermale physicality, and ended up with a straight cash offer. "Just half an hour; nothing elaborate." Marty had guessed what was in the air several minutes before Curtsinger came clean, and had prepared a suitably polite refusal. They parted amicably enough. Such diversions aside, it was a listless time. The rhythm of the house had been broken, and it was impossible to establish a fresh one. The only way Marty could preserve his sanity was by keeping out of the house as much as he could. He ran a great deal that week, often chasing his tail around and around the perimeter of the estate until an exhaustion fugue set in, and he could go back to his room, threading his way through the well-dressed dummies who loitered in every corridor. Upstairs, behind a door that he happily locked (to keep them out, not to keep himself in) he would shower and sleep for long hours the deep, dreamless sleep he enjoyed.

Carys had no such liberty. Since the night the dogs had found Mamoulian she had taken it into her head, on occasion, to play the spy. Why this was, she wasn't certain. She'd never been much interested in goings-on at the Sanctuary. Indeed she'd actively avoided contact with Luther, and Curtsinger, and all the rest of her father's cohorts. Now, however, strange imperatives stirred her without warning: to go into the library, or into the kitchen or the garden, and simply *watch*. She got no pleasure out of this activity. Much that she heard she found impossible to understand; much more was simply the vacuous gossip of financial fishwives. Nevertheless she would sit for hours, until some vague appetite was satisfied, and then she'd move on, perhaps to listen in on another debate. Some of the conversationalists knew who she was; to those who didn't she offered the plainest of introductions. Once her credentials had been established nobody questioned her presence.

She also went to see Lillian and the dogs at that dispiriting compound behind the house. It wasn't because she liked the animals, she simply felt impelled to *see* them, for the sake of seeing; to look at the locks and the cages and at the pups playing around their mother. In her mind she charted the position of the kennels relative to the fence and to the house, pacing it out in case she needed to find them in the dark. Why she would ever need that facility escaped her.

In these trips she was careful not to be seen by Martin, or Toy, or worst of all, her father. It was a game she was playing, though its precise purpose was a mystery. Maybe she was making a map of the place. Was that why she walked from one end of the house to the other several times, checking and rechecking its geography, working out the length of the corridors, memorizing the way the rooms let on to each other? Whatever the reason, this foolish business answered some unspoken need in her, and when it was done, and only then, would that need pronounce itself satisfied, and let her be for a while. By the end of the week she knew the house as she never had before; she'd been in every room except that one room of her father's, which was forbidden even to her. She had checked all the entrances and exits, stairways and passages, with the thoroughness of a thief.

Strange days; strange nights. Was this insanity? she began to wonder.

On the second Sunday—eleven days into the crisis—Marty was summoned to the library. Whitehead was there, looking somewhat tired perhaps, but not substantially cowed by the enormous pressure he was under. He was dressed for the outdoors; the fur-collared coat he'd worn the first day, on that symbolic visit to the kennels.

"I haven't left the house in several days, Marty," he announced, "and my head's getting stale. I think we should take a walk, you and I."

"I'll fetch a jacket."

"Yes. And the gun."

They headed out the back way, avoiding the newly arrived delegations who still thronged the stairs and hallway, waiting for access to the holy of holies.

It was a balmy day; the nineteenth of April. The shadows of light-headed clouds passed across the lawn in dissolute troupes. "We'll go to the woods," the old man said, leading off. Marty walked a respectful couple of yards behind, acutely aware that Whitehead had come out here to clear his mind, not to talk.

The woods were buzzing with activity. New growth poking through the rot of last year's fall; daredevil birds plummeting and rising between the trees, courtship voices on every other branch. They walked for several minutes, following no particular path, without Whitehead so much as looking up from his boots. Out of sight of the house and his disciples, he wore the burden of siege more nakedly. Head bowed, he trudged between the trees, indifferent to birdsong and leaf-burst alike.

Marty was enjoying himself. Whenever he'd crossed this territory before it had been at a run. Now his pace was forcibly slowed, and details of the woods became apparent. The confusion of flowers underfoot, the fungi sprouting in the damp places between the roots: all delighted him. He picked up a selection of pebbles as he went. One bore the fossilized imprint of a fern. He thought of Carys and of the dovecote, and an unexpected longing for her lapped at the edges of his consciousness. Having no reason to prevent its access, he let it come.

Once admitted, the weight of his feeling for her shocked him. He felt conspired against; as though in the last few days his emotions had worked in some secret place in him, transforming mild interest in Carys into something deeper. He had little chance to sort the phenomena out, however. When he glanced up from the stone fern Whitehead had got a good way ahead of him. Putting thoughts of Carys aside, he picked up his pace. Passages of sun and shadow moved through the trees as the light clouds that had sat on the wind earlier gave way to heavier formations. The wind had begun to chill; there was an occasional speckle of rain in it.

Whitehead had pulled his collar up. His hands were plunged into his pockets. When Marty reached him, he was greeted with a question.

"Do you believe in God, Martin?"

The inquiry came out of nowhere. Unprepared for it, Marty could only answer, "I don't know," which was, as answers to that question went, honest enough.

But Whitehead wanted more. His eyes glittered.

"I don't pray, if that's what you mean," Marty offered.

"Not even before your trial? A quick word with the Almighty?"

There was no humor, malicious or otherwise, in this interrogation. Again, Marty answered as honestly as he could.

"I don't remember, exactly . . . I suppose I must have said something then, yes." He paused. Above them, the clouds passed over the sun. "Much good it did me."

"And in prison?"

"No; I never prayed." He was sure of that. "Never once."

"But there were God-fearing men in Wandsworth, surely?"

Marty remembered Heseltine, with whom he'd shared a cell for a few weeks at the beginning of his stretch. An old hand at prison, Tiny had spent more years behind bars than out. Every night he'd murmur a bastardized version of the Lord's Prayer into his pillow before he went to sleep—"*Our Father, who are in Heaven, hello be thy name*"—not understanding the words or their significance, simply saying the prayer by rote, as he had every night of his life, most probably, until the sense was corrupted beyond salvation—"*thine by the King Dome, thine by the Glory, f'ever and f'ever, Amen.*"

Was that what Whitehead meant? Was there respect for a Maker, thanks for Creation, or even some anticipation of Judgment in Heseltine's prayer?

"No," was Marty's reply. "Not really God-fearing. I mean, what's the use . . . ?"

There was more where that thought came from, and Whitehead waited for it with a vulture's patience. But the words sat on

Marty's tongue, refusing to be spoken. The old man prompted them.

"Why no use, Marty?"

"Because it's all down to accident, isn't it? I mean, everything's chance."

Whitehead nodded, almost imperceptibly. There was a long silence between them, until the old man said: "Do you know why I chose you, Martin?"

"Not really."

"Toy never said anything to you?"

"He told me he thought I could do the job."

"Well, a lot of people advised against me taking you. They thought you were unsuitable, for a number of reasons we needn't go into. Even Toy wasn't certain. He liked you, but he wasn't certain."

"But you employed me anyway?"

"Indeed we did."

Marty was beginning to find the cat-and-mouse game insufferable. He said: "Now you're going to tell me why, right?"

"You're a gambler," Whitehead replied. Marty felt he'd known the answer long before it was spoken. "You wouldn't have been in trouble at all, if you hadn't been obliged to pay off large gaming debts. Am I right?"

"More or less."

"You spent every penny you earned. Or so your friends testified at the trial. Frittered it away."

"Not always. I had some big wins. Really big wins."

The look Whitehead gave Marty was scalpel-sharp.

"After all you've been through—all your disease has made you suffer—you still talk about your *big wins*."

"I remember the best times, like anyone would," Marty replied defensively.

"*Flukes.*"

"No! I was good, damn it."

"Flukes, Martin. You said so yourself a moment ago. You said it was all chance. How can you be good at anything that's accidental? That doesn't make sense, does it?"

The man was right, at least superficially. But it wasn't as simple as he made it out to be, was it? It *was* all chance; he couldn't argue with that basic condition. But a sliver of Marty believed something else. What it was he believed, he couldn't describe.

"Isn't that what you said?" Whitehead pressed. "That it was accident."

"It's not always like that."

"Some of us have chance on our side. Is that what you're saying? Some of us have our fingers"—Whitehead's forefinger described a spinning circle—"on the wheel." The circling finger stopped. In his mind's eye, Marty completed the image: the ball jumped from hole to hole and found a niche, a number. Some winner yelped his triumph.

"Not always," he said. "Just sometimes."

"Describe it. Describe how it feels."

Why not? Where was the harm?

"Sometimes it was just easy, you know, like taking sweets from a baby. I'd go to a club and the chips would tingle, and I'd know, Jesus I'd *know*, I couldn't fail to win."

Whitehead smiled.

"But you *did* fail," he reminded Marty, with courteous brutality. "You *often* failed. You failed till you owed everything you had, and more besides."

"I was stupid. I played even when the chips didn't tingle, when I knew I was on a losing streak."

"Why?"

Marty glowered.

"What do you want, a signed confession?" he snapped. "I was greedy, what do you think? And I loved playing, even when I didn't have a chance of winning. I still wanted to play."

"For the game's sake."

"I suppose so. Yes. For the game."

A look, impossibly complex, crossed Whitehead's face. There

was regret in it, and a terrible, aching loss; and more: incomprehension. Whitehead the master, Whitehead the lord of all he surveyed, suddenly showed—all too briefly—another, more accessible, face: that of a man confused to the point of despair.

"I wanted someone with your weaknesses," he explained now, and suddenly *he* was the one doing the confessing. "Because sooner or later I believed a day like today would come; and I'd have to ask you to take a risk with me."

"What sort of risk?"

"Nothing so simple as a wheel, or a game of cards. I wish it were. Then maybe I could explain to you, instead of asking for an act of faith. But it's so complicated. And I'm tired."

"Bill said something—"

Whitehead broke in.

"Toy's left the estate. You won't be seeing him again."

"When did he go?"

"Earlier in the week. Relations between us have been deteriorating for a while." He caught Marty's dismay. "Don't fret about it. Your position here is as secure as it ever was. But you must trust me *absolutely*."

"Sir—"

"No affirmations of loyalty; they're wasted on me. Not because I don't believe you're sincere. But I'm surrounded by people who tell me whatever they think I want to hear. That's how they keep their wives in furs and their sons in cocaine." His gloved fingers clawed at his bearded cheek as he spoke. "So few honest people. Toy was one. Evangeline, my wife, was another. But so *very* few. I just have to trust to instinct; I have to blot out all the talk and follow what my head tells me. And it trusts you, Martin."

Marty said nothing; just listened as Whitehead's voice became quieter, his eyes so intense now a glance from them might have ignited tinder.

"If you stay with me—if you keep me safe—there's nothing you can't be or have. Understand me? *Nothing*."

This was not the first time the old man had offered this

seduction; but circumstances had clearly changed since Marty first arrived at the Sanctuary. There was more at risk now. "What's the worst that can happen?" he asked.

The mazed face had slackened: only the incendiary eyes still showed life.

"The worst?" Whitehead said. "Who knows the worst?" The burning eyes seemed about to be extinguished by tears; he fought them. "I have seen such things. And passed by them on the other side. Never thought . . . not once . . ."

A pattering announced rain; its soft percussion accompanied Whitehead as he stumbled to speak. All his verbal skills had deserted him suddenly; he was bereft. But something—a vast something—demanded to be said.

"Never thought . . . it would ever happen to me."

He bit back more words, and shook his head at his own absurdity.

"Will you help me?" he asked, in place of further explanation.

"Of course."

"Well," he replied. "We'll see, eh?"

Without warning he suddenly stepped past Marty and returned the way they'd come. The jaunt was apparently over. For several minutes they walked as they had, Whitehead taking the lead, with Marty trailing a discreet two yards behind. Just before they came in sight of the house Whitehead spoke again. This time he didn't break the rhythm of his step, but threw the inquiry over his shoulder. Just four words.

"And the Devil, Marty?"

"What, sir?"

"The Devil. Did you ever pray to *him*?"

It was a joke. A little leaden maybe, but the old man's way of making light of his confessional.

"Well, did you?"

"Once or twice," Marty answered, skirting a smile. As the words left his lips Whitehead froze dead in his tracks, a hand outstretched behind him to check Marty.

"Ssh."

Twenty yards ahead, arrested as it crossed their path, was a fox. It hadn't seen its observers yet, but it could only be a matter of moments before their scent reached its nostrils.

"Which way?" Whitehead hissed.

"What?"

"Which way will it run? *A thousand pounds*. Straight bet."

"I haven't got—" Marty began.

"Against a week's pay."

Marty began to smile. What was a week's pay? He couldn't spend it anyway.

"A thousand pounds says it runs to the right," said Whitehead.

Marty hesitated.

"Quickly, man—"

"Done."

Even on the word, the animal caught their scent. Its ears pricked, its head turned, and it saw them. For an instant it was too stupefied by surprise to move; then it ran. For several yards it took off away from them along the path, not veering to one side or the other, its heels kicking up dead leaves as it went. Then, without warning, it sliced away into the cover of the trees, *to the left*. There was no ambiguity about the victory.

"Well done," said Whitehead, pulling off his glove and extending his hand to Marty. When he shook it, Marty felt it tingle like the chips had on a winning night.

By the time they got back, the rain was beginning to come on more heavily. A welcome hush had descended on the house. Apparently Pearl, unable to bear the barbarians in her kitchen any longer, had thrown a fit and left. Though she'd gone, the offending parties seemed well chastened. Their babble was reduced to a murmur, and few of them made any approach to Whitehead as he entered. Those few that did were quickly slapped down. "Are you *still* here, Munrow?" he said to one devotee; to another, who made the error of thrusting a sheaf of papers at him, he quietly suggested the man "choke on them." They reached the study with the minimum of interruptions. Whitehead unlocked the wall safe.

"You would prefer cash, I'm sure."

Marty studied the carpet. Though he'd won the bet fairly, he was embarrassed by the payoff.

"Cash is fine," he murmured.

Whitehead counted out a wad of twenty-pound notes and handed them across.

"Enjoy," he said.

"Thank you."

"Don't thank me," Whitehead said. "It was a straight bet. I lost."

An awkward silence fell while Marty pocketed the money.

"Our talk . . ." the old man said, ". . . is in the strictest confidence, you understand?"

"Of course. I wouldn't—"

Whitehead raised his hand to ward off his protestations.

"—The *strictest* confidence. My enemies have agents."

Marty nodded as though he understood. In a way, of course, he did. Perhaps Whitehead suspected Luther or Pearl. Maybe even Toy, who was so abruptly *persona non grata*.

"These people are responsible for the present fall in my fortunes. It's all meticulously engineered." He shrugged, eyes like slits. God, Marty thought, I'd never want to be on the wrong side of this man. "I don't fret about these things. If they want to plan my ruin, let them. But I wouldn't like to think that my most *intimate* feelings were available to them. Do you see?"

"They won't be."

"No." He pursed his lips; a cold kiss of satisfaction.

"You've seen something of Carys, I gather? Pearl says you spend time together, is that right?"

"Yes."

Whitehead came back with a tone of detachment that was patently fake.

"She seems stable much of the time, but essentially that's a performance. I'm afraid she's not well, and hasn't been for several years. Of course she's seen the best psychiatrists money can buy but I'm afraid it's done no good. Her mother went the same way in the end."

"Are you telling me not to see her?"

Whitehead looked genuinely surprised.

"No, not at all. The companionship may be good for her. But please, bear in mind she's a highly disturbed girl. Don't take her pronouncements *too* seriously. Half the time she doesn't know what she's saying. Well, I think that's it. You'd better go and pay off your fox."

He laughed, gently.

"Clever fox," he said.

In the two and a half months Marty had been at the Sanctuary Whitehead had been an iceberg. Now he had to think about revising that description. Today he'd glimpsed another man altogether: inarticulate, alone; talking of God and prayer. Not just God. There had been that final question, the one he'd thrown away so carelessly:

"And the Devil? Did you ever pray to him?"

Marty felt he'd been handed a pile of jigsaw pieces, none of which seemed to belong to the same portrait. Fragments of a dozen scenes: Whitehead resplendent among his acolytes, or sitting at a window watching the night; Whitehead the potentate, lord of all he surveyed, or betting like a drunken porter on the way a fox might run.

This last fragment puzzled Marty the most. In it, he sensed, was a clue that could unite these disparate images. He had the strangest feeling that the bet on the fox had been fixed. Impossible, of course, and yet, and yet . . . Suppose Whitehead *could* put his finger on the wheel anytime he wanted to, so that even the petty chance of a fox running to the right or left was available to him? Could he know the future before it happened—was that why the chips tingled, and fingers too?—or was he *shaping* it?

An earlier self would have rejected these subtleties out of hand. But Marty had changed. Being in the Sanctuary had changed him, Carys' ellipses had changed him. In a hundred ways he was more complex than he'd been, and part of him longed for a return to the clarity of black and white. But he knew damn well that such simplicity was a lie. Experience was made up of endless ambiguities—of motive, of feeling, of cause and effect—and if he was to win under such circumstances, he had to understand how those ambiguities worked.

No; not *win*. There was no winning and losing here: not in the way that he'd understood before. The fox had run to the left, and he had a thousand pounds folded in his pocket, but he felt none of the exhilaration he had when he'd won on the horses, or at the casino. Just black bleeding into white, and vice versa, until he scarcely knew right from wrong.

30

Toy had rung the estate in the middle of the afternoon, spoken to an irate Pearl, who was just about to make her exit, and left a message for Marty to call him at the Pimlico number. But Marty hadn't rung back. Toy wondered if Pearl had failed to pass the message along, or if Whitehead had somehow intercepted it, and prevented a return call being made. Whatever the reason, he hadn't spoken to Marty, and he felt guilty about it. He'd promised to warn Strauss if events started to go badly awry. Now they were. Nothing observable perhaps; the anxieties Toy was experiencing were born out of instinct rather than fact. But Yvonne had taught him to trust his heart, not his head. Things were going to fall down after all; and he hadn't warned Marty. Perhaps that was why he was having such bad dreams, and waking with memories of ugliness flitting in his head.

Not everyone survived being young. Some died early, victims of their own hunger for life. Toy hadn't been such a victim, though he'd come perilously close. Not that he'd known it at the time. He'd been too dazzled by the new pools he was introduced into by Whitehead to see how lethal those waters could be. And he'd obeyed the great man's wishes with such unquestioning zeal, hadn't he? Never once had he balked at his duty, however criminal it might have seemed. Why should he be surprised then if, after all these years these same crimes, so casually committed, were in silent pursuit of him? That was why he lay now in a clammy sweat, with Yvonne sleeping beside him, and one phrase circling his skull:

Mamoulian will come.

That was the only clear notion he had. The rest—thoughts of Marty, and Whitehead—was a potpourri of shames and accusations. But that plain phrase—*Mamoulian will come*— stood out in the dross of uncertainty as a fixed point to which all his terrors adhered.

No apology would suffice. No humiliation would curb the Last European's anger. Because Toy had been young, and a brute, and he'd had a wicked way with him. Once upon a time, when he'd been too young to know better, he'd made Mamoulian suffer, and the remorse he felt now came too late—twenty, thirty years too late—and after all, hadn't he lived on the profits of his brutality all these years? Oh, Jesus, he said in the unsteady rhythm of his breath, Jesus help me.

Afraid, and ready to admit to being afraid if it meant she'd comfort him, he turned over and reached for Yvonne. She wasn't there. Her side of the bed was cold.

He sat up, momentarily disorientated.

"Yvonne?"

The bedroom door was ajar, and the dimmest of lights from downstairs described the room. It was chaos. They had been packing all evening, and the task had still not been finished when, at one in the morning, they'd retired. Clothes were heaped on the chest of drawers; an open case yawned in the corner; his ties hung over the back of a chair like parched snakes, tongues to the floor.

He heard a noise on the landing. He knew Yvonne's padding step well. She'd gone for a glass of apple juice, or a biscuit, the way she so often did. She appeared at the door, in silhouette.

"Are you all right?" he asked her.

She murmured something like yes. He put his head back on the pillow.

"Hungry again," he said, letting his eyes close. "Always hungry." Cold air seeped into the bed as she raised the sheet to slip in beside him.

"You left the light on downstairs," he chided, as sleep started to slide over him again. She didn't reply. Asleep already, probably: she was blessed with a facility for instant unconsciousness. He turned to look at her in the semidarkness. She wasn't snoring yet, but nor was she entirely silent. He listened more carefully, his coiled innards jittery. It was a liquid sound she was making: as though breathing through mud.

"Yvonne . . . are you all right?"

She didn't answer.

From her face, which was inches from his, the slushing sound went on. He reached for the switch of the lamp above the bed, keeping his eyes on the black mass of Yvonne's head as he did so. Best to do this fast, he reasoned, before my imagination gets the better of me. His fingers located the switch, fumbled with it, then pressed the light on.

What was facing him on the pillow was not recognizably
Yvonne.

He jabbered her name as he scrambled backward out of bed,
eyes fixed on the abomination beside him. How was it possible
that she was alive enough to climb the stairs and get into bed, to
murmur yes to him as she had? The profundity of her wounding
had killed her, surely. Nobody could live skinned and boned like
that.

She half-turned in the bed, eyes closed, as if rolling over in her
sleep. Then—horribly—she said his name. Her mouth didn't
work as it had; blood greased the word on its way. He couldn't
bear to look anymore, or he'd scream, and that would bring
them—whoever did this—bring them howling at him with their
scalpels already wet. They were probably outside the door already;
but nothing could induce him to stay in the same room. Not with
her performing slow gyrations on the bed, still saying his name as
she pulled up her nightdress.

He staggered out of the bedroom and onto the landing. To his
surprise they were not waiting for him there.

At the top of the stairs he hesitated. He was not a brave man;
nor was he foolish. Tomorrow he could mourn her: but for tonight
she was simply gone from him, and there was nothing to be done
but preserve himself from whoever'd done this. Whoever! Why
didn't he admit the name to himself? Mamoulian was responsible:
it had his signature. And he was not alone. The European would
never have laid his purged hands on human flesh the way someone
had on Yvonne; his squeamishness was legendary. But it was
he who'd given her that half-life to live after the murder was done.
Only Mamoulian was capable of that service.

And he would be waiting below now, wouldn't he, in the
undersea world at the bottom of the stairs? Waiting, as he'd
waited so long, for Toy to traipse down to join him.

"Go to Hell," Toy whispered to the dark below, and walked
(the urge was to run, but common sense counseled otherwise)
along the landing toward the spare bedroom. With every step he

anticipated some move from the enemy, but none came. Not until he reached the door of the bedroom anyway.

Then, as he turned the handle, he heard Yvonne's voice behind him:

"Willy . . ." The word was better formed than before.

For the briefest moment he felt his sanity in doubt. Was it possible that if he turned now she would be standing at the bedroom door as disfigured as memory suggested; or was that all a fever-dream?

"Where are you going?" she demanded to know.

Downstairs, somebody moved.

"Come back to bed."

Without turning to refuse her invitation, Toy pushed the door of the spare bedroom open, and as he did so he heard somebody start up the stairs behind him. The footsteps were heavy; their owner eager.

There was no key in the lock to delay his pursuer, and no time to drag furniture in front of the door. Toy crossed the lightless bedroom in three strides, threw open the French windows, and stepped onto the small wrought-iron balcony. It grunted beneath his weight. He suspected it would not hold for long.

Below him, the garden was in darkness, but he had a fair idea of where the flower beds lay, and where the paving stones. Without hesitation—the footsteps loud at his back—he clambered over the balcony. His joints complained at this exertion, and more so when he lowered himself over the other side until he was hanging by his hands, suspended by a grip that was every second in danger of giving out.

A din in the room he'd left drew his glance; his pursuer, a bloated thug with bloody hands and the eyes of something rabid, was in the room—was crossing now toward the windows, growling his displeasure. Toy rocked his body as best he could, praying to miss the paving he knew was directly beneath his bare feet and land in the soft earth of the herbaceous border. There was little chance to fine-tune the maneuver. He let go of the balustrade as the obesity reached the balcony, and for what seemed a long time fell backward through space, the window diminishing above him, until he landed, with no more injury than a bruising, among the geraniums Yvonne had planted only the week before.

He got to his feet badly winded but intact, and ran down the moonlit garden to the back gate. It was padlocked, but he managed to climb over it with ease—adrenaline firing his muscles. There was no sound of further pursuit, and when he glanced back he could see the fat man was still at the French windows, watching his escape as though lacking the initiative to follow. Sick with a sudden excitement, he sprinted away down the narrow passage that led along the backs of all the gardens, caring only to put distance between himself and the house.

It was only when he reached the street, its lamps starting to go out now as dawn edged up over the city, that he realized he was stark naked.

31

Marty had gone to bed a happy man. Though there was still much here he didn't understand, much which the old man— despite his promises of explanations—seemed pleased to keep obscured, finally none of that was his business. If Papa chose to have secrets, so be it. Marty had been hired to look after him, and it appeared that he was fulfilling that obligation to his employer's satisfaction. The results were there in the intimacies the old man had shared with him, and in the thousand pounds beneath his pillow.

Euphoria prevented sleep: Marty's heart seemed to be beating at twice its usual rate. He got up, slipped on his bathrobe, and tried a selection of videos to take his mind off the day's events, but the boxing tapes depressed him; the pornography too. He wandered downstairs to the library, found a dog-eared space opera, then slipped back to his room, making a detour to the kitchen for a beer.

Carys was in his room when he got back, dressed in jeans and a sweater, barefoot. She looked frayed, older than her nineteen years. The smile she offered him was too stage-managed to convince.

"You don't mind?" she said. "Only I heard you walking about."

"Don't you *ever* sleep?"

"Not often."

"Want some beer?"

"No thanks."

"Sit down," he said, throwing a pile of clothes off the single chair for her. She deposited herself on the bed, however, leaving the chair for Marty.

"I have to talk to you," she said.

Marty laid down the book he'd chosen. On the cover a naked woman, her skin a fluorescent green, emerged from an egg on a twin-sunned planet. Carys said:

"Do you know what's going on?"

"Going on? What do you mean?"

"Haven't you felt anything odd in the house?"

"Like what?"

Her mouth had found its favorite shape; corners turned down in exasperation.

"I don't know . . . it's difficult to describe."

"Try."

She hesitated, like a diver at the edge of a high board, then took the plunge.

"Do you know what a *sensitive* is?"

He shook his head.

"It's someone who can pick up waves. Thought waves."

"Mind reading."

"In a way."

He gave her a noncommittal look. "Is it something you can do?" he said.

"Not *do*. I don't *do* anything. It's more like it's done to me."

Marty leaned back in the chair, flummoxed.

"It's as though everything gets sticky. I can't shake it off. I hear people talking without them moving their lips. Most of it's meaningless: just rubbish."

"And it's what they're thinking?"

"Yes."

He couldn't find much to say in response, except that he doubted her, and that wasn't what she wanted to hear. She'd come for reassurance, hadn't she?

"That's not all," she said. "I see shapes sometimes, around people's bodies. Vague shapes . . . like a kind of light."

Marty thought of the man at the fence; of how he'd bled light, or seemed to. He didn't interrupt her, however.

"The point is, I feel things other people don't. I don't think it's particularly clever of me, or anything like that. I just *do* it. And the last few weeks I've felt something in the house. I get odd thoughts in my head, out of nowhere; I dream . . . horrible things." She halted, aware that her description was getting vaguer, and she risked what little credibility this monologue had if she went on.

"The lights you see?" Marty said, backtracking.

"Yes."

"I saw something like them."

She leaned forward.

"When?"

"The man who broke in. I thought I saw light coming from him. From his wounds, I suppose, and his eyes and his mouth." Even as he finished the sentence he was shrugging it off as if fearful of contagion. "I don't know," he said. "I was drunk."

"But you saw something."

"—Yes," he conceded, without pleasure.

She got up and crossed to the window. Like father like daughter, he thought: window freaks, both of them. As she stared out across the lawn—Marty never drew the curtains—he had ample opportunity to look at her.

"Something . . ." she said, ". . . something."

The grace of her crooked leg, the displaced weight of her buttocks; her face, reflected in the cold glass, so intent on this mystery: all enthralled him.

"That's why he doesn't talk to me any longer," she said.

"Papa?"

"He knows I can feel what he's thinking: and he's frightened."

The observation was a cul-de-sac: she started tapping her foot with irritation, her breath ghosting the window intermittently. Then, out of the blue, she said:

"Did you know you had a breast fixation?"

"What?"

"You look at them all the time."

"Do I Hell!"

"*And* you're a liar."

He stood up, not knowing what he intended to do or say until the words were out. At last, smothered in confusion, only the truth seemed appropriate.

"I like looking at you."

He touched her shoulder. At this point, if they chose, the game could stop; tenderness was a breath away. They could take the opportunity or let it be: resume the repartee, or discard it. The moment lay between them, awaiting instructions.

"Babe," she said. "Don't shake."

He moved a half-step closer and kissed the back of her neck. She turned and returned the kiss, her hand moving up his spine to cup the back of his head, as if to sense the weight of his skull.

"At last," she said, when they broke. "I was beginning to think you were too much of a gentleman." They tumbled onto the bed, and she rolled over to straddle his hips. Without hesitation she reached to fumble with the belt of his bathrobe. He was half-hard beneath her, and uncomfortably trapped. Self-conscious, too. She pulled the bathrobe open, and ran her palms across his chest. His body was solid without being heavy; silk hair spread out from his sternum and down the central groove of his abdomen, coarsening as it descended. She sat up a little to release the robe from his groin. His cock, freed, flipped from four to noon. She stroked its underside: it responded in gulps.

"Pretty," she said.

He was getting used to her approbation now. Her calm was infectious. He half-sat up, perching on his elbows to get a better look at her poised above him. She was intent on his erection, putting her index finger into her mouth and transferring a film of saliva to his cock, running fingertips up and down in fluid, lazy motions. He squirmed with pleasure. A rash of heat had appeared on his chest, further signal, if any were needed, of his arousal. His cheeks burned too.

"Kiss me," he asked.

She leaned forward and met his mouth. They collapsed back onto the bed. His hands felt for the bottom of her sweater, and started to ease it up, but she stopped him.

"No," she murmured into his mouth.

". . . want to see you . . ." he said.

She sat back up. He was looking up at her, perplexed.

"Not so fast," she said, and raised the sweater far enough to expose her belly and breasts to him, without taking the garment off. Marty took in her body like a blind man granted sight: the dusting of gooseflesh, the unexpected fullness of her. His hands toured where his eyes went, pressing her bright skin, describing spirals on her nipples, watching the weight of her breasts ride on her rib cage. Mouth now followed eye and hand: he wanted to bathe her with his tongue. She pulled his head against her. Through the mesh of his hair his scalp gleamed a baby pink. She craned to kiss it but couldn't reach, and slid her hand down instead to take hold of his cock. "Be careful," he murmured as she

stroked. There was wetness in her palm; she relinquished her
hold.

Gently, he coaxed her over and they fell side by side across the
bed. She pushed the robe off his neck, while his fingers worked at
the button at the top of her jeans. She made no attempt to assist,
liking the look of concentration he wore. It would be so good to
be completely naked with him: skin to skin. But this wasn't the
time to risk that. Suppose he saw the bruises and the needle
marks, and rejected her. It would be unbearable.

He had successfully undone the button and unzipped the fly,
and now his hands were in her jeans, sliding under the top of her
panties. There was urgency in him, and much as she loved to
watch his intent, she aided the undressing now, raising her hips
from the bed and sliding the jeans and panties down, exposing
her body from nipples to knee. He moved over her, leaving a trail
of saliva to mark his way, licking at her navel, and lower now, face
flushed, his tongue in her, not expert exactly, but eager to learn,
nuzzling out the places that pleased her by the sound of her sighs.

He slid the jeans lower, and when she didn't resist, all the way
off. Her panties followed, and she closed her eyes, blotting out
everything but his exploration. In his eagerness he displayed the
instincts of a cannibal; nothing her body fed him would be
rejected; he pressed as deep as anatomy allowed.

Something itched at the back of her neck, but she ignored it,
too concerned with this other sport. He looked up from her groin,
with doubt on his face.

"Go on," she said.

She wriggled up the bed, inviting him into her. The doubt on
his face persisted.

"What's wrong?"

"No protection," he said.

"Forget it."

He needed no second invitation. Her position, not lying
beneath him but half-sitting, allowed her to watch his sweet
display, pressing the root of his cock until the head darkened and

glossed, before entering her slowly, almost reverentially. Now he relinquished hold of himself, and put his hands on the bed to cither side of her, his back arched, a crescent within a crescent, as his body weight carried him in. His lips parted, and his tongue emerged to lap at her eyes.

She moved to meet him, pressing her hips up to his. He sighed: frowned.

Oh, Jesus, she thought, he's come. But his eyes opened again still raging, and his strokes, after the initial threat of mistiming, were even and slow.

Again, her neck irritated her; it felt more than an itch. It was a bite, a drill hole. She tried to ignore it, but the sensation only intensified as her body gave way to the moment. Marty was too intent on their locked anatomies to register her discomfort. His breath was jagged, hot on her face. She tried to move, hoping the ache was just the tension of this position.

"Marty . . ." she breathed, "roll over."

He wasn't sure of this maneuver at first, but once he was on his back, and she sitting on him, he caught her rhythm easily. He began to climb again: dizzy with the height.

The pain at her neck persisted, but she thrust it out of focus. She bent forward, her face six inches above Marty's, and let saliva fall from her mouth into his, a thread of bubbles that he received with an open grin, pushing up into her as deep as he could go and holding himself there.

Suddenly, something moved in her. Not Marty. Something or *somebody* else, fluttering in her system. Her concentration faltered; her heart too. She lost focus on where she was and what she was. Another set of eyes seemed to look through hers: momentarily she shared their owner's vision. She saw sex as depravity, a raw and bestial exchange.

"No," she said, trying to cancel the nausea that had suddenly risen in her.

Marty opened his eyes to slits, taking her "no" as a command to postpone the finish.

"I'm trying, babe . . ." he said, grinning. "Just don't move."

She couldn't grasp what he meant at first: he was a thousand miles from her, lying below in a foul sweat, wounding her against her wishes. "OK?" he breathed, holding on until it almost hurt. He seemed to swell in her. The sensation drove the double vision out of her head. The other viewer shrank away behind her eyes, revolted by the fullness and the fleshiness of this act; by its reality. Did the intruding mind feel Marty too, she half-thought, its cortex plumbed by a cock-head that was swelling to cream even now?

"God . . ." she said.

With the other eyes in retreat, the joy came back.

"Can't stop, babe," Marty said.

"Go on," she said. "It's all right. It's all right."

Flecks of her sweat hit him as she moved on top of him.

"*Go on. Yes!*" she said again. It was an exclamation of pure delight, and it took him past the point of return. He tried to stave off eruption for a few more trembling seconds. The weight of her hips on him, the heat of her channel, the brightness of her breasts, filled his head.

And then somebody spoke; a low, guttural voice.

"*Stop it.*"

Marty's eyes fluttered open, glancing to left and right. There was nobody else in the room. His head had invented the sound. He canceled the illusion and looked back at Carys.

"Go on," she said. "Please go on." She was dancing on him. The bones of her hips caught the light; the sweat on them ran and ran, glowing.

"Yes . . . yes . . ." he answered, the voice forgotten.

She looked down at him as imminence infested his face, and through the intricacies of her own flaring sensations she felt the second mind again. It was a worm in her budding head, pushing forward, its sickness ready to stain her vision. She fought it.

"Go away," she told it, under her breath, "go away."

But it wanted to defeat her; to defeat them both. What had

seemed like curiosity before was malice now. It wanted to spoil everything.

"I love you," she told Marty, defying the presence in her. "I love you, I love you—"

The invader spasmed, furious with her, and more furious still that she didn't concede to its spoiling. Marty was rigid, on the threshold; blind and deaf to anything but pleasure. Then, with a groan, he began to spurt in her, and she was there too. Her sensations drove all thoughts of resistance out of her head. Somewhere far off she could hear Marty gasping—

"Oh, Jesus," he was saying, "babe . . . babe."

—but he was in another world. They weren't together, even at this moment. She in her ecstasy, he in his; each running a private race to completion.

A wayward spasm made Marty convulse. He opened his eyes. Carys had her hands glued over her face, fingers spread.

"You all right, babe?" he said.

When her eyes opened, he had to bite back a shout. It was, for a moment, not her who stared out between the bars. It was something dredged up from the bottom of the sea. Black eyes swiveling in a gray head. Some primeval genus that viewed him— he knew this to his marrow—with hatred in its bowels.

The hallucination lasted two heartbeats only, but long enough for him to glance down her body and up again to meet the same vile gaze.

"Carys?"

Then her eyelids fluttered, and the fan of her fingers closed across her face. For a lunatic instant he flinched, awaiting the revelation. Her hands dropping from her head; the face transformed: a fish's head. But of course it was her: only her. Here she was now, smiling at him.

"Are you all right?" he ventured.

"What do you think?"

"I love you, babe."

She murmured something as she slumped on him. They lay

there for several minutes, his cock diminishing in a cooling bath of mingled fluids.

"Aren't you getting a cramp?" he asked her after a while, but she didn't reply. She was asleep.

Gently, he slid her sideways, slipping out of her with a wet sound. She lay on the bed beside him, her face impassive. He kissed her breasts, licked her fingers, and fell asleep beside her.

32

Mamoulian felt sick.

She wasn't easy prey, this woman, despite his sentimental claim upon her psyche. But then her strength was to be expected. She was Whitehead's stock: peasant breed, thief breed. Cunning and dirty. Though she couldn't know precisely what she was doing, she'd fought him with the very sensuality he most despised.

But her weaknesses—and she had many—were exploitable. He'd used the heroin fugues at first, gaining access to her when she was pacified to the point of indifference. They warped her perception, which had made his invasion less noticeable, and through her eyes he'd seen the house, listened with her ears to the witless conversation of its occupants, shared with her, though it revolted him, the smell of their cologne and their flatulence. She was the perfect spy, living in the heart of the enemy's camp. And as the weeks had gone by he'd found it easier to slip in and out of her unnoticed. That had made him careless.

It was carelessness not to have looked before he leaped; to commit himself to her head without first checking what she was doing. He hadn't even thought she might be with the bodyguard; and by the time he'd realized his error he was sharing her sensations—her ridiculous rapture—and it had left him trembling. He would not make such a mistake again.

He sat in the bare room in the bare house he had bought for himself and Breer, and tried to forget the turbulence he'd experienced, the look in Strauss' eyes as he stared up at the girl. Had the thug glimpsed, perhaps, the face *behind* her face? The European guessed so.

No matter; none of them would survive. It wouldn't just be the old man, the way he'd planned at first. All of them—his acolytes, his serfs, *all*—would go to the wall with their master.

The memories of Strauss' assaults lingered in the European's entrails; he longed to evacuate them. The sensation shamed and disgusted him.

Downstairs, he heard Breer come in or go out; on his way to some atrocity or home from one. Mamoulian concentrated on the blank wall opposite him, but try as he might to exile the trauma, he still felt the intrusion: the spurting head, the heat of the act.

Forget, he said aloud. Forget the brown fire off them. It's no risk to you. See only the emptiness: the promise of the void.

His innards shook. Beneath his gaze, the paint on the wall seemed to blister. Venereal eruptions disfigured its emptiness. Illusions; but horribly real to him nevertheless. Very well: if he couldn't dislodge the obscenities, he would transform them. It wasn't difficult to smudge sexuality into violence, turn sighs into screams, thrusts into convulsions. The grammar was the same; only the punctuation differed. Picturing the lovers in death together, the nausea he'd felt receded.

In the face of that void what was their substance? Transitory. Their promises? Pretension.

He began to calm. The sores on the wall had started to heal, and he was left, after a few minutes, with an echo of the nothingness he had come to need so much. Life came and went. But absence, he knew, went on forever.

33

"Oh, by the way, there was a telephone call for you. From Bill Toy. Day before yesterday."

Marty looked up at Pearl from his plate of steak, and pulled a face.

"Why didn't you tell me?"

She looked contrite.

"It was the day I lost my wick with those damn people. I left a message for you—"

"I didn't get it."

"—on the pad beside the telephone."

It was still there: "Call Toy," and a number. He dialed, and waited a full minute before the phone was picked up at the other end. It wasn't Toy. The woman who repeated the number had a soft, lost voice, slurred as if by too much drink.

"Can I speak to William Toy, please?" he asked.

"He's gone," the woman replied.

"Oh, I see."

"He won't be coming back. Not ever."

The quality of the voice was eerie. "Who is this?" it asked of him.

"It doesn't matter," Marty replied. His instinct rebelled against giving his name.

"Who is this?" she asked again.

"I'm sorry to have bothered you."

"Who is this?"

He put the receiver down on the slushing insistence at the other end. Only when he had did he realize that his shirt was clinging to a cold sweat that had suddenly sprung from his chest and spine.

I n the love nest in Pimlico, Yvonne asked the vacated line "Who is this?" for half an hour or more before letting the telephone drop. Then she went to sit down. The couch was damp: large, sticky stains were spreading on it from the place where she always sat. She assumed it was something to do with her, but she couldn't work out how or why. Nor could she explain the flies that congregated all over her, in her hair, in her clothes, whining away.

"Who is this?" she asked again. The question remained perfectly pertinent, though she was no longer speaking to the stranger on the phone. The rotting skin of her hands, the blood she left in the tub after bathing, the horrid look the mirror gave her—all inspired the same hypnotic inquiry: *"Who is this?"*

"Who is this? Who is this? Who is this?"

VI. THE TREE

34

Breer hated the house. It was cold, and the natives in this part of the city were inhospitable. He was regarded with suspicion as soon as he stepped out of the front door. There were, he had to concede, reasons for this. In recent weeks a smell had begun to linger around him; a sickly, syrupy smell that made him almost ashamed to get too close to the pretty ones along the schoolyard railing, for fear they would put their fingers to their noses, making a "poo-poo" sound, and run off calling him names. When they did that, it made him want to die.

Though there was no heating in the house, and he had to bathe in cold water, he nevertheless washed from head to foot three or four times a day, hoping to dislodge the smell. When that didn't work he bought perfume—sandalwood in particular—and doused his body with it after each ablution. Now the comments they called after him weren't about excreta but about his sex life. He took the brunt of their remarks with equanimity.

Nevertheless, dull resentments festered in him. Not just about the way he was treated in the district. The European, after a courtship that had been polite, was more and more treating him with contempt: as a lackey rather than an ally. It irritated him, the way he was sent to this haunt or that looking for Toy—asked to comb a city of millions in search of a shriveled old man whom Breer had last seen scrambling over a wall stark naked, his scrawny buttocks white in the moonlight. The European was losing his sense of proportion. Whatever crimes this Toy had committed against Mamoulian they could scarcely be profound, and it made Breer weak with tiredness to contemplate another day wandering the streets.

Despite his weariness, the capacity for sleep seemed to have deserted him almost entirely. Nothing, not even the fatigue that killed his nerves, could persuade his body to close down for more than a few eye-fluttering minutes, and even then his mind dreamed such things, such dreadful things, it was scarcely possible to call the slumber blissful. The only comfort remaining to him was his pretties.

That was one of the few advantages in this house: it had a cellar. Just a dry, cool space, which he was systematically clearing of the rubbish left by the previous owners. It was a long job, but he was gradually getting the place the way he wanted it, and though he had never much liked enclosed spaces there was something about the darkness, and the sense of being *underground*, that answered an unarticulated need in him. Soon he would have it all scrubbed. He would put colored paper chains around the walls, and flowers in vases on the floor. A table maybe, with a cloth on it, smelling of violets; comfortable chairs for his guests. Then he could begin to entertain friends in the manner to which he hoped they would become accustomed.

All his arrangements could be effected much more quickly if he weren't forever interrupted by the damn-fool errands the European sent him on. But the time for such servitude, he'd decided, had come to an end. Today, he would tell Mamoulian that he wouldn't be blackmailed or bullied into playing this game. He'd threaten to leave if it came to the worst. He'd go north. There were places north where the sun didn't come up for five months of the year—he'd read about such places—and that seemed fine to him. No sun; and deep caves to live in, holes where not even moonlight could stray. The time had come to lay his cards on the table.

If the air in the house was cold, it was even colder in Mamoulian's room. The European seemed to exhale a breath that was mortuary-chilled.

Breer stood in the doorway. He'd only been in this room once before, and he had a niggling fear of it. It was too plain. The

European had asked Breer to nail boards across the window: this he had done. Now, by the light of a single wick, burning in a dish of oil on the floor, the room looked bleak and gray; everything in it seemed insubstantial, even the European. He sat in the dark wood chair that was the only furnishing and looked at Breer with eyes so glazed he could have been blind.

"I didn't call you up here," Mamoulian said.

"I wanted . . . to talk to you."

"Close the door, then."

Though this was against his better judgment, Breer obeyed. The lock clicked at his back; the room was now centered on that single flame and the fitful luminosity it offered. Sluggishly Breer looked around the room for someplace to sit, or at least lean. But there was no comfort here: its austerity would have shamed an ascetic. Just a few blankets on the bare boards in the corner, where the great man slept; some books stacked against the wall; a pack of cards; a jug of water and a cup; little else. The walls, except for the rosary that hung from a hook, were naked.

"What do you want, Anthony?"

All Breer could think was: I hate this room.

"Say what you have to say."

"I want to go . . ."

"Go?"

"Away. The flies bother me. There are so many flies."

"No more than there are in any other May. It is perhaps a little warmer than usual. All the signs are that the summer will be blistering."

The thought of heat and light made Breer sick. And that was another thing: the way his belly revolted if he put food into it. The European had promised him a new world—health, wealth and happiness—but he was suffering the torments of the damned. It was a cheat: all a cheat.

"Why didn't you let me die?" he said, without thinking what he was saying.

"I need you."

"But I feel ill."

"The work will soon be over."

Breer looked straight at Mamoulian, something he very rarely mustered the courage to do. But desperation was a rod at his back.

"You mean finding Toy?" he said. "We won't find him. It's impossible."

"Oh, but we will, Anthony. That I insist upon."

Breer sighed. "I wish I was dead," he said.

"Don't say that. You've got all the freedom you want, haven't you? You feel no guilt now, do you?"

"No . . ."

"Most people would happily suffer your minor discomforts to be guiltless, Anthony: to commit their heart's desire to flesh and never be called to regret it. Rest today. Tomorrow we're going to be busy, you and I."

"Why?"

"We're going to visit Mr. Whitehead."

Mamoulian had told him about Whitehead and the house and the dogs. The damage they'd done to the European was conspicuous. Though his torn hand had healed quickly, the tissue damage was irreparable. A finger and a half missing, ugly scars raking palm and face, a thumb that would no longer move properly: his facility with the cards was permanently spoiled. It was a long and sorry tale he'd told Breer the day he'd returned, bloodied from his encounter with the dogs. A history of promises broken and trust despised; of atrocities committed against friendship. The European had wept freely in the telling of it, and Breer had glimpsed the profundity of pain in him. They were both despised men, conspired against and spat upon. Remembering the European's confessional, the sense of injustice Breer had felt at the time was reawoken. And here was he, who owed the European so much—his life, his sanity—planning to turn his back on his Savior. The Razor-Eater felt ashamed.

"Please," he said, eager to make amends for his petty complaints, "let me go and kill this man for you."

"No, Anthony."

"I can," Breer insisted. "I'm not afraid of dogs. I feel no pain; not now, not since you came back. I can kill him in his bed."

"I'm sure you could. And I will certainly need you, to keep the dogs off me."

"I'll tear them apart."

Mamoulian looked deeply pleased.

"You do that, Anthony. I loathe the species. Always have. You deal with them while I have words with Joseph."

"Why bother with him? He's so old."

"So am I," Mamoulian replied. "Older than I look, believe me. But a bargain is a bargain."

"It's difficult," said Breer, his eyes wet with phlegmy tears.

"What is?"

"Being the Last."

"Oh, yes."

"Needing to do everything properly; so that the tribe's remembered . . ." Breer's voice broke. All the glories he'd missed, not being born into a Great Age. What must that dream time have been like, when the Razor-Eaters and the Europeans, and all the other tribes, held the world in their hands? There would never come such an Age again; Mamoulian had said so.

"You won't be forgotten," the European promised.

"I think I will."

The European stood up. He seemed bigger than Breer remembered him; and darker.

"Have a little faith, Anthony. There is so much to look forward to."

Breer felt a touch at the back of his neck. It seemed a moth had alighted there and was stroking his nape with its furred antennae. His head had begun to buzz, as though the flies that beset him had laid eggs in his ears, and they were suddenly hatching. He shook his head to try to dislocate the sensation.

"It's all right," he heard the European say through the whirring of their wings. "Be calm."

"I don't feel well," Breer protested meekly, hoping his weakness would make Mamoulian merciful. The room was fragmenting around him, the walls separating from the floor and ceiling, the six sides of this gray box coming apart at the seams and letting all kinds of nothingness in. Everything had disappeared into a fog: furniture, blankets, even Mamoulian.

"There's so much to look forward to," he heard the European repeat, or was it an echo, coming back to him from some far-off cliff face? Breer was terrified. Though he could no longer even see his outstretched arm, he knew that this place went on forever and he was lost in it. The tears came thicker. His nose ran, his guts knotted.

Just as he thought he must scream or lose his mind, the European appeared out of the nothingness in front of him, and by the lightning flash of his eclipsed consciousness Breer saw the man transformed. Here was the source of all flies, all blistering summers and killing winters, all loss, all fear, floating before him more naked than any man had right to be, naked to the point of not-being. Now he spread his good hand toward Breer. In it were bone dice, carved with faces Breer almost recognized, and the Last European was crouching, and was tossing the dice, faces and all, into the void, while somewhere close by a thing with fire for a head wept and wept until it seemed they would all drown in tears.

35

Whitehead took the vodka glass, and the bottle, and went down to the sauna. It had become a favorite retreat of his during the weeks of Crisis. Now, though the danger was far from

over, he had lost focus on the state of the Empire. Large sectors
of the corporation's European and Far Eastern operations had
already been sold off to cut their losses; receivers had been called
in to a couple of smaller firms; there were mass redundancies
planned for some of the chemical plants in Germany and
Scandinavia: last-ditch attempts to stave off closure or sale. Joe
had other problems on his mind, however. Empires could be
regained, life and sanity could not. He'd sent the financiers away,
and the government think-tank men: sent them back to their
banks and their report-lined offices in Whitehall. There was
nothing they could tell him that he wanted to hear. No graphs, no
computer displays, no predictions interested him. In the five weeks
since the beginning of the Crisis he remembered with interest only
one conversation: the debate he'd had with Strauss.

He liked Strauss. More to the point, he *trusted* Strauss, and
that was a commodity rarer than uranium in the bazaar Joe
bartered in. Toy's instinct about Strauss had been correct; Bill had
been a man with a nose for integrity in others. Sometimes,
particularly when the vodka filled him with sentiment and
remorse, he missed Toy badly. But he was damned if he'd mourn:
that had never been his style, and he wasn't about to start now.
He poured himself another glass of vodka and raised it.

"To the Fall," he said, and drank.

He'd worked up a good head of steam in the white-tiled room,
and sitting on the bench in the half-light, blotched and florid, he
felt like some fleshy plant. He enjoyed the sensation of sweat in
the folds of his belly, at his armpits and groin; simple physical
stimuli that distracted him from bad thoughts.

Maybe the European wouldn't come after all, he thought.
Pray God.

Somewhere in the benighted house a door opened and closed,
but the drink and the steam made him feel quite aloof from events
elsewhere. The sauna was another planet; his, and his alone. He
put the drained glass down on the tiles and closed his eyes, hoping
to drowse.

B reer went to the gate. There was a hum of electricity off it, and the sour smell of power in the air.

"You're strong," the European said. "You told me so. Open the gate."

Breer put his hand on the wire. The boasts were true: he felt only the slightest tremor. There was just a cooking smell and the sound of his teeth chattering as he started to tear the gate apart. He was stronger than he'd imagined. There was no fear in him, and its absence made him Herculean. Now the dogs had started to bark along the fence, but he just thought: let them come. He wasn't going to die. Perhaps he would *never* die.

Laughing like a loon, he ripped the gate open; the hum stopped as the circuit was broken. The air was tinged with blue smoke.

"That's good," said the European.

Breer tried to drop the section of wire he was holding, but some of it had welded itself into his palm. He had to tear it out with his other hand. He looked down incredulously at his seared flesh. It was blackened, and smelled appetizing. Soon, surely, it must begin to hurt a little. No man—not even a man like him, guiltless and sublimely strong—could receive a wound like this and not suffer. But there was no sensation.

Suddenly—out of the dark—a dog.

Mamoulian backed off, fear convulsing him, but Breer was its intended victim. A few paces from its target the dog leaped, and its bulk struck Breer center chest. The impact toppled him over onto his back, and the dog was swiftly on top of him, jaws snapping at his throat. Breer was armed with a long-bladed kitchen knife, but he seemed uninterested in the weapon, though it was within easy reach. His fat face broke into a laugh as the dog scrabbled to get access to the man's neck. Breer simply took hold of the dog's lower jaw. The animal snapped down, clamping Breer's hand in its mouth. Almost immediately it realized its error. Breer reached around the back of the dog's head with his free hand, grabbed a fistful of fur and muscle, and jerked neck and head in opposite directions. There was a grinding sound. The dog roared in its throat, still unwilling to let go of its executioner's hand, even as blood sprang from between its clenched teeth. Breer gave the dog another lethal wrench. Its eyes showed white and its limbs stiffened. It slumped down onto Breer's chest, dead.

Other dogs barked in the distance, responding to the death-yelp they'd heard. The European looked nervously to right and left along the fence.

"Get up! Quickly!"

Breer loosed his hand from the dog's maw and shrugged the corpse off. He was still laughing.

"Easy," he said.

"There's more."

"Take me to them."

"Maybe too many for you to take on all at once."

"Was this the one?" Breer asked, kicking the dead dog over so that the European could see it better.

"The one?"

"That took off your fingers?"

"I don't know," the European replied, avoiding Breer's blood-spattered face as it grinned at him, eyes sparkling like an adolescent's in love.

"The kennels?" he suggested. "Finish them off there."

"Why not?"

The European led off from the fence in the direction of the kennels. Thanks to Carys, the layout of the Sanctuary was as familiar to him as the palm of his own hand. Breer kept pace with him, stinking of blood already, a spring in his heavy step. He had seldom felt so alive.

Life was so good, wasn't it? So *very* good.

The dogs barked.

In her room Carys pulled the pillow over her head to shut out the din. Tomorrow she'd pluck up her courage and tell Lillian

that she resented being kept awake half the night by hysterical
hounds. If she was ever going to be healthy she'd have to start
learning the rhythms of a normal life. That meant going about her
business while the sun shone, and sleeping at night.

As she turned over to find a portion of the bed that was still
cool an image flashed into her head. It was gone again before she
could entirely grasp it but she caught enough to wake her with a
start. She saw a man—faceless, but familiar—crossing a tract of
grass. At his heels, a tide of filth. It crept close behind him, in
blind adoration, its waves sibilant as snakes. She didn't have time
to see what the waves contained, and perhaps that was a good
thing.

She turned over a third time, and ordered herself to forget
these nonsenses.

Curiously, the dogs had stopped barking.

And what, after all, was the worst he could do, what was *the very
worst*? Whitehead had tried on this particular question so often
it felt like a familiar coat. The possible physical torments were
endless, of course. Sometimes, in the clammy hug of a three-A.M.
sweat, he would deem himself worthy of them all—if a man could
die a dozen, two dozen times—because the crimes of power he
had committed were not easily paid for. The things, oh, Jesus in
Heaven, the things he had done.

But then, damn it, who would not have crimes to confess,
when the time came? Who would not have acted out of greed, and
envy; or grappled for station, and having gained it, been absolute
in authority rather than relinquish it? He couldn't be held
responsible for everything the corporation had done. If, once in a
decade, a medical preparation that deformed fetuses had slipped
onto the market, was he to blame because there'd been profit
made? That kind of moral accounting was for the writers of
revenge fiction: it didn't belong in the real world, where most
crimes went punished only with wealth and influence; where the

worm seldom turned, and when it did was immediately crushed; where the best a man could hope was that having risen to his ambition's height by wit, stealth or violence there was some smidgen of pleasure in the view. That was the real world, and the European was as familiar with its ironies as *he* was. Hadn't Mamoulian shown him so much of it himself? How, in all conscience, could the European turn around and punish his student for learning his lessons too well?

I'll probably die in a warm bed, Whitehead thought, with curtains partially drawn against a yellow spring sky, and surrounded by admirers. "There is nothing to fear," he said aloud. The steam billowed. The tiles, laid with an obsessive's precision, sweated with him: but coldly, where he was hot.

Nothing to fear.

36

From the door of the doghouse Mamoulian watched Breer at work. It was an efficient slaughter this time, not the trial of strength he'd had with the dog at the gate. The fat man simply opened the cages and then the throats of the dogs one by one, using his long-bladed knife. Cornered in their cells the dogs were easy prey. All they could do was turn and turn, snapping uselessly at their assassin, somehow knowing the battle was lost before it was truly entered. They dropped turds as they slumped down, slashed necks and flanks spurting, brown eyes turned up to look at Breer like painted saints. He killed the pups too; tearing them from their mother's lap and cracking their heads open in his hand. Bella fought back with more vehemence than the other dogs, determined to inflict as much damage as she could on the killer before she too was killed. He returned the favor, mutilating her body after he'd silenced her; wounds in return for the wounds she'd given him. Once the clamor was over, and the only movement in the cages was the twitch of a leg or the splash of a bladder giving vent, Breer pronounced himself finished. They went together toward the house.

There were two more dogs here; the last of them. The Razor-Eater made short work of them both. By now he looked more like an abattoir worker than a sometime librarian. The European thanked him. It had been easier than he'd expected.

"I have business inside the house now," he told Breer.

"Do you want me to come?"

"No. But you could open the door for me, if you would."

Breer went to the back door and punched out the glass, then reached through and unlocked it, letting Mamoulian into the kitchen.

"Thank you. Wait here for me."

The European disappeared into the blue gloom of the interior. Breer watched him go, and once his master was out of sight, entered the Sanctuary after him, blood and smiles wreathing his face.

Though the pall of steam muffled the sound, Whitehead had the impression that somebody was moving around in the house. Strauss, probably: the man had become restless recently. Whitehead let his eyes drift closed again.

Somewhere close by, he heard a door opening and closing, the door of the antechamber beyond the steam room. He stood up, and quizzed the gloom.

"Marty?"

There was no answer from Marty or anybody else. The certainty of having heard a door at all faltered. It wasn't always easy to judge sound here. Nor vision. The steam had thickened considerably; he could no longer see across to the other side of the room.

"Is there somebody there?" he asked.

The steam was a dead, gray wall in front of his eyes. He cursed himself for letting it get so heavy.

"Martin?" he said again. Though there was neither sight nor sound to confirm his suspicions, he knew he wasn't alone. Somebody was very close, and yet not answering. When he spoke he reached, inch by tremulous inch, across the tiles to the towel folded at his side. His fingers investigated the fold while his eyes stayed fixed on the steam-wall; in the towel was a gun. His grateful fingers located it.

This time more quietly, he addressed the invisible visitor. The gun gave him confidence.

"I know you're there. Show yourself, you bastard. I won't be terrorized."

Something moved in the steam. Eddies began, and multiplied. Whitehead could hear the double thump of his heart in his ears. Whoever it was (*let it not be him, oh, Christ, let it not be him*) he was ready. And then, without warning, the steam divided, killed by a sudden cold. The old man raised the gun. If it *was* Marty out there, and he was playing some sick joke, he was going to regret it. The hand that held the gun had begun to tremble.

And now, finally, there was a figure in front of him. It was still indecipherable in the mist. At least it was until a voice he'd heard a hundred times in his vodka-sodden dreams said:

"*Pilgrim.*"

The steam shrank back. The European was there, standing in front of him. His face had scarcely conceded the seventeen years since last they'd met. The domed brow, the eyes set so deep in their orbits they glinted like water at the bottom of a well. He had changed so little, as though time—in awe of him—had passed him by.

"Sit down," he said.

Whitehead didn't move; the gun was still pointed directly at the European.

"*Please*, Joseph. Sit down."

Might it be better if he sat? Might the death blows be avoided

by a feigned meekness? Or was it melodrama to think that this
man would stoop to blows? What kind of dream have I been
living in, Whitehead chided himself, to think he'd come here to
bruise me, to bleed me? Such eyes have more than bruising on
their mind.

He sat down. He was aware of his nakedness, but he didn't
much care. Mamoulian wasn't seeing his flesh; he looked deeper
than fat and bone. Whitehead could feel the stare in him now; it
stroked his heart. How else was he to explain the relief he felt,
seeing the European at last?

"It's so long . . ." was all he could say: a limping banality. Did
he sound like a hopeful lover, longing for a reconciliation? Perhaps
that wasn't so far from the truth. The singularity of their mutual
hatred had the purity of love.

The European studied him.

"Pilgrim," he murmured reproachfully, glancing at the gun,
"there's no need. Or use."

Whitehead smiled and laid the gun down on the towel beside him.

"I was afraid of you coming," he said, by way of explanation.
"That's why I bought the dogs. You know how I loathe dogs. But
I knew you loathed them more."

Mamoulian put his finger to his lips to hush Whitehead's talk.

"I forgive the dogs," he said. Whom was he forgiving: the
animals or the man who'd used them against him?

"Why did you have to come back?" Whitehead said. "You
must have known I wouldn't welcome you."

"You know why I came."

"No I don't. *Really*. I don't."

"Joseph," Mamoulian sighed. "Don't treat me like one of your
politicians. I'm not to be paid off in promises, then thrown away
when your fortunes change. You can't treat me like that."

"I didn't."

"No lies, please. Not now. Not with so little time left to us.
This time, this *last* time, let us be honest with each other. Let us
spill our hearts. There won't be any more opportunities."

"Why not? Why can't we start again?"

"We're old. And tired."

"I'm not."

"Why haven't you fought for your Empire, then, if not because of fatigue?"

"That was your doing?" Whitehead asked, already certain of the reply.

Mamoulian nodded. "You're not the only man I've helped to fortune. I've got friends in the highest circles; all, like you, students of Providence. They could buy and sell half the world if I asked them to; they owe me that. But none of them were ever quite like you, Joseph. You were the hungriest, and the ablest. Only with you did I see a chance of—"

"Go on," Whitehead prompted. "Chance of what?"

"Salvation," Mamoulian replied, then laughed the thought off. "Of all things," he said quietly.

Whitehead had never imagined it would be like this: a hushed debate in a white-tiled room, two old men exchanging hurts. Turning the memories over like stones, and watching the lice scuttle away. It was so much more gentle and so much more painful. Nothing scourged like loss.

"I made mistakes," he said, "and I'm genuinely sorry for them."

"Tell me the *truth*," Mamoulian scolded.

"That *is* the truth, damn it. I'm sorry. What more do you want? Land? Companies? *What do you want?*"

"You amaze me, Joseph. Even now, in extremis, you try to make bargains. What a loss you are. What a terrible loss. I could have made you great."

"I *am* great."

"You know better than that, Pilgrim," he said gently. "What would you have been, without me? With your glib tongue and your fancy suits. An actor? A car salesman? *A thief?*"

Whitehead flinched, not just at the taunts. The steam had become uneasy behind Mamoulian, as if ghosts had begun to move in it.

"You were *nothing*. At least have the good grace to admit that."

"I took you on," Whitehead pointed out.

"Oh, yes," said Mamoulian. "You had appetite, I grant you. You had *that* in abundance."

"You needed me," Whitehead retorted. The European had wounded him; now, despite his better judgment, he wanted to wound in return. This was *his* world, after all. The European was a trespasser here: unarmed, unaided. And he had asked for the truth to be told. Well, he'd hear it, ghosts or no ghosts.

"Why would I need you?" Mamoulian asked. There was sudden contempt in his tone. "What are you worth?"

Whitehead held off answering for a moment; and then he was spilling the words, careless of the consequences.

"To live for you, because you were too bloodless to do it for yourself! That was why you picked me up. To taste it all through me. The women, the power: all of it."

"No . . ."

"You're looking sick, Mamoulian—"

He called the European by his name. See that? God, the ease of it. He called the bastard by his name, and he didn't look away when those eyes glinted, because he was telling the *truth* here, wasn't he? They both knew it. Mamoulian was pale; almost insipid. Drained of the will to live. Suddenly, Whitehead began to know he could win this confrontation, if he was clever.

"Don't try to fight," Mamoulian said. "I will have my due."

"Which is?"

"You. Your death. Your soul, for want of a better word."

"You had all I owed you and more, years ago."

"That wasn't the bargain, Pilgrim."

"We all make deals and then change the rules."

"That's not playing the game."

"There is only *one* game. You taught me that. As long as I win that one . . . the rest don't matter."

"I will have what's mine," Mamoulian said with quiet determination. "It's a foregone conclusion."

"Why not just have me killed?"

"You know me, Joseph. I want this to finish cleanly. I'm granting you time to organize your affairs. To close the books, clean the slates, give the land back to those you stole it from."

"I didn't take you for a Communist."

"I'm not here to debate politics. I came to tell you my terms."

So, Whitehead thought, the execution date is a while away. He quickly put all thoughts of escape out of his head, for fear the European sniff them out. Mamoulian had reached into his jacket pocket. The mutilated hand brought out a large envelope, folded on itself. "You will dispose of your assets in strict accordance with these directions."

"All to friends of yours, presumably."

"I have no friends."

"It's fine by me." Whitehead shrugged. "I'm glad to be rid of it."

"Didn't I warn you it would become burdensome?"

"I'll give it all away. Become a saint, if you like. Will you be satisfied then?"

"As long as you die, Pilgrim," the European said.

"No."

"You and I together."

"I'll die in my time," Whitehead said, "not in yours."

"You won't want to go alone." Behind the European the ghosts were getting restless. The steam simmered with them.

"I'm not going *anywhere*," Whitehead said. He thought he glimpsed faces in the billows. Perhaps defiance wasn't wise, he decided. ". . . Where's the harm?" he muttered, half-standing to ward off whatever the steam contained. The sauna lights were dimming. Mamoulian's eyes shone in the deepening murk, and there was illumination spilling up from his throat too, staining the air. The ghosts were taking substance from it, growing more palpable by the second.

"Stop," Whitehead begged, but it was a vain hope.

The sauna had vanished. The steam was discharging its passengers. Whitehead could feel their prickling gaze on him. Only now did he feel naked. He bent for the towel, and when he stood upright again, Mamoulian had gone. He clutched the towel to his groin. He could feel how the ghosts in the darkness smirked at his breasts, at his shrunken pudenda, at the sheer absurdity of his old flesh. They had known him in rarer times; when the chest had been broad, the pudenda arrogant, the flesh impressive whether naked or dressed.

"Mamoulian . . ." he murmured, hoping the European might yet undo this misery before it got out of control. But nobody answered his appeal.

He took a faltering step across the slippery tiles toward the door. If the European had gone, then he could simply walk out of the place, find Strauss and a room where he could hide. But the ghosts weren't finished with him yet. The steam, which had darkened to a bruise, lifted a little, and in its depths something shimmered. He couldn't make sense of it at first: the uncertain whiteness, the fluttering, as of snowflakes.

Then, from nowhere, a breeze. It belonged to the past: and smelled of it. Of ash and brick dust; of the dirt on bodies unwashed for decades; of burning hair, of anger. But there was another smell that wove between these, and when he breathed it the significance of that shimmering air came clear, and he forsook the towel and covered his eyes, tears and pleas coming and coming.

But the ghosts pressed in nevertheless, carrying the scent of petals with them.

37

Carys stood on the small landing outside Marty's room, and listened. From inside, there came the sound of steady sleep. She hesitated a moment—unsure of whether or not to go in—then slipped down the stairs again, leaving him un-woken. It was too convenient to slide into bed beside him, to weep into the crook of his neck where his pulse ticked, to unburden herself of all her fretting and beg him to be strong for her. Convenient and dangerous. It wasn't real safety, there in his bed. She'd find that *by* herself and *in* herself, nowhere else.

Halfway down the second flight of stairs she stopped. There was a curious tingle in the darkened hallway. A chill of night air: and more. She waited, shadow-thin, on the stairs, until her eyes accustomed themselves to the dark. Perhaps she should just go back upstairs, lock her bedroom door behind her, and find a few pills to while away the hours until the sun came up. It would be so much easier than living as she was, with every nerve electric. Along the hall toward the kitchen she caught a movement. A black bulk was framed against the doorway, and then gone.

It's just the dark, she told herself, playing tricks. She smoothed her hand over the wall, feeling the design of the wallpaper ripple under her fingertips, until she found the light switch. She flipped it on. The corridor was empty. The stairway at her back was empty. The landing was empty. She muttered "Stupid" to herself, and padded down the last three stairs and along the corridor to the kitchen.

Before she got there, her suspicions about the chill were confirmed. The back door was in direct line with the kitchen door, and both were open. It was odd, almost shocking in fact, to see the house, which was usually hermetically sealed, exposed to the night. The open door was like a wound in its flank.

She stepped through from the carpeted hallway onto the cool linoleum of the kitchen and was halfway to closing the door when she caught the glass glinting on the floor. The door had not been left open accidentally; somebody had forced his way in. A smell—sandalwood—was pricking her nostrils. It was sickly; but what it covered was sicklier still.

She had to inform Marty; that was the first priority. No need to go back upstairs. There was a phone on the kitchen wall.

Her mind divided. Part of her coolly assessed the problem and its solutions: where the phone was, what she must say to Marty when he answered it. Another part, the part that embraced H, that was always frightened, dissolved in panic. There's somebody close (sandalwood), it said, somebody lethal in the dark, rotting in the dark.

The cooler self kept control. She walked—glad now to be barefoot because she made scarcely a sound—across to the phone. She picked up the receiver and dialed nineteen, the number of Marty's bedroom. It rang once, then again. She willed him to wake quickly. Her reserves of control were, she knew, strictly limited.

"Come on, come on . . ." she breathed.

Then there was a sound behind her; heavy feet crunched the glass into smaller pieces. She turned to see who it was, and there was a nightmare standing in the doorway with a knife in his hand and a dogskin slung over one shoulder. The phone slipped from her fingers, and the part of her that had advised panic all along took the reins.

Told you so, it shouted. *Told you so!*

A phone rang in Marty's dreams. He dreamed he woke, put it to his ear, and spoke to death on the other end of the line. But the ringing went on even though he'd picked the phone up and he surfaced from sleep to find the receiver in his hand and no one on the line.

He put it back in its cradle. Had it rung at all? He thought not. Still, the dream wasn't worth going back to: his conversation with death had been gobbledygook. Swinging his legs out of bed he pulled on his jeans and was at the door, bleary-eyed, when from downstairs there came the crash of breaking glass.

The butcher had lurched toward her—throwing off the dog's skin to make an embrace easier. She ducked him once; twice. He was ponderous, but she knew if he once got his hands on her, that was the end. He was between her and the exit into the house now; she was obliged to maneuver her way toward the back door.

"I wouldn't go out there—" he advised, his voice, like his smell, mixing sweetness and rot. "It's not safe."

His warning was the best recommendation she'd heard. She slipped around the kitchen table and out through the open door, trying to skip across the glass shards. She contrived to pull the door closed behind her—more glass fell and shattered—and then she was away from the house. Behind her, she heard the door pulled open so roughly it might have been wrenched off its hinges. Now she heard the dog-killer's footsteps—thunder in the ground— coming after her.

The brute was slow: she was nimble. He was heavy: she was light to the point of invisibility. Instead of clinging to the walls of the house, which would only take her around to the front eventually, where the lawn was illuminated, she struck out away from the building, and hoped to God the beast couldn't see in the dark.

Marty stumbled down the stairs, still shaking sleep from his head. The cold in the hall slapped him fully awake. He followed the draft to the kitchen. He only had a few seconds to take in the glass and the blood on the floor before Carys started screaming.

From some unimaginable place, someone cried out. Whitehead heard the voice, a girl's voice, but lost as he was in a wilderness, he couldn't fix the cry. He had no idea how long he'd been weeping here, watching the damned come and go: it seemed an age. His head swam with hyperventilation; his throat was hoarse with sobs.

"Mamoulian . . ." he pleaded again, "don't leave me here."

The European had been right—he *didn't* want to go alone into this nowhere. Though he had begged to be saved from it a hundred times without result, now, at last, the illusion began to relent. The tiles, like shy white crabs, scuttled back into place at his feet; the smell of his own stale sweat reassaulted him, more welcome than any scent he'd ever smelled. And now the European was here in front of him, as if he had never moved.

"Shall we talk, Pilgrim?" he asked.

Whitehead was shivering, despite the heat. His teeth chattered. "Yes," he said.

"Quietly? With dignity and politeness?"

Again: "Yes."

"You didn't like what you saw."

Whitehead ran his fingers across his pasty face, his thumb and forefinger digging into the pits at the bridge of his nose, as if to push the sights out. "No, damn you," he said. The images would not be dislodged. Not now, not ever.

"Perhaps we could talk somewhere else," the European suggested. "Don't you have a room we could retire to?"

"I heard Carys. She screamed."

Mamoulian closed his eyes for a moment, fetching a thought from the girl. "She's quite all right," he said.

"Don't hurt her. Please. She's all I've got."

"There's no harm done. She simply found a piece of my friend's handiwork."

Breer had not only skinned the dog, he'd disemboweled it. Carys had slipped in the muck of its innards, and the scream had escaped before she could stop herself. When its reverberations died she listened for the butcher's footsteps. Somebody was running in her direction.

"Carys!" It was Marty's voice.

"I'm over here."

He found her staring down at the dog's skinned head.

"Who the fuck did this?" he snapped.

"He's here," she said. "He followed me out."

He touched her face. "Are you all right?"

"It's only a dead dog," she said. "It was just a shock."

As they returned to the house, she remembered the dream she'd woken from. There'd been a faceless man crossing this very lawn—were they treading in his footprints now?—with a surf of shit at his heels.

"There's somebody else here," she said, with absolute certainty, "besides the dog-killer."

"Sure."

She nodded, face stony, then took Marty's arm. "This one's worse, babe."

"I've got a gun. It's in my room."

They'd come to the kitchen door; the dog's skin still lay discarded beside it.

"Do you know who they are?" he asked her. She shook her head.

"He's fat," was all she could say. "Stupid-looking."

"And the other one. You know him?"

The other? Of course she knew him: he was as familiar as her own face. She had thought of him a thousand times a day in the last weeks; something told her she had always known him. He was the Architect who paraded in her sleep, who dabbled his fingers at her neck, who had come now to unleash the flood of filth that had followed him across the lawn. Was there ever a time when she hadn't lived in his shadow?

"What are you thinking?"

He was giving her such a sweet look, trying to put a heroic face on his confusion.

"I'll tell you sometime," she said. "Now we should get that damn gun."

They threaded their way through the house. It was absolutely
still. No bloody footsteps, no cries. He fetched the gun from his
room.

"Now for Papa," he said. "Check that he's all right."

With the dog-killer still loose the search was stealthy, and
therefore slow. Whitehead wasn't in any of the bedrooms, or his
dressing rooms. The bathrooms, the library, the study and the
lounges were similarly deserted. It was Carys who suggested the
sauna.

Marty flung the door of the steam room open. A wall of humid
heat met his face, and steam curled out into the hallway. The
place had certainly been used recently. But the steam room, the
Jacuzzi and solarium were all empty. When he'd made a quick
search of the rooms he came back to find Carys leaning unsteadily
on the doorjamb.

". . . I suddenly feel sick," she said. "It just came over me."

Marty supported her as her legs gave.

"Sit down for a minute." He guided her across to a bench.
There was a gun on it, sweating.

"I'm all right," she insisted. "You go and find Papa, I'll stay
here."

"You look bloody awful."

"Thank you," she said. "Now will you please go? I'd prefer to
throw up with nobody watching, if you don't mind."

"You sure?"

"*Go on*, damn you. Leave me be. I'll be fine."

"Lock the door after me," he stressed.

"Yes, sir," she said, throwing him a queasy look. He left her
in the steam room, and waited until he heard the bolt drawn
across. It didn't completely reassure him, but it was better than
nothing.

He cautiously made his way back into the vestibule, and
decided to take a quick look around the front of the house. The

lawn lights were on, and if the old man was there he'd soon be picked out. That made Marty an easy target too, of course, but at least he was armed. He unlocked the front door and stepped out onto the gravel. The floodlights poured unflinching illumination down. It was whiter than sunlight, but curiously dead. He scanned the lawn to right and left. There was no sign of the old man.

Behind him, in the hallway, Breer watched the hero stride out in search of his master. Only when he was well out of sight did the Razor-Eater slouch out of hiding and lope, bloody-handed, toward his heart's desire.

38

Having bolted the door Carys returned, groggily, to the bench and concentrated on controlling her mutinous system. She wasn't certain what had brought the nausea on, but she was determined to get the better of it. When she had, she'd go after Marty and help him search for Papa. The old man had been here recently, that much was apparent. That he'd left without his gun did not augur well.

An insinuating voice stirred her from her meditation, and she looked up. There was a smudge in the steam, in front of her, a paleness projected onto the air. She squinted to try to make sense of it. It seemed to have the texture of white dots. She stood up, and—far from vanishing—the illusion strengthened. Filaments were spreading to connect one dot to the next, and she almost laughed with recognition as all at once the puzzle came clear. It was blossom she was looking at, brilliant white heads of it caught in sun or starlight. Twitched by some sourceless wind, the branches threw down flurries of petals. They seemed to graze her

face, though when she put her fingers to the places there was
nothing there.

In her years of addiction to H she'd never dreamed an image
that was so superficially benign and yet so charged with threat. It
wasn't hers, this tree. She hadn't made it from her own head. It
belonged to someone who'd been here before her: the Architect,
no doubt. He'd shown this spectacle to Papa, and its echoes
lingered.

She tried to look away, around to the door, but her eyes were
glued to the tree. She couldn't seem to unfix them. She had the
impression that the blossom was swelling, as if more buds were
coming into bloom. The blankness of the tree—its horrid purity—
was filling her eyes, the whiteness congealing and fattening.

And then, somewhere beneath these swaying, laden branches,
a figure moved. A woman with burning eyes lifted her broken
head in Carys' direction. Her presence brought the nausea back.
Carys felt faint. This wasn't the time to lose consciousness. Not
with the blossom still bursting and the woman beneath the tree
moving out of hiding toward her. She had been beautiful, this
one: and used to admiration. But chance had intervened. The
body had been cruelly maimed, the beauty spoiled. When, finally,
she emerged from hiding, Carys knew her as her own.

"Mama."

Evangeline Whitehead opened her arms, and offered her
daughter an embrace she had never offered while alive. In death,
had she discovered the capacity to love as well as be loved? No.
Never. The open arms were a trap, Carys knew it. If she fell into
them the tree, and its Maker, would have her, forever.

Her head thundering, she forced herself to look away. Her
limbs were like jelly; she wondered if she had the strength to
move. Unsteadily, she craned her head toward the door. To her
shock she saw that it was wide open. The bolt had been wrenched
off as the door was beaten open.

"Marty?" she said.

"No."

She turned again, this time to her left, and the dog-killer was standing no more than two yards from her. He had washed his hands and face of bloodstains, and he smelled strongly of perfume.

"You're safe with me," he said.

She glanced back at the tree. It was dissolving, its illusory life dispersed by the brute's interruption. Carys' mother, arms still outstretched, was growing thin and wretched. At the last instant before she disappeared she opened her mouth and vomited a stream of black blood toward her daughter. Then the tree and its horrors were gone. There was only the steam, and the tiles, and a man with dog's blood under his fingernails standing beside her. She'd heard nothing of his forced entry: the reverie at the tree had muted the outside world.

"You shouted," he explained. "I heard you shout."

She didn't remember doing so. "I want Marty," she told him.

"No," he replied politely.

"Where is he?" she demanded, and made a move, albeit weakly, toward the open door.

"I said *no*!" He stepped in her path. He didn't need to touch her. His very proximity was sufficient to halt her. She contemplated trying to slip by him, and out into the hallway, but how far could she get before he caught her? There were two basic rules when dealing with mad dogs and psychotics. The first: don't run. The second: show no fear. When he reached out toward her she tried not to recoil.

"I won't let anybody hurt you," he said. He ran the ball of his thumb across the back of her hand, finding a speck of sweat there, and brushing it away. His stroke was feather-light; and ice-cold.

"Will you let me look after you, pretty?" he asked.

She said nothing; his touch appalled her. Not for the first time tonight she wished she weren't a sensitive: she'd never felt such distress at another human's touch.

"I would like to make you comfortable," he was saying. "Share . . ." He stopped, as though the words escaped him. ". . . your secrets."

She looked up into his face. The muscles of his jaw fluttered as he made his proposals, nervous as an adolescent.

"And in return," he proposed, "I'll show you *my* secrets. You want to see?"

He didn't wait for an answer. His hand had plunged into the pocket of his stained jacket and was taking out a clutch of razors. Their edges glinted. It was too absurd: like a fairground sideshow, but played without the razzmatazz. This clown, smelling of sandalwood, was about to eat razors to win her love. He put out his dry tongue and laid the first blade on it. She didn't like this one bit; razors made her nervous, and always had.

"Don't," she said.

"It's all right," he told her, swallowing hard. "I'm the last of the tribe. See?" He opened his mouth and put out his tongue. "All gone."

"Extraordinary," she said. It was. Revolting, but extraordinary.

"That's not all," he said, pleased by her response.

It was best to let him go on with this bizarre display, she reasoned. The longer he took showing her these perversities, the more chance there was of Marty coming back.

"What else can you do?" she asked.

He let go of her hand and started to unbuckle his belt.

"I'll show you," he replied, unbuttoning.

Oh, Christ, she thought, stupid, stupid, stupid. His arousal at this exhibition was absolutely plain even before he had his trousers down.

"I'm past pain now," he explained courteously. "No pain, whatever I do to myself. The Razor-Eater feels nothing."

He was naked beneath his trousers. "See?" he said, proudly.

She saw. His groin was completely shaved, and the region sported an array of self-inflicted adornments. Hooks and rings transfixing the fat of his lower belly and his genitals. His testicles bristled with needles.

"Touch me," he invited.

"No . . . thank you," she said.

He frowned; his upper lip curled to expose teeth that in his pale flesh looked bright yellow.

"I want you to touch me," he said, and reached for her.

"*Breer.*"

The Razor-Eater stood absolutely still. Only his eyes flickered.

"Let her alone."

She knew the voice; too well. It was the Architect, of course; her dream-guide.

"I didn't hurt her," Breer mumbled. "Did I? Tell him I didn't hurt you."

"Cover yourself up," the European said.

Breer hoisted up his trousers like a boy caught masturbating, and moved away from Carys, throwing her a conspiratorial glance. Only now did the speaker come into the steam room. He was taller than she'd dreamed he'd be, and more doleful.

"I'm sorry," he said. His tone was that of the perfect maitre d', apologizing for a gauche waiter.

"She was sick," Breer said. "That's why I broke in."

"Sick?"

"Talking to the wall," he blustered. "Calling after her mother."

The Architect understood the observation immediately. He looked at Carys keenly.

"So you saw?" he said.

"What was it?"

"Nothing you need ever suffer again," he replied.

"My mother was there. Evangeline."

"Forget it all," he said. "That horror's for others, not for you." Listening to his calm voice was mesmeric. She found it difficult to recall her nightmares of nullity; his presence canceled memory.

"I think perhaps you should come with me," he said.

"Why?"

"Your father's going to die, Carys."

"Oh?" she said.

She felt utterly removed from herself. Fears were a thing of the past in his courteous presence.

"If you stay here, you'll only suffer with him, and there's no need for that."

It was a seductive offer; never to live under the old man's thumb again, never to endure his kisses, that tasted so old. Carys glanced at Breer.

"Don't be afraid of him," the Architect reassured her, laying a hand on the back of her neck. "He is nothing and no one. You're safe with me."

"She could run away," Breer protested, when the European had let Carys go off to her room to gather up her belongings.

"She will never leave me," Mamoulian replied. "I mean her no harm and she knows it. I rocked her once, in these arms."

"Naked, was she?"

"A tiny thing: so vulnerable." His voice dropped to a near-whisper: "She deserved better than him."

Breer said nothing; simply lolled insolently against the wall, peeling dried blood from under his nails with a razor. He was deteriorating faster than the European had anticipated. He'd hoped Breer would survive until all of this chaos was over, but knowing the old man, he'd wheedle and prevaricate, and what should have taken days would occupy weeks, by which time the Razor-Eater's condition would be poor indeed. The European felt weary. Finding and controlling a substitute for Breer would be a drain on his already depleted energies.

Presently, Carys came downstairs.

In some ways he regretted losing his spy in the enemy camp, but there were too many variables remaining if he didn't take her. For one, she had knowledge of him, deeper knowledge than she was perhaps aware of. She knew instinctively his terrors of the flesh; witness the way she had driven him out when she and Strauss had been together. She knew too his weariness, his dwindling faith. But there was another reason to take her. Whitehead had said that she was his only comfort. If they took her now the pilgrim would be alone, and that would be agony. Mamoulian trusted it would prove unendurable.

39

After searching as much of the grounds as was lit by the floodlights, and finding no sign of Whitehead, Marty went back upstairs. It was time to break Whitehead's commandment, and look for the old man in forbidden territory. The door to the room at the end of the top corridor, beyond Carys' and Whitehead's bedrooms, was closed. Heart in mouth, Marty approached, and tapped on it.

"Sir?"

At first there was no sound from within. Then came Whitehead's voice; vague, as if woken from sleep: "Who is it?"

"Strauss, sir."

"Come in."

Marty pushed the door gently and it swung open.

When he had imagined the interior of this room it had always been a treasure house. But the truth was quite the reverse. The room was Spartan: its white walls and its spare furnishings a chilly spectacle. It did boast one treasure. An altarpiece stood against one of the bare walls, its richness quite out of place in such an austere setting. Its central panel was a crucifixion of sublime sadism; all gold and blood.

Its owner sat, dressed in an opulent dressing gown, at the far end of the room, behind a large table. He looked at Marty with neither welcome nor accusation on his face, his body slumped in the chair like a sack.

"Don't stand in the doorway, man. Come in."

Marty closed the door behind him.

"I know what you told me, sir, about never coming up here. But I was afraid something had happened to you."

"I'm alive," Whitehead said, spreading his hands. "All's well."

"The dogs—"

"—are dead. I know. Sit."

He gestured to the empty chair opposite him across the table.

"Shouldn't I call the police?"

"There's no need."

"They could still be on the premises."

Whitehead shook his head. "They've gone. Sit down, Martin. Pour yourself a glass of wine. You look as if you've been running hard."

Marty pulled out the chair that had been neatly placed under the table and sat down. The unadorned bulb that burned in the middle of the room threw an unflattering light on everything. Heavy shadows, ghastly highlights: a ghost show.

"Put down the gun. You won't be needing it."

He lay the weapon down on the table beside the plate, on which there were still several wafer-thin slices of meat. Beyond the plate, a bowl of strawberries, partially devoured, and a glass of water. The frugality of the meal matched the environment: the meat, sliced to the point of transparency, rare and moist; the casual arrangement of cups and strawberry bowl. An arbitrary precision invested everything, an eerie sense of chance beauty. Between Marty and Whitehead a mote of dust turned in the air, fluctuating between the light bulb and table, its direction influenced by the merest exhalation.

"Try the meat, Martin."

"I'm not hungry."

"It's superb. My guest brought it."

"You know who they are, then."

"Yes, of course. Now eat."

Reluctantly Marty cut a piece of the slice in front of him, and tasted it. The texture dissolved on the tongue, delicate and appetizing.

"Finish it off," Whitehead said.

Marty did as the old man had invited: the night's exertions had given him an appetite. A glass of red wine was poured for him; he drank it down.

"Your head's full of questions, no doubt," Whitehead said. "Please ask away. I'll do my best to answer."

"Who are they?" he asked.

"Friends."

"They broke in like assassins."

"Is it not possible that friends, with time, can *become* assassins?" Marty hadn't been prepared for that particular paradox. "One of them sat where you're sitting now."

"How can I be your bodyguard if I don't know your friends from your enemies?"

Whitehead paused, and looked hard at Marty.

"Do you care?" he asked after a beat.

"You've been good to me," Marty replied, insulted by the inquiry. "What kind of coldhearted bastard do you take me for?"

"My God . . ." Whitehead shook his head. "Marty . . ."

"*Explain to me*. I want to help."

"Explain what?"

"How you can invite a man who wants to kill you to eat dinner with you."

Whitehead watched the dust mote turning between them. He either thought the question beneath contempt, or had no answer for it.

"You want to help me?" he said eventually. "Then bury the dogs."

"Is that all I'm good for?"

"The time may come—"

"So you keep telling me," Marty said, standing up. He wasn't going to get any answers; that much was apparent. Just meat and good wine. Tonight, that wasn't enough.

"Can I go now?" he asked, and without waiting for a reply turned his back on the old man and went to the door.

As he opened it, Whitehead said: "Forgive me," very quietly. So quietly in fact that Marty wasn't sure whether the words were intended for him or not.

He closed the door behind him and went back through the house to check that the intruders had indeed gone; they had. The steam room was empty. Carys had obviously returned to her room.

Feeling insolent, he slipped into the study and poured himself a treble whisky from the decanter, and then sat in Whitehead's chair by the window, sipping and thinking. The alcohol did nothing for the clarity of his mind: it simply dulled the ache of frustration he felt. He slipped away to bed before dawn described the ragged bundles of fur on the lawn too distinctly.

VII. NO LIMITS

40

It was no morning for burying dead dogs; the sky was too high and promising. Jets, trailing vapor, crossed to America, the woods budded and winged with life. Still, the work had to be done, however inappropriate.

Only by the uncompromising light of day was it possible to see the full extent of the slaughter. In addition to killing the dogs around the house, the intruders had broken into the kennels and systematically murdered all its occupants, including Bella and her offspring. When Marty arrived at the kennels Lillian was already there. She looked as though she'd been weeping for days. In her hands she cradled one of the pups. Its head had been crushed, as if in a vise.

"Look," she said, proffering the corpse.

Marty hadn't managed to eat anything for breakfast: the thought of the job ahead had taken the edge off his appetite. Now he wished he'd forced something down: his empty belly echoed on itself. He felt almost light-headed.

"If only I'd been here," she said.

"You probably would have ended up dead yourself," he told her. It was the simple truth.

She laid the pup back on the straw, and stroked the matted fur of Bella's body. Marty was more fastidious than she. Even wearing a pair of thick leather gloves he didn't want to touch the corpses. But whatever he lacked in respect he made up for in efficiency, using his disgust as a spur to hurry the work along. Lillian, though she had insisted on being there to help, was useless in the face of the fact. All she could do was watch while Marty wrapped the bodies in black plastic refuse bags, loaded the forlorn parcels into the back of the jeep, and then drove this makeshift hearse across to a clearing he'd chosen in the woods. It was here that they were to be buried, at Whitehead's request, out of sight of the house. He'd brought two spades, hoping that Lillian would assist, but she was clearly incapable. He was left to do it single-handed, while she stood, hands thrust into the pockets of her filthy anorak, staring at the leaking bundles.

It was difficult work. The soil was a network of roots, crisscrossing from tree to tree, and Marty soon worked up a sweat, hacking at the roots with the blade of his spade. Once he'd dug a shallow grave, he rolled the bodies into it and began to shovel the earth back on top of them. It rattled on their plastic shrouds, a dry rain. When the filling was done he patted the soil into a rough mound.

"I'm going back to the house for a beer," he told Lillian. "You coming?"

She shook her head. "Last respects," she muttered.

He left her among the trees and headed back across the lawn to the house. As he walked, he thought of Carys. She must be awake by now, surely, though the curtains at the window were still drawn. How fine to be a bird, he thought, to peer through the gap in the curtains and spy on her stretching naked on the bed, sloth that she was, her arms thrown up above her head, fur at her armpits, fur where her legs met. He walked into the house wearing a smile and an erection.

He found Pearl in the kitchen, told her he was hungry, and went upstairs to shower. When he came down again she had a cold spread laid out for him: beef, bread, tomatoes. He dug in with a will.

"Seen Carys this morning?" he asked, mouth crammed.

"No," she replied. She was at her most uncommunicative today, her face pinched up with some fermenting grievance. He wondered, watching her move around the kitchen, what she was like in bed: for some reason he was full of dirty thoughts today, as if his mind, refusing to be depressed by the burial, was eager for uplifting sport. Chewing on a mouthful of salted beef he said:

"Was it veal you fed the old man last night?"

Pearl didn't look up from her labors as she said: "He didn't eat last night. I left fish for him, but he didn't touch it."

"But he had meat," Marty said. "I finished it off for him. And strawberries."

"He must have come down and got those for himself. Always strawberries," she said. "He'll choke on them one of these days."

Now Marty came to think of it, Whitehead had said something about his guest providing the meat.

"It was good, whatever it was," he said.

"None of my doing," Pearl said, offended as a wife discovering her husband's adultery.

Marty put the conversation to rest; it was no use trying to raise her spirits when she was in this kind of mood.

The meal finished, he went up to Carys' room. The house was pin-drop still: after the lethal farce of the previous night it had regained its composure. The pictures that lined the staircase, the carpets underfoot, all conspired against any rumor of distress. Chaos here was as unthinkable as a riot in an art gallery: all precedent forbade it.

He knocked on Carys' door, lightly. There was no answer, so he knocked again, more loudly this time.

"Carys?"

Perhaps she didn't want to speak to him. He'd never been able to predict from one day to the next whether they were lovers or enemies. Her ambiguities no longer distressed him, however. It was her way of testing him, he guessed, and it was fine by him as long as she finally admitted that she loved him more than any other fucker on the face of the earth.

He tried the handle; the door wasn't locked. The room beyond was empty. Not only did it not contain Carys, it contained no trace of her existence there. Her books, her toiletries, her clothes, her ornaments, everything that marked out the room as hers had been removed. The sheets had been stripped from the bed, the pillowcases from the pillow. The bare mattress looked desolate.

Marty closed the door and started downstairs. He'd asked for explanations more than once and he'd been granted precious few. But this was too much. He wished to God Toy was still around: at least he'd treated Marty as a thinking animal.

Luther was back in the kitchen, his feet up on the table among a clutter of unwashed dishes. Pearl had clearly left her province to the barbarians.

"Where's Carys?" was Marty's first question.

"You never quit, do you?" Luther said. He stubbed out his cigarette on Marty's lunch plate, and turned a page of his magazine.

Marty felt detonation approaching. He'd never liked Luther, but he'd taken months of sly remarks from the bastard because the system forbade the kind of response he really wanted to give. Now that system was crumbling, rapidly. Toy gone, dogs dead, heels on the kitchen table: who the hell cared any longer if he beat Luther to pulp?

"I want to know where Carys is."

"No lady by that name here."

Marty took a step toward the table. Luther seemed to sense that his repartee had gone sour. He slung down the magazine; the smile disappeared.

"Don't get edgy, man."

"Where is she?"

He smoothed the page in front of him, palm down across the sleek nude.

"She's gone," he said.

"Where?"

"Gone, man. That's all. You deaf, stupid, or both?"

Marty crossed the kitchen in one second flat and hauled Luther out of his chair. Like most spontaneous violence, there was no grace in it. The ragged attack threw them both off-balance. Luther half-fell back, an outflung arm catching a coffee cup, which leaped and smashed as they staggered across the kitchen. Finding his balance first, Luther brought his knee up into Marty's groin.

"Je-sus!"

"You get your fucking hands off me, man!" Luther yelled, panicked by the outburst. "I don't want no fight with you, right?" The demands became a plea for sanity—"Come on, man. Calm down."

Marty replied by launching himself at the other man, fists flying. A blow, more chance than intention, connected with Luther's face, and Marty followed through with three or four punches to stomach and chest. Luther, stepping back to avoid this assault, slid in cold coffee and fell. Breathless and bloodied, he stayed down on the floor where he was safe, while Marty, eyes streaming from the blow to his balls, rubbed his aching hands.

"Just tell me where she is . . ." he gasped.

Luther spat out a wad of blood-tinted phlegm before speaking.

"You're out of your fucking mind, man, you know that? I don't know where she's gone. Ask the big white father. He's the one who feeds her fucking heroin."

Of course; in that revelation lay the answer to half a dozen mysteries. It explained her reluctance to leave the old man; it explained her lassitude too, that inability to see beyond the next day, the next fix.

"And you supply the stuff? Is that it?"

"Maybe I do. But I never addicted her, man. I never did that. That was him; all along it was *him*! He did it to keep her. To fucking keep her. Bastard." It was spoken with genuine contempt. "What kind of father does that? I tell you, that fucker could teach us both a few lessons in dirty tricks." He paused to finger the inside of his mouth; he clearly had no intention of standing up again until Marty's bloodlust had subsided. "I don't ask no questions," he said. "All I know is I had to clear out her room this morning."

"Where's her stuff gone?"

He didn't answer for several seconds. "Burned most of it," he said finally.

"In God's name, why?"

"Old man's orders. You finished?"

Marty nodded. "I've finished."

"You and I," Luther said, "we never liked each other from the start. You know why?"

"Why?"

"We're both shit," he said grimly. "Worthless shit. Except I know what I am. I can even live with it. But you, you poor bastard, you think if you brown-nose around long enough one of these days someone's going to forgive you your trespasses."

Marty snorted mucus into his hand and wiped it on his jeans.

"Truth hurt?" Luther jibed.

"All right," Marty came back, "if you're so good with the truth maybe you can tell me what's going on around here."

"I told you: I don't ask questions."

"You never wondered?"

"Of course I fucking wondered. I wondered every day I brought the kid dope, or saw the old man sweat when it started to get dark. But why should there be any sense to it? He's a lunatic; that's your answer. He lost his marbles when his wife went. Too sudden. He couldn't take it. He's been out of his mind ever since."

"And that's enough to explain everything that's going on?"

Luther wiped a spot of bloody spittle off his chin with the back of his hand. "Hear no evil, speak no evil, see no evil," he said.

"I'm no monkey," Marty replied.

41

It wasn't until the middle of the evening that the old man would consent to see Marty. By that time the edge had been taken off his anger, which was presumably the intention of the delay. Whitehead had forsaken the study and the chair by the window tonight. He sat in the library instead. The only lamp that burned in the room had been placed a little way behind his chair. As a consequence, it was almost impossible to see his face, and his voice was so drained of color that no clue to his mood could be caught from it. But Marty had half-expected the theatrics, and was prepared for them. There were questions to be asked, and he wasn't about to be intimidated into silence.

"Where's Carys?" he demanded.

The head moved a little in the cove of the chair. The hands closed a book on his lap and placed it on the table. One of the science fiction paperbacks; light reading for a dark night.

"What business is it of yours?" Whitehead wanted to know.

Marty thought he'd predicted all the responses—bribery, prevarication—but this question, throwing the onus of inquiry back onto him, he hadn't expected. It begged other questions: did Whitehead know about his relationship with Carys, for instance? He'd tortured himself all afternoon with the idea that she'd told him everything, gone to the old man after that first night, and the subsequent nights, to report his every clumsiness, every naïveté.

"I need to know," he said.

"Well, I see no reason why you shouldn't be told," the dead voice replied, "though God knows it's a private hurt. Still, there are very few people I have left to confide in."

Marty tried to locate Whitehead's eyes, but the light behind the chair dazzled him. All he could do was listen to the even modulation of the voice, and try to dig out the implications beneath the flow.

"She's been taken away, Marty. At my request. Somewhere where her problems can be dealt with in a proper manner."

"The drugs?"

"You must have realized her addiction has worsened considerably in the last few weeks. I had hoped to contain it by giving her enough to keep her content, while slowly reducing her supply. It was working too, until recently." He sighed; a hand went up to his face. "I've been stupid. I should have conceded defeat a long time ago, and sent her to a clinic. But I didn't want to have her taken from me; it was as simple as that. Then last night—our visitors, the slaughter of the dogs—I realized how selfish I was, subjecting her to such pressures. It's too late in the day for possessiveness or pride. If people find out my daughter's a junkie, then so be it."

"I see."

"You were fond of her."

"Yes."

"She's a beautiful girl; and you're lonely. She spoke warmly of you. In time we'll have her back amongst us, I'm sure."

"I'd like to visit her."

"Again, in time. I'm told they demand isolation in the first few weeks of treatment. But rest assured, she's in good hands."

It was all so persuasive. But *lies*. Surely, lies. Carys' room had been stripped: was that in anticipation of her being "amongst them again" in a few weeks? This was all another fiction. Before Marty could protest, however, Whitehead was speaking again, a measured cadence.

"You're so close to me now, Marty. The way Bill used to be. In fact, I really think you should be welcomed into the inner circle, don't you? I'm having a dinner party next Sunday. I'd like you to be there. Our guest of honor." This was fine, flattering talk. Effortlessly, the old man had gained the upper hand. "In the week I think you should go down to London and buy yourself something decent to wear. I'm afraid my dinner parties are rather formal."

He reached for the paperback again and opened it.

"Here's a check." It lay in the fold of the book, already signed, ready for Marty. "It should cover the price of a good suit, shirts, shoes. Whatever else you want to treat yourself to." The check was proffered between fore and middle finger. "Take it, please."

Marty stepped forward and took the check.

"Thank you."

"It can be cashed at my bank in the Strand. They'll be expecting you. Whatever you don't spend, I want you to gamble."

"Sir?" Marty wasn't certain he was hearing the invitation properly.

"I *insist* you gamble it, Marty. Horses, cards, whatever you like. Enjoy it. Would you do that for me? And when you come back you can make an old man envious with tales of your adventures."

So it *was* bribery after all. The fact of the check made Marty more certain than ever that the old man was lying about Carys, but he lacked the courage to press the issue. It wasn't just cowardice, however, that made him hold back: it was burgeoning excitement. He had been bribed twice. Once with the money; again with the invitation to gamble it. It was years since he'd had a chance like this. Money in abundance, and time on his hands. The day might come when he'd hate Papa for waking the virus in his system: but before then a fortune could be won and lost and won again. He stood in front of the old man with the fever already on him.

"You're a good man, Strauss." Whitehead's words rose from the shadowed chair like a prophet's from a cleft rock. Though he couldn't see the potentate's face, Marty knew he was smiling.

42

Despite her years on the sunshine island, Carys had a healthy sense of reality. Or had, until they took her to that cold, bare house on Caliban Street. There, nothing was certain anymore. It was Mamoulian's doing. That, perhaps, was the only thing that was certain. Houses weren't haunted, only human minds.

Whatever moved in the air there, or flitted along the bare boards with the dust balls and the cockroaches, whatever scintillated, like light on water, at the corners of her eyes, it was all of Mamoulian's manufacture.

For three days after her arrival at the new house she had refused even to speak to her host or captor, whichever he was. She couldn't recall why she'd come, but she knew he'd conned her into it—his mind breathing at her neck—and she'd resented his manipulations. Breer, the fat one, had brought her food, and, on the second day, dope too, but she wouldn't eat or say a word. The room they'd locked her in was quite comfortable. She had books, and a television too, but the atmosphere was too unstable for her to be at ease. She couldn't read, nor could she watch the inanities on the box. Sometimes she found it difficult to remember her own name; it was as if his constant proximity was wiping her clean. Perhaps he could do that. After all, he'd got into her head, hadn't he? Surreptitiously wormed his way into her psyche God knows how many times. He'd been in her, *in her* for Christ's sake, and she'd never known.

"Don't be frightened."

It was three A.M. on the fourth day, and another sleepless night. He had come into her room so silently she'd looked down to see if his feet were making contact with the floor.

"I hate this place," she informed him.

"Would you like to explore, rather than being locked up in here?"

"It's haunted," she said, expecting him to laugh at her. He didn't, however. So she went on. "Are you the ghost?"

"What I am is a mystery," he replied, "even to myself." His voice was softened by introspection. "But I'm no ghost. You may be certain of that. Don't fear me, Carys. Anything you feel, I share, in some measure."

She remembered acutely this man's revulsion at the sex act. What a pale, sickly thing he was, for all his powers. She couldn't bring herself to hate him, though she had reason enough.

"I don't like to be *used*," she said.

"I did you no harm. I do you no harm *now*, do I?"

"I want to see Marty."

Mamoulian had started to try to clench his mutilated hand. "I'm afraid that's not possible," he said. The scar tissue of his hand, pulled tight, shone, but the mishealed anatomy wouldn't give.

"Why not? Why won't you let me see him?"

"You'll have everything you need. Ample supplies of food; of heroin."

It suddenly crossed her mind that Marty might be on the European's execution list. Might, in fact, already be dead.

"Please don't harm him," she said.

"Thieves come and thieves go," he replied. "I can't be responsible for what happens to him."

"I'll never forgive you," she said.

"Yes you will," he replied, his voice so soft now it was practically illusory. "I'm your protector now, Carys. Had I been allowed, I would have nurtured you from childhood, and you would have been spared the humiliations he's made you suffer. But it's too late. All I can do is shelter you from further corruption."

He gave up trying to make a fist. She saw how the wounded hand disgusted him. He would cut it off if he could, she thought; it's not just sex he loathes, it's flesh.

"No more," he said, apropos of the hand, or debate, or nothing at all.

When he left her to sleep, he didn't lock the door behind him.

The next day, she began her exploration of the house. There was nothing very remarkable about the place; it was simply a large, empty, three-story house. In the street beyond the dirty windows ordinary people passed by, too locked in their heads even to glance around. Though her first instinct was to knock on the glass, to mouth some appeal to them, the urge was easily conquered by reason. If she slipped away what would she be escaping from, or to? She had safety here, of a kind, and drugs. Though at first she resisted them, they were too attractive to flush away down the toilet. And after a few days of the pills, she gave in to the heroin too. It came in steady supply: never too much, never too little, and always good stuff.

Only Breer, the fat one, upset her. He would come, some days, and watch her, his eyes sloppy in his head like partially poached eggs. She told Mamoulian about him, and the next day he didn't linger; just brought the pills and hurried away. And the days flowed into one another; and sometimes she didn't remember where she was or how she'd got here; sometimes she remembered her name, sometimes not. Once, maybe twice, she tried to think her way to Marty, but he was too far from her. Either that, or the house subdued her powers. Whichever, her thoughts lost their way a few miles from Caliban Street, and she returned there sweating and afraid.

She had been in the house almost a week when things took a turn for the worse.

I'd like you to do something for me," the European said.

"What?"

"I'd like you to find Mr. Toy. You do remember Mr. Toy?"

Of course she remembered. Not well, but she remembered. His broken nose, those cautious eyes that had always looked at her so sadly.

"Do you think you could locate him?"

"I don't know how to."

"Let your mind go to him. You know the way, Carys."

"Why can't *you* do it?"

"Because he'll be expecting me. He'll have defenses, and I'm too tired to fight with him at the moment."

"Is he afraid of you?"

"Probably."

"Why?"

"You were a babe in arms when Mr. Toy and I last met. He and I parted as enemies; he presumes we are still enemies . . ."

"You're going to harm him," she said.

"That's my business, Carys."

She stood, sliding up the wall against which she'd been slumped.

"I don't think I want to find him for you."

"Aren't we friends?"

"No," she said. "No. Never."

"Come now."

He stepped toward her. The broken hand touched her: the contact was feather-light.

"I think you *are* a ghost," she said.

She left him standing in the corridor, and went up to the bathroom to think this through, locking the door behind her. She knew without a shadow of a doubt that he'd harm Toy if she led him to the man.

"Carys," he said quietly. He was outside the bathroom door. His proximity made her scalp creep.

"You can't make me," she said.

"Don't tempt me."

Suddenly the European's face loomed in her head. He spoke again: "I knew you before you could walk, Carys. I've held you in my arms, often. You've sucked on my thumb." He was speaking with his lips close to the door; his low voice reverberated in the wood she had her back against.

"It's no fault of yours or mine that we were parted. Believe me, I'm glad you carry your father's gifts, because he never used them. He never once understood the wisdom there was to be found with them. He squandered it all: for fame, for wealth. But you . . . I could *teach* you, Carys. Such things."

The voice was so seductive it seemed to reach through the door and enfold her, the way his arms had, so many years ago. She was suddenly minute in his grasp; he cooed at her, made foolish faces to bring a cherubic smile to bloom.

"Just find Toy for me. Is it so much to ask for all my favors to you?"

She found herself rocking with the rhythm of his cradling.

"Toy never loved you," he was saying, "nobody has *ever* loved you."

That was a lie: and a tactical error. The words were cold water on her sleepy face. She *was* loved! Marty loved her. The runner; *her* runner.

Mamoulian sensed his miscalculation.

"Don't defy me," he said; the cooing had gone from his voice.

"Go to Hell," she replied.

"As you wish . . ."

There was a falling note in his words, as though the issue was closed and done with. He didn't leave his station by the door, however. She felt him close. Was he waiting for her to tire, and come out? she wondered. Persuasion by physical violence wasn't his style, surely; unless he was going to use Breer. She hardened herself against the possibility. She'd claw his watery eyes out.

Minutes passed, and she was sure the European was still outside though she could hear neither movement nor breath.

And then, the pipes began to rumble. Somewhere in the system, a tide was moving. The sink made a sucking sound, the water in the toilet bowl splashed, the toilet lid flapped open and slammed closed again as a gust of fetid air was discharged from below. This was his doing somehow, though it seemed a vacuous exercise. The toilet farted again: the smell was noxious.

"What's happening?" she asked under her breath.

A gruel of filth had started to seep over the lip of the toilet and dribble onto the floor. Wormy shapes moved in it. She shut her eyes. This was a fabrication, conjured up by the European to subdue her mutiny: she would ignore it. But even with canceled sight the illusion persisted. The water splashed more loudly as the flood rose, and in the stream she heard wet heavy things flopping onto the bathroom floor.

"Well?" said Mamoulian.

She cursed the illusions and their charmer in one vitriolic breath.

Something skittered across her bare foot. She was damned if she was going to open her eyes and give him another sense to assault, but curiosity forced them open.

The dribbles from the toilet had become a stream, as if the sewers had backed up and were discharging their contents at her feet. Not simply excrement and water; the soup of hot dirt had bred monsters. Creatures that could be found in no sane zoology: things that had been fish once, crabs once; fetuses flushed down clinic drains before their mothers could wake to scream; beasts that fed on excrement whose bodies were a pun on what they devoured. Everywhere in the silt forsaken stuff, offal and dregs, raised itself on queasy limbs and flapped and paddled toward her.

"Make them go away," she said.

They had no intention of retreat. The scummy tide still edged forward: the fauna the toilet was vomiting up was getting larger.

"Find Toy," the voice on the other side of the door bargained. Her sweaty hands slid on the handle, but the door refused to open. There was no hint of a reprieve.

"Let me *out*."

"Just say yes."

She flattened herself against the door. The toilet lid flew open in the strongest gust yet, and this time stayed open. The flood thickened and the pipes creaked as something that was almost too large for them began to force its way toward the light. She heard its claws rake the sides of the pipes, she heard the chatter of its teeth.

"Say yes."

"No."

A glistening arm was thrown up from the belching bowl, and flailed around until its digits fixed on the sink. Then it began to haul itself up, its water-rotted bones rubbery.

"*Please!*" she screamed.

"Just say yes."

"Yes! Yes! Anything! *Yes!*"

As she spat out the words the handle of the door moved. She turned her back on the emerging horror and put her weight down on the handle at the same time as her other hand fumbled with the key. Behind her, she heard the sound of a body contorting itself to fetch itself free. She turned the key the wrong way, and then the right. Muck splashed on her shin. It was almost at her heels. As she opened the door sodden fingers snatched at her ankle, but she threw herself out of the bathroom before it could catch her, and onto the landing, slamming the door behind her.

Mamoulian, his victory won, had gone.

After that, she couldn't bring herself to go back into the bathroom. At her request the Razor-Eater supplied a bucket for her to use, which he brought and took away again with reverence.

The European never spoke of the incident again. There was no need. That night she did as he had asked her. She opened up her head and went to look for Bill Toy and, within a matter of minutes, she found him. So, soon after, did the Last European.

43

Not since the halcyon days of his big wins at the casinos had Marty possessed so much money as he did now. Two thousand pounds was no fortune to Whitehead, but it raised Marty to blind heights. Perhaps the old man's story about Carys *had* been a lie. If so, he'd wheedle the truth out of him in time. Slowee, slowee, catchee monkey, as Feaver used to say. What would Feaver say to see Marty now, with money lapping at his feet?

He left the car near Euston, and caught a cab to the Strand to cash the check. Then he went in search of a good evening suit. Whitehead had suggested an outfitter off Regent Street. The fitters treated him with some brusqueness at first, but once he showed them the color of his money the tune changed to sycophancy. Curbing his smiles, Marty played the fastidious buyer; they fawned and fussed; he let them. Only after three-quarters of an hour of their fey attentions did he alight on something he liked: a conservative choice, but immaculately styled. The suit, and the accompanying wardrobe—shoes, shirts, a selection of ties—bit more deeply into the cash than he'd anticipated, but he let it go, like water, through his fingers. The suit, and one set of accoutrements, he took with him. The rest he had sent to the Sanctuary.

It was lunchtime when he emerged, and he wandered around looking for somewhere to eat. There'd been a Chinese restaurant on Gerard Street that he and Charmaine had frequented whenever funds allowed: he returned there now. Though its façade had been modernized to accommodate a large neon sign, the interior was much the same; the food as good as he remembered. He sat in splendid isolation and ate and drank his way through the menu, happy to play the rich man to the hilt. He ordered half a dozen cigars after the meal, downed several brandies and tipped like a millionaire. Papa would be proud of me, he thought. When he was full, drunk and satisfied, he headed out into the balmy afternoon. It was time he followed the rest of Whitehead's instructions.

He made his way through Soho, wandering for a few minutes until he found a betting office. As he entered the smoky interior, guilt assailed him, but he told his spoilsport conscience to go hang. He was obeying orders in coming here.

There were races at Newmarket, Kempton Park and Doncaster—each name evoked some bittersweet association— and he bet freely on every one on the board. Soon the old enthusiasm had killed the last smidgen of guilt. It was like living, this game, but it tasted stronger. It dramatized, with its promised gains, its too-easy losses, the sense he had had as a child of what adult life must be like. Of how, once one grew out of boredom and into the secret, bearded, erectile world of manhood, every word would be loaded with risk and promise, every breath taken won in the face of extraordinary odds.

At first, the money dribbled away from him; he didn't bet heavily, but the frequency of the losses began to dwindle his reserves. Then, three-quarters of an hour into the session things took a turn for the better; horses he plucked from thin air romped home at ridiculous odds, one after the other. In one race he made back what he'd lost in the previous two, and more. The enthusiasm turned to euphoria. This was the very feeling he'd tried so hard to describe to Whitehead—of being in charge of chance.

Finally, the wins began to bore him. Pocketing his winnings without taking any proper account of them, he left. The money in his jacket was a thick wedge; it ached to be spent. On instinct, he sauntered through the crowds to Oxford Street, selected an expensive shop, and bought a nine-hundred-pound fur coat for Charmaine, then hailed a cab to take it to her. It was a slow journey; the wage-slaves were beginning to make their escape, and the roads were snarled. But his mood forbade irritation.

He had the taxi drop him off at the corner of the street, because he wanted to walk the length of it. Things had changed since he'd last been here, two and a half months before. Early spring was now early summer. Now, at almost six in the evening, the warmth of the day hadn't dissipated; there was growing time in it still. Nor, he thought, was it just the season that had advanced, become riper; he had too.

He felt real. God in Heaven, that was it. At last he was able to operate in the world again, affect it, shape it.

Charmaine came to the door looking flustered. She looked more flustered still when Marty stepped in, kissed her, and put the coat box in her arms.

"Here. I bought you something."

She frowned. "What is it, Marty?"

"Take a look. It's for you."

"No," she said. "I can't."

The front door was still open. She was ushering him back toward it, or at least attempting to. But he wouldn't go. There was something beneath the look of embarrassment on her face: anger, panic even. She pressed the box back at him, unopened.

"Please go," she said.

"It's a surprise," he told her, determined not to be repelled.

"I don't want any surprises. Just go. Ring me tomorrow."

He wouldn't take the proffered box, and it fell between them, breaking open. The sumptuous gleam of the coat spilled out; she couldn't help but stoop to pick it up.

"Oh, Marty . . ." she whispered.

As he looked down at her gleaming hair someone appeared at the top of the stairs.

"What's the problem?"

Marty looked up. Flynn was standing on the half-landing, dressed only in underwear and socks. He was unshaven. For a few seconds he said nothing, juggling the options. Then the smile, his panacea, swarmed across his face.

"Marty," he exclaimed, "what's buzzing?"

Marty looked at Charmaine, who was looking at the floor. She had the coat in her arms, bundled up like a dead animal.

"I see," Marty said.

Flynn descended a few stairs. His eyes were bloodshot.

"It's not what you think. Really it isn't," he said, stopping halfway down, waiting to see which way Marty would jump.

"It's exactly what you think, Marty," Charmaine said quietly. "I'm sorry you had to find out like this, but you never rang. I said ring before you come round."

"How long?" Marty murmured.

"Two years, more or less."

Marty glanced up at Flynn. They'd played together with that black girl—Ursula, was it?—only a few weeks past, and when the milk was spilt Flynn had slid away. He'd come back here, to Charmaine. Had he washed, Marty wondered, before he'd joined Charmaine in their double bed? Probably not.

"Why him?" he found himself asking. "Why him, for Christ's sake? Couldn't you have improved on that?"

Flynn said nothing in his own defense.

"I think you should leave, Marty," Charmaine said, clumsily attempting to rebox the coat.

"He's such a shit," Marty said. "Can't you see what a shit he is?"

"*He was there*," she retorted bitterly. "You weren't."

"He's a fucking pimp, for Christ's sake!"

"Yes," she said, letting the box lie, and standing up at last, eyes furious, to spit all the truth out. "Yes, that's right. Why do you think I took up with him?"

"No, Char—"

"Hard times, Marty. Nothing to live on but fresh air and love letters."

She'd whored for him; the fucker had made her whore. On the stairs, Flynn had gone a sickly color. "Hold up, Marty," he said. "No way did I make her do a damn thing she didn't want to do."

Marty moved to the bottom of the stairs.

"Isn't that right?" Flynn appealed to Charmaine. "Tell him, woman! Did I make you do a thing you didn't want to do?"

"*Dont*," Charmaine said, but Marty was already starting up the stairs. Flynn stood his ground for two steps only, then retreated backward. "Hey, come on . . ." Palms up, to keep the blows at bay.

"You made my wife a whore?"

"Would I do that?"

"*You made my wife a fucking whore?*"

Flynn turned and made a bid for the landing. Marty stumbled up the stairs after him.

"Bastard!"

The escape ploy worked: Flynn was safely behind the door and wedging a chair against it before Marty could get to the landing. All he could do was beat on the panels, demanding, uselessly, that Flynn let him in. But it took only a small interruption to spoil his anger. By the time Charmaine got to the top of the stairs he'd left off haranguing the door, and was leaning back on the wall, eyes stinging. She said nothing; she had neither the means nor the desire to cross the chasm between them.

"Him," was all he could say. "Of all people."

"He's been very good to me," she replied. She had no intention of pleading their case; Marty was the intruder here. She owed him no apology.

"It wasn't as if I walked out."

"It was your doing, Marty. You lost for *both* of us. I never got a say in the matter." She was trembling, he saw, with fury, not with sorrow. "You gambled everything we had. Every damn thing. And lost it for us both."

"We're not dead."

"I'm thirty-two. I feel twice that."

"He makes you tired."

"You're so stupid," she said, without feeling; her cool contempt withered him. "You never saw how fragile everything was: you just went on being the way it suited you to be. Stupid and selfish."

Marty bit at his upper lip, watching her mouth as it spoke the truth at him. He wanted to hit her, but that wouldn't make her any less right; just bruised and right. Shaking his head, he stepped past her and thundered down the stairs. She was silent above.

He passed the box, the discarded fur. They could fuck on it, he thought: Flynn would like that. He picked up the bag containing his suit, and left. The glass in the window rattled he slammed the door so hard.

"You can come out now," Charmaine said to the closed bedroom door. "The shooting's over."

44

Marty couldn't get one particular thought out of his head: that she'd told Flynn all about him: spilling the secrets of their life together. He pictured Flynn lying on the bed with his socks on, stroking her, and laughing, as she poured out all the dirt. How Marty'd spent all the money on horses or poker; how he'd never had a winning streak in his life that lasted more than five minutes (you should have seen me today, he wanted to tell her, things are different now, I'm shit-hot now); how he was only good in bed on the infrequent occasions that he'd won and uninterested the rest of the time; how he'd first lost the car to Macnamara, then the television, then the best of the furniture, and still owed a small fortune. How he'd then gone out and tried to steal his way out of debt. Even that had failed miserably.

He lived the pursuit again, sharp as ever. The car smelling of the shotgun Nygaard was nursing; the sweat on Marty's face pricking in his pores as it cooled in the draft from the open window, fluttering up into his face like petals. It was all so clear, it might have happened yesterday. Everything since then, almost a decade of his life, pivoted on those few minutes. It made him almost physically sick to think of it. Waste. All waste.

It was time to get drunk. The money he had left in his pocket— still well into four figures—was burning a hole, demanding to be spent or gambled. He wandered down to the Commercial Road, and hailed another cab, not entirely certain of what to do next. It was barely seven; the night ahead needed careful planning. What would Papa do? he thought. Betrayed and shat on, what would the great man do?

Whatever his heart desired, came the answer; whatever his fucking heart desired.

He went to Euston Station and spent half an hour in the bathroom there, washing and changing into the new shirt and new suit, emerging transformed. The clothes he'd been wearing he gave to the attendant, along with a ten-pound note.

Some of the old mellowness had crept back into his system by the time he'd changed. He liked what the mirror told him: the evening might turn out to be a winner yet, as long as he didn't whip it too hard. He drank in Covent Garden, enough to lace his blood and breath with spirits, then had a meal in an Italian restaurant. When he came out the theaters were emptying; he garnered a clutch of appreciative glances, mostly from middle-aged women and well-coiffured young men. I probably look like a gigolo, he thought; there was a disparity between his dress and his face that signaled a man playing a role. The thought pleased him. From now on he would play Martin Strauss, man of the world, with all the bravura he could muster. Being himself had not got him very far. Perhaps a fiction would improve his rate of advancement.

He idled down Charing Cross Road and into the tangle of traffic and pedestrians at Trafalgar Square. There'd been a fight on the steps on St. Martin's-in-the-Field; two men were exchanging curses and accusations while their wives looked on.

Off the square, at the back of the Mall, the traffic quietened. It took him several minutes to orient himself. He knew where he was going, and had thought he knew how to get there, but now he wasn't so certain. It was a long time since he'd been in the area, and when he eventually hit the small mews that contained the Academy—Bill Toy's club—it was more by chance than design.

His heart beat a little faster as he sauntered up the steps. Ahead lay a major piece of playacting, which, if it failed, would ruin the evening. He paused a moment to light a cigar, then entered.

In his time he'd frequented a number of high-class casinos; this one had the same slightly passé grandeur as others he'd been in; dark-wood paneling, damson carpeting, portraits of forgotten luminaries on the walls. Hand in trouser pocket, jacket unbuttoned to reveal the gloss of the lining, he crossed the mosaic foyer to the desk. Security would be tight: the moneyed expected safety. He wasn't a member, nor could expect to become one on the spot: not without sponsors and references. The only way he'd get a good night's gaming was by bluffing his way through.

The English rose at the desk smiled promisingly. "Good evening, sir."

"How are you tonight?"

Her smile didn't falter for a moment, even though she couldn't possibly know who he was.

"Well. And you?"

"Lovely night. Is Bill here yet?"

"I'm sorry, sir?"

"Mr. Toy. Has he arrived yet?"

"Mr. Toy." She consulted the guest book, running a lacquered finger down the list of tonight's gamblers. "I don't think he's—"

"He won't have signed in," Marty said. "He's a member, for God's sake." The slight irritation in his voice took the girl off-balance.

"Oh . . . I see. I don't think I know him."

"Well, no matter. I'll just go straight up. Tell him I'm at the tables, will you?"

"Wait, sir. I haven't—"

She reached out, as if to tug at his sleeve, but thought better of it. He flashed her a disarming smile as he started up the stairs.

"Who shall I say?"

"Mr. Strauss," he said, affecting a tiny barb of exasperation.

"Yes. Of course." Artificial recognition flooded her face. "I'm sorry, Mr. Strauss. It's just that—"

"No problem," he replied, benignly, as he left her below, staring up at him.

It took him only a few minutes to acquaint himself with the

layout of the rooms. Roulette, poker, blackjack; all and more were available. The atmosphere was serious: frivolity was not welcome where money could be won or lost on such a scale. If the men and few women who haunted these hushed enclaves were here to enjoy themselves they showed no sign of it. This was work; hard, serious work. There were some quiet exchanges on the stairs and in the corridors—and of course calls from the tables, otherwise the interior was almost reverentially subdued.

He sauntered from room to room, standing on the fringe of one game then another, familiarizing himself with the etiquette of the place. Nobody gave him more than a glance; he fitted into this obsessive's paradise too well.

Anticipation of the moment when he eventually sat down to join a game exhilarated him; he indulged it awhile longer. He had all night to enjoy, after all, and he knew only too well that the money in his pocket would disappear in minutes if he wasn't careful. He went into the bar, ordered a whisky and water, and scanned his fellow drinkers. They were all here for the same reason: to pit their wits against chance. Most drank alone, psyching themselves up for the games ahead. Later, when fortunes had been won, there might be dancing on the tables, an impromptu striptease from a drunken mistress. But it was early yet.

The waiter appeared. A young man, twenty at most, with a mustache that looked drawn on; he'd already achieved that mixture of obsequiousness and superiority that marked his profession.

"I'm sorry, sir—" he said.

Marty's stomach lurched. Was somebody going to call his bluff?

"Yes?"

"Scotch or bourbon, sir?"

"Oh. Er . . . Scotch."

"Very well, sir."

"Bring it to the table."

"Where will you be, sir?"

"Roulette."

The waiter withdrew. Marty went to the cashier and bought eight hundred pounds of chips, then went into the roulette room.

He'd never been much of a card-player. It required techniques that he'd always been too bored to learn; and much as he admired the skill of great players, that very skill blurred the essential confrontation. A good card-player *used* luck, a great one rode it. But roulette, though it too had its systems and its techniques, was a purer game. Nothing had the glamor of the spinning wheel: its numbers blurring, the ball rattling as it lodged and jumped again.

He sat down at the table between a highly perfumed Arab who spoke only French, and an American. Neither said a word to him: there were no welcomes or farewells here. All the niceties of human intercourse were sacrificed to the matter at hand.

It was an odd disease. Its symptoms were like infatuation— palpitations, sleeplessness. Its only certain cure, death. On one or two occasions he'd caught sight of himself in a casino bar mirror or in the glass of the cashier's booth, and met a hunted, hungry look. But nothing—not self-disgust, not the disparagement of friends—nothing had ever quite rooted out the appetite.

The waiter brought the drink to his elbow, its ice clinking. Marty tipped him heavily.

There was a spin of the wheel, though Marty had joined the table too late to place money. All eyes were fixed on the circling numbers . . .

It was an hour or more before Marty left the table, and then only to relieve his bladder before returning to his seat. Players came and went. The American, indulging the aquiline youth who accompanied him, had left the decisions to his companion, and lost a small fortune before retiring. Marty's reserves were running low. He'd won, and lost, and won; then lost and lost and lost. The defeats didn't distress him overmuch. It wasn't his money, and as Whitehead had often observed, there was plenty more where that came from. With enough chips left for one more bet of any consequence, he withdrew from the table for a breather. He'd sometimes found that he could change his luck by retiring from the field for a few minutes and returning with new focus.

As he got up from his seat, his eyes full of numbers, somebody walked past the door of the roulette room and glanced in before moving on to another game. Fleeting seconds were enough for recognition.

When Marty'd last met that face it had been ill-shaven and waxen with pain, lit by the floods along the Sanctuary fence. Now Mamoulian was transformed. No longer the derelict, cornered and anguished. Marty found himself walking toward the door like a man hypnotized. The waiter was at his side—"Another drink, sir?"—but the inquiry went ignored as Marty stepped out of the roulette room and into the corridor. Contrary feelings ran in him: he was half-afraid to confirm his sighting of the man, yet curiously excited that the man was here. It was no coincidence, surely. Perhaps Toy was with him. Perhaps the whole mystery would unravel here and now. He caught sight of Mamoulian walking into the baccarat room. A particularly fierce match was going on there, and spectators had drifted in to watch its closing stages. The room was full; players from other tables had deserted their own games to enjoy the battle at hand. Even the waiters were lingering on the periphery trying to catch a glimpse.

Mamoulian threaded his way through the crowd to get a better view, his thin gray figure parting the throng. Having found himself a vantage point he stood, light shining up from the baize onto his pale face. The wounded hand was lodged in his jacket pocket, out of sight; the wide brow was clear of the least expression. Marty watched him for upward of five minutes. Not once did the European's eyes flicker from the game in front of him. He was like a piece of porcelain: a glazed façade onto which a nonchalant artisan had scrawled a few lines. The eyes pressed into the clay were incapable, it seemed, of anything but that relentless stare. Yet there was power in the man. It was uncanny to see how people kept clear of him, cramming themselves into knots rather than press too close to him at the tableside.

Across the room, Marty caught sight of the pen-mustache waiter. He pushed his way between the spectators to where the young man stood.

"A word," he whispered.

"Yes, sir?"

"That man. In the gray suit."

The waiter glanced toward the table, then back to Marty.

"Mr. Mamoulian."

"Yes. What do you know about him?"

The waiter gave Marty a reproving look.

"I'm sorry, sir. We're not at liberty to discuss members."

He turned on his heel and went into the corridor. Marty followed. It was empty. Downstairs, the girl on the desk—not the same he'd spoken with—was giggling with the coat-check clerk.

"Wait a moment."

When the waiter looked back, Marty was producing his wallet, still amply enough filled to present a decent bribe. The other man stared at the notes with undisguised greed.

"I just want to ask a few questions. I don't need the number of his bank account."

"I don't know it anyway." The waiter smirked. "Are you police?"

"I'm just interested in Mr. Mamoulian," Marty said, proffering fifty pounds in tens. "Some bare essentials."

The waiter snatched the money and pocketed it with the speed of a practiced bribee.

"Ask away," he said.

"Is he a regular here?"

"A couple of times a month."

"To play?"

The waiter frowned.

"Now you mention it I don't think I've ever seen him actually play."

"Just to watch, then?"

"Well, I can't be sure. But I think if he did play I'd have seen him by now. Strange. Still, we have a few members who do that."

"And does he have any friends? People he arrives with, leaves with?"

"Not that I remember. He used to be quite pally with a Greek woman who used to come in. Always won a fortune. Never failed."

That was the gambler's equivalent of the fisherman's tale, the story of the player with a system so flawless it never faltered. Marty had heard it a hundred times, always the friend of a friend, a mythical somebody whom you never got to meet face-to-face. And yet, when he thought of Mamoulian's face, so calculating in its supreme indifference, he could almost imagine the fiction real.

"Why are you so interested in him?" the waiter asked.

"I have an odd feeling about him."

"You're not the only one."

"What do you mean?"

"He's never said or done anything to me, you understand," the waiter explained. "He always tips well, though God knows all he ever drinks is distilled water. But we had one fellow came here, this is a couple of years ago now, he was American, over from Boston. He saw Mamoulian and let me tell you—he freaked out. Seems he'd played with a guy who was his spitting image, this is in the 1920s. That caused quite a buzz. I mean, he doesn't look like the type to have a father, does he?"

The waiter had something there. It was impossible to imagine this Mamoulian as a child or a pimply adolescent. Had he suffered infatuation, the death of pets, of parents? It seemed so unlikely as to be laughable.

"That's all I know, really."

"Thank you," said Marty. It was enough.

The waiter walked away, leaving Marty with an armful of

possibilities. Apocryphal tales, most likely: the Greek with the system, the panicking American. A man like Mamoulian was bound to collect rumors; his air of lost aristocracy invited invented histories. Like an onion, unwrapped and unwrapped and unwrapped again, each skin giving way not to the core but to another skin.

Tired, and dizzy with too much drink and too little sleep, Marty decided to call it a night. He'd use the hundred or so left in his wallet to bribe a taxi driver to drive him back to the estate, and leave the car to be picked up another day. He was too drunk to drive. He glanced one final time into the baccarat room. The game was still going on; Mamoulian had not moved from his station.

Marty went downstairs to the bathroom. It was a few degrees colder than the interior of the club, its rococo plasterwork facetious in the face of its lowly function. He glanced at his weariness in the mirror, then went to relieve himself at the urinal.

In one of the stalls, somebody had begun to sob, very quietly, as if attempting to stifle the sound. Despite his aching bladder, Marty found he was unable to piss; the anonymous grief distressed him too much. It was coming from behind the locked door of the stalls. Probably some optimist who'd lost his shirt on a roll of the dice, and was now contemplating the consequences. Marty left him to it. There was nothing he could say or do; he knew that from bitter experience.

Out in the foyer, the woman on the desk called after him.

"Mr. Strauss?" It was the English rose. She showed no sign of wilting, despite the hour. "Did you find Mr. Toy?"

"No, I didn't."

"Oh, that's odd. He was here."

"Are you sure?"

"Yes. He came with Mr. Mamoulian. I told him you were here, and that you'd asked after him."

"And what did he say?"

"Nothing," the girl replied. "Not a word." She dropped her

voice. "Is he well? I mean, he looked really terrible, if you don't mind me saying so. Awful color."

Marty glanced up the stairs, scanned the landing.

"Is he still here?"

"Well, I haven't been on the desk all evening, but I didn't see him leave."

Marty took the stairs two at a time. He wanted to see Toy so much. There were questions to ask, confidences to exchange. He scoured the rooms, looking for that worn-leather face. But though Mamoulian was still there, sipping his water, Toy was not with him. Nor was he to be found in any of the bars. He had clearly come and gone. Disappointed, Marty went back downstairs, thanked the girl for her help, tipped her well, and left.

It was only when he had put a good distance between himself and the Academy, walking in the middle of the road to waylay the first available taxi, that he remembered the sobbing in the bathroom. His pace slowed. Eventually he stopped in the street, his head echoing to the thump of his heart. Was it just hindsight, or had that ragged voice sounded familiar, as it chewed on its grief? Had it been Toy sitting there in the questionable privacy of a toilet stall, crying like a lost child?

Dreamily, Marty glanced back the way he'd come. If he suspected Toy was still at the club, shouldn't he go back and find out? But his head was making unpleasant connections. The woman at the Pimlico number whose voice was too horrid to listen to; the desk-girl's question: "Is he well?"; the profundity of despair he had heard from behind the locked door. No, he couldn't go back. Nothing, not even the promise of a faultless system to beat every table in the house, would induce him to return. There was, after all, such a thing as reasonable doubt; and on occasion it could be a balm without equal.

VIII. RAISING CAIN

45

The day of the Last Supper, as he was to come to think of it, Marty shaved three times, once in the morning and twice in the afternoon. The initial flattery of the invitation had long since faded. Now all he prayed for was some convenient get-out clause, a means by which he could politely escape what he was certain would be an excruciating evening. He had no place in Whitehead's entourage. Their values were not his; their world was one in which he was no more than a functionary. There could be nothing about him that would give them more than a moment's entertainment.

It wasn't until he put on the evening jacket again that he began to feel more courageous. In this world of appearances, why shouldn't he carry off the illusion as well as the next man? After all, he'd succeeded at the Academy. The trick was to get the superficies right—the proper dress code, the correct direction in which to pass the port. He began to view the evening ahead as a test of his wits, and his competitive spirit began to rise to the challenge. He would play them at their own game, among the clinking glasses and the chatter of opera and high finance.

Triply shaved, dressed and cologned, he went down to the kitchen. Oddly, Pearl wasn't in the house: Luther had been left in charge of the night's gourmandizing. He was opening bottles of wine: the room was fragrant with the mingled bouquets. Though Marty had understood the gathering to be small, several dozen bottles were assembled on the table; the labels on many were dirtied to illegibility. It looked as though the cellar were being stripped of its finest vintages.

Luther looked Marty up and down.

"Who'd you steal the suit off?"

Marty picked up one of the open bottles and sniffed it, ignoring the remark. Tonight he wasn't going to be needled: tonight he had things figured out, and he'd let no one burst the bubble.

"I said: where'd you—"

"I heard you first time. I bought it."

"What with?"

Marty put the bottle down heavily. Glasses on the table clinked together.

"Why don't you shut up?"

Luther shrugged. "Old man give it to you?"

"I told you. Shove it."

"Seems to me you're getting in deep, man. You know you're guest of honor at this shindig?"

"I'm going along to meet some of the old man's friends, that's all."

"You mean Dwoskin and those fuckheads? Aren't you the lucky one?"

"And what are you tonight: the wine-boy?"

Luther grimaced as he pulled the cork on another bottle. "They don't have no waiters at their special parties. They're *very* private."

"What do you mean?"

"What do I know?" Luther said, shrugging. "I'm a monkey, right?"

B etween eight and eight-thirty, the cars started to arrive at the Sanctuary. Marty waited in his room for a summons to join the rest of the guests. He heard Curtsinger's voice, and those of women; there was laughter, some of it shrill. He wondered if it was just the wives they'd brought, or their daughters too.

The phone rang.

"Marty." It was Whitehead.

"Sir?"

"Why not come up and join us? We're waiting for you."

"Right."

"We're in the white room." Another surprise. That bare room, with its ugly altarpiece, seemed an unlikely venue for a dinner party.

Evening was drawing on outside, and before going on up to the room, Marty switched the lawn floods on. They blazed, their illumination echoing through the house. His earlier trepidation had been entirely replaced by a mixture of defiance and fatalism. As long as he didn't spit in the soup, he told himself, he'd get through.

"Come on in, Marty."

The atmosphere inside the white room was already chokingly thick with cigar and cigarette smoke. No attempt had been made to prettify the place. The only decoration was the triptych: its crucifixion as vicious as Marty remembered it. Whitehead stood as Marty entered, and extended his hand in welcome, an almost garish smile on his face.

"Close the door, will you? Come on in and sit down."

There was a single empty place at the table. Marty went to it.

"You know Felix, of course."

Ottaway, the fan-dancing lawyer, nodded. The bare bulb threw light on his pate, and exposed the line of his toupee.

"And Lawrence."

Dwoskin—the lean and trollish—was in the middle of a sip of wine. He murmured a greeting.

"And James."

"Hello," said Curtsinger. "How nice to see you again." The cigar he held was just about the largest Marty had ever set eyes on.

The familiar faces accounted for, Whitehead introduced the three women who sat between the men.

"Our guests for tonight," he said.

"Hello."

"This is my sometime bodyguard, Martin Strauss."

"Martin." Oriana, a woman in her mid-thirties, gave him a slightly crooked smile. "Pleased to meet you."

Whitehead used no second name, which left Marty wondering if this was the wife of one of the men, or just a friend. She was a good deal younger than either Ottaway or Curtsinger, between whom she sat. Perhaps she was a mistress. The thought tantalized.

"This is Stephanie."

Stephanie, the first woman's senior by a good ten years, graced Marty with a look that seemed to strip him naked from head to foot. It was disconcertingly plain, and he wondered if anyone else around the table had caught it.

"We've heard so much about you," she said, laying a caressing hand on Dwoskin's. "Haven't we?"

Dwoskin smirked. Marty's distaste for the man was as thoroughgoing as ever. It was difficult to imagine how or why any human would want to touch him.

"—And, finally, Emily."

Marty turned to greet the third new face at the table. As he did so, Emily knocked over a glass of red wine.

"Oh Jesus!" she said.

"Doesn't matter," Curtsinger said, grinning. He was already drunk, Marty now registered; the grin was too lavish for sobriety. "Couldn't matter less, sweet. Really it couldn't."

Emily looked up at Marty. She too had already drunk too much, to judge by her flushed complexion. She was by far the youngest of the three women, and almost winsomely pretty.

"Sit down. Sit down," Whitehead said. "Never mind the wine, for God's sake." Marty took his place beside Curtsinger. The wine Emily had spilled dribbled off the edge of the table, unarrested.

"We were just saying—" Dwoskin chimed in, "what a pity Willy couldn't have been here."

Marty shot a glance at the old man to see if the mention of Toy—the sound of weeping came back as he thought of him—had brought any response. There was none. He too, Marty now saw, was the worse for drink. The bottles that Luther had been opening—the clarets, the burgundies—forested the table; the atmosphere was more that of an *ad hoc* picnic rather than a dinner party. There was none of the ceremony he'd anticipated: no meticulous ordering of courses, no cutlery in regiments. What food there was—tins of caviar with spoons thrust into them, cheeses, thin biscuits—took a poor second place to the wine. Though Marty knew little about wine his suspicions about the old man emptying his cellar were confirmed by the babble around the table. They had come together tonight to drink the Sanctuary dry of its finest, its most celebrated, vintages.

"Drink!" Curtsinger said. "It's the best stuff you'll ever swallow, believe me." He fumbled for a specific bottle among the throng. "Where's the Latour? We haven't finished it, have we? Stephanie, are you hiding it, darling?"

Stephanie looked up from her cups. Marty doubted if she even knew what Curtsinger was talking about. These women weren't wives, he was certain of it. He doubted if they were even mistresses.

"Here!" Curtsinger sloppily filled a glass for Marty. "See what you make of that."

Marty had never much liked wine. It was a drink to be sipped and swilled around the mouth, and he had no patience with it. But the bouquet off the glass spoke quality, even to his uneducated nose. It had a richness that made him salivate before he'd downed a mouthful, and the taste didn't disappoint: it was superb.

"Good, eh?"

"Tasty."

"Tasty," Curtsinger bellowed to the table in mock outrage. "The boy pronounces it *tasty*."

"Better pass it back over before he downs the lot," Ottaway remarked.

"It's all got to go," Whitehead said, "tonight."

"All of it?" said Emily, glancing over at the two dozen other bottles that stood against the wall: liqueurs and cognacs among the wines.

"Yes, everything. One blowout, to finish the best of the stuff."

What was this about? They were like a retreating army razing a place rather than leaving anything for those who followed to occupy.

"What are you going to drink next week?" Oriana asked, a heaped spoonful of caviar hovering above her cleavage.

"Next week?" Whitehead said. "No parties next week. I'm joining a monastery." He looked across at Marty. "Marty knows what a troubled man I am."

"Troubled?" said Dwoskin.

"Concerned for my immortal soul," said Whitehead, not taking his eyes off Marty. This earned a spluttered guffaw from Ottaway, who was rapidly losing control of himself.

Dwoskin leaned across and refilled Marty's glass. "Drink up," he said. "We've got a lot to get through."

There was no slow savoring of the wine going on around the table: the glasses were being filled, guzzled and refilled as though the tipple were water. There seemed something desperate in their appetite. But he should have known Whitehead did nothing by halves. Not to be outdone, Marty downed his second glass in two gulps, and filled it to brimming again immediately.

"Like it?" Dwoskin asked.

"Willy would not approve," said Ottaway.

"What; of Mr. Strauss?" Oriana said. The caviar had still not found her mouth.

"Not of Martin. Of this indiscriminate consumption—"

He was barely able to get his tongue around the last two words. There was some pleasure in seeing the lawyer tongue-twisted, no more the Fan-Dancer.

"Toy can go fuck himself," Dwoskin said. Marty wanted to say something in Bill's defense, but the drink had slowed his responses and before he could speak Whitehead had lifted his glass. "A toast," he announced.

Dwoskin stumbled to his feet, knocking over an empty bottle which in turn felled another three. Wine gurgled out of one of the spilled bottles, weaving across the table and splashing onto the floor.

"To Willy!" Whitehead said, "wherever he is."

Glasses raised and tapped together, even Dwoskin's. A chorus of voices offered up—

"To Willy!"

—and the glasses were noisily drained. Marty's glass was filled up by Ottaway.

"Drink, man, drink!"

The drink, on Marty's empty stomach, was causing ructions. He felt dislocated from events in the room: from the women, the Fan-Dancer, the crucifixion on the wall. His initial shock seeing the men like this, wine on their bibs and chins, mouthing obscenities, had long since faded. Their behavior didn't matter. Getting more of these vintages down his throat did. He exchanged a baleful look with Christ. "Fuck you," he said under his breath.

Curtsinger caught the comment. "My very words," he whispered back.

"Where *is* Willy?" Emily was asking. "I thought he'd be here."

She offered the question to the table, but nobody seemed willing to take it up.

"He's gone," Whitehead replied eventually.

"He's such a nice man," the girl said. She dug Dwoskin in the ribs. "Didn't you think he was a nice man?"

Dwoskin was irritated by the interruptions. He had taken to fumbling at the zip on the back of Stephanie's dress. She made no objection to this public advance. The glass he held in the other hand was spilling wine into his lap. He either didn't notice or didn't care.

Whitehead caught Marty's eye.

"Entertaining you, are we?" he said.

Marty wiped the nascent smile off his face.

"Don't you approve?" Ottaway asked Marty.

"Not up to me."

"I always got the impression the criminal classes were quite puritanical at heart. Is that right?"

Marty looked down from the Fan-Dancer's drink-puffed features and shook his head. The jibe was beneath contempt, as was the jiber.

"If I were you, Marty," Whitehead said from the other end of the table, "I'd break his neck."

Marty shrugged. "Why bother?" he said.

"Seems to me, you're not so dangerous after all," Ottaway went on.

"Who said I was dangerous?"

The smirk the lawyer wore deepened. "I mean. We were expecting an *animal* act, you know?" Ottaway moved a bottle to get a better look at Marty. "We were promised—" The conversation around the table had ground to a halt, but Ottaway didn't seem to notice. "Still, nothing's quite as advertised, is it?" he said. "I mean, you ask any one of these godforsaken gentlemen." The table was a still-life; Ottaway's arm swept around to include everyone in his tirade. "We know, don't we? We know how disappointing life can be."

"Shut up," Curtsinger snapped. He stared woozily at Ottaway. "We don't want to hear."

"We may not get another chance, my dear James," Ottaway replied, his courtesy contemptuous. "Don't you think we should all admit the truth? We are *in extremis*! Oh yes, my friends. We should all get down on our knees and confess!"

"Yes, yes," said Stephanie. She was trying to stand but her legs were of another mind. Her dress, the back unzipped, threatened to slip. "Let's all confess," she said.

Dwoskin pulled her back into her chair.

"We'll be here all night," he said. Emily giggled. Ottaway, undeterred, was still talking.

"Seems to me," he said, "*he's* probably the only innocent one amongst us." Ottaway pointed at Marty. "I mean, look at him. He doesn't even know what I'm talking about."

The remarks were beginning to irritate Marty. But there'd be precious little satisfaction in threatening the lawyer. In his present state Ottaway would crumble under one blow. His bleary eyes didn't look far from unconsciousness. "You disappoint me," Ottaway murmured, with genuine regret in his voice, "I thought we'd end better than this . . ."

Dwoskin stood up. "I've got a toast," he announced. "I want to toast the women."

"Now there's an idea," Curtsinger said. "But we'll need a fire." Oriana thought this the funniest remark she'd heard all night.

"The women!" Dwoskin declared, raising his glass. But nobody was listening. Emily, who had been lamblike so far, had suddenly taken it into her head to strip off. She'd pushed her chair back and was now unbuttoning her blouse. She wore nothing beneath; her nipples looked rouged, as if in preparation for this unveiling. Curtsinger applauded; Ottaway and Whitehead joined in with a chorus of encouraging remarks.

"What do you think?" Curtsinger asked Marty. "Your type, is she? And they're all her own, aren't they, sweetheart?"

"You want to feel?" Emily offered. She'd discarded her blouse; she was now naked from the waist up. "Come on," she said, taking hold of Marty's hand and pressing it against her breast, working it around, and around.

"Oh, yes," said Curtsinger, leering at Marty. "He likes that. I can tell he likes that."

"Of course he does," Marty heard Whitehead say. His gaze, not too focused, slid in the old man's direction. Whitehead met it head-on: the hooded eyes were devoid of humor or arousal. "Go on," he said. "She's all yours. That's what she's here for." Marty heard the words but couldn't make proper sense of them. He pulled his hand off the girl's flesh as if scalded.

"Go to Hell," he said.

Curtsinger had stood up. "Now don't be a spoilsport," he rebuked Marty, "we only want to see what you're made of."

Down the table, Oriana had started to laugh again, Marty

wasn't sure at what. Dwoskin was banging his hand, palm down, on the table. The bottles jumped in rhythm.

"Go on," Whitehead told Marty. They were all looking at him. He turned to face Emily. She was standing a yard away from him, attempting the catch of her skirt. There was something undeniably erotic about her exhibitionism. Marty's trousers felt tight: his head too. Curtsinger had his hands on Marty's shoulders and was trying to slip off his jacket. The tattoo Dwoskin was beating on the table, which Ottaway had now taken up, made Marty's head dance.

Emily had succeeded with the catch, and her skirt was at her feet. Now, without prompting, she pulled off her panties and stood in front of the assembled company wearing only pearls and high-heeled shoes. Naked, she looked young enough to be jailbait: fourteen, fifteen, at most. Her skin was creamy. Somebody's hand—Oriana's, he thought, was massaging Marty's erection. He half-turned: it wasn't her at all, but Curtsinger. He pushed the hand away. Emily had stepped toward him and was unbuttoning his shirt from the bottom up. He tried to stand to say something to Whitehead. The words weren't there yet, but he badly wanted to find them: wanted to tell the old man what a cheat he was. More than a cheat: he was scum; dirty-minded scum. This was why he'd been invited up here, plied with wine and dirty talk. The old man had wanted to see him naked and rutting.

Marty pushed Curtsinger's hand away a second time: the touch was horribly expert. He looked along the table to Whitehead, who was pouring himself another glass of wine. Dwoskin's gaze was fixed on Emily's nakedness; Ottaway's on Marty. Both had given up slapping the table. The lawyer's stare said everything: he was sickly pale, sweaty anticipation on his face.

"Go on," he said, his breath ragged, "go on, take her. Give us a show to remember. Or haven't you got anything worth displaying?"

Marty heard the sense too late to reply; the naked child was

pressing herself against him, and somebody (Curtsinger) was
trying to unbutton the top of his trousers. He made one last,
ungainly lunge at equilibrium.

"Stop this," he murmured, looking at the old man.

"What's the problem?" Whitehead asked lightly.

"Joke over," Marty said. There was a hand in his trousers,
reaching for his erection. "*Get the fuck off me!*" He shoved
Curtsinger back with more force than he'd planned. The big man
stumbled and fell against the wall. "*What's wrong with you
people?*" Emily took a step back from him to avoid Marty's flailing
arm. The wine was boiling up in his belly and throat. His trousers
jutted. He looked, he knew, absurd. Oriana was still laughing: not
just her, Dwoskin too, and Stephanie. Ottaway just stared.

"You never seen a fucking hard-on before?" he spat at them all.

"Where's your sense of humor?" Ottaway said. "We just want
a floor show. Where's the harm?"

Marty jabbed a finger in Whitehead's direction. "*I trusted
you,*" he said. It was all he could find to shape his hurt.

"That was an error then, wasn't it?" Dwoskin commented. He
spoke as if to an imbecile.

"You fucking *shut up!*" Fighting back the urge to break
somebody's face—anybody's would do—Marty pulled on his
jacket, and with one back-sweep of his hand cleared a dozen
bottles, most of them full, off the table. Emily screamed as they
shattered around her feet, but Marty didn't wait to see how much
damage he'd done. He backed off from the table and stumbled
toward the door. The key was in the lock; he opened it and
stepped into the hallway. Behind him Emily had begun to bawl
like a baby just woken from a nightmare; he could hear her all the
way down the darkened corridor. He hoped to God his jittering
limbs would bear him up. He wanted *out*: into the air, into the
night. He lurched down the back staircase, hand outstretched
against the wall for support, the steps receding beneath his feet.
He reached the kitchen having fallen only once, and opened the
back door. The night was waiting. Nothing to see him; nothing

to know him. He breathed in cold black air, and it burned in his nostrils and lungs. He staggered across the lawn, almost blind, not knowing which direction he was going in, until he thought of the woods. Taking a moment to reorientate himself, he ran toward them, begging their discretion.

46

He ran, the undergrowth dragging at his legs, until he was so deep in the stand of trees he could see neither the house nor its lights. Only then did he stop, his whole body thumping like one vast heart. His head felt loose on his neck; bile gurgled at the back of his throat.

"Jesus. Jesus. Jesus."

For a moment, his gyrating head lost control: his ears whined, his eyes blurred. He was suddenly certain of *nothing*, not even his physical existence. Panic crawled up from his bowels, raking the tissue of his gut and his stomach as it came.

"Get down," he told it. Only once before had he felt so close to losing his mind—to throwing back his head and screaming— and that had been the first night at Wandsworth, the first of many years of nights locked in a cell twelve by eight. He'd sat on the edge of the mattress and felt what he was feeling now. The blind beast ascending, squeezing adrenaline from his spleen. He'd mastered the terror then, and he could do it again. Brutally, he stuck his fingers as far down his throat as he could reach, and was rewarded with a surge of nausea. The reflex begun, he let his body do the rest, throwing up a system full of undigested wine. It was a filthy, cleansing experience, and he made no effort to control the spasms until there was nothing left to vomit.

262 CLIVE BARKER

His stomach muscles aching from the contractions, he uprooted some ferns and wiped his mouth and chin, then washed his hands in the damp soil and stood up. The rough treatment had done its job; there was a marked improvement in his condition.

He turned his back on his spilled stomach and wandered further away from the house. Though the thatch of leaves and branches was heavy above, some starlight trickled down, enough illumination to give a tenuous solidity to trunk and brush. Walking in the ghost-wood enchanted him. He let the gentle spectacle of light and leaf-shade heal his wounded vanity. He saw how all his dreams of finding a permanent and trusted place in Whitehead's world had been pretension. He was, and always would be, a marked man.

He walked quietly here, where the trees thickened and the undergrowth, light-starved, thinned. Small animals scuttled ahead of him; night insects whirred in the grass. He stood still to hear the nocturne better. As he did so he caught a movement out of the corner of his eye. He looked toward it, seeking focus through the receding corridor of trunks. It was no trick. There was somebody, gray as the trees, standing thirty or so yards from him—now still, now moving again. Concentrating, he fixed the figure in the matrix of shadow and deeper shadow.

It was a ghost surely. So quiet, so casual. He watched it as a deer might watch a hunter; not certain if he had been seen but unwilling to break cover. Fear ran in his scalp. Not of an open blade; he'd long ago faced those terrors and mastered them. This was the prickly heat fear of childhood; the essential fear. And paradoxically, it made him whole. It didn't matter if he was four or thirty-four, he was the same creature at heart. He'd dreamed of such woods, of such encompassing night. He touched his terror reverently, frozen to the spot, while the gray figure—too taken with its own business to notice him—watched the earth between the trees.

They stood in that relation, ghost and he, for what seemed like several minutes. Certainly a good time passed before he heard a noise that was neither owl, nor rodent, filtering between the trees. It had been there all along, he had just failed to interpret it for what it was: the sound of digging. The rattle of tiny stones, the fall of earth. The child in him said *bad*: leave it be, leave it *all* be. But he was too curious to ignore it. He took two experimental steps toward the ghost. It made no sign of seeing or hearing him. Taking courage, he advanced a few more steps, attempting to keep as close to a tree as possible, so that should the ghost look his way he could find cover quickly. In this way he advanced ten yards toward his quarry. Close enough to see the ghost in enough detail for recognition.

It was Mamoulian.

The European was still staring down at the earth at his feet. Marty slid into hiding behind a trunk and flattened himself there, his back to the scene. There was obviously somebody digging, at Mamoulian's feet; he conceivably had other cohorts in the vicinity. The only safety was in lying doggo and hoping to God no one had been spying on him as he had spied on the European.

At length the digging stopped; and so, as if on an unspoken cue, did the nocturne. It was bizarre. The whole assembly, insect and animal alike, seemed to hold its breath, aghast.

Marty slid down the trunk into crawling position, his ears straining for every clue as to what was going on. He chanced a look. Mamoulian was moving off in what Marty guessed to be the direction of the house. Undergrowth obscured his view: he could see nothing of the digger, or the other disciples who were accompanying the European. He heard their passage, however; the brush of their dragging steps. Let them go, he thought. He was past protecting Whitehead. That bargain was defunct.

He sat, knees hugged against his chest, and waited until Mamoulian had woven between the trees and disappeared. Then he counted to twenty and stood up. Pins and needles pricked at his lower legs, and he had to rub the circulation back into them. Only then did he start toward the spot where Mamoulian had lingered.

Even as he approached he recognized the glade, though he had previously come to it from the direction of the house. His late-evening walk had taken him in a semicircle. He was standing now in the place he'd buried the dogs.

The grave was open and empty; the black plastic shrouds had been torn apart, their contents unceremoniously removed. Marty stared into the hole not quite comprehending the joke. What use were dead dogs?

There was a movement in the grave; something shifted beneath the plastic sheets. He stepped back from the edge, his gorge too susceptible for this. A nest of maggots presumably, or perhaps a worm the size of his arm, grown fat on dogmeat; who knew what hid in the earth?

Turning his back on the hole, he walked toward the house, following the trail Mamoulian had taken, until the trees thinned and the starlight brightened. There, on the borderland between wood and lawn, he stayed, until the sounds of the night reestablished themselves around him.

47

Stephanie excused herself from the table, and went out to the bathroom, leaving the hysteria behind her. As she closed the door one of the men—Ottaway, she thought—suggested she come back in and piss in a bottle for him. She didn't grace the remark with a reply. However well they paid, she wasn't going to get involved in that kind of activity; it wasn't clean.

The hallway was in semidarkness; the sheen of vases, the richness of the carpet underfoot—all of it spoke wealth, and on previous visits she'd enjoyed the extravagance of the place. But tonight they were so uneasy—Ottaway, Dwoskin, the old man himself—there was an air of desperation in their drinking and their innuendo, and it took any pleasure out of being here. On the other nights they'd all got pleasantly drunk and then there'd been the usual performances, sometimes developing into something more serious with one or two of them. Just as often they were content to watch. And at the end of the night there'd been generous payment. But tonight was different. There was cruelty in it, which she disliked. Money or no money, she wouldn't come here again. It was time she retired anyway; leave it to younger girls, who at least looked less raddled than she did.

She bent close to the bathroom mirror and tried to reapply her eyeliner, but her hand was shaky with drink, and it slipped. She cursed, and dug in her purse for a tissue to clean off the error. As she did so there was a scuffling sound in the hallway. Dwoskin, she guessed. She didn't want the gargoyle touching her again, at least not until she was too paralytic with drink to care. She tiptoed to the door and locked it. The sounds outside had stopped. She went back to the sink and turned on the tap; cold water, to splash on her tired face.

D woskin *had* gone out after Stephanie. He intended to suggest something outrageous for her to perform on him, something gross for this night of nights.

"Where are you going?" somebody asked him, as he traipsed the hall, or did he just imagine the words? He'd taken a few pills before the party—that always loosened him up—but it tended to put voices in his head, mostly his mother's. Whether somebody had asked the question or not, he chose not to answer; he just wandered down the corridor, calling for Stephanie. The woman was extraordinary, or so his drugged libido had decided. She had superb buttocks. He wanted to be smothered by those cheeks; to die under them.

"Stephanie," he demanded. She didn't reappear. "Come on," he reassured her, "it's only me."

There was a smell in the corridor: just a hint of sewer. He inhaled it. "Foul," he announced, not unappreciatively. The smell was getting stronger, as though its source was close by, and approaching. "Lights," he told himself and peered along the wall looking for a switch.

A few yards down the corridor something started to move toward him. The light was too dim to see properly by, but it was a man, and the man was not alone. There were other shapes, knee-high, mustering in the darkness. The smell was becoming overpowering. Dwoskin's head had started to dance with color; disgraceful images flickered in the air to accompany the smell. It took him a moment to grasp that this air graffiti was not his doing. It was coming from the man ahead of him. Dashes and dots of light flared and whirled away into the air.

"Who are you?" Dwoskin demanded. In answer, the graffiti ignited into a full-blown literature. Not certain if any sound was coming out, the Troll-King began to screech.

Stephanie dropped the eyeliner into the sink as the scream reached her. She didn't recognize the voice. It was high enough to be a woman's, but it was neither Emily nor Oriana.

The shakes suddenly worsened. She held on to the edge of the sink to steady herself as the noises multiplied: howls now, and running feet. Somebody was shouting; all but incoherent orders. It was Ottaway, she thought, but she wasn't going out to check. Whatever was going on beyond the door—pursuit, capture, murder even—she needed none of it. She turned off the light in the bathroom in case it spilled under the door. Somebody ran by, calling on God: now *there* was desperation. Feet thudded down the stairs; somebody fell. Doors slammed: screams mounted.

She backed away from the door and sat on the edge of the bath. There, in the darkness, she started to sing "Abide with Me"—or what little she could remember of it—very quietly.

M arty heard the screams too, though he didn't want to. Even at such a distance, they carried a freight of blind panic that made him clammy.

He knelt down in the dirt between the trees and stopped his ears. The earth smelled ripe beneath him, and his mind seethed with unwelcome thoughts of lying faceup in the ground, dead perhaps, but anticipating resurrection. Like a sleeper on the verge of waking, nervous of the day.

After a while the din became intermittent. Soon, he told himself, he must open his eyes, stand up and go back to the house to see the hows and the whys of all this commotion. Soon; but not yet.

W hen the noise in the hallway and on the stairs had long stopped, Stephanie crept to the bathroom door, unlocked it and peered out. The corridor was in complete darkness now. The lamps had either been turned off or shattered. But her eyes, accustomed to the blackness of the bathroom, soon pierced the feeble light from the stairwell. The gallery was empty in both directions. There was just a smell in the air like a bad butcher's shop on a hot day.

She slipped off her shoes, and started to the top of the stairs. The contents of a handbag were scattered down the steps, and there was something wet underfoot. She looked down: the carpet was stained: either wine or blood. She hurried on down into the hallway. It was chilly; both front and vestibule doors were wide open. Again, there was no sign of life. The cars had gone from the driveway; the downstairs rooms—library, reception rooms, kitchen—all were forsaken. She rushed back upstairs to collect her belongings from the white room and leave.

As she retraced her steps along the gallery she heard a soft padding behind her. She turned. There was a dog at the top of the stairs; it had presumably followed her up. She could scarcely make it out in the bad light, but she wasn't afraid. "Good boy," she said, glad of its living presence in the abandoned house.

It didn't growl, nor did it wag its tail, it simply hobbled towards her. Only then did she realize her error in welcoming it. The butcher's shop was here, on all fours: she backed off.

"No . . ." she said, "I don't . . . oh, Christ . . . leave me alone."

Still it came; and with every step it took toward her she saw more of its condition. The innards that looped from its underside. The decayed face, all teeth and putrescence. She headed toward the white room, but it covered the distance between them in three strides. Her hands slid on its body as it leaped at her, and to her disgust fur and flesh separated, her grasp skinning the creature's flanks. She fell back; it advanced, head rocking uneasily on its scrappy neck, its jaws closing around her throat and shaking her. She couldn't scream—it was devouring her voice—but her arm thrust up into the cold body and found its spine. Instinct made her grasp the column, muscle dividing in slimy threads, and the beast let her go, arching back as her grip snapped one vertabra from the next. It let out a prolonged hiss as she dragged her arm out. Her other hand cupped her throat: blood was hitting the carpet with thudding sounds: she must get help or bleed to death.

She started to crawl back toward the top of the stairs. Miles away from her, somebody opened a door. Light fell across her. Too numb to feel pain, she looked around. Whitehead was silhouetted in a distant doorway. Between them stood the dog. Somehow, it had got up, or rather its front portion had, and it was dragging itself across the shining carpet toward her, most of its bulk useless now, its head barely raised from the ground. But still moving, as it would move until its resurrector granted it rest.

She raised her arm to signal her presence to Whitehead. If he saw her in the gloom he made no sign.

She had reached the top of the stairs. She had no strength left in her. Death was coming quickly. Enough, her body said, enough.

Her will conceded, and she slumped down, the blood, loosed from her wounded neck, flowing down the stairs as her darkening eyes watched. One step, two steps.

Counting games were a perfect cure for insomnia.

Three steps, four.

She didn't see the fifth step, or any other in the creeping descent.

M arty was loath to go back into the house, but whatever had happened there was surely over, and he was getting chilly where he knelt. His expense-account suit was dirtied beyond reclamation; his shirt was stained and torn, his immaculate shoes clay-caked. He looked like a derelict. The thought almost pleased him.

He meandered back across the lawn. He could see the lights of the house somewhere ahead. They burned reassuringly, though he knew such reassurance was delusion. Not every house was a refuge. Sometimes it was safer to be out in the world, under the sky, where no one could come knocking and looking for you, where no roof could fall on your trusting head.

Halfway between house and trees a jet growled overhead, high up, its lights twin stars. He stood and watched it pass over him at his zenith. Perhaps it was one of the monitoring planes that he'd read passed perpetually over Europe—one American, one Russian—their electric eyes scanning the sleeping cities; judgmental twins upon whose benevolence the lives of millions depended. The sound of the jet diminished to a murmur, and then to silence. Gone to spy on other heads. The sins of England would not prove fatal tonight, it seemed.

He began to walk toward the house with fresh resolution, taking a route that would lead him around to the front and into the false day of the floodlights. As he crossed the stage toward the front door the European stepped out of the house.

There was no way to avoid being seen. Marty stood, rooted to

the spot, while Breer emerged, and the two unlikely companions
moved away from the house. Whatever job they'd come to do was
clearly completed.

A few steps across the gravel Mamoulian glanced around. His
eyes found Marty immediately. For a long moment the European
simply stared across the expanse of bright grass. Then he nodded,
a short, sharp nod that was simply acknowledgment. I see you, it
said, and look! I do you no harm. Then he turned and walked
away, until he and the gravedigger were obscured by the cypresses
that lined the drive.

PART FOUR
THE THIEF'S TALE

Civilisations do not degenerate through fear, but because they forget that fear exists.

—FREYA STARK, *PERSEUS IN THE WIND*

48

Marty stood in the hallway and listened for footsteps or voices. There were neither. The women had obviously gone, as had Ottaway, Curtsinger and the Troll-King. Perhaps the old man too.

Few lights burned in the house. Those that did rendered the place almost two-dimensional. Power had been unleashed here. Its remnants skittered in the metalwork; the air had a bluish tinge. He made his way upstairs. The second floor was in darkness, but he found his way along it by instinct, his feet kicking the porcelain shards—some smashed treasure or other—as he went. There was more than porcelain underfoot. Things damp, things torn. He didn't look down, but made his way toward the white room, anticipation mounting with every step.

The door was ajar, and a light, not electric but candle, burned inside. He stepped over the threshold. The single flame offered a panicky illumination—his very presence had it jumping—but he could see that every bottle in the room had been smashed. He stepped into a swamp of broken glass and spilled wine: the room was pungent with the dregs. The table had been overturned and several of the chairs reduced to matchwood.

Old Man Whitehead was standing in the corner of the room. There were spatters of blood on his face, but it was difficult to be certain if it was his. He looked like a man pictured in the aftermath of an earthquake: shock had bled his features white.

"He came early," he said, disbelief in every hushed syllable. "Imagine that. I thought he believed in covenants. But he came *early* to catch me out."

"Who is he?"

He wiped tears from his cheeks with the heel of his hand, smearing the blood. "The bastard lied to me," he said.

"Are you hurt?"

"No," Whitehead said, as if the question were utterly ridiculous. "He wouldn't lay a hand on me. He knows better than that. He wants me to go willingly, you see?"

Marty didn't.

"There's a body in the hallway," Whitehead observed matter-of-factly. "I moved her off the stairs."

"Who?"

"Stephanie."

"He killed her?"

"Him? No. His hands are clean. You could drink milk from them."

"I'll call the police."

"No!"

Whitehead took several ill-advised steps through the glass to catch Marty's arm.

"No! No police."

"But somebody's dead."

"Forget her. You can hide her away later, eh?" His tone was almost ingratiating, his breath, now he was close, toxic. "You'll do that, won't you?"

"After all you've done?"

"A little joke," Whitehead said. He tried a smile; his grip on Marty's arm was blood-stopping. "*Come on;* a joke, that's all." It was like being buttonholed by an alcoholic on a street corner.

Marty loosed his arm. "I've done all I'm going to do for you," he said.

"You want to go back home, is that it?" Whitehead's tone soured on an instant. "Want to go back behind bars where you can hide your head?"

"You've tried that trick."

"Am I getting repetitive? Oh, dear. Oh, Christ in Heaven." He waved Marty away. "Go on then. Piss off; you're not in my class."

He staggered back to the crutch of the wall and leaned there. "What the fuck am I doing, expecting you to take a stand?"

"You set me up," Marty snarled in reply, "all along!"

"I told you . . . a joke."

"Not just tonight. All along. Lying to me . . . bribing me. You said you needed someone to trust, and then you treat me like shit. No wonder they all run out on you in the end!"

Whitehead wheeled on him. "All right," he shouted back, "what do you want?"

"*The truth.*"

"Are you sure?"

"Yes, damn you, *yes!*"

The old man sucked at his lip, debating with himself. When he spoke again, the voice had quietened. "All right, boy. All right." The old glitter flared in his eyes, and momentarily the defeat was burned away by a new enthusiasm. "If you're so eager to hear, I'll tell you." He pointed a shaky finger at Marty. "Close the door."

Marty kicked a smashed bottle out of the way, and pushed the door shut. It was bizarre to be closing the door on murder simply to listen to a story. But this tale had waited so long to be told; it could be delayed no longer.

"When were you born, Marty?"

"In 1948. December."

"The war was over."

"Yes."

"You don't know what you missed."

It was an odd beginning for a confession.

"Such times."

"You had a good war?"

Whitehead reached for one of the less damaged chairs and righted it; then he sat down. For several seconds he didn't say anything.

"I was a thief, Marty," he said at last. "Well . . . black marketeer has a more impressive ring, I suppose, but it amounts to the same thing. I was able to speak three or four languages adequately, and I was always quick-witted. Things fell my way very easily."

"You were lucky."

"Luck had no bearing on it. Luck's out for people with no *control*. I *had* control; though I didn't know it at the time. I made my own luck, if you like." He paused. "You must understand, war isn't like you see in the cinema; or at least my war wasn't. Europe was falling apart. Everything was in flux. Borders were changing, people were being shipped into oblivion: the world was up for grabs." He shook his head. "You can't conceive of it. You've always lived in a period of relative stability. But war changes the rules you live by. Suddenly it's *good* to hate, it's *good* to applaud destruction. People are allowed to show their true selves—"

Marty wondered where this introduction was taking them, but Whitehead was just getting into the rhythm of his telling. This was no time to divert him.

"—and when there's so much uncertainty all around, the man who can shape his own destiny can be king of the world. Forgive the hyperbole, but it's how I felt. King of the World. I was clever, you see. Not *educated*, that came later, but clever. Streetwise, you'd call it now. And I was determined to make the most of this wonderful war God had sent me. I spent two or three months in Paris, just before the Occupation, then got out while the going was good. Later on, I went south. Enjoyed Italy; the Mediterranean. I wanted for nothing. The worse the war became the better it was for me. Other people's desperation made me into a rich man.

"Of course I frittered the money away. Never really held on to my earnings for more than a few months. When I think of the paintings I had through my hands, the *objets d'art*, the sheer loot. Not that I knew that when I pissed in the bucket I splashed a Raphael. I bought and sold these things by the jeepload."

"Towards the end of the European war I took off north, into Poland. The Germans were in a bad way: they knew the game was coming to an end, and I thought I could strike a few deals. Eventually—it was an error really—I wound up in Warsaw. There

was practically nothing left by the time I got there. What the
Russians hadn't flattened, the Nazis had. It was one wasteland
from end to end." He sighed, and pulled a face, making an effort
to find the words. "You can't imagine it," he said. "This had been
a great city. But now? How can I make you understand? You have
to see through my eyes, or none of this makes sense."

"I'm trying," Marty said.

"You live in *yourself*," Whitehead went on. "As I live in *myself*.
We have very strong ideas of what we are. That's why we value
ourselves; by what's unique in us. Do you follow what I'm
saying?"

Marty was too involved to lie. He shook his head.

"No; not really."

"The *isness* of things: that's my point. The fact that everything
of any value in the world is very specifically *itself*. We celebrate
the individuality of appearance, of being, and I suppose we
assume that some part of that individuality goes on forever, if
only in the memories of the people who experienced it. That's
why I valued Evangeline's collection, because I delight in the
special thing. The vase that was unlike any other, the carpet
woven with special artistry."

Then suddenly, they were back in Warsaw—

"There'd been such glories there, you know. Fine houses;
beautiful churches; great collections of paintings. So much. But
by the time I arrived it was all gone, pounded to dust.

"Everywhere you walked it was the same. Underfoot there was
muck. Gray muck. It caked your boots, its dust hung in the air, it
coated the back of your throat. When you sneezed, your snot was
gray; your shit the same. And if you looked closely at that filth
you could see it wasn't just dirt, it was flesh, it was rubble, it was
porcelain fragments, newspapers. All of Warsaw was in that mud.
Its houses, its citizens, its art, its history: all ground down to
something that you scraped off your boots."

Whitehead was hunched up. He looked his seventy years; an
old man lost in remembering. His face was knotted up, his hands

were fists. He was older than Marty's father would have been had he survived his lousy heart: except that his father would never have been able to speak this way. He'd lacked the power of articulation, and, Marty thought, the depth of pain. Whitehead was in agonies. The memory of muck. More than that: the *anticipation* of it.

Thinking of his father, of the past, Marty alighted upon a memory that made some sense of Whitehead's reminiscences. He'd been a boy of five or six when a woman who'd lived three doors down the terrace died. She'd had no relatives apparently, or none that cared sufficiently to remove what few possessions she'd had from the house. The council had reclaimed the property and summarily emptied it, carting off her furniture to be auctioned. The day after, Marty and his playmates had found some of the dead woman's belongings dumped in the alley behind the row of houses. The council workmen, pressed for time, had simply emptied all the drawers of worthless personal effects into a pile, and left them there. Bundles of ancient letters roughly tied up with faded ribbon; a photograph album (she was there repeatedly: as a girl; as a bride; as a middle-aged harridan, diminishing in size as she dried up); much valueless bric-a-brac; sealing wax, inkless pens, a letter opener. The boys had fallen on these leavings like hyenas in search of something nourishing. Finding nothing, they scattered the torn-up letters down the alley; they dismembered the album, and laughed themselves silly at the photographs, although some superstition in them prevented them tearing those. They had no need to do so. The elements soon vandalized them more efficiently than their best efforts could have done. In a week of rain and night-frost the faces on the photographs had been spoiled, dirtied and finally eroded entirely. Perhaps the last existing portraits of people now dead went to mush in that alley, and Marty, passing down it daily, had watched the gradual extinction; seen the ink on the scattered letters rained off until the old woman's memorial was gone away utterly, just as her body had gone. If you'd upended the tray that held her ashes onto the trampled remains of her belongings they would have been virtually indistinguishable: both gray dirt, their significance irretrievably lost. Muck held the whip hand.

All this Marty recalled mistily. It wasn't quite that he saw the letters, the rain, the boys—as much as retouching the feelings the events had aroused: the buried sense that what had happened in that alley was unbearably poignant. Now his memory meshed with Whitehead's. All the old man had said about muck, about the isness of things, made some sense.

"I see," he murmured.

Whitehead looked up at Marty.

"Perhaps," he said.

"I was a gambling man in those days; far more than I am now. War brings it out in you, I think. You hear stories all the time, about how some lucky man escaped death because he sneezed, or died for the same reason. Tales of benign providence, or fatal bad fortune. And after a while you get to look at the world a little differently: you begin to see chance at work everywhere. You become alive to its mysteries. And of course to its flip side; to determinism. Because take it from me there are men who make their own luck. Men who can *mold* chance like putty. You talked of feeling a tingle in your hands. As though today, whatever you did, you couldn't lose."

"Yes . . ." That conversation seemed an age away; ancient history.

"Well, while I was in Warsaw, I heard about a man who never once lost a game. A card-player."

"Never lost?" Marty was incredulous.

"Yes, I was as cynical as you. I treated the stories I heard as fable, at least for a while. But wherever I went, people told me about him. I got to be curious. In fact I decided to stay in the city, though God knows there was precious little to keep me there, and find this miracle worker for myself."

"Who did he play against?"

"All comers, apparently. Some said he'd been there in the last days before the Russian advance, playing against Nazis, and then when the Red Army entered the city he stayed on."

"Why play in the middle of nowhere? There can't have been much money around."

"Practically none. The Russians were betting their rations, their boots."

"So again: why?"

"That's what fascinated me. I couldn't understand it either. Nor did I believe he won every game, however good a player he was."

"I don't see how he kept finding people to play him."

"Because there's always somebody who thinks he can bring the champion down. I was one. I went searching for him to prove the stories wrong. They offended my sense of reality, if you like. I spent every waking hour of every day searching the city for him. Eventually I found a soldier who'd played against him, and of course lost. Lieutenant Konstantin Vasiliev."

"And the card-player . . . what was his name?"

"I think you know . . ." Whitehead said.

"Yes," Marty replied, after a moment. "Yes, you know I saw him. At Bill's club?"

"When was this?"

"When I went to buy my suit. You told me to gamble what was left of the money."

"Mamoulian was at the Academy? And did he play?"

"No. Apparently he never does."

"I tried to get him to play, when he came here last, but he wouldn't."

"But in Warsaw? You played him there?"

"Oh, yes. That's what he'd been waiting for. I see that now. All these years I pretended I was in charge, you know? That I'd gone to him, that I'd won by my own skills—"

"You won?" Marty exclaimed.

"Certainly I won. But he let me. It was his way of seducing me, and it worked. He made it look difficult, of course, to give some weight to the illusion, but I was so full of myself I never once contemplated the possibility that he'd lost the game deliberately. I mean, there was no reason for him to do that, was there? Not that I could see. Not at the time."

"Why did he let you win?"

"I told you: seduction."

"What, do you mean he wanted you in bed?"

Whitehead made the gentlest of shrugs. "It's possible, yes." The thought seemed to amuse him; vanity bloomed on his face. "Yes, I think I probably was a temptation." Then the smile faded. "But sex is nothing, is it? I mean, as possessions go, to fuck somebody is trite stuff. What he wanted me for went far deeper and was far more permanent than any physical act."

"Did you always win when you played him?"

"I never played against him again, that was the first and only time. I know it sounds unlikely. He was a gambler and so was I. But as I told you, he wasn't interested in cards for the betting."

"It was a test."

"Yes. To see if I was worthy of him. Fit to build an Empire. After the war, when they started rebuilding Europe, he used to say there were no *real* Europeans left—they'd all been wiped out by one holocaust or another—and he was the last of the line. I believed him. All the talk of Empires and traditions. I was flattered to be lionized by him. He was more cultured, more persuasive, more penetrating than any man I had met or have met since." Whitehead was lost in this reverie, hypnotized by the memory. "All that's left now is a husk, of course. You can't really appreciate what an impression he made. There was nothing he couldn't have been or done if he'd put his mind to it. But when I said to him: why do you bother with the likes of me, why don't you go into politics, some sphere where you can wield power directly, he'd give me this look, and say: it's all been done. At first I thought he meant those lives were predictable. But I think he meant something else. I think he was telling me that he'd *been* these people, *done* those things."

"How's that possible? One man."

"I don't know. It's all conjecture. It was from the beginning. And here I am forty years later, still juggling rumors."

He stood up. By the look on his face it was obvious that his sitting position had caused some stiffness in the joints. Once he was upright, he leaned against the wall, and put his head back, staring up at the blank ceiling.

"He had one great love. One all-consuming passion. Chance. It obsessed him. 'All life is chance,' he used to say. 'The trick is learning how to use it.'"

"And all this made sense to you?"

"It took time; but I came to share his fascination over a period of years, yes. Not out of intellectual interest. I've never had much of that. But because I knew it could bring power. If you can make Providence work for you"—he glanced down at Marty—"work out its *system* if you like—the world succumbs to you." The voice soured. "I mean, look at me. See how well I've done for myself . . ." He let out a short, bitter laugh. ". . . He cheated," he said, returning to the beginning of their conversation. "He didn't obey the rules."

"This was to be the Last Supper," Marty said. "Am I right? You were going to escape before he came for you."

"In a way."

"How?"

Whitehead didn't reply. Instead he began the story again, where he'd left off.

"He taught me so much. After the war we traveled around for a while, picking up a small fortune. Me with my skills, him with his. Then we came to England, and I went into chemicals."

"And got rich."

"Beyond the dreams of Croesus. It took a few years, but the money came, the power came."

"With his help."

Whitehead frowned at this unwelcome observation. "I applied

his principles, yes," he replied. "But *he* prospered every bit as much as I did. He shared my houses, my friends. Even my wife."

Marty made to speak, but Whitehead cut him off.

"Did I tell you about the lieutenant?" he said.

"You mentioned him. Vasiliev."

"He died, did I tell you *that*?"

"No."

"He didn't pay his debts. His body was dragged out of the sewers of Warsaw."

"Mamoulian killed him?"

"Not personally. But yes, I think—" Whitehead stopped in midflow, almost cocked his head, listening. "Did you hear something?"

"What?"

"No. It's all right. In my head. What was I saying?"

"The lieutenant."

"Oh, yes. This piece of the story . . . I don't know if it'll mean too much to you . . . but I have to explain, because without it the rest doesn't quite make sense. You see, the night I found Mamoulian was an incredible evening. Useless to try to describe it really, but you know the way the sun can catch the tops of clouds; they were blush-colored, love-colored. And I was so full of myself, so *certain* that nothing could ever harm me." He stopped and licked his lips before going on. "I was an imbecile." Self-contempt stung the words from him. "I walked through the ruins—smell of putrefaction everywhere, muck under my feet— and I *didn't care*, because it wasn't *my* ruin, *my* putrefaction. I thought I was above all that: especially that night. I felt like the victor, because *I* was alive and the dead were dead." The words stopped pressing forward for a moment. When he spoke again, it was so quietly it hurt the ears to catch the words. "What did I know? Nothing at all." He covered his face with his shaking hand, and said, "Oh, Jesus," quietly into it.

In the silence that followed, Marty thought he heard something outside the door: a movement in the hallway. But the sound was too soft for him to be certain, and the atmosphere in the room demanded his absolute fixedness. To move now, to speak, would ruin the confessional, and Marty, like a child hooked by a master storyteller, wanted to hear the end of this narrative. At that moment it seemed to him more important than anything else.

Whitehead's face was concealed behind his hand as he attempted to stem tears. After a moment he took up the tail of the story again—carefully, as if it might strike him dead.

"I've never told anyone this. I thought if I kept my silence—if I let it become another rumor—sooner or later it would disappear."

There was another noise in the hall, a whine like wind through a tiny aperture. And then, a scratching at the door. Whitehead didn't hear it. He was in Warsaw again, in a house with a bonfire and a flight of steps and a room with a table and a guttering flame. Almost like the room they were in now, in fact, but smelling of old fire rather than souring wine.

"I remember," he said, "when the game was over Mamoulian stood up and shook hands with me. Cold hands. Icy hands. Then the door opened behind me. I half-turned to see. It was Vasiliev."

"The lieutenant?"

"Horribly burned."

"He'd survived," Marty breathed.

"No," came the reply. "He was quite dead."

Marty thought maybe he'd missed something in the story that would justify this preposterous statement. But no; the insanity was presented as plain truth. "Mamoulian was responsible," Whitehead went on. He was trembling, but the tears had stopped, boiled away by the glare of the memory. "He'd raised the lieutenant from the dead, you see. Like Lazarus. He needed functionaries, I suppose."

As the words faltered the scratching began again at the door, an unmistakable appeal for entry. This time Whitehead heard it. His moment of weakness had passed, apparently. His head jerked up. "Don't answer it," he commanded.

"Why not?"

"It's him," he said, eyes wild.

"No. The European's gone. I saw him leave."

"Not the European," Whitehead replied. "It's the lieutenant. *Vasiliev*."

Marty looked incredulous. "No," he said.

"You don't know what Mamoulian can do."

"You're being ridiculous!"

Marty stood up, and picked his way through the glass. Behind him, he heard Whitehead say "no" again, "please, Jesus, no," but he turned the handle and opened the door. Meager candlelight found the would-be entrant.

It was Bella, the Madonna of the kennels. She stood uncertainly on the threshold, her eyes, what was left of them, turned balefully up to look at Marty, her tongue a rag of maggoty muscle that hung from her mouth as if she lacked the strength to withdraw it. From somewhere in the pit of her body, she exhaled a thin whistle of air, the whine of a dog seeking human comfort.

Marty took two or three stumbling steps back from the door.

"It isn't him," Whitehead said, smiling.

"Jesus Christ."

"It's all right, Martin. It isn't him."

"Close the door!" Marty said, unable to move and do it himself. Her eyes, her stench, kept him at bay.

"She doesn't mean any harm. She used to come up here sometimes, for tidbits. She was the only one of them I trusted. Vile species."

Whitehead pushed himself away from the wall and walked across to the door, kicking broken bottles ahead of him as he went. Bella shifted her head to look at him, and her tail began to wag. Marty turned away, revolted, his reason thrashing around to find some sane explanation, but there was none to be had. The dog had been dead: he'd parceled her up himself. There was no question of premature burial.

Whitehead was staring at Bella across the threshold.

"No, you can't come in," he told her, as if she were a living thing.

"Send it away," Marty groaned.

"She's lonely," the old man replied, chiding him for his lack of compassion. It crossed Marty's mind that Whitehead had lost his wits. "I don't believe this is happening," he said.

"Dogs are nothing to him, believe me."

Marty remembered watching Mamoulian standing in the woods, staring down at the earth. He had seen no gravedigger because there'd been none. They'd exhumed themselves; squirming out of their plastic shrouds and pawing their way to the air.

"It's easy with dogs," Whitehead said. "Isn't it, Bella? You're trained to obey."

She was sniffing at herself, content now that she'd seen Whitehead. Her God was still in his Heaven, and all was well with the world. The old man left the door ajar, and turned back to Marty.

"There's nothing to be afraid of," he said. "She's not going to do us any harm."

"He brought them to the house?"

"Yes; to break up my party. Pure spite. It was his way of reminding me of what he's capable of."

Marty stooped and righted another chair. He was shaking so violently, he feared if he didn't sit down he'd fall down.

"The lieutenant was worse," the old man said, "because he didn't obey like Bella. He knew what had been done to him was an abomination. That made him angry."

Bella had woken with an appetite. That was why she'd made her way up to the room she remembered most fondly; a place where a man who knew the best spot to scratch behind her ear would coo soft words to her and feed her morsels off his plate. But tonight she'd come up to find things changed. The man was odd with her, his voice jangling, and there was someone else in the room, one she vaguely knew the scent of, but couldn't place. She was *still* hungry, such deep hunger, and there was an appetizing smell very close to her. Of meat left in the earth, the way she liked it, still on the bone and half gone to putrescence. She sniffed, almost blind, looking for the source of the smell, and having found it, began to eat.

"Not a pretty sight."

She was devouring her own body, taking gray, greasy bites from the decayed muscle of her haunch. Whitehead watched as she pulled at herself. His passivity in the face of this new horror broke Marty.

"Don't let her!" he pushed the old man aside.

"But she's hungry," he responded, as though this horror were the most natural sight in the world.

Marty picked up the chair he'd been sitting on and slammed it against the wall. It was heavy, but his muscles were brimming, and the violence was a welcome release. The chair broke.

The dog looked up from her meal; the meat she was swallowing fell from her cut throat.

"Too much," Marty said, picking up a leg of the chair and crossing the room to the door before Bella could register what he intended. At the last moment she seemed to understand that he meant her harm, and tried to get to her feet. One of her back legs, the haunch almost chewed through, would no longer support her, and she staggered, teeth bared, as Marty swung his makeshift weapon down on her. The force of his blow shattered her skull. The snarling stopped. The body backed off, dragging the ruined head on a rope of a neck, the tail tucked between its back legs in fear. Two or three trembling steps of retreat and it could go no further.

Marty waited, hoping to God he wouldn't have to strike a second time. As he watched the body seemed to deflate. The swell of its chest, the remnants of its head, the organs hanging in the vault of its torso all collapsed into an abstraction, one part indistinguishable from the next. He closed the door on it, and dropped the blooded weapon at his side.

Whitehead had taken refuge across the room. His face was as gray as Bella's body.

"How did he do this?" Marty said. "*How* is it possible?"

"He has power," Whitehead stated. It was as simple as that, apparently. "He can steal life, and he can give it."

Marty dug in his pocket for the linen handkerchief he'd bought specially for this night of dining and conversation. Shaking it out, its edges pristine, he wiped his face. The handkerchief came away dirtied with specks of rot. He felt as empty as the sac in the hall outside.

"You asked me once if I believed in Hell," he said. "Do you remember?"

"Yes."

"Is that what you think Mamoulian is? Something"—he wanted to laugh—"something from Hell?"

"I've considered the possibility. But I'm not by nature a supernaturalist. Heaven and Hell. All that paraphernalia. My system revolts at it."

"If not devils, what?"

"Is it so important?"

Marty wiped his sweaty palms on his trousers. He felt contaminated by this obscenity. It would take a long time to wash the horror out, if he ever could. He'd made the error of digging too deep, and the story he'd heard—that and the dog at the door—were the consequence.

"You look sick," Whitehead said.

"I never thought . . ."

"What? That the dead can get up and walk? Oh, Marty, I took you for a Christian, despite your protestations."

"I'm getting out," Marty said. "Both of us."

"*Both?*"

"Carys and me. We'll go away. From him. From you."

"Poor Marty. You're more bovine than I thought you were. You won't see her again."

"Why not?"

"She's with *him*, damn you! Didn't it occur to you? *She went with him!*" So that had been the unthinkable solution to her abrupt vanishing trick. "Willingly, of course."

"No."

"Oh, yes, Marty. He had a claim on her from the beginning. He rocked her in his arms when she was barely born. Who knows what kind of influence he has. I won her back, of course, for a while." He sighed. "I made her love me."

"She wanted to be away from you."

"Never. She's *my* daughter, Strauss. She's as manipulative as I am. Anything between you and her was purely a marriage of her convenience."

"You're a fucking bastard."

"That's a given, Marty. I'm a monster; I concede the point." He threw up his hands, palms out, innocent of everything but guilt.

"I thought you said she loved you. Still she went."

"I told you: she's my daughter. She thinks the way I do. She went with him to learn how to use her powers. I did the same, remember?"

This line of argument, even from vermin like Whitehead, made a kind of sense. Beneath her strange conversation hadn't there always lurked a contempt for Marty and the old man alike, contempt earned by their inability to sum her up? Given the opportunity, wouldn't Carys go dance with the Devil if she felt she'd understand more of herself by doing so?

"Don't concern yourself with her," Whitehead said. "Forget her; she's gone."

Marty tried to hold on to the image of her face, but it was deteriorating. He was suddenly very tired, exhausted to his bones.

"Get some rest, Marty. Tomorrow we can bury the whore together."

"I'm not getting involved in this."

"I told you once, didn't I, if you stayed with me, there was nowhere I couldn't take you. It's more true now than ever. You know Toy's dead."

"When? How?"

"I didn't ask the details. The point is, he's gone. There's only you and I now."

"You made a fool out of me."

Whitehead's face was a portrait of persuasion. "An error of taste," he said. "Forgive me."

"Too late."

"I don't want you to leave me, Marty. *I won't let you leave me!* You hear?" His finger jabbed the air. "You came here to help me! What have you done? Nothing! *Nothing!*"

Blandishment had turned into accusations of betrayal in mere seconds. One moment tears, the next curses, and behind it all, the same terror of being left alone. Marty watched the old man's trembling hands fist and unfist.

"Please . . ." he appealed, ". . . don't leave me."

"I want you to finish the story."

"*Good* boy."

"Everything, you understand me. Everything."

"What more is there to tell?" Whitehead said. "I became rich. I had entered one of the fastest-growing postwar markets: pharmaceuticals. Within half a decade I was up there with the world leaders." He smiled to himself. "What's more, there was very little illegality in the way I made my fortune. Unlike many, I played by the rules."

"And Mamoulian? Did he help you?"

"He taught me not to agonize over the moral issues."

"And what did he want in return?"

Whitehead narrowed his eyes. "You're not so stupid, are you?" he said appreciatively. "You manage to get right to the hurt when it suits you."

"It's an obvious question. You'd made a deal with him."

"No!" Whitehead interrupted, face set. "I made no deal, not in the way you mean it anyway. There was, perhaps, a gentleman's agreement, but that's long past. He's had all he's getting from me."

"Which was?"

"To live through me," Whitehead replied.

"Explain," Marty said, "I don't understand."

"He *wanted* life, like any other man. He had *appetites*. And he satisfied them through me. Don't ask me how. I don't understand myself. But sometimes I could feel him at the back of my eyes . . ."

"And you let him?"

"At first I didn't even know what he was doing: I had other calls on my attention. I was getting richer by the hour, it seemed. I had houses, land, art, women. It was easy to forget that he was always there, watching; living by proxy.

"Then in 1959 I married Evangeline. We had a wedding that would have shamed royalty: it was written up in newspapers from here to Hong Kong. Wealth and Influence marries Intelligence and Beauty: it was the ideal match. It crowned my happiness, it really did."

"You were in love."

"It was impossible not to love Evangeline. I think"—he sounded surprised as he spoke—"I think she even loved me."

"What did she make of Mamoulian?"

"Ah, there's the rub," he said. "She loathed him from the start. She said he was too puritanical; that his presence made her feel perpetually guilty. And she was right. He loathed the body; its functions disgusted him. But he couldn't be free of it, or its appetites. That was a torment to him. And as time went by that streak of self-hatred worsened."

"Because of her?"

"I don't know. Perhaps. Now I think back, he probably *wanted* her, the way he'd wanted beauties in the past. And of course she despised him, right from the beginning. Once she was mistress of the house this war of nerves just escalated. Eventually she told me to get rid of him. This was just after Carys was born. She said she didn't like him handling the baby—which he seemed to like to do. She just didn't want him in the house. I'd known him two decades by now—he'd lived in my house, he'd shared my life—and I realized I knew *nothing* about him. He was still the mythical card-player I'd met in Warsaw."

"Did you ever ask him?"

"Ask him what?"

"Who he was? Where he came from? How he got his skills?"

"Oh, yes, I asked him. On each occasion the answer was a little different from the time before."

"So he was lying to you?"

"Quite blatantly. It was a sort of joke, I think: his idea of a party piece, never to be the same person twice. As if he didn't quite exist. As if this man called *Mamoulian* was a construction, covering something else altogether."

"What?"

Whitehead shrugged. "I don't know. Evangeline used to say: he's empty. That was what she found foul about him. It wasn't his presence in the house that distressed her, it was his *absence*, the nullity of him. And I began to think maybe I'd be better getting rid of him, for Evangeline's sake. All the lessons he had to teach me I'd learned. I didn't need him anymore.

"Besides, he'd become a social embarrassment. God, when I think back I wonder—I really wonder—how we let him rule us for so long. He'd sit at the dinner table and you could feel the spell of depression he'd cast on the guests. And the older he got the more his talk was all futility.

"Not that he visibly aged; he didn't. He doesn't look a year older now than when I first met him."

"No change at all?"

"Not physically. There's something altered maybe. He's got an air of defeat about him now."

"He didn't seem defeated to me."

"You should have seen him in his prime. He was terrifying then, believe me. People would fall silent when he stepped through the door: he seemed to soak up the joy in anyone; kill it on the spot. It got to the point where Evangeline couldn't bear to be in the same room with him. She got paranoid about him plotting to kill her and the child. She had somebody sit with Carys every night, to make certain that he didn't touch her. Come to think of it, it was Evangeline who first coaxed me into buying the dogs. She knew he had an abhorrence of them."

"But you didn't do as she asked? I mean, you didn't throw him out."

"Oh, I knew I'd have to act sooner or later; I just lacked the balls to do it. Then he started petty power games, just to prove I still needed him. It was a tactical error. The novelty value of an in-house puritan had worn very thin. I told him so. Told him he'd have to change his whole demeanor or go. He refused, of course. I knew he would. All I wanted was an excuse to break our association off, and he gave it to me on a plate. Looking back, of course, I realize he knew damn well what I was doing. Anyway, the upshot was—I threw him out. Well, not me personally. Toy did the deed."

"Toy worked for you personally?"

"Oh, yes. Again, it was Evangeline's idea: she was always so protective of me. She suggested I hire a bodyguard. I chose Toy. He'd been a boxer, and he was as honest as the day's long. He was always unimpressed by Mamoulian. Never had the least qualm about speaking his mind. So when I told him to get rid of the man, he did just that. I came home one day and the card-player had gone.

"I breathed easy that day. It was as though I'd been wearing a stone around my neck and not known it. Suddenly it was gone: I was light-headed.

"Any fears I'd had about the consequences proved utterly groundless. My fortune didn't evaporate. I was as successful as ever without him. More so, perhaps. I found new confidence."

"And you didn't see him again?"

"Oh, no, I saw him. He came back to the house twice, each time unannounced. Things hadn't gone well for him, it seemed. I don't know what it was, but he'd lost the magic touch somehow.

The first time he came back he was so decrepit I scarcely recognized him. He looked ill, he smelled foul. If you'd seen him in the street you'd have crossed over the road to avoid him. I could scarcely credit the transformation. He didn't want even to step into the house—not that I would have let him—all he wanted was money, which I gave him, and then he went away."

"And it was genuine?"

"What do you mean, *genuine*?"

"The beggar performance: it was real, was it? I mean, it wasn't another story . . . ?"

Whitehead raised his eyebrows. "All these years . . . I never thought of that. Always assumed . . ." He stopped, and began again on a different tack. "You know, I'm not a sophisticated man, despite appearances to the contrary. I'm a thief. My father was a thief, and probably his father too. All this culture I surround myself with, it's a façade. Things I've picked up from other people. Received good taste, if you like.

"But after a few years you begin to believe your own publicity; you begin to think you actually *are* a sophisticate, a man of the world. You start to be ashamed of the instincts that got you where you are, because they're part of an embarrassing history. That's what happened to me. I lost any sense of what I was.

"Well, I think it's time the thief had his say again: time I started to use *his* eyes, *his* instinct. You taught me that, though Christ knows you weren't aware of it."

"Me?"

"We're the same. Don't you see? Both thieves. Both victims."

The self-pity in Whitehead's pronouncement was too much. "You can't tell me you're a victim," Marty said, "the way you've lived."

"What do you know about my feelings?" Whitehead snapped back. "Don't *presume*, you hear me? Don't think you understand, because you don't! He took everything away from me; *everything*! First Evangeline, then Toy, now Carys. Don't tell me whether I've suffered or not!"

"What do you mean, he *took* Evangeline? I thought she died in an accident?"

Whitehead shook his head. "There's a limit to what I can tell you," he said. "Some things I can't express. Never will." The voice was ashen. Marty let the point go, and moved on.

"You said he came back twice."

"That's right. He came again, a year or two after his first visit. Evangeline wasn't at home that night. It was November. Toy answered the door, I remember, and though I hadn't heard Mamoulian's voice I *knew* it was him. I went into the hallway. He was standing on the step, in the porch light. It was drizzling. I can see him now, the way his eyes found me. 'Am I welcome?' he said. Just stood there and said, 'Am I welcome?'

"I don't know why, but I let him in. He didn't look in bad shape. Maybe I thought he'd come to apologize, I can't remember. Even then I would have been friends with him, if he'd offered. Not on the old basis. As business acquaintances, perhaps. I let my defenses down. We started talking about the past together"— Whitehead chewed the memory over, trying to get a better taste of it—"and then he started to tell me how lonely he was, how he needed my companionship. I told him Warsaw was a long time gone. I was a married man, a pillar of the community, and I had no intention of changing my ways. He started to get abusive: accused me of ingratitude. Said I'd cheated him. Broken the covenant between us. I told him there'd never been a covenant, I'd just won a game of cards once, in a distant city, and as a result, he'd chosen to help me, for his own reasons. I said I felt I'd acceded to his demands sufficiently to feel that any debt to him had been paid. He'd shared my house, my friends, my *life* for a decade: everything that I had, had been his to share. 'It's not enough,' he said, and he began again: the same pleas as before, the same demands that I give up this pretense to respectability and go off somewhere with him, be a wanderer, be his pupil, learn new, terrible lessons about the way of the world. And I have to say he made it sound almost attractive. There were times when I tired of the masquerade; when I smelled war, dirt; when I saw the clouds over Warsaw, and I was homesick for the thief I used to be. But I wasn't going to throw everything away for nostalgia's sake. I told him so. I think he must have known I was immovable, because he became desperate. He started to ramble, started to tell me he was frightened without me, lost. I was the one he'd given years of his life and his energies to, and how could I be so callous and unloving? He laid hands on me, wept, tried to paw my face. I was horrified by the whole thing. He disgusted me with his melodrama; I wanted no part of it, or him. But he wouldn't leave. His demands turned into threats, and I suppose I lost my temper. No suppose about it. I've never been so angry. I wanted an end to him and all he stood for: my grubby past. I hit him. Not hard at first, but when he wouldn't stop staring at me I lost control. He didn't make any attempt to defend himself, and his passivity only inflamed me more. I hit him and hit him, and he just took it. Kept offering up his face to be beaten—" He took a trembling breath. "—God knows I've done worse things. But nothing I feel so ashamed of. I didn't stop till my knuckles began to split. Then I gave him to Toy, who really worked him over. And all the time not a peep out of him. I go cold to think about it. I can still see him against the wall, with Bill at his throat and his eyes not looking at where the next blow was coming from but at me. Just at me.

"I remember he said: 'Do you know what you've done?' Just like that. Very quietly, blood coming out with the words.

"Then something happened. The air got thick. The blood on his face started to crawl around like it was alive. Toy let him go. He slid down the wall; left a smear down it. I thought we'd killed him. It was the worst moment of my life, standing here with Toy, both of us staring down at this bag of bones we'd beaten up. That was our mistake, of course. We should never have backed down. We should have finished it then and there, and killed him."

"Jesus."

"Yes! Stupid, not to have finished it. Bill was loyal: there would have been no comeback. But we didn't have the courage. *I* didn't have the courage. I just made Toy clean Mamoulian up, then drive him to the middle of the city and dump him."

"You wouldn't have killed him," Marty said.

"Still you insist on reading my mind," Whitehead replied, wearily. "Don't you see that's what he wanted? *What he'd come for?* He would have let me be his executioner then, if I'd only had the nerve to follow through. He was sick of life. I could have put him out of his misery, and that would have been the end of it."

"You think he's mortal?"

"Everything has its season. His is past. He knows it."

"So all you need do is wait, right? He'll die, given time." Marty was suddenly sick of the story now; of thieves, of chance. The whole sorry tale, true or untrue, repulsed him. "You don't need me anymore," he said. He stood and crossed to the door. The sound of his feet in the glass was too loud in the small room.

"Where are you going?" the old man wanted to know.

"Away. As far as I can get."

"You promised to stay."

"I promised to listen. I *have* listened. And I don't want any of this bloody place."

Marty began to open the door. Whitehead addressed his back.

"You think the European'll let you be? You've seen him in the flesh, you've seen what he can do. He'll have to silence you sooner or later. Have you thought of that?"

"I'll take the risk."

"You're safe here."

"Safe?" Marty repeated incredulously. "You can't be serious. *Safe?* You really are pathetic, you know that?"

"If you go—" Whitehead warned.

"What?" Marty turned on him, spitting contempt. "What will you do, *old man?*"

"I'll have them after you in two minutes flat; you're skipping parole."

"And if they find me, I'll tell them everything. About the heroin, about her out there in the hall. Every dirty thing I can dig up to tell them. I don't give a monkey's toss for your fucking threats, you hear?"

Whitehead nodded. "So. Stalemate."

"Looks like it," Marty replied, and stepped out into the corridor without looking back.

There was a morbid surprise awaiting him: the pups had found Bella. They had not been spared Mamoulian's resurrecting hand, though they could not have served any practical purpose. Too small, too blind. They lay in the shadow of her empty belly, their mouths seeking teats that had long since gone. One of them was missing, he noted. Had it been the sixth child he'd seen move in the grave, either buried too deeply, or too profoundly degenerated, to follow where the rest went?

Bella raised her neck as he sidled past. What was left of her head swung in his general direction. Marty looked away, disgusted; but a rhythmical thumping made him glance back.

She had forgiven him his previous violence, apparently. Content now, with her adoring litter in her lap, she stared, eyeless, at him, while her wretched tail beat gently on the carpet.

I n the room where Marty had left him Whitehead sat slumped with exhaustion.

Though it had been difficult to tell the story at first, it had become easier with the telling, and he was glad to have unburdened it. So many times he'd wanted to tell Evangeline. But she had signaled, in her elegant, subtle way, that if there were indeed secrets he had from her, she didn't want to know them. All those years, living with Mamoulian in the home, she had never directly asked Whitehead *why*, as though she'd known the answer would be no answer at all, merely another question.

Thinking about her brought many sorrows to his throat; they brimmed in him. The European had killed her, he had no doubt of that. He or his agents had been on the road with her; her death had not been chance. Had it been chance he would have known.

His unfailing instinct would have sensed its rightness, however terrible his grief. But there had been no such sense, only the recognition of his oblique complicity in her death. She had been killed as revenge upon him. One of many such acts, but easily the worst.

And had the European taken her, after death? Had he slipped into the mausoleum and touched her into life, the way he had the dogs? The thought was repugnant, but Whitehead entertained it nevertheless, determined to think the worst for fear that if he didn't Mamoulian might still find terrors to shake him with.

"*You won't*," he said aloud to the room of glass. Won't: *frighten me, intimidate me, destroy me.* There were ways and means. He could escape still, and hide at the ends of the earth. Find a place where he could forget the story of his life.

There *was* something he hadn't told; a fraction of the Tale, scarcely pivotal but of more than passing interest, that he'd withheld from Strauss as he would withhold it from any interrogator. Perhaps it was unspeakable. Or perhaps it touched so centrally, so profoundly, upon the ambiguities that had pursued him through the wastelands of his life that to speak it was to reveal the color of his soul.

He pondered this last secret now, and in a strange way the thought of it warmed him:

He had left the game, that first and only game with the European, and scrambled through the half-choked door into Muranowski Square. No stars were burning; only the bonfire at his back.

As he'd stood in the gloom, reorienting himself, the chill creeping up through the soles of his boots, the lipless woman had appeared in front of him. She'd beckoned. He assumed she intended to lead him back the way he'd come, and so followed. She'd had other intentions, however. She'd led him away from the square to a house with barricaded windows, and—ever curious, he'd pursued her into it, certain that tonight of all nights no harm could possibly come to him.

In the entrails of the house was a tiny room whose walls were draped with pirated swaths of cloth, some rags, others dusty lengths of velvet that had once framed majestic windows. Here, in this makeshift boudoir, there was one piece of furniture only. A bed, upon which the dead Lieutenant Vasiliev—whom he had so recently seen in Mamoulian's gaming room—was making love. And as the thief stepped through the door, and the lipless woman stood aside, Konstantin had looked up from his labors, his body continuing to press into the woman who lay beneath him on a mattress strewn with Russian and German and Polish flags.

The thief stood, disbelieving, wanting to tell Vasiliev that he was performing the act incorrectly, that he'd mistaken one hole for another, and it was no natural orifice he was using so brutally, but a wound.

The lieutenant wouldn't have listened, of course. He grinned as he worked, the red pole rooting and dislodging, rooting and dislodging. The corpse he was pleasuring rocked beneath him, unimpressed by her paramour's attentions.

How long had the thief watched? The act showed no sign of consummation. At last the lipless woman had murmured *"Enough?"* in his ear, and he had turned a little way to her while she had put her hand on the front of his trousers. She seemed not at all surprised that he was aroused, though in all the years since he had never understood how such a thing was possible. He had long ago accepted that the dead could be woken. But that he had felt heat in their presence—that was another crime altogether, more terrible to him than the first.

There is no Hell, the old man thought, putting the boudoir and its charred Casanova out of his mind. *Or else Hell is a room and a bed and appetite everlasting, and I've been there and seen its rapture and, if the worst comes to the worst, I will endure it.*

PART FIVE

THE DELUGE

Out of a fired ship, which, by no way
But drowning, could be rescued from the flame,
Some men leap'd forth, and as ever as they came
Near the foes' ships, did by their shot decay;
So all were lost, which in the ship were found,
They in the sea being burnt, they in the burnt ship drown'd.

—JOHN DONNE, "A BURNT SHIP"

IX. BAD FAITH

49

The Deluge descended in the driest July in living memory; but then no revisionist's dream of Armageddon is complete without its paradox. Lightning appearing out of a clear sky; flesh turned to salt; the meek inheriting the earth: all unlikely phenomena.

That July, however, there were no spectacular transformations. No celestial lights appeared in the clouds. No rains of salamanders or children. If angels came and went that month—if the looked-for Deluge broke—then it was, like the truest Armageddons, metaphor.

There are, it's true, some freakish occurrences to be recounted, but most of them take place in backwaters, in ill-lit corridors, in shunned wastelands among rain-sodden mattresses and the ashes of old bonfires. They are local; almost private. Their shock waves—at best—made gossip among wild dogs.

Most of these miracles, however—games, rains and salvations—were slipped with such cunning behind the façade of ordinary life that only the sharpest-sighted, or those in search of the unlikely, caught a glimpse of the Apocalypse showing its splendors to a sun-bleached city.

50

The city didn't welcome Marty back with open arms, but he was glad to be away from the house once and for all, his back turned on the old man and his madness. Whatever the consequences of his departure in the long term—and he would have to think very carefully about whether he now turned himself in—he at least had a breathing space; time to think things through.

The tourist season was under way. London was thronged with visitors, making familiar streets unfamiliar. He spent the first couple of days just wandering around, getting used to being footloose and fancy-free again. He had precious little money left: but he could turn his hand to a laboring job if need be. With summer at its height the building trade was hungry for fit workhorses. The thought of an honest day's work, its production of sweat paid for in cash, was attractive. If necessary he would sell the Citroën that he'd taken from the Sanctuary in one last, and probably ill-advised, gesture of rebellion.

After two days of liberty, his thoughts turned to an old theme: America. He'd had it tattooed on his arm as a keepsake of his prison dreams. Now, perhaps, was the time for him to make it a reality. In his imagination, Kansas beckoned, its grain fields running to the eye's limit in every direction, and not a man-made thing in sight. He'd be safe there. Not just from the police and Mamoulian, but from *history*, from stories told again and again, round in circles, world without end. In Kansas, there would be a new story: a story that he could not know the end of. And wasn't that a working definition of freedom, unspoiled by European hand, European certainty?

To keep himself off the streets while he planned his escape he found a room in Kilburn, a dingy one-room flat with a toilet two flights down, which was shared, the landlord informed him, with six other people. In fact there were at least fifteen occupants of the seven rooms in the house, including a family of four in one. The bawling of the youngest child kept his sleep fitful, so he'd rise early and leave the house to its own devices all day, only returning when the pubs were closed, and then only grudgingly. Still, he reassured himself, it wasn't for long.

There were problems about the departure, of course, not the least of which was getting a passport with a visa stamp in it. Without it he would not be allowed to step onto American soil. Securing himself these documents would have to be a speedy operation. For all he knew his parole-jumping had been reported by Whitehead and damn what tales Marty told. Perhaps the authorities were already combing the streets for him.

On the third day of July, a week and a half after leaving the estate, he decided to take fate by the horns and visit Toy's place. Despite Whitehead's insistence that Bill was dead, Marty kept hope intact. Papa had lied before, many times: why not in this instance?

The house was in an elegant backwater in Pimlico; a road of hushed façades and expensive automobiles straddling the narrow pavements. He rang the doorbell half a dozen times, but there was no sign of life. The venetian blinds were drawn on the downstairs windows; there was a fat wedge of mail—circulars mostly—thrust in the mailbox.

He was standing on the step staring dumbly at the door, knowing full well it wasn't going to open, when a woman appeared on the next-door step. Not the owner of the house, he was sure: more likely a cleaner. Her tanned face—who wasn't tanned this blistering summer?—bore the suppressed delight of a bad-news bringer.

"Excuse me. Can I help you?" she inquired hopefully.

He was suddenly glad he'd dressed in jacket and tie to come to the house; this woman looked the kind who'd report her slightest suspicions to the police.

"I was looking for Bill. Mr. Toy."

She clearly disapproved; if not of him, of Toy.

"He's not here," she said.

"Do you happen to know where he's gone?"

"Nobody knows. He just left her. He just upped and left."

"Left who?"

"His wife. Well . . . lady friend. She was found in there a couple of weeks ago, didn't you read about it? It was all over the papers. They interviewed me. I told them; I said he wasn't a pretty piece of work: not at all."

"I must have missed it."

"It was all over the papers. They're looking for him at the moment."

"Mr. Toy?"

"Murder Squad."

"Really."

"You're not a reporter?"

"No."

"Only I'm willing, you know, to tell my story, if the price is right. The things I could tell you."

"Really."

"She was in a terrible state, apparently . . ."

"What do you mean?"

Mindful of her salability, the matron had no intention of divulging the details, even if she knew them, which Marty doubted. But she was willing to offer a tantalizing trailer. "There was mutilation," she promised, "unrecognizable, even to her nearest and dearest."

"Are you sure?"

The woman looked affronted by this smear on her authenticity.

"She either did it to herself, or else somebody did it to her and kept her in there, locked up, bleeding to death. For days and days. The smell when they opened the door—"

The sound of the slushy, lost voice that had answered the telephone came back to Marty, and he knew without doubt that Toy's lady had already been dead when she spoke. Mutilated and dead, but resurrected as a telephonist to keep up appearances for a useful while. The syllables ran in his ear: "Who is this?" she'd asked, hadn't she? Despite the heat and light of a brilliant July, he started to shiver. Mamoulian had been here. He'd crossed this very threshold in search of Toy. He had a score to settle with Bill, as Marty now knew; what might a man not plan, while the humiliations festered, in return for such violence?

Marty caught the woman staring at him.

"Are you all right?" she said.

"Thank you. Yes."

"You need some sleep. I have the same problems. Hot nights like these: I get restless."

He thanked her again and hurried away from the house, without looking back. Too easy to imagine the horrors; they came without warning, out of nowhere.

Nor would they go away. Not now. The memory of Mamoulian was with him—night and day and restless night—from then on. He became aware (was it just his dream life, denied its span in sleepless nights, spreading into wakefulness?) of another world, hovering beyond or behind the façade of reality.

There was no time for prevarication. He *had* to leave; forget Whitehead and Carys and the law. Trick his way out of the country and into America any way he could; away to a place where real was real, and dreams stayed under the eyelids, where they belonged.

51

Raglan was an expert at the fine art of forgery. Two telephone calls located him, and Marty struck a deal with the man. The appropriate visa could be forged in a passport for a modest fee. If Marty could bring along a photograph of himself the job could be done in a day; two at the most.

It was the fifteenth of July: the month was simmering, a few degrees off the boil. The radio, blaring from the room next door, had promised a day as faultlessly blue as the one preceding, and the one preceding that. Not even blue; white. The sky was blind white these days.

Marty set out for Raglan's house early, partially to avoid the worst of the heat, and partially because he was eager to get the forgery made, buy his ticket, and be away. As it was, he got no further than Kilburn High Road Tube Station. It was there, on the cover of the *Daily Telegraph*, that he read the headline: MILLIONAIRE RECLUSE FOUND DEAD AT HOME. Beneath it, a picture of Papa; a younger, beardless Whitehead, snapped at the height of his looks and influence. He bought the paper, and two others that carried the story on their covers, and read them standing in the middle of the pavement, while harried commuters nudged and tutted at him as they surged down the stairs into the station.

"*The death was announced today of Joseph Newzam Whitehead, the millionaire head of the Whitehead Corporation, whose pharmaceutical products had, until recent falls, made it one of the most successful companies in Western Europe. Mr. Whitehead, sixty-eight, was found at his hideaway sanctum in*

Oxfordshire in the early hours of yesterday morning by his chauffeur. He is believed to have died of heart failure. Police say there are no suspicious circumstances. For Obituary; see page seven."

The obituary was the usual amalgam of information gleaned from the pages of *Who's Who*, with a brief outline of the fortunes of the Whitehead Corporation, plus a spicing of conjecture, mostly concerning the corporation's recent fall from financial grace. There was a potted history of Whitehead's life, though the early years were skimpily reported, as though there was some doubt as to the details. The rest of the design was there, albeit threadbare. The marriage to Evangeline; the spectacular rise in the boom years of the late fifties; the decades of consolidation and achievement; then the withdrawal, after Evangeline's death, into mysterious and unilluminating silence.

He was dead.

Despite all the brave talk, all the defiance, all the contempt for the machinations of the European, the battle was lost. Whether it was indeed a natural death, as the papers reported, or Mamoulian's doing, Marty could not know. But there was no denying the curiosity he felt. More than curiosity, grief. That he had a capacity for sorrow at the old man's death came as a shock; perhaps more of a shock than the sorrow itself. He hadn't counted on the ache of loss he felt.

He canceled the meeting with Raglan and went back to the flat, there to study the newspapers over and over again, squeezing out every drop from the text about the circumstances of Whitehead's death. There were few clues, of course: all the reports were couched in the bland and formal language of such announcements. Having exhausted the written word he went next door and asked to borrow his neighbor's radio. The young woman who occupied the room, a student, he thought, took some persuading, but she eventually relinquished it. He listened to the half-hourly bulletins from midmorning on, while the heat rose in his room. The story had some prominence until noon, but thereafter events in Beirut and a drugs coup in Southampton claimed the bulk of the time, the report of Whitehead's death steadily slipping from a major story to news-in-brief, and thence, by midafternoon, into invisibility.

He returned the radio, declining a cup of coffee with the girl and her cat, the smell of whose uneaten food hung around the narrow room like the threat of thunder, and returned to his own quarters to sit and think. If Mamoulian had indeed murdered Whitehead—and he didn't doubt that the European had the skill to do it undetected by the acutest pathologist—it was indirectly *his* fault. Perhaps, had he remained at the house, the old man would still be alive. It was unlikely. Far more likely, he too would be dead. But the guilt still nagged.

For the next couple of days he did very little: entropy had poured lead into his bowels. His thoughts were circular, almost obsessional. In the private cinema of his skull he ran the home movies he'd accrued; from those first, uncertain glimpses of the private life of power to his later memories—almost too sharp, too detailed—of the man alone in a glass-floored cage; the dogs; the dark. Through most, though not all, the face of Carys appeared, sometimes quizzical, sometimes careless: often sealed from him, peering up between the bars of her downcast lashes as if envying him. Late at night, when the baby had fallen asleep in the flat below, and the only sound was the traffic on the High Road, he'd rerun those most private moments between them, moments too precious to be conjured up indiscriminately for fear their power to revive him wane with repetition.

For a time he had tried to forget her: it was more convenient that way. Now he clung to thoughts of that face, bereft. He wondered if he would see her again.

The Sunday newspapers all carried further reports on the death. The *Sunday Times* gave over the front of its Review section to a thumbnail sketch of BRITAIN'S MOST MYSTERIOUS MILLIONAIRE, written by Lawrence Dwoskin, *"longtime associate and confidant of England's Howard Hughes."* Marty

read the piece through twice, unable to scan the printed words
without hearing Dwoskin's insinuating tone in his ear—

"... *he was in many ways a paragon,*" it read, "... *though the
almost hermitlike history of his latter years gave rise, inevitably,
to reams of gossip and tittle-tattle, much of it hurtful to a man
of Joseph's sensibilities. Through all his years in public life,
exposed to the scrutiny of a press that was not always beneficent,
he never hardened himself to criticism, implied or explicit. To we
few who knew him well he revealed a nature more susceptible to
barbs than his outward show of indifference would ever have
suggested. When he found rumors of misconduct or excess being
circulated about him, the criticism bit deeply, especially as, since
his beloved wife Evangeline's death in 1965, he had become the
most fastidious of sexual and moral beings.*"

Marty read this simpering cant with a bitter taste in his throat.
The canonization of the old man had already begun. Soon,
presumably, would come the biographies, authorized—and then
bowdlerized—by his estate, turning his life into a series of
flattering fables by which he would be remembered. The process
nauseated him. Reading the platitudes in Dwoskin's text he found
himself fiercely and unpredictably defensive of the old man's
foibles, as though everything that had made him unique—made
him *real*—now stood in danger of being whitewashed away.

He read Dwoskin's article to its maudlin end and put it down.
The only detail in its length that was of interest was mention of
the funeral service, which was to be held in a small church at
Minster Lovell the following day. The body was then to be
cremated. Dangerous though it might be, Marty felt the need to
go and pay his last respects.

52

In fact the service attracted so many onlookers, from casual observers to diehard scandal-sniffers, Marty's presence went entirely unnoticed. The whole event had an unreal air to it, as if contrived to have the entire world know that the great man was dead. There were correspondents and photographers from all over Europe in addition to the clan from Fleet Street; and among the mourners some of the most famous faces in public life: politicians, professional pundits, captains of industry; even a smattering of movie stars whose only claim to fame was fame itself. The presence of so many celebrities attracted dedicated Peeping Toms in their hundreds. The small church, the yard around it, and the road around that were overrun. The service itself was relayed to those outside the building via loudspeakers; a curious, dislocating detail. The voice of the presiding clergyman sounded tinny and theatrical through the sound system, his eulogy punctuated by an amplified percussion of coughs and shufflings.

Marty didn't like hearing the service this way, any more than he liked the tourists, ill-dressed for a funeral, who lolled on the gravestones and littered the grass, waiting with barely suppressed impatience for this tiresome interruption in their stargazing to be concluded. Whitehead had encouraged a dormant misanthropy in Marty: it now had a permanent place in his worldview. Looking around the graveyard at this heat-flushed, dull-eyed congregation he felt contempt well up in him. He itched to turn his back on the farrago and slip away. But the desire to see this final scene played out overwhelmed the desire to leave, so he waited in the throng while wasps buzzed at children's sticky heads and a woman with the physique of a stick insect flirted with him from the top of a tomb.

Somebody was now reading the lesson. An actor, to judge by the self-regarding tone. It was announced as a passage from the Psalms, but Marty didn't recognize it.

As the reading was drawing to a close, a car drew up at the main gate. Heads turned and cameras clicked as two figures emerged. A buzz spread through the crowd; people who'd taken to lying down stood up again to see what could be seen. Something roused Marty from his lethargy, and he too stood on tiptoe to glimpse the latecomers: it was quite an entrance they were making. He peered between the heads of the crowd to catch a look; caught sight, then lost it again; said "no," quietly to himself, not believing; then pushed his way through the crowd trying to keep pace as Mamoulian, a veiled Carys at his side, glided down the pathway from gate to porch and disappeared into the church. "Who was it?" somebody asked him. "Do you know who it was?"

Hell, he wanted to answer. *The Devil himself.*

Mamoulian was here! In broad daylight, sun on the back of his neck, walking with Carys arm in arm like man and wife, letting the cameras catch him for tomorrow's edition. He had no fear, apparently. This late appearance, so measured, so ironic, was a final gesture of contempt. And why did she play his game? Why didn't she throw off his hand and denounce him for the unnatural thing he was? Because she'd gone willingly into his entourage, the very way Whitehead had told him she would. In search of what? Someone to celebrate that strain of nihilism in her; to educate her in the fine art of dying? And what might she give in return? Ah, there was the prickly question.

At long last the service came to an end. Suddenly, to the delight and outrage of the congregation, a raucous saxophone broke the solemnity, and a jazz rendering of "Fools Rush In" was blaring over the loudspeakers. Whitehead's final joke, presumably. It earned its laughs; some of the crowd even applauded. From inside the church there came the clatter of people rising from their pews.

Marty craned to get a better view of the porch, and failing, threaded his way back through the press of people to a tomb that offered a view. There were birds in the heat-drooped trees, and their pursuits distracted him, catching him up in their swooping play. When he looked back the coffin was almost parallel with him, shouldered, among others, by Ottaway and Curtsinger. The plain box seemed almost indecently exposed. He wondered what they'd dressed the old man in at the last; if they'd trimmed his beard and sewed his eyelids shut.

The procession of mourners followed on the heels of the pallbearers, a black cortège that parted the candy-colored sea of tourists. To right and left the shutters tutted; some damn fool called, "Watch the birdy." The jazz played on. It was all gratifyingly absurd. The old man, Marty guessed, would be smiling in his box.

Finally Carys and Mamoulian emerged from the shade of the porch into the brilliance of the afternoon, and Marty was sure he caught the girl cautiously scanning the crowd, fearful that her companion would notice. She was looking for *him*; he was certain of it. She knew he'd be there, somewhere, and she was looking for him. His mind raced, tripping over itself in its turmoil. If he made a sign to her, however subtle, there was every chance Mamoulian would see it, and that was surely dangerous for them both. Better to hide his head then, painful as it was not to lock glances with her.

Reluctantly, he stepped down off the tomb as the clump of mourners came abreast of him, and spied what he could from the shelter of the crowd. The European scarcely raised his head from its bowed position, and from what Marty could glimpse between the bobbing heads Carys had given up her search—perhaps despairing of his being there. As the coffin and its black tail wound out of the churchyard, Marty ducked away and over the wall to watch events proceed from a better vantage point.

In the road Mamoulian was speaking to one or two of the mourners. Handshakes were exchanged; commiserations offered to Carys. Marty watched impatiently. Perhaps she and the

European would separate in the throng, and he'd get a chance to show himself, if only momentarily, and reassure her of his presence. But no such opportunity presented itself. Mamoulian was the perfect guardian, keeping Carys close to him every moment. Pleasantries and farewells exchanged, they got into the back of a dark green Rover and drove away. Marty raced to the Citroën. He mustn't lose her now, whatever happened: this was perhaps his last chance to locate her. The pursuit proved difficult. Once off the small country roads and onto the highway the Rover accelerated with insolent ease. Marty gave chase as discreetly as the twin imperatives of tactics and excitement would allow.

In the back seat of the car Carys had a strange, flickering thought. Whenever she closed her lids to blink or shut out the day's glare, a figure appeared: a runner. She recognized him in seconds: the gray track suit, a cloud of steam emerging from the hood, named him before she glimpsed his face. She wanted to glance over her shoulder, to see if he was, as she guessed, behind them somewhere. But she knew better. Mamoulian would guess something was going on, if he hadn't already.

The European looked across at her. She was a secret one, he thought. He never really knew what she was thinking. She was, in that regard, her mother's child. Whereas he had learned, with time, to read Joseph's face, Evangeline had seldom let a glimmer of her true feelings show. For the space of several months he'd assumed her to be indifferent to his presence in the house; only time had told the true story of her machinations against him. He sometimes suspected Carys of similar pretenses. Wasn't she simply *too* compliant? Even now she wore the faintest trace of a smile.

"It amused you?" he inquired.

"What?"

"The funeral."

"No," she said lightly. "No, of course not."

"You were smiling."

The trace evaporated; her face slackened. "It had some grotesquerie value, I suppose," she said, her voice dull, "watching them all play up to the cameras."

"You didn't trust their grief?"

"They never loved him."

"And you did?"

She seemed to weigh the question up. "Love . . ." she said, floating the word on the hot air to see, it seemed, what it would become. "Yes. I suppose I did."

She made Mamoulian uneasy. He wanted a better grip on the girl's mind, but it refused his best endeavors. Fear of the illusions he might evoke for her had certainly given her a veneer of obsequiousness, but he doubted they'd truly made a slave of her. Terrors were a useful goad, but the law of diminishing returns pertained; each time she fought him he was obliged to find some new, more awesome fright: it exhausted him.

And now, to add insult to injury, Joseph was dead. He had perished—according to the talk at the funeral—"peacefully in his sleep." Not even *died*; that vulgarity had been exorcised from the vocabulary of all concerned. He had passed on, or over, or away; he had gone to sleep. But never died. The cant and sentimentality that followed the thief to the grave disgusted the European. But he disgusted himself more. He had let Whitehead go. Not once, but twice, undone by his own desire to have the game concluded with due attention to detail. That, and his concern to persuade the thief to come willingly into the void. Prevarication had proved his undoing. While he had threatened, and juggled visions, the old goat had slipped away.

That might not have been the end of the story. After all, he possessed the facility to follow Whitehead into death, and bring him out of it, had he been able to get to the corpse. But the old man had been wise to such an eventuality. His body had been kept from viewing, even by his closest companions. It had been locked in a bank safe (how appropriate!) and guarded night and day, much to the delight of the tabloids, who reveled in such eccentricities. By this evening it would be ash; and Mamoulian's last opportunity for permanent reunion would have been lost.

And yet . . .

Why did he feel as if the games they'd played all these years—the Temptation games, the Revelation games, the Rejection, Vilification and Damnation games—were not *quite* over? His intuition, like his strength, was dwindling: but he was certain that something was amiss. He thought of the way the woman at his side smiled; the secret on her face.

"Is he dead?" he suddenly asked her.

The question appeared to flummox her. "Of course he's dead," she replied.

"*Is he*, Carys?"

"We just saw his funeral, for God's sake."

She felt his mind, a solid presence, at the back of her neck. They had played this scene many times in the preceding weeks—the trial of strength between wills—and she knew that he was weaker by the day. Not so weak as to be negligible, however: he could still deliver terrors, if it suited him.

"Tell me your thoughts . . ." he said, ". . . so I don't have to dig for them."

If she didn't answer his questions, and he entered her forcibly, he'd see the runner for certain.

"Please," she said, making a sham of cowardice, "don't hurt me."

The mind withdrew a little.

"Is he dead?" Mamoulian inquired again.

"The night he died . . ." she began. What could she tell but the truth? No lie would suffice: he would know. ". . . the night *they said* he died I felt nothing. There was no change. Not like when Mama died."

She threw a cowed look at Mamoulian, to reinforce the illusion of servility.

"What do you construe from that?" he asked.

"I don't know," she replied quite honestly.

"What do you *guess*?"

Again, honestly: "That he isn't dead."

The first smile Carys had ever seen on the European's face appeared. It was merest hint, but it was there. She felt him withdraw the horns of his thought and content himself with musing. He would not press her further. Too many plans to plan.

"Oh, Pilgrim," he said under his breath, chiding his invisible enemy like a much-loved but errant child, "you almost had me fooled."

M arty followed the car off the highway and across the city to the house on Caliban Street. It was early evening by the time the pursuit ended. Parked at a prudent distance he watched them get out of the car. The European paid the driver and then, after some delay unlocking the front door, he and Carys stepped into a house whose dirtied lace curtains and peeling paintwork suggested nothing abnormal in a street whose houses were all in need of renovation. A light went on at the middle floor: a blind was drawn.

He sat in the car for an hour, keeping the house in view, though nothing happened. She did not appear at the window; no letters were thrown, wrapped in stones and kisses, out to her waiting hero. But he hadn't really expected such signs; they were fictional devices, and this was real. Dirty stone, dirty windows, dirty terrors skulking at his groin.

He hadn't eaten properly since the announcement of Whitehead's death; now, for the first time since that morning, he felt healthily hungry. Leaving the house to creeping twilight, he went to find himself sustenance.

53

Luther was packing. The days since Whitehead's death had been a whirlwind, and he was dizzied by it. With so much money in his pocket, every minute a new option occurred to him, a fantasy now realizable. For the short term at least he'd decided to go home to Jamaica for a long holiday. He had left when he was eight, nineteen years ago; his memories of the island were gilded. He was prepared to be disappointed, but if he didn't like the place, no matter. A man of his newfound wealth needed no specific plans: he could move on. Another island; another continent.

He had almost finished his preparations for departure when a voice called him from downstairs. It wasn't a voice he knew.

"Luther? Are you there?"

He went to the top of the stairs. The woman he'd once shared this small house with had gone, left him six months ago, taking their children. The house should have been empty. But there was somebody in the hall; not one but two people. His interlocutor, a tall, even stately man, stared up the stairs at him, light from the landing shining on his wide, smooth brow. Luther recognized the face; from the funeral perhaps? Behind him, in shadow, was a heavier figure.

"I'd like a word," said the first.

"How did you get in here? Who the hell are you?"

"Just a word. About your employer."

"Are you from the press, is that it? Look, I've told you everything I know. Now get the hell out of here before I call the police. You've got no right breaking in here."

The second man stepped out of the shadows and looked up the

stairs. IIis face was made-up, that much was apparent even from a distance. The flesh was powdered, the cheeks rouged: he looked like a pantomime dame. Luther stepped back from the top of the stairs, mind racing. "Don't be afraid," the first man said, and the way he said it made Luther more afraid than ever. What capacities might such politeness harbor?

"If you're not out of here in ten seconds—" he warned.

"Where is Joseph?" the polite man asked.

"Dead."

"Are you sure?"

"Of course I'm sure. I saw you at the funeral, didn't I? I don't know who you are—"

"My name is Mamoulian."

"Well, you were there, weren't you? You saw for yourself. He's dead."

"I saw a box."

"He's dead, man," Luther insisted.

"You were the one who found him, I gather," the European said, moving a few silent paces across the hallway to the bottom of the stairs.

"That's right. In bed," Luther replied. Maybe they *were* press, after all. "I found him in bed. He died in his sleep."

"Come down here. Furnish the details, if you would."

"I'm fine where I am."

The European looked up at the chauffeur's frowning face; felt, tentatively, at the nape of his neck. There was too much heat and dirt in there; he wasn't resilient enough for an investigation. There were other, cruder methods, however. He half-gestured toward the Razor-Eater, whose sandalwood presence he smelled close.

"This is Anthony Breer," he said. "He has in his time dispatched children and dogs—you remember the dogs, Luther?—with admirable thoroughness. He is not afraid of death. Indeed he enjoys an extraordinary empathy with it."

The pantomime face gleamed up from the stairwell, desire in its eyes.

"Now, please," Mamoulian said, "for both our sakes; the truth."

Luther's throat was so dry the words scarcely came. "The old man's dead," he said. "That's all I know. If I knew any more I'd tell you."

Mamoulian nodded; the look on his face as he spoke was compassionate, as if he genuinely feared for what must happen next.

"You tell me something I want to believe; and you say it with such conviction I almost do. In principle I can leave, content, and you can go about your business. Except"—he sighed, heavily—"except that I don't *quite* believe you enough."

"Look, this is my fucking house!" Luther blustered, sensing that extreme measures were needed now. The man called Breer had unbuttoned his jacket. He wore no shirt underneath. There were skewers threaded through the fat of his chest, transfixing his nipples, crossways. He reached up and drew two out; no blood came. Armed with these steel needles, he shuffled to the bottom of the stairs.

"I've done nothing," Luther pleaded.

"So you say."

The Razor-Eater began to mount the stairs. The unpowdered breasts were hairless and yellowish.

"Wait!"

At Luther's shout, Breer paused.

"Yes?" said Mamoulian.

"You keep him off me!"

"If you have something to tell me, spit it out. I'm more than eager to listen."

Luther nodded. Breer's face registered disappointment. Luther swallowed hard before speaking. He'd been paid what was to him a small fortune not to say what he was about to say, but Whitehead hadn't warned him that it would be like this. He'd expected a gaggle of inquisitive reporters, perhaps even a lucrative offer for his story to go into the Sunday papers, but not this: not this ogre, with his doll's face and his bloodless wounds. There was a limit to the amount of silence any money could buy, for Christ's sake.

"What have you got to say?" Mamoulian asked.

"He's not dead," Luther replied. There: it wasn't so difficult to do, was it? "It was all set up. Only two or three people knew: I was one of them."

"Why you?"

Luther wasn't certain on this point. "I suppose he trusted me," he said, shrugging.

"Ah."

"Besides, somebody had to find the body, and I was the most believable candidate. He just wanted to make a clean getaway. Start again where he'd never be found."

"And where was that?"

Luther shook his head. "I don't know, man. Anywhere, I suppose, where nobody knows his face. He never told me."

"He must have hinted."

"No."

Breer took heart at Luther's reticence; his look brightened.

"Now come on," Mamoulian coaxed. "You've given me the motherlode; where's the harm in telling me the rest?"

"There *is* no more."

"Why make pain for yourself?"

"*He never told me, man!*" Breer took a step up the stairs; and another; and another.

"He must have given you some idea," Mamoulian said. "Think! Think! You said he trusted you."

"Not that much! Hey, keep him off me, will you?"

The skewers glittered.

"For Christ's sake keep him off me!"

There were many pities. The first was that one human being was capable of such smiling brutality to another. The second that Luther had known nothing. His fund of information had been, as he'd claimed, strictly limited. But by the time the European was certain of Luther's ignorance the man was past recall. Well; that wasn't strictly true. Resurrection was perfectly plausible. But Mamoulian had better things to do with his waning stamina; and besides, letting the man remain dead was the one way he could compensate for the suffering the chauffeur had vainly endured.

Joseph. Joseph. Joseph," Mamoulian chided. And the dark flowed on.

X. NOTHING; AND AFTER

54

Having secured himself all he needed for a long vigil at the house on Caliban Street—reading material, food, drink— Marty returned there and watched through most of the night, with a bottle of Chivas Regal and the car radio for company. Just before dawn he deserted his watch and drove drunkenly back to his room, sleeping through until almost noon. When he woke his head felt the size of a balloon, and as stalely inflated; but there was purpose in the day ahead. No dreams of Kansas now; just the fact of the house and Carys locked up in it.

After a breakfast of hamburgers he returned to the street, parking far enough away to be inconspicuous, yet close enough to see the comings and goings. He spent the next three days—in which the temperature rose from the high seventies into the middle eighties—in the same location. Sometimes he'd catch a few minutes of cramped sleep in the car; more often he returned to Kilburn to snatch an hour or two. The furnace of the street became familiar to him in all its moods. He saw it just before dawn, flickering into solidity. He saw it in midmorning, young wives out with children, business in their walk; in the gaudy afternoon too; and in the evening, when the sugar-pink light of a declining sun made brick and slate exult. The private and public lives of the Calibanese unfolded to him. A spastic child at Number Sixty-seven, whose anger was a secret vice. The woman at Number Eighty-one who welcomed a man to the house daily at twelve-forty-five. Her husband, a policeman to judge by shirt and tie, was welcomed home each night with a ration of doorstep ardor in direct proportion to the time wife and lover had spent together at lunchtime. More too: a dozen, two dozen stories, interlocking, dividing again.

As to the house itself, he saw occasional activity there, but not once did he glimpse Carys. The blinds at the middle windows were kept drawn throughout the day and only lifted in the late afternoon, when the strongest of the sun was past. The single top-story window looked to be permanently shuttered from inside.

Marty concluded that there were only two people in the house besides Carys. One, of course, was the European. The other was the butcher that they'd almost faced back at the Sanctuary; the dog-killer. He came and went once, sometimes twice, daily; usually about some trivial business. An unpalatable sight, with his cosmeticized features, his hobbled walk, the sly looks he gave the children as they played.

In those three days Mamoulian didn't leave the house; at least Marty didn't see him leave. He might appear fleetingly at the downstairs window, glancing out down the sunlit street; but that, infrequently. And as long as he was in the house Marty knew better than to attempt a rescue. No amount of courage—and he did not possess that attribute in limitless supply—would arm him against the powers the European wielded. No; he must sit it out and wait for a safer opportunity to present itself.

On the fifth day of his surveillance, with the heat still rising, luck came his way. About eight-fifty in the evening, as dusk invaded the street, a taxi drew up outside the house, and Mamoulian, dressed for the casino, got into it. Almost an hour later the other man appeared at the front door, his face a blur in the deepening night, but hungry somehow. Marty watched him lock the door, then glance up and down the pavement before setting off. He waited until the shambling figure disappeared around the corner of Caliban Street before he got out of the car. Determined not to risk the least error in this—his first, and probably only, chance at rescue—he went to the corner to check that the butcher was not simply taking a late-evening constitutional. But the man's bulk was unmistakable as he headed toward the city, hugging the shadows as he went. Only when he was completely out of sight did Marty go back to the house.

All the windows were locked, back and front; there were no visible lights. Perhaps—the doubt niggled—she was not even in the house; perhaps she'd gone out while he was dozing in the car. He prayed not; and praying, forced open the back door with a jimmy he'd bought for that very purpose. That and a flashlight: the standbys of any self-respecting burglar.

Inside, the atmosphere was sterile. He began a room-by-room search of the ground floor, determined to be as systematic as possible. This was no time for unprofessional behavior: no shouting, no rushing about; just a cautious, efficient investigation. The rooms were all empty, of people and of furniture. A few items, discarded by the previous occupants of the house, emphasized rather than alleviated the sense of desolation. He ascended a flight.

On the second floor he found Breer's room. It stank; an unwholesome mingling of perfume and rancid meat. In the corner a large-screened black-and-white television had been left on, its sound turned down to a sibilant whisper; some sort of quiz show was playing. The quizmaster howled soundlessly in mock despair at a contestant's defeat. The fluttering, metallic light fell on the few articles of furniture in the room: a bed with a bare mattress and several stained cushions; a mirror propped on a chair, the seat of which was littered with cosmetics and toilet waters. On the walls were photographs torn from a book of war atrocities. He did no more than glimpse at them, but their details, even in the doubtful light, were appalling. He closed the door on the squalor and tried the next. It was the toilet. Beside that, the bathroom. The fourth and last door on this floor was tucked around a half-corridor, and it was locked. He turned the handle once, twice, back and forth, and then pressed his ear to the wood, listening for some clue from within.

"Carys?"

There was no reply: no sound of occupancy either.

"Carys? It's Marty. Can you hear me?" He rattled the handle again, more fiercely. "It's Marty."

Impatience overtook him. She was there, just beyond the door—he was suddenly seized by the absolute conviction of her presence. He kicked the door, more out of frustration than anything; then, raising his heel to the lock, he booted it with all his strength. The wood began to splinter beneath his assault. Half a dozen further blows and the lock cracked; he put his shoulder to the door and forced it open.

The room smelled of her; was hot with her. Other than her presence and her heat, however, it was practically empty. Just a bucket in the corner, and a selection of empty dishes; a scattering of books, a blanket, a small table on which lay her gear: needles, hypodermic, dishes, matches. She was lying, curled up on herself, in a corner of the room. A lamp, with a low-voltage bulb in it, stood in another corner, its shade partially draped with a cloth to keep the light level lower yet. She was wearing only a T-shirt and a pair of panties. Other articles of clothing, jeans, sweaters, shirts, lay strewn around. When she looked up at him he could see how the sweat on her brow made her hair cling.

"Carys."

At first she didn't seem to recognize him.

"It's me. It's Marty."

A tick of a frown creased her shiny forehead. "Marty?" she said, her voice in miniature. The frown deepened: he wasn't sure she even saw him; her eyes swam. "Marty," she repeated, and this time the name seemed to mean something to her.

"Yes, it's me."

He crossed the room to her, and she seemed almost shocked by the suddenness of his approach. Her eyes sprang open, recognition flooding into them, with fear in attendance. She half-sat up, the T-shirt clinging to her sweaty torso. The crook of her arm was punctured and bruised.

"Don't come near me."

"What's wrong?"

"Don't come near me."

He took a step back at the ferocity of her order. What the hell had they done to her?

She sat up fully, and put her head between her legs, elbows on her knees.

"Wait . . ." she said, still whispering.

Her breath became very regular. He waited, aware for the first time that the room seemed to buzz. Perhaps not just the room: perhaps this whine—as if a generator were humming away to itself somewhere in the building—had been in the air since he'd first come in. If so, he hadn't noticed it. Now, waiting for her to finish whatever ritual she was engaged upon, it irritated him. Subtle, yet so pervasive it was impossible, after a few seconds of hearing it, to know if it was more than a whine in the inner ear. He swallowed hard: his sinuses clicked. The sound went on, a monotone. At last, Carys looked up.

"It's all right," she said. "He isn't here."

"I could have told you that. He left the house two hours ago. I watched him go."

"He doesn't need to be here physically," she said, rubbing the back of her neck.

"Are you all right?"

"I'm fine." From the tone of her voice they might have seen each other only the day before. He felt foolish, as though his relief, his desire to pick her up and run, was inappropriate, even redundant.

"We have to go," he said. "They may come back."

She shook her head. "No use," she told him.

"What do you mean, no use?"

"If you knew what he can do."

"Believe me, I've seen."

He thought of Bella, poor dead Bella, with her pups suckling rot. He'd seen enough, and more.

"There's no use trying to escape," she insisted. "He's got access to my head. I'm an open book to him." This was an overstatement. He was less and less able to control her. But she was tired of the fight: almost as tired as the European. She wondered sometimes if he hadn't infected her with his world-weariness; if a trace of him in her cortex hadn't tainted every possibility with the knowledge of its dissolution. She saw that now, in Marty, whose face she'd dreamed, whose body she'd wanted. Saw how he would age, would wind down and die, as everything wound down and died. Why stand up at all, the disease in her system asked, if it's only a matter of time before you fall down again?

"Can't you block him out?" Marty demanded.

"I'm too weak to resist him. With you I'll be weaker still."

"Why?" The remark appalled him.

"As soon as I relax, he'll get through. Do you see? The moment I surrender to anything, *anyone*, he can break in."

Marty thought about Carys' face on the pillow, and the way, for an insane moment, another face had seemed to peer down between her fingers. The Last European had been watching, even then; sharing the experience. A *ménage à trois* for male, female and occupying spirit. Its obscenity touched deeper chords of anger in him: not the superficial rage of a righteous man, but a profound rejection of the European in all his decadence. Whatever happened as a consequence, he would not be talked into leaving Carys to Mamoulian's devices. If need be he'd take her against her will. When she was out of this buzzing house, with the despair peeling the wallpaper, she'd remember how good life could be; he'd *make* her remember. He stepped toward her again, and went down on his haunches to touch her. She flinched.

"He's occupied—" he reassured her, "—he's at the casino."

"He'll kill you," she said simply, "if he finds you've been here."

"He'll kill me whatever happens now. I've interfered. I've seen his hidey-hole, and I'm going to do damage to it before we go, just so he remembers me."

"Do whatever you want to do." She shrugged. "It's up to you. But leave me be."

"So Papa was right," Marty said bitterly.

"Papa? What did he tell you?"

"That you wanted to be with Mamoulian all along."

"No."

"You want to be *like* him!"

"No, Marty, *no!*"

"I suppose he supplies the best-quality dope, eh? And I can't, can I?" She didn't deny this; just looked sullen. "What the fuck am I doing here?" he said. "You're happy, aren't you? Christ; you're happy."

It was laughable to think how he'd misunderstood the politics of this rescue. She was content in this hovel, as long as she was supplied. Her talk of Mamoulian's invasions were window dressing. In her heart she could forgive him every crime he perpetrated as long as the dope kept coming.

He stood up. "Where's his room?"

"No, Marty."

"I want to see where he sleeps. Where is it?"

She pulled herself up on his arm. Her hands were hot and damp.

"Please leave, Marty. This isn't a game. It's not all going to be forgiven when we come to the end, you know? It doesn't even stop when you die. Do you understand what I'm saying?"

"Oh, yes," he said, "I understand." He put his palm on her face. Her breath smelled sour. His too, he thought, but for the whisky.

"I'm not an innocent any longer. I know what's going on. Not all of it, but enough. I've seen things I pray I never see again; I've heard stories . . . Christ, *I understand*." How could he impress it upon her forcibly enough? "I'm shit-scared. I've never been so scared in my life."

"You've got reason," she said coldly.

"Don't you care what happens to you?"

"Not much."

"I'll find you dope," he said. "If that's all that's keeping you here; I'll get it for you."

Did a doubt cross her face? He pressed the point home. "I saw you looking for me at the funeral."

"You were there?"

"Why were you looking if you didn't want me to come?"

She shrugged. "I don't know. I thought maybe you'd gone with Papa."

"Dead, you mean?"

She frowned at him. "No. Gone away. Wherever he's gone."

It took a moment for her words to sink in. At last, he said: "You mean he's not dead?"

She shook her head. "I thought you knew. I thought you'd be involved with his getaway."

Of course the old bastard wasn't dead. Great men didn't just lie down and die offstage. They bided their time through the middle acts—revered, mourned and vilified—before appearing to play some final scene or other. A death scene; a marriage.

"Where is he?" Marty asked.

"I don't know, and neither does Mamoulian. He tried to get me to find him, the way I found Toy; but I can't do it. I've lost focus. I even tried to find *you* once. It was useless. I could scarcely think my way beyond the front door."

"But you found Toy?"

"That was at the beginning. Now . . . I'm used up. I tell him it hurts. Like something's going to break inside me." Pain, remembered and actual, registered on her face.

"And you still want to stay?"

"It'll be over soon. For all of us."

"Come with me. I've got friends who can help us," he appealed to her, gripping her wrists. "Gentle God, can't you see I need you? *Please*. I need you."

"I'm no use. I'm weak."

"Me too. I'm weak too. We deserve each other."

The thought, in its cynicism, seemed to please her. She pondered it a moment before saying, "Maybe we do," very quietly. Her face was a maze of indecision; dope and doubt. Finally she said: "I'll dress."

He hugged her, hard, breathing the staleness of her hair, knowing that this first victory might be his only one, but jubilating nevertheless. She gently broke his embrace and turned to the business of preparing to go. He watched her while she pulled on her jeans, but her self-consciousness made him leave her to it. He stepped onto the landing. Out of her presence, the hum filled his ears; louder now, he thought, than it had been. Switching on his flashlight he climbed the last flight of stairs to Mamoulian's room. With each step he took the whine deepened; it sounded in the boards of the stairs and in the walls—a living presence.

On the top landing there was only one door; the room beyond it apparently spread over the entire top floor. Mamoulian, the natural aristocrat, had taken the choicest space for himself. The door had been left open. The European feared no intruder. When Marty pushed, it swung inward a few inches, but his reluctant flashlight beam failed to penetrate more than an arm's length into the darkness beyond. He stood on the threshold like a child hesitating in front of a ghost-train ride.

During his peripheral association with Mamoulian he had come to feel an intense curiosity about the man. There was harm there, no doubt of that, perhaps terrible capacities for violence. But just as Mamoulian's face had appeared beneath Carys', there was probably a face under that of the European. More than one, perhaps. Half a hundred faces, each stranger than the one before, regressing toward some state that was older than Bethlehem. He had to have one peep, didn't he? One look, for old times' sake. Girding his loins, he pushed forward into the living darkness of the room.

"Marty!"

Something flickered in front of him, a bubble burst in his head as Carys called up to him.

"Marty! I'm ready!" The hum in the room seemed to have risen as he entered. Now, as he withdrew, it lowered itself to a moan of disappointment. *Don't go,* it seemed to sigh. *Why go? She can wait. Let her wait. Stay awhile up here and see what's to be seen.*

"There's no time," Carys said.

Almost angered to have been summoned away, Marty closed the door on the voice, and went down.

"I don't feel good," she said, when he joined her on the lower landing.

"Is it him? Is he trying to get to you?"

"No. I'm just dizzy. I didn't realize that I'd got so weak."

"There's a car outside," he said, offering a supportive hand. She waved him off.

"There's a parcel of my things," she said. "In the room."

He went back to get it, and was picking it up when she made a small noise of complaint, and stumbled on the stairs.

"Are you all right?"

"Yes," she said. When he appeared on the stairs beside her, pillowcase parcel in hand, she gave him an ashen look. "The house wants me to stay," she whispered.

"We'll take it steady," he said, and went ahead of her, for fear she stumble again. They reached the hallway without further incident.

"We can't go by the front door," she said. "It's double-locked from the outside."

As they made their way back through the hall, they heard the unmistakable sound of the back door opening.

"Shit," Marty said, under his breath. He let go of Carys' arm and slipped back through the gloom to the front door, and tried to open it. It was, as Carys had warned, double-locked. Panic was rising in him, but in its confusion a still voice, which he knew to be the voice of the room, said: *No need to worry. Come up. Be safe in me. Hide in me.* He thrust the temptation aside. Carys' face was turned to his:

"It's Breer," she breathed. The dog-killer was in the kitchen. Marty could hear him, smell him. Carys tapped at Marty's sleeve, and pointed to a bolted door under the well of the stairs. Cellar, he guessed. White-faced in the murk, she pointed down. He nodded.

Breer, about some business, was singing to himself. Strange, to think of him happy, this lumbering slaughterer; content enough with his lot to sing.

Carys had slid the bolt open on the cellar door. Steps, dimly illuminated by the thrown light from the kitchen, led down into the pit. A smell of disinfectant and wood shaving: healthy smells. They crept down the stairs; cringing at each scraped heel, each creaking step. But the Razor-Eater was too busy to hear, it seemed. There was no howl of pursuit. Marty closed the cellar door on them, desperately hoping Breer would not notice that the bolts had been drawn, and listened.

In time, the sound of running water; then the clink of cups, a teapot perhaps: the monster was brewing camomile.

Breer's senses were not as acute as they had been. The heat of the summer made him listless and weak. His skin smelled, his hair was falling out, his bowels would scarcely move these days. He needed a holiday, he'd decided. Once the European had found Whitehead, and dispatched him—and that was surely only a matter of days away—he'd go and see the aurora borealis. That would mean leaving his houseguest—he felt her proximity, mere feet away—but by that time she would have lost her appeal anyway. He was more fickle than he used to be, and beauty was transient. In two weeks, three in cool weather, all their charms dispersed.

He sat down at the table and poured a cup of the camomile. Its scent, once a great joy to him, was too subtle for his clogged sinuses, but he drank it for tradition's sake. Later he'd go up to his room and watch the soap operas he loved so much; maybe he'd look in on Carys and watch her while she slept; oblige her, if she woke, to pass water in his presence. Lost in a reverie of toilet training, he sat and sipped his tea.

Marty had hoped the man would retire to his room with his brew, leaving them access to the back door, but Breer was clearly staying put for a while.

He reached back in the dark to Carys. She was on the stairs behind him, trembling from head to toe, as was he. Foolishly he'd left his jimmy, his only weapon, somewhere in the house; probably in Carys' room. Should it come to a face-to-face confrontation, he was weaponless. Worse; time was passing. How long before Mamoulian came home? His heart sank at the thought. He slid down the stairs, hands on the cold brick of the wall, past Carys and into the body of the cellar itself. Perhaps there was a weapon of some kind down here. Even, hope of hopes, another exit from the house. There was very little light, however. He could see no chinks to suggest a trapdoor or coalhole. Certain that he was out of direct line with the door, he switched on his flashlight. The cellar was not entirely empty. There was a tarpaulin strung up to divide it, an artificial wall.

He put his hand up to the low roof and guided himself across the cellar step by tentative step, clinging to the pipes on the ceiling for equilibrium. He pulled the tarpaulin aside, and aimed the flashlight beam into the space beyond. As he did so his stomach leaped up into his mouth. A cry almost came; he stifled it an instant before it escaped.

A yard or two from where he stood was a table. At it sat a young girl. She was staring at him.

He put his fingers to his mouth to hush her before she cried out. But there was no need. She neither moved nor spoke. The glazed look on her face was not mental deficiency. The child was dead, he now understood. There was dust on her.

"Oh, Christ," he said, very quietly.

Carys heard him. She turned, and made her way to the bottom of the steps.

"Marty?" she breathed.

"Stay away," he said, unable to unglue his eyes from the dead girl. There was more than the body to feast his eyes upon. There were the knives and the plate on the table in front of her, with a napkin lovingly shaken out and spread in her lap. The plate, he saw, had meat on it, sliced thinly as if by a master butcher. He moved past the body, trying to slide from under its gaze. As he passed the table he brushed the silk napkin; it slid through the divide of the girl's legs.

Two horrors came, brutal twins, one upon the other. The napkin had neatly covered a place on the girl's inner thigh from which the meat on her plate had been carved. In the same moment came another recognition: that he had eaten such meat, at Whitehead's encouragement, in the room at the estate. It had been the tastiest of delicacies; he'd left his plate clean.

Nausea swept up him. He dropped the flashlight as he tried to fight the sickness back, but it was beyond his physical control. The bitter odor of stomach acid filled the cellar. All at once there was no hiding, no help for this insanity but to throw it up and take the consequences.

Overhead, the Razor-Eater raised himself from his tea, pushed back his chair and came out of the kitchen.

"Who?" his thick voice demanded. "Who's down there?"

He crossed unerringly to the cellar door and pulled it open. Dead fluorescent light rolled down the stairs.

"Who's there?" he said again, and now he was coming down in pursuit of the light, his feet thundering on the wooden steps. *"What are you doing?"* He was shouting, his voice was at hysteria pitch. *"You can't come down here!"*

Marty looked up, dizzied by breathlessness, to see Carys crossing the cellar toward him. Her eyes alighted on the tableau at the table but she kept admirable control, ignoring the body and reaching for the knife and fork that sat beside the plate. She snatched them both up, catching the tablecloth in her haste. The plate and its flyblown serving spun to the floor; knives cluttered beside it.

Breer had paused at the bottom of the stairs to take in the desecration of his temple. Now, appalled, he came careering toward the infidels, his size lending awesome momentum to the attack. Dwarfed by him, Carys half-turned as he reached for her, roaring. She was eclipsed. Marty couldn't make out who was where. But the confusion lasted only seconds. Then Breer was raising his gray hands as if to push Carys off, his head shaking to and fro. A howl was issuing from him, more of complaint than pain.

Carys ducked his flailing, and slipped sideways out of harm's way. The knife and fork she had held were no longer in her hands. Breer had run straight onto them. He seemed not to be aware of their presence in his gut, however. His concern was for the girl whose body was even now toppling and falling into a rubber-jointed heap on the cellar floor. He rushed to her comfort, ignoring the desecraters in his anguish. Carys caught sight of Marty, his face a greaseball, hauling himself upright by hanging on to the ceiling pipes.

"Move!" she yelled at him. She waited long enough to see that he had responded and then made for the stairs. As she clattered up the steps toward the light, she heard the Razor-Eater behind him, shouting: "No! No!" She glanced over her shoulder. Marty gained the bottom of the stairs just as Breer's hands—manicured, perfumed and lethal—grabbed for him. Marty threw an ill-aimed swipe backward, and Breer lost his hold. It was a moment's grace, however, no more. Marty was only halfway up the stairs before his attacker was back on his heels. The rouged face was smeared as it peered up from the cellar depths, the features so contorted by outrage that they appeared scarcely human.

This time Breer's grasp caught Marty's trousers, the fingers digging deeply into the muscle of his skin. Marty yelped as cloth tore and blood ran. He flung out a hand to Carys, who loaned what strength she had left to the contest, pulling Marty up toward her. Breer, badly balanced, lost his snatched grip, and Marty stumbled up the stairs, pressing Carys ahead of him. She tumbled into the hallway, and Marty followed, with Breer at his back. At the top of the stairs Marty suddenly turned and kicked. His heel struck the Razor-Eater's punctured belly. Breer fell backward, hands clawing the air for support; there was none to be had. His nails managed to rake the brickwork as he toppled and fell heavily down the steps, hitting the stone floor of the cellar with a lazy thud. There, sprawled, he lay still; a painted giant.

Marty slammed the door on him, and bolted it. He felt too squeamish to look at the gouging on his leg, but he could tell by the warmth soaking into sock and shoe that it was bleeding badly.

"Can you . . . you get something . . ." he said, ". . . just to cover it?"

Too breathless to reply, Carys nodded, and rounded the corner into the kitchen. There was a towel on the draining board, but it was too unsavory to be used on an open wound. She started to search for something clean, however primitive. It was time they were gone; Mamoulian would not stay out all night.

In the hallway, Marty listened for any sound from the cellar. He heard none.

Another noise infiltrated, however, one that he'd almost forgotten about. The buzz of the house was back in his head, and that mellow voice was threaded into it, a dreamy undercurrent. Common sense told him to shut it out. But when he listened, trying to sort out its syllables, it seemed the nausea and the pain in his leg subsided.

On the back of a kitchen chair Carys had found one of Mamoulian's dark-gray shirts. The European was fastidious about his laundry. The shirt had been recently laundered; an ideal bandage. She tore it up—though its fine-quality cotton resisted— then soaked a length of it in cold water to clean the wound, and made strips of the rest to bind the leg up. When she was done, she went out into the hallway. But Marty had gone.

55

He had to see. Or if seeing wouldn't do (What was seeing anyway? Mere sensuality) then he would learn a new way of knowing. That was the promise the room whispered in his ear: a new thing to know and a way of knowing it. He pulled himself up the banisters, hand over hand, less and less aware of the pain as he climbed to the buzzing darkness. He wanted so much to take the ghost-train ride. There were dreams in there he'd never dreamed, would never have a chance to dream again. Blood squelched in his shoe; he laughed at it. A spasm had begun in his leg; he ignored it. The last steps were ahead: he climbed them with steady work. The door was ajar.

He achieved the summit of the stairs and limped toward it.

Though it was totally dark in the cellar, that scarcely concerned the Razor-Eater. It was many weeks since his eyes had worked as well as they used to: he'd learned to substitute touch for sight. He stood up and tried to think clearly. Soon the European would come home. There would be punishment for leaving the house unattended and letting this escape take place. Worse than that, he would not see the girl anymore; no longer be able to watch her pass water, that fragrant water he preserved for special occasions. He was desolate.

He heard her moving even now in the hallway above him; she was going up the stairs. The rhythm of her tiny feet was familiar to him, he'd listened long nights and days to her padding back and forth in her cell. In his mind's eye the ceiling of the cellar became transparent; he looked up between her legs as she climbed the stairs; that lavish slit gaped. It made him angry to be losing it, and her. She was old, of course, not like the pretty at the table, or the others on the streets, but there had been times when her presence had been the one thing keeping him from insanity.

He went back, stumbling in the pitch, in the direction of his little autocannibal, whose dining had been so rudely interrupted. Before he got to her, his foot kicked at one of the carving knives he'd left on the table should she want to help herself. He went down on all fours and patted the ground until he found it, and then he crawled back up the stairs and started to hack at the wood where the light through the door crack showed the bolts to be.

C arys didn't want to go to the top of the house again. There was so much up there she feared. Innuendo rather than fact, but enough to make her weak. Why Marty had gone up—and that was the only place he *could* have gone—confounded her. Despite his claim to understanding, there was still so much he had to learn.

"Marty?" she'd called, at the foot of the stairs, hoping he'd appear at the top, smiling, and limp down to her without her having to go up and fetch him. But her inquiry was met with silence, and the night wasn't getting any younger. The European might come to the door at any moment.

Unwillingly, she started up the stairs.

M arty had never understood until now. He'd been a virgin, living in a world innocent of this deep and exhilarating penetration, not simply of body, of mind too. The air in the room closed around his head as soon as he stepped into it. The plates of his skull seemed to grind against each other; the voice of the room, no longer needing its whispered tones, shouted in his brain. *So you came? Of course you came. Welcome to Wonderland.* He was dimly aware that it was his own voice that was speaking these words. It had probably been his voice all along. He had been talking to himself like a lunatic. Even though he'd now seen through the trick, the voice came again, lower this time—*This is a fine place to find yourself in, don't you think?*

At the question, he looked around. There was nothing to see, not even walls. If there were windows in the room, they were hermetically sealed. Not a chink of the outside world belonged in here.

"I don't see anything," he murmured in reply to the room's boast.

The voice laughed; he laughed with it.

Nothing here to be frightened of, it said. Then, after a smirking pause: *Nothing here at all.*

And that was right, wasn't it? Nothing at all. It wasn't just darkness that kept him sightless, it was the room itself. He glanced giddily over his shoulder: he could no longer see the door behind him, even though he knew he had left it open when he came in. There should have been at least a glimmer of light from downstairs spilling into the room. But that illumination had been eaten up, as was the beam of his flashlight. A smothering gray fog pressed so close to his eyes that even if he lifted his hand up in front of him he could see nothing.

You're all right here, the room soothed him. *No judges here; no bars here.*

"Am I blind?" he asked.

No, the room replied. *You're seeing truly for the first time.*

"I . . . don't . . . like it."

Of course you don't. But you'll learn in time. Living's not for you. Ghosts of ghosts, the living are. You want to lie down; be done with that caper. Nothing's essential, boy.

"I want to leave."

Would I tell you lies?

"I want to leave . . . please."

You're in safe hands.

"Please."

He stumbled forward, confused as to which way the door was.

In front, or behind? Arms spread before him like a blind man on a cliff edge, he reeled, looking for some point of security. This wasn't the adventure he'd thought it would be; it was nothing. *Nothing is essential.* Once stepped into, this boundless nowhere had neither distance nor depth, north nor south. And everything outside it—the stairs, the landing, the stairs below that, the hallway, Carys—all of it was like a fabrication. A dream of palpability, not a true place. There *was* no true place but here. All he'd lived and experienced, all he'd taken joy in, taken pain in, it was insubstantial. Passion was dust. Optimism, self-deception. He doubted now even the memory of senses: the textures, the temperatures. Color, form, pattern. All diversions—games the mind had invented to disguise this unbearable *zero*. And why not? Looking too long into the abyss would madden a man.

Not mad, surely? said the room, savoring the thought.

Always, even in his blackest moments (lying on a bunk in a hothouse cell, listening to the man in the bed below sob in his sleep) there had been something to look forward to: a letter, a dawn, release; some glimpse of meaning.

But here, meaning was *dead*. Future and past were *dead*. Love and life were *dead*. Even death was dead, because anything that excited emotion was unwelcome here. Only nothing: once and for all, nothing.

"Help me," he said, like a lost child.

Go to Hell, the room respectfully replied; and for the first time in his life, he knew exactly what that meant.

On the second landing, Carys stopped. She could hear voices; not, now she listened more closely, plural, but the same voice—Marty's voice—speaking and answering itself. It was difficult to know where the exchange was coming from; the words seemed to be everywhere and nowhere. She glanced into her room, then into Breer's. Finally, steeling herself for a repeat of her nightmare, she looked into the bathroom. He was in none of them. There was no avoiding the unpalatable conclusion. He'd gone upstairs, back to Mamoulian's room.

Even as she crossed the landing to the flight of stairs that led up to the top story, another sound caught her attention: somewhere below a blade was hacking wood. She knew at once it was the Razor-Eater. He was up and itching to come for her. What a house this is, she thought, for all its bland façade. It would take another Dante to describe its depths and heights: dead children, Razor-Eaters, addicts, madmen and all. Surely the stars that hung at its zenith squirmed in their settings; in the earth beneath it, the magma curdled.

In the European's room, Marty cried out, a bewildered plea. Calling his name in answer, and hoping to God he heard her, she scrambled to the top of the stairs and crossed, heart in mouth, toward the door.

He had fallen to his knees; what was left of his self-preservation was a tattered and hopeless thought, gray on gray. Even the voice had stopped now. It was bored with the banter. Besides, it had taught its lesson well. *Nothing is essential*, it had said, and shown him the why and how; or rather dug up that part of him that had known all along. Now he would just wait for the progenitor of this elegant syllogism to come and dispatch him. He lay down, not certain if he was alive or dead, if the man who would presently come would kill him or resurrect him: only certain that to lie down was easiest, in this, the emptiest of all possible worlds.

Carys had been in this Nowhere before. She'd tasted its flat, futile air. But in the past few hours she had glimpsed something beyond its aridity. There had been victories today; not large, perhaps, but victories nevertheless. She thought of the way Marty had come, his eyes with more than lust in them. That was a victory, wasn't it? She'd won that feeling out of him, earned it in some incalculable way. She would not be beaten by this last oppressor, this stale beast that smothered her senses. It was only the European's residue, after all. His sloughings, left to decorate his bower. Scurf; dross. It and he were contemptible.

"Marty," she said. "Where are you?"

"Nowhere . . ." came a voice.

She followed it, stumbling. Desolation pressed in, insisting on her.

B reer paused for a moment. A long way off, he heard voices. He couldn't make out the words, but the sense was academic. They hadn't escaped yet, that was the important thing. He had plans for them once he got out: especially the man. He would divide him into tiny pieces, until not even his loved ones could tell which part was his finger, which his face.

He began to hack at the wood with renewed fervor. Under his relentless attack the door finally began to splinter.

C arys followed Marty's voice through the fog, but he eluded her. Either he was moving around or else the room was somehow deceiving her, echoing his voice off the walls, or even impersonating him. Then his voice called her name, close by. She turned in the murk, utterly without bearings. There was no sign of the door she'd entered by—it had disappeared, as had the windows. The pieces of her resolve began to unglue. Doubt seeped in, smirking.

Well, well. And who are you? somebody asked. Perhaps herself.

"I know my name," she breathed. It wasn't going to unseat her that way. "I know my name."

She was a pragmatist, damn it! She wasn't prone to believing that the world was all in the mind. That's why she'd gone to H: the world was *too real*. Now here was this vapor in her ears, telling her she was nothing, everything was nothing; nameless muck.

"Shit," she told it. "You're shit. *His* shit!"

It didn't deign to reply; she took the advantage while she had it.

"Marty. Can you hear me?" There was no answer. "It's just a room, Marty. Can you hear me? That's all it is! Just a room."

You've been in me before, the voice in her head pointed out. *Remember?*

Oh, yes; she remembered. There was a tree in this fog somewhere; she'd seen it in the sauna. It was a blossom-laden freak of a tree, and under it she'd glimpsed such horrid sights. Was that where Marty had gone? Was he hanging from it even now: new fruit?

Damn it, no! She mustn't give in to such thoughts. It was just a room. She could find the walls if she concentrated, even find the window maybe.

Careless of what she might stumble over, she turned to her right, and walked four paces, five, until her outstretched hands hit the wall: it was shockingly, splendidly solid. Ha! she thought, fuck you and your tree! Look what I've found. She put her palms flat on the wall. Now; left or right? She threw up an imaginary coin. It came down heads, and she started to edge along to her left.

No you don't, the room whispered.

"Try stopping me."

Nowhere to go, it spat back, *just round and round. You've always gone round and round, haven't you? Weak, lazy, ridiculous woman.*

"You call *me* ridiculous. You. A talking *fog*."

The wall she was moving steadily along seemed to stretch on and on. After half a dozen paces she began to doubt the theory she was testing. Perhaps this *was* a manipulable space after all. Perhaps she was moving away from Marty along some new Wall of China. But she clung to the cold surface as tenaciously as a climber to a sheer cliff. If necessary she would make her way around the entire room until she found the door, Marty, or both.

Pure cunt, the room said. *That's all you are. Can't even find your way out of a little maze like this. Better just lie down and take what's coming to you, the way good cunts should.*

Did she sense a note of desperation in this fresh assault?

Despair? said the room. *I thrive on it. Cunt.*

She had reached a corner of the room. Now she turned along the next wall.

No you don't, said the room.

Yes I do, she thought.

I wouldn't go that way. Oh, no. Really I wouldn't. The Razor-Eater's up here with you. Can't you hear him? He's just a few inches ahead of you. No, don't! Oh, please don't! I hate the smell of blood.

Pure histrionics; that was all it could muster. The more the room panicked, the more her spirits rose.

Stop! For your own sake! Stop!

Even as it shouted in her head her hands found the window. This was what it was so frightened she'd discover.

CUNT! it shrieked. *You'll be sorry. I promise you. Oh, yes.*

There were no curtains or shutters; the window had been entirely boarded up so that nothing could spoil this perfect nullity. Her fingers scrabbled for purchase on one of the planks: it was time she let some outside world *in*. The wood had been very firmly nailed in place, however. Though she tugged, there was little or no give.

"Shift, damn you!"

The plank creaked, splinters sprang off it. "Yes," she coaxed, "here we are." Light, a fractured, all-too-uncertain thread of it, filtered between the planks. "Come on," she cajoled, pulling harder. The top joints of her fingers were bent back in her effort to wrest the wood from its place, but the thread of light had now widened to a beam. It fell on her, and through a veil of dirty air she began to make out the shape of her own hands.

It wasn't daylight that spilled between the planks. Just the glimmer of streetlamps and car headlights, of starlight perhaps, of televisions blazing in a dozen houses along Caliban Street. It was sufficient, though. With every inch the gap increased, more certainty invaded the room; edge and substance.

Elsewhere in the room, Marty too felt the light. It irritated him, like someone throwing open spring-morning curtains on a dying man. He crabbed his way across the floor, trying to bury himself in the fog before it dispersed, seeking out the reassuring voice that would tell him nothing was essential. But it had gone. He was deserted, and the light was falling in broader and yet broader strokes. He could see a woman outlined against the window. She had wrenched off one plank and thrown it down. Now she was pulling at a second. "Come to Mama," she was saying, and the light came, defining her within ever more nauseating detail. He wanted none of it; it was a burden, this *being* business. He exhaled a little whistle of pain and exasperation.

She turned to him. "There you are," she said, crossing to him and pulling him to his feet. "We've got to be quick."

Marty was staring at the room, which was now revealed in all its banality. A mattress on the floor; an upturned porcelain cup; beside it, a water jug.

"Wake up," Carys said, shaking him.

No need to go, he thought; nothing to lose if I stay here and the gray comes again.

"For Christ's sake, Marty!" she yelled at him. From below came the sound of wood shrieking. He's coming, ready or not, she thought.

"Marty," she shouted at him. "Can you hear? It's Breer."

The name awoke horrors. A cold girl, sitting at her table laid with her own meat. His terrible, unspeakable joke. The image slapped the fog from Marty's head. The thing that had performed that horror was downstairs; he remembered now, all too well. He looked at Carys with clear, if tearful, eyes.

"What happened?"

"No time," she said.

He limped after her toward the door. She was still carrying

one of the planks she'd pulled from the window, its nails still in place. The noise from below mounted still, the din of unhinged door and mind.

The pain in Marty's torn leg, which the room had so skillfully dulled, now raged up again. He needed support from Carys to make his way down the first flight of stairs. They made the descent together, his hand, bloody from touching the wound, marking their passage on the wall.

Halfway down the second flight of stairs, the cacophony from the cellar stopped.

They stood still, waiting for Breer's next move. From below there came a thin creak as the Razor-Eater pushed the cellar door wide. Other than the dim light from the kitchen, which had several corners to round before it reached the hallway, there was nothing to illuminate the scene. Hunter and prey, both camouflaged by darkness, hung on to this tenuous moment, neither knowing if the next would bring catastrophe. Carys left Marty behind and slipped down the remaining steps to the bottom of the stairs. Her feet were all but silent on the carpetless stairs, but after the sense deprivation of Mamoulian's room Marty heard her every heartbeat.

Nothing moved in the hallway; she beckoned Marty down after her. The passageway was still, and apparently empty. Breer was near, she knew: but where? He was large and cumbersome: hiding places would be difficult to find. Perhaps, she prayed, he hadn't escaped after all, merely given up, exhausted. She stepped forward.

Without warning, the Razor-Eater emerged from the door of the front room, roaring. The carving knife descended in a swooping stroke. She succeeded in sidestepping the blow, but in doing so all but lost her balance. It was Marty's hand that caught her arm, and dragged her out of the way of Breer's second slash. The force of the Razor-Eater's charge propelled him past her. He slammed against the front door; the glass rattled.

"Out!" Marty said, seeing the way clear along the passage. But this time Carys had no intention of running. There was a time for running and a time for confrontation; she might never have another opportunity to thank Breer for his many humiliations. She shrugged Marty's hold off and took the wooden club she still carried in a two-handed grasp.

The Razor-Eater had righted himself, the knife still in his hand, and now he took a raging step toward her. She preempted his attack, however. She raised the plank and ran at him, delivering a blow to the side of his head. His neck, already fractured by his fall, snapped. The nails in the plank pierced his skull, and she was obliged to relinquish her weapon, leaving it fixed like a fifth limb to the side of Breer's head. He fell to his knees. His twitching hand dropped the knife while the other scrabbled for the plank and wrenched it from his head. She was glad of the darkness; the slosh of blood and the tattoo his feet beat on the bare boards were more than enough to appall. He knelt upright for several moments, then pitched forward, pressing the cutlery in his belly all the way home.

She was satisfied. This time, when Marty pulled at her, she went with him.

As they made their way along the corridor there was a sharp rapping on the wall. They stopped. What now? More possessing spirits?

"What is it?" he asked.

The rapping ceased, then began again, this time accompanied by a voice.

"Be quiet, will you? There's people trying to sleep in here."

"Next door," she said. The thought of their complaints struck her as funny, and by the time they'd made their way out of the house, past the wreckage of the cellar door and Breer's cooling camomile, they were both laughing.

They slipped away down the darkened alleyway behind the house to the car, where they sat for several minutes, tears and laughter coming on them in alternating waves; two mad people, the Calibanese might have guessed; or else adulterers, amused by a night of adventures.

XI. KINGDOM COME

56

Chad Schuckman and Tom Loomis had been bringing the message of the Church of the Resurrected Saints to the populace of London for three weeks now, and they were sick to the back teeth of it. "Some way to spend a vacation," Tom grumbled daily as they planned their day's route. Memphis seemed a long way off, and they were both homesick for it. Besides, the whole campaign was proving a failure. The sinners they encountered on the doorsteps of this godforsaken city were as indifferent to the Reverend's message of imminent Apocalypse as they were to his promise of Deliverance.

Despite the weather (or maybe because of it), sin wasn't hot news in England these days. Chad was contemptuous: "They don't know what they've got coming," he kept telling Tom, who knew all the descriptions of the Deluge by heart but also knew they sounded better from the lips of a golden boy like Chad than from himself. He even suspected that those few people who did stop to listen did so more because Chad had the looks of a corn-fed angel than because they wanted to hear the Reverend's inspired word. Most simply slammed their doors.

But Chad was adamant. "There's sin here," he assured Tom, "and where there's sin there's guilt. And where there's guilt there's money for the Lord's Work." It was a simple equation: and if Tom had some doubts about its ethics he kept them to himself. Better his silence than Chad's disapprobation; all they had was each other in this foreign city, and Tom wasn't about to lose his guiding light.

Sometimes, though, it was difficult to keep your faith intact. Especially on blistering days like this, when your polyester suit was itching at the back of your neck and the Lord, if He was in His Heaven, was keeping well out of sight. Not a hint of a breeze to cool your face; not a rain cloud in sight.

"Isn't this *from* something?" Tom asked Chad.

"What's that?" Chad was counting the pamphlets they still had left to distribute today.

"The name of the street," Tom said. "Caliban. It's from something."

"That so?" Chad had finished counting. "We only got rid of five pamphlets."

He handed the armful of literature to Tom and fished for a comb in the inside pocket of his jacket. Despite the heat, he looked cool and unruffled. By comparison, Tom felt shabby, overheated and, he feared, easily tempted from the path of righteousness. By *what*, he wasn't certain, but he was open to suggestions. Chad put the comb through his hair, restoring in one elegant sweep the perfect sheen of his halo. It was important, the Reverend taught, to look your best. "You're agents of the Lord," he'd said. "He wants you to be clean and tidy; to shine through every nook and cranny."

"Here," Chad said, exchanging the comb for the pamphlets. "Your hair's a mess."

Tom took the comb; its teeth had gold in them. He made a desultory attempt to control his coxcomb, while Chad looked on. Tom's hair wouldn't lie flat the way Chad's did. The Lord probably tutted at that: He wouldn't like it at all. But then what *did* the Lord like? He disapproved of smoking, drinking, fornication, tea, coffee, Pepsi, roller coasters, masturbation. And for those weak creatures who indulged in any or, God help them, *all* of the above the Deluge hovered.

Tom just prayed that the waters, when they came, would be cool.

The guy in the dark suit who answered the door of Number Eighty-two Caliban Street reminded both Tom and Chad of the Reverend. Not physically, of course. Bliss was a tanned, glutinous man, while this dude was thin and sallow. But there was the same implicit authority about them both; the same seriousness of purpose. He was drawn to the pamphlets too, the first real interest they'd had all morning. He even quoted Deuteronomy at them—a text they were unfamiliar with—and then, offering them both a drink, invited them into the house.

It was like home from home. The bare walls and floors; the smell of disinfectant and incense, as though something had just been cleaned up. Truth to tell, Tom thought this guy had taken the asceticism to extremes. The back room he led them into boasted two chairs, no more.

"My name is Mamoulian."

"How do you do? I'm Chad Schuckman, this is Thomas Loomis."

"Both saints, eh?" The young men looked mystified. "Your names. Both names of saints."

"Saint *Chad*?" the blond one ventured.

"Oh, certainly. He was an English bishop; we're speaking of the seventh century now. Thomas, of course, the great Doubter."

He left them awhile to fetch water. Tom squirmed in his chair.

"What's your problem?" Chad snapped. "He's the first sniff of a convert we've had over here."

"He's weird."

"You think the Lord cares if he's weird?" Chad said. It was a good question, and one for which Tom was shaping a reply when their host came back in.

"Your water."

"Do you live alone?" Chad asked. "It's such a big house for one person."

"Of late I've been alone," Mamoulian said, proffering the glasses of water. "And I must say, I'm in serious need of help."

I bet you are, Tom thought. The man looked at him as the idea flashed through his head, almost as though he'd said it aloud. Tom flushed, and drank his water to cover his embarrassment. It was warm. Had the English never heard of refrigerators? Mamoulian turned his attention back to Saint Chad.

"What are you two doing in the next few days?"

"The Lord's work," Chad returned patly.

Mamoulian nodded. "Good," he said.

"Spreading the word."

"'I will make you fishers of men.' "

"Matthew. Chapter Four," Chad returned.

"Perhaps," said Mamoulian, "if I allowed you to save my immortal soul, you might help me?"

"Doing what?"

Mamoulian shrugged: "I need the assistance of two healthy young animals like yourself."

Animals? That didn't sound too fundamentalist. Had this poor sinner never heard of Eden? No, Tom thought, looking at the man's eyes; no, he probably never has.

"I'm afraid we've got other commitments," Chad replied politely. "But we'll be very happy to have you come along when the Reverend arrives, and have you baptized."

"I'd like to meet the Reverend," the man returned. Tom wasn't certain if this wasn't all a charade. "We have so little time before the Maker's wrath descends," Mamoulian was saying. Chad nodded fervently. "Then we shall be as flotsam—shall we not?—as flotsam in the flood."

The words were the Reverend's almost precisely. Tom heard them falling from this man's narrow lips, and that accusation of being a Doubter came home to roost. But Chad was entranced. His face had that evangelical look that came over it during sermons; the look that Tom had always envied, but now thought positively rabid.

"Chad . . ." he began.

"Flotsam in the flood," Chad repeated, "*Hallelujah*."

Tom put his glass down beside his chair. "I think we should be going," he said, and got up. For some reason the bare boards he stood on seemed far more than six feet away from his eyes: more like sixty. As though he was a tower about to topple, his foundations dug away. "We've got so many streets to cover," he said, trying to focus on the problem at hand, which was, in a nutshell, how to get out of this house before something terrible happened.

"The Deluge," Mamoulian announced, "is almost upon us."

Tom reached toward Chad to wake him from his trance. The fingers at the end of his outstretched arm seemed a thousand miles from his eyes. "Chad," he said. Saint Chad; he of the halo, pissing rainbows.

"Are you all right, boy?" the stranger asked, swiveling his fish eyes in Tom's direction.

"I . . . feel . . ."

"What do you feel?" Mamoulian asked.

Chad was looking at him too, face innocent of concern; innocent, in fact, of all feeling. Perhaps—this thought dawned on Tom for the first time—*that* was why Chad's face was so perfect. White, symmetrical and completely empty.

"Sit down," the stranger said. "Before you fall down."

"It's all right," Chad reassured him.

"No," Tom said. His knees felt disobedient. He suspected they'd give out very soon.

"Trust me," Chad said. Tom wanted to. Chad had usually been right in the past. "Believe me, we're on to a good thing here. Sit down, like the gentleman said."

"Is it the heat?"

"Yes," Chad told the man on Tom's behalf. "It's the heat. It gets hot in Memphis; but we've got air-conditioning." He turned to Tom and put his hand on his companion's shoulder. Tom let himself give in to weakness, and sat down. He felt a fluttering at the back of his neck, as though a hummingbird were hovering there, but he didn't have the willpower to flick it away.

"You call yourselves agents?" the man said, almost under his breath. "I don't think you know the meaning of the word."

Chad was quick to their defense.

"The Reverend says—"

"The Reverend?" the man interrupted contemptuously. "Do you think he had the slightest idea of your value?"

This flummoxed Chad. Tom tried to tell his friend not to be flattered, but the words wouldn't come. His tongue lay in his mouth like a dead fish. Whatever happens now, he thought, at least it'll happen to us together. They'd been friends since first grade; they'd tasted pubescence and metaphysics together; Tom thought of them as inseparable. He hoped the man understood that where Chad went, Tom went too. The fluttering at his neck had stopped; a warm reassurance was creeping over his head. Things didn't seem so bad after all.

"I need help from you young men."

"To do what?" Chad asked.

"To begin the Deluge," Mamoulian replied. A smile, uncertain at first but broadening as the idea caught his imagination, appeared on Chad's face. His features, too often sober with zeal, ignited.

"Oh, yes," he said. He glanced across at Tom. "Hear what this man's telling us?"

Tom nodded.

"You hear, man?"

"I hear. I hear."

All his blissful life Chad had waited for this invitation. For the first time he could picture the literal reality behind the destruction he'd threatened on a hundred doorsteps. In his mind waters—red, raging waters—mounted into foam-crested waves and bore down on this pagan city. We are as flotsam in the flood, he said, and the words brought images with them. Men and women—but mostly women—running naked before these curling tides. The water was hot; rains of it fell on their screaming faces, their gleaming, jiggling breasts. This was what the Reverend had promised all along; and here was this man asking them to help make it all possible, to bring this thrashing, foamy Day of Days to consummation. How could they refuse? He felt the urge to thank the man for considering them worthy. The thought fathered the action. His knees bent, and he fell to the floor at Mamoulian's feet.

"Thank you," he said to the man with the dark suit.

"You'll help me, then?"

"Yes . . ." Chad replied; wasn't this homage sign enough? "Of course."

Behind him, Tom murmured his own concession.

"Thank you," Chad said. "Thank you."

But when he looked up the man, apparently convinced by their devotion, had already left the room.

57

Marty and Carys slept together in his single bed: long, rewarding sleep. If the baby in the room below them cried in the night, they didn't hear it. Nor did they hear the sirens on Kilburn High Road, police and fire engines going to a conflagration in Maida Vale. Dawn through the dirty window didn't wake them either, though the curtains had not been drawn. But once, in the early hours, Marty turned in his sleep and his eyes flickered open to see the first light of day at the glass. Rather than turning away from it, he let it fall on his lids as they flickered down again.

They had half a day together in the flat before the *need* began; bathing themselves, drinking coffee, saying very little. Carys washed and bound the wound on Marty's leg; they changed their clothes, ditching those they'd worn the previous night.

It wasn't until the middle of the afternoon that they started to talk. The dialogue began quite calmly, but Carys' nervousness escalated as she felt hungrier for a fix, and the talk rapidly became a desperate diversion from her jittering belly. She told Marty what life with the European had been like: the humiliations, the deceptions, the sense she had that he knew her father, and her too, better than she guessed. Marty in his turn attempted to paraphrase the story Whitehead had told him on that last night, but she was too distracted to concentrate properly. Her conversation became increasingly agitated.

"I have to have a fix, Marty."

"Now?"

"Pretty soon."

He'd been waiting for this moment and dreading it. Not because he couldn't find her a supply; he knew he could. But because he'd hoped somehow she'd be able to resist the need when she was with him.

"I feel really bad," she said.

"You're all right. You're with me."

"He'll come, you know."

"Not now, he won't."

"He'll be angry, and he'll come."

Marty's mind went back and back again to his experience in the upstairs room of Caliban Street. What he had seen there, or rather *not* seen there, had terrified him more profoundly than the dogs or Breer. Those were merely physical dangers. But what had gone on in the room was a danger of another order altogether. He had felt, perhaps for the first time in his life, that his *soul*—a notion he had hitherto rejected as Christian flim-flam—had been threatened. What he meant by the word he wasn't certain; not, he suspected, what the pope meant. But some part of him more essential than limb or life had been almost eclipsed, and Mamoulian had been responsible. What more could the creature unleash, if pressed? His curiosity was more now than an idle desire to know what was behind the veil: it had become a necessity. How could they hope to arm themselves against this demagogue without some clue to his nature?

"I don't want to know," Carys said, reading his thoughts. "If he comes, he comes. There's nothing we can do about it."

"Last night—" he began, about to remind her of how they had won the skirmish. She waved the thought away before it was finished. The strain on her face was unbearable; her need was flaying her.

"Marty . . ."

He looked across at her.

". . . you promised," she said accusingly.

"I haven't forgotten."

He'd done the mental arithmetic in his head: not the cost of the drug itself, but of lost pride. He would have to go to Flynn for the heroin; he knew no one else he could trust. They were both fugitives now, from Mamoulian and from the law.

"I'll have to make a phone call," he said.

"Make it," she replied.

She seemed to have physically altered in the last half-hour. Her skin was waxy; her eyes had a desperate gleam in them; the shaking was worsening by the minute.

"Don't make it easy for him," she said.

He frowned: "Easy?"

"He can make me do things I don't want to," she said. Tears had started to run. There was no accompanying sob, just a free-fall from the eyes. "Maybe make me hurt you."

"It's all right. I'll go now. There's a guy lives with Charmaine, he'll be able to get me stuff, don't worry. You want to come?"

She hugged herself. "No," she said. "I'll slow you down. Just go."

He pulled on his jacket, trying not to look at her; the mixture of frailty and appetite scared him. The sweat on her body was fresh; it gathered in the soft passage behind her clavicles; it streamed on her face.

"Don't let anybody in, OK?"

She nodded, her eyes searing him.

When he'd gone she locked the door behind him and went back to sit on the bed. The tears started to come again, freely. Not grief tears, just salt water. Well, perhaps there was some grief in them: for this rediscovered fragility, and for the man who had gone down the stairs.

He was responsible for her present discomfort, she thought. He'd been the one to seduce her into thinking she could stand on her own two feet. And where had it brought her; brought them both? To this hot-house cell in the middle of a July afternoon with so much malice ready to close in on them.

It wasn't love she felt for him. That was too big a burden of feeling to carry. It was at best infatuation, mingled with that sense of impending loss she always tasted when close to somebody, as though every moment in his presence she was internally mourning the time when he would no longer be there.

Below, the door slammed as he stepped into the street. She lay back on the bed, thinking of the first time they'd made love together. Of how even that most private act had been overlooked by the European. The thought of Mamoulian, once begun, was like a snowball on a steep hill. It rolled, gathering speed and size as it went, until it was monstrous. An avalanche, a whiteout.

For an instant she doubted that she was simply remembering: the feeling was so clear; so *real*. Then she had no doubts.

She stood up, the bedsprings creaking. It wasn't memory at all. *He was here.*

58

Flynn?"

"Hello." The voice at the other end of the line was gruff with sleep. "Who is this?"

"It's Marty. Have I woken you up?"

"What the hell do you want?"

"I need some help."

There was a long silence at the other end of the phone.

"Are you still there?"

"Yeah. Yeah."

"I need heroin."

The gruffness left the voice; incredulity replaced it.

"You on it?"

"I need it for a friend." Marty could sense the smile spreading on Flynn's face. "Can you get me something? *Quickly.*"

"How much?"

"I've got a hundred quid."

"It's not impossible."

"Soon?"

"Yeah. If you like. What time is it now?" The thought of easy money had got Flynn's mind oiled and ready to go. "One-fifteen? OK." He paused for calculations. "You come around in about three-quarters of an hour."

That was efficient; unless, as Marty suspected, Flynn was involved with the market so deeply he had easy access to the stuff: his jacket pocket, for instance.

"I can't guarantee, of course," he said just to keep the

desperation simmering. "But I'll do my best. Can't say fairer than that, can I?"

"Thanks," Marty replied. "I appreciate this."

"Just bring the cash, Marty. That's all the appreciation I need."

The phone went dead. Flynn had a knack of getting the last word in. "Bastard," Marty said to the receiver, and slammed it down. He was shaking slightly; his nerves were frayed. He slipped into a newsstand, picked up a packet of cigarettes, and then got back into the car. It was lunchtime; the traffic in the middle of London would be thick, and it would take the best part of forty-five minutes to get to the old stamping ground. There was no time to go back and check on Carys. Besides, he guessed she wouldn't have thanked him for delaying his purchase. She needed dope more than she needed him.

The European appeared too suddenly for Carys to hold his insinuating presence at bay. But weak as she felt, she *had* to fight. And there was something about this assault that was different from others. Was it that he was more desperate in his approach this time? The back of her neck felt physically bruised by his entrance. She rubbed it with a sweating palm.

I found you, he said in her head.

She looked around the room for a way to drive him out.

No use, he told her.

"Leave us alone."

You've treated me badly, Carys. I should punish you. But I won't; not if you give me your father. Is that so much to ask? I have a right to him. You know that in your heart of hearts. He belongs to me.

She knew better than to trust his coaxing tones. If she found Papa, what would he do then? Leave her to live her life? No; he would take her too, the way he'd taken Evangeline and Toy and only he knew how many others; to that tree, to that Nowhere.

Her eyes came to rest on the small electric cooker in the corner of the room. She got up, her limbs jangling, and walked unsteadily across to it. If the European had caught wind of her plan, then all the better. He *was* weak, she could sense it. Tired and sad; one eye on the sky for kites, his concentration faltering. But his presence was still distressing enough to muddy her thought processes. Once she reached the cooker she could hardly think of why she was there. She pressed her mind into higher gear. Refusal! That was it. The cooker was refusal! She reached out and turned on one of the two electric rings.

No, Carys, he told her. *This isn't wise.*

His face appeared in her mind's eye. It was vast, and it blotted out the room around her. She shook her head to rid herself of him, but he wouldn't be dislodged. There was a second illusion too, besides his face. She felt arms around her: not a stranglehold, but a sheltering embrace. They rocked her, those arms.

"I don't belong to you," she said, fighting off the urge to succumb to his cradling. In the back of her head she could hear a song being sung; its rhythm matched the soporific rhythm of the rocking. The words weren't English, but Russian. It was a lullaby, she knew that without understanding the words, and as it ran, and she listened, it seemed all the hurts she'd felt disappeared. She was a babe-in-arms again; in his arms. He was rocking her to sleep to this murmured song.

Through the lace of approaching sleep she caught sight of a bright pattern. Though she couldn't fix its significance, she remembered that it *had* been important, this orange spiral that glowed not far from her. But what did it mean? The problem vexed her, and kept the sleep she wanted at bay. So she opened her eyes a little wider to work out what the pattern was, once and for all, and so be done with it.

The cooker came into focus in front of her, the ring glowing. The air above it shimmered. *Now* she remembered, and the memory thrust sleepiness away. She stretched out her arm toward the heat.

Don't do this, the voice in her head advised. *You'll only hurt yourself.*

But she knew better. Slumber in his arms was more dangerous than any pain the next few moments would bring. The heat was uncomfortable, though her skin was still inches from its source, and for a desperate moment her willpower faltered.

You'll be scarred for life, the European said, sensing her equivocation.

"Let me alone."

I just don't want to see you hurt, child. I love you too much. The lie was a spur. She found the vital ounce of courage, raised her hand and pressed it, palm down, onto the electric ring.

The European screamed first; she heard his voice begin to rise in the instant before her own cry began. She pulled her hand off the cooker as the smell of burning hit her. Mamoulian withdrew from her; she felt his retreat. Relief flooded her system. Then the pain overwhelmed her, and a quick dark came down. She didn't fear it, though. It was quite safe, that dark. He wasn't in it.

"Gone," she said, and collapsed.

When she came to, less than five minutes later, her first thought was that she was holding a fistful of razors.

She edged her way across to the bed and put her head on it until she'd fully regained her consciousness. When she had courage enough, she looked at her hand. The design of the rings was burned quite clearly onto her palm, a spiral tattoo. She stood up and went to the sink to run the wound under cold water. The process calmed the pain somewhat; the damage was not as severe as she had thought. Though it had seemed an age, her palm had probably only been in direct contact with the ring for a second or two. She wrapped her hand up in one of Marty's T-shirts. Then she remembered she'd read somewhere that burns were best left to the open air, and she undid her handiwork. Exhausted, she lay on the bed and waited for Marty to bring her a piece of the Island.

59

The Reverend Bliss' boys stayed in the downstairs back room of the house on Caliban Street, lost in a reverie of watery death, for well over an hour. In that time Mamoulian had gone in search of Carys, found her and been driven out again. But he had discovered her whereabouts. More than that, he had gleaned that Strauss—the man he had so foolishly ignored at the Sanctuary—had now gone to fetch the girl heroin. It was time, he thought, to stop being so compassionate.

He felt like a beaten dog: all he wanted to do was to lie down and die. It seemed today—especially since the girl's skillful rejection of him—that he felt every hour of his long, long life in his sinews. He looked down at his hand, which still ached with the burn he'd received through Carys. Perhaps the girl would understand, finally, that all of this was inevitable. That the endgame he was about to enter was more important than her life or Strauss' or Breer's or those of the two idiot Memphisites he'd left dreaming two floors below.

He went down to the first landing and into Breer's room. The Razor-Eater was recumbent on his mattress in the corner of the room, his neck akimbo, his stomach impaled, gaping up at him like a lunatic fish. At the bottom of the mattress, drawn up close because of Breer's failing eyesight, the television gabbled its inanities.

"We'll be leaving soon," Mamoulian said.

"Did you find her?"

"Yes, I found her. A place called Bright Street. The house—" he seemed to find this thought amusing, "is painted yellow. The second floor, I think."

"Bright Street," said Breer, dreamily. "Shall we go and find her then?"

"No; not *we*."

Breer turned a little more toward the European; he had braced his broken neck with a makeshift splint, and it made movement difficult. "I want to see her," he said.

"You shouldn't have let her go in the first place."

"*He* came; the one from the house. I told you."

"Oh, yes," said Mamoulian. "I have plans for Strauss."

"Shall I find him for you?" Breer said. The old images of execution sprang into his head, as if fresh from a book of atrocities. One or two of them were sharper than ever, as if they were close to being realized.

"No need," the European replied. "I have two eager acolytes willing to do that job for me."

Breer sulked. "What can I do, then?"

"You can prepare the house for our departure. I want you to burn what few possessions we have. I want it to be as though we never existed, you and I."

"The end's near, is it?"

"Now I know where she is, yes."

"She may run off."

"She's too weak. She won't be able to move until Strauss brings her drug. And of course he'll never do that."

"You're going to have him killed?"

"Him, and anyone who gets in my way from this moment on. I've no energy left for compassion. That's been my error so often: letting the innocent escape. You've got your instructions, Anthony. Be about your business."

He withdrew from the fetid room, and went downstairs to his new agents. The Americans stood respectfully when he opened the door.

"Are you ready?" he asked.

The blond one, who had been the more compliant from the outset, started to express his undying thanks over again, but

Mamoulian silenced him. He gave them their orders, and they took them as if he were dispensing sweets.

"There are knives in the kitchen," he said. "Take them and use them in good health."

Chad smiled. "You want us to kill the wife too?"

"The Deluge has no time to be selective."

"Suppose she hasn't sinned?" Tom said, not sure of why he thought this foolish thought.

"Oh, she's sinned," the man replied, with glittering eyes, and that was good enough for the Reverend Bliss' boys.

Upstairs, Breer hoisted himself off his mattress with difficulty, and stumbled into the bathroom to look at himself in the cracked mirror. His injuries had long ago stopped seeping, but he looked terrible.

"Shave," he told himself. "And sandalwood."

He was afraid that things were moving too fast now, and if he wasn't careful he was going to be left out of the calculations. It was time he acted on his own behalf. He would find a clean shirt, a tie and a jacket and then he would go out courting. If the endgame was so close that the evidence had to be destroyed, then he had better be quick. Better finish his romance with the girl before she went the way of all flesh.

60

It took considerably longer than three-quarters of an hour to cross London. A large antinuclear march was underway; various sections of the main body were assembling around the city, then marching toward a mass rally in Hyde Park. The center of the city, which was at best difficult to navigate, was so thick with marchers and arrested traffic as to be virtually impassable. None of which Marty had realized until he was in the thick of it, by which time retreat and rerouting was out of the question. He cursed his lack of attention: there had surely been police signs warning incoming motorists of the delay. He had noticed none of them.

There was nothing to be done, however, except perhaps to desert the car and set out on foot or by subway. Neither option was particularly attractive. The subway would be packed, and walking in today's blistering heat would be debilitating. He needed what small reserves of energy he still possessed. He was living on adrenaline and cigarettes, and had been for too long. He was weak. He only hoped—vain hope—that the opposition was weaker.

It was the middle of the afternoon by the time he reached Charmaine's place. He drove around the block, looking for somewhere to park, and eventually found a space around the corner from the house. His feet were somewhat reluctant; the abasement ahead wasn't particularly attractive. But Carys was waiting.

The front door was just slightly ajar. He rang the bell nevertheless, and waited on the pavement, unwilling simply to step into the house. Perhaps they were upstairs in bed, or taking a cool shower together. The heat was still furious, even though the afternoon was well advanced.

Down at the end of the street an ice-cream van, playing an off-key version of "The Blue Danube," appeared and stopped by the curb to await patrons. Marty glanced toward it. The waltz had already attracted two customers. They drew his attention for a moment: sober-suited young men whose backs were turned to him. One of them boasted bright yellow hair: it shone in the sun. They were taking possession of their ice creams now; money was exchanged. Satisfied, they disappeared around the corner without looking over their shoulders.

Despairing of an answer to his bell-ringing, Marty pushed the door open. It grated across the coconut matting, which bore a threadbare "*Welcome.*" A pamphlet, stuck halfway through the mailbox, dislodged and fell on the inside, facedown. The sprung mailbox snapped loudly back into place.

"Flynn? Charmaine?"

His voice was an intrusion; it carried up the stairs, where dust motes thronged the sunlight through the half-landing window; it ran into the kitchen, where yesterday's milk was curdling on the board beside the sink.

"Is anybody in?"

Standing in the hallway, he heard a fly. It circled his head, and he waved it off. Unconcerned, it buzzed off down the hallway toward the kitchen, tempted by something. Marty followed it, calling Charmaine's name as he went.

She was waiting for him in the kitchen, as was Flynn. They had both had their throats cut.

Charmaine had sunk down against the washing machine. She sat, one leg bent beneath her, staring at the opposite wall. Flynn had been placed with his head over the sink as though bending to douse his face. The illusion of life was almost successful, even to the splashing sound.

Marty stood in the doorway, while the fly, not as finicky as he, flew around and around the kitchen, ecstatic. Marty just stared. There was nothing to be done: all that was left was to look. They were dead. And Marty knew without the effort of thinking about it that the killers were dressed in gray, and had turned that far corner, ice creams in hand, accompanied by "The Blue Danube."

They'd called Marty the Dancer of Wandsworth—those who'd called him anything at all—because Strauss was the Waltz King. He wondered if he'd ever told Charmaine that, in any of his letters. No, he probably hadn't: and now it was too late. Tears had begun to sting the rims of his eyes. He fought them back. They would interrupt the view, and he hadn't finished looking yet.

The fly who'd brought him here was circling close to his head again.

"The European," he murmured to it. "He sent them."

The fly zigzagged, excitedly. "Of course," it buzzed.

"I'll kill him."

The fly laughed. "You don't have any idea what he is. He could be the Devil himself."

"Fucking fly. What do you know?"

"Don't get so grand with me," the fly replied. "You're a shit-walker, same as I am.

He watched it rove, looking for a place to put its dirty feet. It landed, at last, on Charmaine's face. Atrocious that she didn't raise a lazy hand to swat it away; terrible that she just sprawled there, leg bent, neck slit, and let it crawl on her cheek, up to her eye, down to her nostril, supping here and there, careless.

The fly was right. He *was* ignorant. If they were to survive, he had to root out Mamoulian's secret life, because that knowledge was power. Carys had been wise all along. There was no closing your eyes and turning your back on the European. The only way to be free of him was to *know* him; to look at him for as long as courage allowed and see him in every ghastly particular.

He left the lovers in the kitchen and went to look for the heroin. He didn't have to search far. The packet was in the inside of Flynn's jacket, which was casually thrown over the sofa in the front room. Pocketing the fix Marty went to the front door, aware that stepping out of this house into the open sunlight was tantamount to inviting a murder charge. He would be seen and easily recognized: the police would be after him in hours. But there was no help for it; escaping by the back door would look every bit as suspicious.

At the door he stooped and snatched up the pamphlet that had slid from the letterbox. It bore the smiling face of an evangelist, one Reverend Bliss, who was standing, microphone in hand, raising his eyes to Heaven. "*Join the Crowd*," the banner proclaimed, "*and*

Feel the Power of God in Operation. Hear the Words! Feel the Spirit!" He pocketed it for future reference.

On his way back to Kilburn he stopped at a telephone box and reported the murders. When they asked him who he was he told them, admitting that he was a parole jumper to boot. When they told him to turn himself in to the nearest police station, he replied that he would, but first he had to attend to some personal business.

As he drove back to Kilburn through streets now littered with the aftermath of the march, his mind turned over every possible lead to Whitehead's whereabouts. Wherever the old man was, there, sooner or later, Mamoulian would be. He could try to get Carys to find her father of course. But he had another request to make of her, one that it might take more than gentle persuasion to get her to concede to. He would have to locate the old man by his own ingenuity.

It was only as he drove back, and caught sight of a signpost to Holborn, that he remembered Mr. Halifax and the strawberries.

61

Marty smelled Carys as soon as he opened the door, but for a few seconds he mistook the scent for pork cooking. Only when he crossed to the bed did he see the burn on her open hand.

"I'm all right," she told him very coolly.

"He's been here."

She nodded. "But he's gone now."

"Didn't he leave me any messages?" he asked, with a crooked smile.

She sat up. Something was horribly wrong with him. His voice was odd; his face was the color of fishmeat. He stood off from her, as if the merest touch would shatter him. Looking at him made her almost forget the appetite that still consumed her.

"Message," she said, "for you?" She didn't understand. "Why? What's happened?"

"They were dead."

"Who?"

"Flynn. Charmaine. Somebody slit their throats."

His face came within an ace of crumpling up. This was the nadir, surely. They had no further to fall.

"Oh, Marty . . ."

"He knew I was going back to my house," he said. She looked for accusation in his voice, but there was none. She defended herself nevertheless.

"It couldn't have been me. I don't even know where you live."

"Oh, but he does. I'm sure he makes it his business to know everything."

"Why kill them? I don't see why."

"Mistaken identity."

"Breer knows who you are."

"It wasn't Breer who did it."

"You saw who?"

"I think so. Two kids." He fished for the pamphlet he'd found behind the door. The assassins had delivered it, he guessed. Something about their sober suits, and that glimpsed halo of blond hair, suggested doorstep evangelists, fresh-faced and lethal. Wouldn't the European delight in such a paradox?

"They made an error," he said, slipping off his jacket and starting to unbutton his sweat-soaked shirt. "They just went into the house and murdered the first man and woman they met. Only it wasn't me, it was Flynn." He pulled his shirt out of his trousers and slung it off. "It's so easy, isn't it? He doesn't care about the law—he thinks he's above all that." Marty was forcibly aware of how ironic this was. He, the ex-con, the despiser of uniforms, cleaving to the notion of law. It wasn't a pretty refuge, but it was the best he'd got at the moment. "What is he, Carys? What makes him so certain he's immune?"

She was staring down at the fervent face of the Reverend Bliss. "Baptism in the Holy Ghost!" he promised, blithely.

"What does it matter what he is?" she said.

"Otherwise it's over."

She made no reply. He went to the sink and washed his face and chest in cold water. As far as the European was concerned, they were like sheep in a pen. Not just in this room, in any room. Wherever they hid he'd find their refuge in time, and come. There might be a small struggle—do sheep fight the oncoming execution? he wondered. He should have asked the fly. The fly would have known.

He turned from the sink, water dripping from his jawline, to look at Carys. She was staring at the floor, scratching herself.

"Go to him," he said without warning.

He'd tried a dozen ways to open this conversation as he drove back, but why try to sweeten the pill?

She looked up at him, empty-eyed. "What did you say?"

"Go to him, Carys. Go *into* him, the way he goes into you. Reverse the procedure."

She almost laughed; there was a sneer mustering in reply to this obscenity. "*Into* him?" she said.

"Yes."

"You're insane."

"We can't fight what we don't know. And we can't know unless we *look*. You can do that; you can do it for both of us." He started across the room toward her, but she bowed her head again. "Find out *what* he is. Find a weakness, a hint of a weakness, anything that can help us survive."

"No."

"Because if you don't, whatever we try to do, wherever we try to go, he's going to come, him or one of his cohorts, and slit my throat the way he did Flynn's. And you? God knows, I think you'll be wishing you'd died the way I did." This was brutal stuff, and he felt dirtied by the very saying of it, but he knew how passionately she'd resist. If bullying didn't work, he still had the heroin. He squatted on his haunches in front of her, looking up at her.

"*Think* about it, Carys. Give the idea a chance."

Her face hardened. "You saw his room," she said. "It'd be like locking myself in an asylum."

"He wouldn't even know," he said. "He wouldn't be prepared."

"I'm not going to discuss it. Give me the smack, Marty." He stood up, face slack. Don't make me cruel, he thought.

"You want me to shoot up, and then wait, is that it?"

"Yes," she said, faintly. Then more strongly: "*Yes*."

"Is that all you think you're worth?" She didn't reply. Her face was impossible to read. "If you thought that, why'd you burn yourself?"

"I didn't want to go. Not without . . . seeing you again. Being with you." She was trembling. "We can't win," she said.

"If we can't win, what's to lose?"

"I'm tired," she replied, shaking her head. "Give me the smack. Maybe tomorrow, when I'm feeling better." She looked up at him, eyes shining in the bruises of her eye sockets. "Just give me the smack!"

"Then you can forget all about it, eh?"

"Marty, don't. It's going to spoil—" She stopped.

"Spoil what? Our last few hours together?"

"I need the dope, Marty."

"That's very convenient. Fuck what happens to me." He suddenly felt this to be indisputably true; that she didn't care what he suffered and never really had. He'd run into her life and now, once he'd brought her dope, he could fade out of it again and leave her to her dreams. He wanted to hit her. He turned his back on her before he did.

Behind him, she said: "We could have some dope—you too, Marty, why not? Then we could be together."

He didn't reply for a long moment. When he did he said:

"No fix."

"Marty?"

"No fix until you go to him."

It took Carys several seconds to register the full impact of his blackmail. Hadn't she said, a long time ago, that he'd disappointed her because she'd expected a brute? She'd spoken too soon.

"He'll know," she breathed, "he'll know the moment I get near him."

"Tread softly. You can; you know you can. You're clever. You've crept into my head often enough."

"I can't," she protested. Didn't he understand what he was asking?

He made a face, sighed, and crossed to his jacket, which was where he'd dropped it on the floor. He rummaged around in the pocket until he found the heroin. It was a pitifully small packet, and if he knew Flynn, the stuff was cut. But that was her business, not his. She stared, transfixed, at the packet.

"It's all yours," he said, and threw it over to her. It landed on the bed beside her. "You're welcome to it."

She still stared; now at his empty hand. He broke her look to pick up his stale shirt, and slip it back on.

"Where are you going?"

"I've seen you high on that crap. I've heard the garbage you talk. I don't want to remember you like that."

"I have to have it."

She hated him; she looked at him standing in a patch of late-afternoon sun, with his bare belly and his bare chest, and she hated every fiber of him. The blackmail she could understand. It was crude, but functional. This desertion was a worse kind of trick altogether.

"Even if I was to do as you say . . ." she began; the thought seemed to shrink her. ". . . I won't find out anything."

He shrugged. "Look, the smack's yours," he said. "You've got what you wanted."

"And what about you? What do you want?"

"I want to live. And I think this is our only chance."

Even then it was such a slim chance; the slimmest crack in the wall through which they might, if fate loved them, slip.

She weighed up the options; why she even contemplated his idea she wasn't certain. On another day she might have said: for love's sake. Finally she said: "You win."

He sat down and watched her prepare for the journey ahead. First, she washed. Not just her face, her whole body, standing on a spread towel at the little sink in the corner of the room, with the gas-fired water heater roaring as it spat water into the bowl. Watching her, he got an erection, and he felt ashamed that he should be thinking of sex when so much was at issue. But that was just the puritan talking; he should feel whatever felt right. She'd taught him that.

When she'd finished she put her underwear back on, and a T-shirt. It was what she'd been wearing when he'd arrived at Caliban Street, he noted: simple unconfining clothes. She sat on a chair. Her skin rippled with gooseflesh. He wanted to be forgiven by her; to be told that his manipulation was justified and—whatever happened from now on—she understood that he'd acted for the best. She offered no such disclaimer. She just said:

"I think I'm ready."

"What can I do?"

"Very little," she replied. "But be here, Marty."

"And if . . . you know . . . if anything seems to be wrong? Can I help you?"

"No," she answered.

"When will I know that you're there?" he asked.

She looked at him as though his question was an idiot's, and said: "You'll know."

62

It wasn't difficult to find the European: her mind went to him with almost distressing readiness, as if into the arms of a long-lost compatriot. She could distinctly feel the pull of him, though not, she thought, a conscious magnetism. When her thoughts arrived at Caliban Street and entered the room at the top of the stairs, her suspicions about his passivity were verified. He was lying on the bare boards of the room in a posture of utter exhaustion. Perhaps, she thought, I *can* do this after all. Like a teasing mistress, she crept to his side, and slipped into him.

She murmured.

Marty flinched. There were movements in her throat, which were so thin he felt he could almost see the words shaping in it. Speak to me, he willed her. Say it's all right. Her body had become rigid. He touched her. Her muscle was stone, as though she'd exchanged glances with the basilisk.

"Carys?"

She murmured again, her throat palpitating, but no words came; there was barely breath.

"Can you hear me?"

If she could, she made no sign of it. Seconds passed into minutes and still she was a wall, his questions fracturing against her and falling into silence.

And then she said: "I'm here." Her voice was insubstantial, like a foreign station found on a radio; words from some unfixable place.

"With him?" he asked.

"Yes."

No prevarication now, he charged himself. She'd gone to the European, as he'd asked. Now he had to use her courage as efficiently as possible and call her back before anything went wrong. He asked the most difficult question first, and the one he most needed an answer to.

"What is he, Carys?"

"I don't know," she said.

The tip of her tongue flickered out to spread a film of spit across her lips.

"So dark," she muttered.

It *was* dark in him: the same palpable darkness as in the room at Caliban Street. But, for the moment at least, the shadows were passive. The European didn't expect intruders here. He'd left no guardian terrors at the gates of his brain. She stepped deeper into his head. Darts of light burst at the corners of her thought's sight, like the colors that came after she'd rubbed her eyes, only more brilliant and more momentary. They came and went so quickly she was not certain if she saw anything in them or illuminated by them, but as she progressed and the bursts became more frequent, she began to see patterns there: commas, lattices, bars, dots, spirals.

Marty's voice interrupted the reverie, some foolish question that she had no patience with. She ignored it. Let him wait. The lights were becoming more intricate, their patterns cross-fertilizing, gaining depth and weight. Now she seemed to see tunnels and tumbling cubes; seas of rolling light; fissures opening and sealing; rains of white noise. She watched, entranced by the way they grew and multiplied, the world of his thought appearing in flickering Heavens above her; falling in showers on her and about her. Vast blocks of intersecting geometries thundered over, hovering inches above her skull, the weight of small moons.

Just as suddenly: gone. All of them. Darkness again, as relentless as ever, pressed on her from every side. For a moment she had the sensation of being smothered; she grabbed for breath, panicking.

"Carys?"

"I'm all right," she whispered to the distant inquirer. He was a world away, but he cared for her, or so she dimly remembered.

"Where are you?" he wanted to know.

She didn't have a clue, so she shook her head. Which way should she advance, if at all? She waited in the darkness, readying herself for whatever might happen next.

Suddenly the lights began again, at the horizon. This time—for their second performance—pattern had become form. Instead of spirals she saw rising columns of burning smoke. In place of seas of light, a landscape, with intermittent sunshine stabbing distant hillsides. Birds rose on burning wings then turned into leaves of books, fluttering up from conflagrations that were even now flaring on every side.

"Where are you?" he asked her again. Her eyes roved maniacally behind her closed lids, taking in this burgeoning province. He could share none of it, except through her words, and she was dumb with admiration or terror, he couldn't tell which.

There was sound here too. Not much; the promontory she walked on had suffered too many ravages to shout. Its life was almost out. Bodies sprawled underfoot, so badly disfigured they might have been dropped out of the sky. Weapons; horses; wheels. She saw all of this as if by a show of lurid fireworks, with no sight glimpsed more than once. In the instant of darkness between one light-burst and the next the entire scene would change. One moment she was standing on an open road with a naked girl running toward her, bawling. The next, on a hillside looking down on a razed valley, snatched through a pall of smoke. Now a silver birch copse, now not. Now a ruin, with a headless man at her feet; again, not. But always the fires somewhere near; the smuts and the shrieks dirtying the air; the sense of relentless pursuit. She felt it could go on forever, these scenes changing before her—one moment a landscape, the next an atrocity—without her having time to correlate the disparate images.

Then, as abruptly as the first patterns had ceased, the fires did also, and the darkness was everywhere about her again.

"Where?"

Marty's voice found her. He was so agitated in his confusion, she answered him.

"I'm almost dead," she said, quite calmly.

"Carys?" He was terrified that naming her would alert Mamoulian, but he had to know if she spoke for herself, or for him.

"Not Carys," she replied. Her mouth seemed to lose its fullness; the lips thinning. It was Mamoulian's mouth, not hers.

She raised her hand a little way from her lap as if making to touch her face.

"Almost dead," she said again. "Lost the battle, you see. Lost the whole bloody war . . ."

"Which war?"

"Lost from the beginning. Not that it matters, eh? Find myself another war. There's always one around."

"Who are you?"

She frowned. "What's it to you?" she snapped at him. "None of your business."

"It doesn't matter," Marty returned. He feared pushing the interrogation too hard. As it was, his question was answered in the next breath.

"My name's Mamoulian. I'm a sergeant in the Third Fusiliers. Correction: *was* a sergeant."

"Not now?"

"No, not now. I'm nobody now. It's safer to be nobody these days, don't you think?"

The tone was eerily conversational, as though the European knew exactly what was happening, and had chosen to talk with Marty through Carys. Another game, perhaps?

"When I think of the things I've done," he said, "to stay out of trouble. I'm such a coward, you see? Always have been. *Loathe* the sight of blood." He began to laugh in her, a solid, unfeminine laugh.

"You're just a man?" Marty said. He could scarcely credit what he was being told. There was no Devil hiding in the European's cortex, just this half-mad sergeant, lost on some battlefield. "Just a man?" he said again.

"What did you want me to be?" the sergeant replied, quick as a flash. "I'm happy to oblige. Anything to get me out of this shit."

"Who do you think you're talking to?"

The sergeant frowned with Carys' face, puzzling this one out.

"I'm losing my mind," he said dolefully. "I've been talking to myself for days now on and off. There's no one left, you see? The Third's been wiped out. And the Fourth. And the Fifth. All blown to Hell!" He stopped and pulled a wry face. "Got no one to play cards with, damn it. Can't play with dead men, can I? They've got nothing I want . . ." The voice trailed away.

"What date is it?"

"Sometime in October, isn't it?" the sergeant came back. "I've lost track of time. Still, it's fucking cold at night, I tell you that much. Yes, must be October at least. There was snow in the wind yesterday. Or was it the day before?"

"What year is it?"

The sergeant laughed. "I'm not that far gone," he said. "It's 1811. That's right. I'm thirty-two on the ninth of November. And I don't look a day over forty."

It was 1811. If the sergeant was answering truthfully that made Mamoulian two centuries old.

"Are you sure?" Marty asked. "The year is 1811; you're certain?"

"Shut your mouth!" the answer came.

"What?"

"Trouble."

Carys had drawn her arms up against her chest, as though constricted. She felt enclosed—but by what she wasn't certain. The open road she'd been standing on had abruptly disappeared, and now she sensed herself lying down, in darkness. It was warmer here than it had been on the road, but not a pleasant heat. It smelled putrid. She spat, not once but three or four times, to rid herself of a mouthful of muck. Where was she, for God's sake?

Close by she could hear the approach of horses. The sound was muffled, but it made her, or rather the man she occupied, panic. Off to her right, somebody moaned.

"Ssh . . ." she hissed. Didn't the moaner hear the horses too? They'd be discovered; and though she didn't know why, she was certain discovery would prove fatal.

"What's happening?" Marty asked.

She didn't dare reply. The horsemen were too close to dare a word. She could hear them dismounting and approaching her hiding place. She repeated a prayer, soundlessly. The riders were talking now; they were soldiers, she guessed. An argument had erupted among them as to who would tackle some distasteful duty. Maybe, she prayed, they'd give up their search before they started. But no. The debate was over, and they were grunting and complaining as several set about their labors. She heard them moving sacks, and flinging them down. A dozen; two dozen. Light seeped through to where she lay, scarcely breathing. More sacks were moved; more light fell on her. She opened her eyes, and finally recognized what refuge the sergeant had chosen.

"God Almighty," she said.

They weren't sacks she lay among, but bodies. He had hidden himself in a mound of corpses. It was the heat of putrefaction that made her sweat.

Now the hillock was being taken apart by the horsemen, who were pricking each of the bodies as they were hauled from the heap, in order to distinguish living from dead. The few who still breathed were pointed out to the officer. He dismissed them all as past the point of no return; they were swiftly dispatched. Before a bayonet could pierce his hide, the sergeant rolled over and showed himself.

"I surrender," he said. They jabbed him through the shoulder anyway. He yelled. Carys too.

Marty reached to touch her; her face was scrawled with pain. But he thought better of interfering at what was clearly a vital juncture: it might do more harm than good.

"Well, well," said the officer, high on the horse. "You don't look very dead to me."

"I was practicing," the sergeant replied. His wit earned him a second jab. To judge by the looks of the men who surrounded him, he'd be lucky to avoid a disemboweling. They were ready for some sport.

"You're not going to die," the officer said, patting his mount's gleaming neck. The presence of so much decay made the thoroughbred uneasy. "We need answers to some questions first. Then you can have your place in the pit."

Behind the officer's plumed head the sky had darkened. Even as he spoke the scene began to lose coherence, as though Mamoulian had forgotten how it went from here.

Under her lids Carys' eyes began to twitch back and forth again. Another welter of impressions had overtaken her, each moment delineated with absolute precision, but all coming too fast for her to make any sense of.

"Carys? Are you all right?"

"Yes, yes," she said breathlessly. "Just moments . . . living moments."

She saw a room, a chair. Felt a kiss, a slap. Pain; relief; pain again. Questions; laughter. She couldn't be certain, but she guessed that under pressure the sergeant was telling the enemy everything they wanted to know and more. Days passed in a heartbeat. She let them run through her fingers, sensing that the European's dreaming head was moving with mounting velocity toward some critical event. It was best to let him lead the way; he knew better than she the significance of this descent.

The journey finished with shocking suddenness.

A sky the color of cold iron opened above her head. Snow drifted from it, a lazy fall of goosedown, which instead of warming her made her bones ache. In the claustrophobic one-room flat, with Marty sitting bare-chested and sweating opposite her, Carys' teeth began to chatter.

The sergeant's captors were done with their interrogation, it seemed. They had led him and five other ragged prisoners out into a small quadrangle. He looked around. This was a monastery, or had been until its occupation. One or two monks stood in the shelter of the cloister walkway and watched events in the yard unfold with philosophical gaze.

The six prisoners waited in a line while the snow fell. They were not bound. There was nowhere in this square for them to run to. The sergeant, on the end of the line, chewed his nails and tried to keep his thoughts light. They were going to die here, that was an unavoidable fact. They were not the first to be executed this afternoon. Along one wall, arranged neatly for posthumous inspection, lay five dead men. Their lopped heads had been placed, the ultimate defamation, at their groins. Open-eyed, as if startled by the killing stroke, they stared at the snow as it descended, at the windows, at the one tree that was planted in a square of soil among the stones. In summer, it surely bore fruit; birds made idiot song in it. Now, it was leafless.

"They're going to kill us," she said matter-of-factly.

It was all very informal. The presiding officer, a fur coat pulled around his shoulders, was standing with his hands at a blazing brazier, his back to the prisoners. The executioner was with him, his bloody sword jauntily leaned on his shoulder. A fat, lumbering man, he laughed at some joke the officer made and downed a cup of something warming before turning back to his business.

Carys smiled.

"What's happening now?"

She said nothing; her eyes were on the man who was going to kill them; she smiled on.

"Carys. What's happening?"

The soldiers had come along the line, and pushed them to the ground in the middle of the square. Carys had bowed her head, to expose the nape of her neck. "We're going to die," she whispered to her distant confidant.

At the far end of the line the executioner raised his sword and brought it down with one professional stroke. The prisoner's head seemed to leap from the neck, pushed forward by a geyser of blood. It was lurid against the gray walls, the white snow. The head fell face-forward, rolled a little way and stopped. The body curled to the ground. Out of the corner of his eye Mamoulian watched the proceedings, trying to stop his teeth from chattering. He wasn't afraid, and didn't want them to think he was. The next man in line had started to scream. Two soldiers stepped forward at the officer's barked command and seized the man. Suddenly, after a calm in which you could hear the snow pat the ground, the line erupted with pleas and prayers; the man's terror had opened a floodgate. The sergeant said nothing. They were lucky to be dying in such style, he thought: the sword was for aristocrats and officers. But the tree was not yet tall enough to hang a man from. He watched the sword fall a second time, wondering if the tongue still wagged after death, sitting in the draining palate of the dead man's head.

"I'm not afraid," he said. "What's the use of fear? You can't buy it or sell it, you can't make love to it. You can't even wear it if they strip off your shirt and you're cold."

A third prisoner's head rolled in the snow; and a fourth. A soldier laughed. The blood steamed. Its meaty smell was appetizing to a man who hadn't been fed for a week.

"I'm not losing anything," he said in lieu of prayer. "I've had a useless life. If it ends here, so what?"

The prisoner at his left was young: no more than fifteen. A drummer-boy, the sergeant guessed. He was quietly crying.

"Look over there," Mamoulian said. "Desertion if ever I saw it."

He nodded toward the sprawled bodies, which were already being vacated by their various parasites. Fleas and nits, aware that their host had ceased, crawled and leaped from head and hem, eager to find new residence before the cold caught them.

The boy looked and smiled. The spectacle diverted him in the moment it took for the executioner to position himself and deliver the killing stroke. The head sprang; heat escaped onto the sergeant's chest.

Idly, Mamoulian looked around at the executioner. He was slightly blood-spattered; otherwise his profession was not written upon him. It was a stupid face, with a shabby beard that needed trimming, and round, parboiled eyes. Shall I be murdered by this? the sergeant thought; well, I'm not ashamed. He spread his arms to either side of his body, the universal gesture of submission, and bowed his head. Somebody pulled at his shirt to expose his neck.

He waited. A noise like a shot sounded in his head. He opened his eyes, expecting to see the snow approaching as his head leaped from his neck; but no. In the middle of the square one of the soldiers was falling to his knees, his chest blown open by a shot from one of the upper cloister windows. Mamoulian glanced behind him. Soldiers were swarming from every side of the quadrangle; shots sliced the snow. The presiding officer, wounded, fell clumsily against the brazier, and his fur coat caught fire. Trapped beneath the tree, two soldiers were mowed down, slumping together like lovers under the branches.

"Away." Carys whispered the imperative with his voice: "Quickly. Away."

He belly-crawled across the frozen stone as the factions fought above his head, scarcely able to believe that he'd been spared. Nobody gave him a second glance. Unarmed and skeletal-thin, he was no danger to anyone. Once out of the square, and into the backwaters of the monastery, he took a breath. Smoke had started to drift along the icy corridors. Inevitably, the place was being put to the torch by one side or the other: perhaps both. They were all imbeciles: he loved none of them. He began his way through the maze of the building, hoping to find his way out without encountering any stray fusiliers.

In a passageway far from the skirmishes he heard footsteps— sandaled, not booted—coming after him. He turned to face his pursuer. It was a monk, his scrawny features every inch the ascetic's. He arrested the sergeant by the tattered collar of his shirt.

"You're God-given," he said. He was breathless, but his grip was fierce.

"Let me alone. I want to get out."

"The fighting's spreading through the building; it's not safe anywhere."

"I'll take the risk." The sergeant grinned.

"You were chosen, soldier," the monk replied, still holding on. "Chance stepped in on your behalf. The innocent boy at your side died, but *you* survived. Don't you see? Ask yourself why."

He tried to push the shaveling away; the mixture of incense and stale sweat was vile. But the man held fast, speaking hurriedly: "There are secret tunnels beneath the cells. We can slip away without being slaughtered."

"Yes?"

"Certainly. If you'll help me."

"How?"

"I've got writings to salvage; a life's work. I need your muscle, soldier. Don't fret yourself, you'll get something in return."

"What have you got that I'd want?" the sergeant said. What could this wild-eyed flagellant possibly possess?

"I need an acolyte," the monk said. "Someone to give my learning to."

"Spare me your spiritual guidance."

"I can teach you so much. How to live forever, if that's what you want." Mamoulian had started to laugh, but the monk went on with his dream-talk. "How to take life from other people, and have it for yourself. Or if you like, give it to the dead to resurrect them."

"Never."

"It's old wisdom," the monk said. "But I've found it again, written out in plain Greek. Secrets that were ancient when the hills were young. *Such* secrets."

"If you can do all that, why aren't you tsar of all the Russians?" Mamoulian replied.

The monk let go of his shirt, and looked at the soldier with contempt freshly squeezed from his eyes. "What man," he said slowly, "what man with true ambition in his soul would want to be *merely* tsar?"

The reply wiped the soldier's smile away. Strange words, whose significance—had he been asked—he would have had difficulty explaining. But there was a promise in them that his confusion couldn't rob them of. Well, he thought, maybe this is the way wisdom comes; and the sword didn't fall on me, did it?

"Show me the way," he said.

C arys smiled: a small but radiant smile. In the space of a wing-beat winter melted away. Spring blossomed, the ground was green everywhere, especially over the burial pits.

"Where are you going?" Marty asked her. It was clear from her delighted expression that circumstances had changed. For several minutes she had spat out clues to the life she was sharing in the European's head. Marty had barely grasped the gist of what was going on. He hoped she would be able to furnish the details later. What country this was; what war.

Suddenly, she said: "I'm finished." Her voice was light; almost playful.

"Carys?"

"Who's Carys? Never heard of him. Probably dead. They're all dead but me."

"What have you finished?"

"Learning, of course. All he can teach me. And it was true. Everything he promised: all true. Old wisdom."

"What have you learned?"

She raised her hand, the burned one, and spread it. "I can steal life," she said. "Easily. Just find the place, and drink. Easy to take; easy to give."

"Give?"

"For a while. As long as it suits me." She extended a finger: God to Adam. "Let there be life."

He began to laugh in her again.

"And the monk?"

"What about him?"

"Is he still with you?"

The sergeant shook Carys' head.

"I killed him, when he'd taught me everything he could." Her hands reached out and strangled the air. "I just throttled him one night, when he was sleeping. Of course he woke when he felt my grip around his throat. But he didn't struggle; he didn't make the slightest attempt to save himself." The sergeant was leering as he described the act. "He just let me murder him. I could scarcely believe my luck; I'd been planning the thing for weeks, terrified that he'd read my thoughts. When he went so easily, I was ecstatic—" The leer suddenly vanished. "Stupid," he murmured in her throat. "So, so *stupid*."

"Why?"

"I didn't see the trap he'd set. Didn't see how he'd planned it all along, nurtured me like a son *knowing* that I'd be his executioner when the time came. I never realized—not once— that I was just his tool. *He wanted to die*. He wanted to pass his wisdom"—the word was pronounced derisively—"along to me, and then have me put an end to him."

"Why did he want to die?"

"Don't you see how terrible it is to live when everything around you perishes? And the more the years pass the more the thought of death freezes your bowels, because the longer you avoid it the worse you imagine it must be? And you start to long— oh, *how* you long—for someone to take pity on you, someone to embrace you and share your terrors. And, at the end, someone to go into the dark with you."

"And you chose Whitehead," Marty said, almost beneath his breath, "the way *you* were chosen; by chance."

"Everything is chance; and so nothing is," the sleeping man pronounced; then laughed again, at his own expense, bitterly.

THE DAMNATION GAME 389

"Yes, I chose him, with a game of cards. And then I made a bargain with him."

"But he cheated you."

Carys nodded her head, very slowly, her hand inscribing a circle on the air.

"Round and round," she said. "Round and round."

"What will you do now?"

"Find the pilgrim. Wherever he is, find him! Take him with me. I swear I won't let him escape me. I'll take him, and show him."

"Show him what?"

No answer came. In its place, she sighed, stretching a little, and moving her head from left to right and back again. With a shock of recognition Marty realized that he was still watching her repeat Mamoulian's movements: that all the time the European had been asleep, and now, his energies repleted, he was preparing to wake. He snapped his previous question out again, determined to have an answer to his last, vital inquiry.

"Show him *what*?"

"*Hell*," Mamoulian said. "He cheated me! He squandered all my teachings, all my knowledge, threw it away for greed's sake, for power's sake, for the life of the body. *Appetite!* All gone for appetite. All my precious love, wasted!" Marty could hear, in his litany, the voice of the puritan—a monk's voice, perhaps?—the rage of a creature who wanted the world purer than it was and lived in torment because it saw only filth and flesh sweating to make more flesh, more filth. What hope of sanity in such a place? Except to find a soul to share the torment, a lover to hate the world with. Whitehead had been such a partner. And now Mamoulian was being true to his lover's soul: wanting, at the end, to go into death with the only other creature he had ever trusted. "We'll go to nothing . . ." he breathed, and the breath was a promise. "All of us, go to nothing. Down! Down!"

He was waking. There was no time left for further questions, however curious Marty was.

"Carys."

"Down! Down!"

"Carys! Can you hear me? Come out of him! Quickly!"

Her head rolled on her neck.

"Carys!"

She grunted.

"Quickly!"

In Mamoulian's head the patterns had begun again, as enchanting as ever. Spurts of light that would become pictures in a while, she knew. What would they be this time? Birds, flowers, trees in blossom. What a wonderland it was.

"Carys."

The voice of someone she had once known was calling her from some very distant place. But so were the lights. They were resolving themselves even now. She waited, expectantly, but this time they weren't memories that burst into view—

"Carys! Quickly!"

—they were the real world, appearing as the European opened his lids. Her body tensed. Marty reached for her hand, and seized it. She exhaled, slowly, the breath coming out as a thin whine between her teeth, and suddenly she was awake to her imminent danger. She flung her thought out of the European's head and back across the miles to Kilburn. For an agonized instant she felt her will falter, and she was falling backward, back into his waiting head. Terrified, she gasped like a stranded fish while her mind fought for propulsion.

Marty dragged her to a standing position, but her legs buckled. He held her up with his arms wrapped around her.

"Don't leave me," he whispered into her hair. "Gentle God, don't leave me."

Suddenly, her eyes flickered open.

"Marty," she mumbled. "Marty."

It was her: he knew her look too well for the European to deceive him.

"You came back," he said.

They didn't speak for several minutes, simply held on to each other. When they did talk, she had no taste for retelling what she'd experienced. Marty held his curiosity in check. It was enough to know they had no Devil on their backs.

Just old humanity, cheated of love, and ready to pull down the world on its head.

63

So perhaps they had a chance of life after all. Mamoulian was a man, for all his unnatural faculties. He was two hundred years old, perhaps, but what were a few years between friends?

The priority now was to find Papa and warn him of what Mamoulian intended, then plan as best they could against the European's offensive. If Whitehead wouldn't help, that was his prerogative. At least Marty would have tried, for old times' sake. And in the light of the murder of Charmaine and Flynn, Whitehead's crimes against Marty diminished to sins of discourtesy. He was easily the lesser of two evils.

As to the *how* of finding Whitehead, the only lead Marty had was the strawberries. It had been Pearl who'd told him that Old Man Whitehead had never let a day go by without strawberries. Not in twenty years, she'd claimed. Wasn't it possible, then, that he'd continued to indulge himself, even in hiding? It was a slender line of inquiry. But appetite, as Marty had so recently learned, was at the crux of this conundrum.

He tried to persuade Carys to come with him, but she was wrung out to the point of collapse. Her journeys, she said, were

over; she'd seen too much for one day. All she wanted now was
the sunshine island, and on that point she would not be moved.
Reluctantly, Marty left her to her fix, and went off to discuss
strawberries with Mr. Halifax of Holborn.

L eft alone, Carys found forgetfulness very quickly. The sights
 she had witnessed in Mamoulian's head were dismissed to the
dim past from which they'd come. The future, if there was to be
one, was ignored here, where there was only tranquility. She
bathed under a sun of nonsenses, while outside a soft rain began.

XII. THE FAT MAN DANCES

64

Breer didn't mind the change in the weather. It was altogether too sultry on the street, and the rain, with its symbolic cleansing, made him feel more comfortable. Though it was many weeks since he'd felt the least spasm of pain, he did itch in the heat. Not even an itch really. It was a more fundamental irritation: a crawling sensation on or beneath his skin that no ointment allayed. The drizzle seemed to subdue it a measure, however, for which he was grateful. Either the rain, or the fact that he was going to see the woman he loved. Though Carys had attacked him several times (he wore the wounds like trophies) he forgave her her trespasses. She understood him better than anyone else. She was unique—a goddess, despite her body hair—and he knew that if he could only see her again, display himself for her, touch her, all would be well.

But first he had to get to the house. It had taken him a while to find a taxi that would stop for him, and when one obliged the driver only took him part of the way before telling him to get out because, he claimed, the smell was so repulsive he wouldn't be able to get another fare all day. Shamed by this all-too-public rejection—the taxi driver harangued him from his cab as he drove away—Breer took to the back streets, where he hoped he wouldn't be sneered and sniggered at.

It was in one such backwater, just a few minutes' walk from where Carys was waiting for him, that a young man with blue swallows tattooed on his neck stepped out of a doorway to offer the Razor-Eater some assistance.

"Hey, man. You look sick, you know that? Let me lend you a hand."

"No, no," Breer grunted, hoping the Good Samaritan would leave him alone. "I'm fine, really."

"But I insist," Swallows said, picking up his pace to overtake Breer, then standing in the Razor-Eater's way. He glanced up and down the road to check for witnesses before pushing Breer into the doorway of a bricked-up house.

"You keep your mouth shut, man," he said, whipping out a knife and pressing it to Breer's bandaged throat, "and you'll be OK. Just empty your pockets. Quick! Quick!"

Breer made no move to comply. The suddenness of the attack had disoriented him; and the way the youth had seized his splinted neck had made him giddy. Swallows pushed the knife a little way into the bandaging to make his point clear. The victim smelled bad, and the thief wanted the job over and done with as soon as possible.

"Pockets, man! You deaf?" He pushed the knife deeper. The man didn't flinch. "I'll do it, man," the thief warned, "I'll slit your fucking throat."

"Oh," said Breer, unimpressed. More to quiet the tick than out of fear, he rummaged in the pocket of his coat and found a handful of possessions. Some coins, a few peppermints that he'd continued to suck until his saliva supply dried up, and a bottle of aftershave. He proffered them with faint apology on his rouged face.

"That all you've got?" Swallows was outraged. He tore open Breer's coat.

"Don't," the Razor-Eater suggested.

"Bit hot to be wearing a coat, isn't it?" said the thief. "What are you hiding?"

The buttons gave as he tore at the jacket Breer was wearing beneath his coat, and now the thief was staring, open-mouthed, at the handles of the knife and fork that were still buried in the

Razor-Eater's abdomen. The stains of dried fluids that ran from the wounds were only marginally less disgusting than the brown rot that was spreading down from his armpits and up from his groin. In his panic, the thief pressed the knife more deeply into Breer's throat.

"Christ, man—"

Anthony, having lost his dignity, his self-esteem, and, did he but know it, his life—had only his temper left to lose. He reached up and took hold of the inquiring knife in a greasy palm. The thief relinquished it a moment too late. Breer, swifter than his bulk suggested, twisted blade and hand back, and broke his assailant's wrist.

Swallows was seventeen. He had lived, he thought, a full life for a seventeen-year-old. He'd seen two violent deaths, he'd lost his virginity—to his half-sister—at fourteen, he'd raised whippets, he'd watched snuff movies, he'd taken every kind of pill he could get his trembling hands on: it had been, he thought, a busy existence, full of acquired wisdom. But this was new. Nothing like this, ever. It made his bladder ache.

Breer still had hold of the thief's useless arm.

"Let me go . . . please."

Breer just looked at him, his jacket still swinging open, those bizarre wounds displayed.

"What do you want, man? You're hurting me."

Swallows' jacket was also open. Inside was another weapon, thrust into a deep pocket.

"Knife?" Breer said, looking at the handle.

"No, man." Breer reached for it. The youth, eager to oblige, pulled the weapon out and dropped it at Breer's feet. It was a machete. Its blade was stained, but its edge keen.

"It's yours, man. Go on, take it. Only let go of my arm, man."

"Pick it up. Get down and pick it up," Breer said, releasing the injured wrist. The youth went down onto his haunches and picked the machete up, then handed it to Breer. The Razor-Eater took it.

The tableau, with him standing over his kneeling victim, blade in hand, meant something to Breer, but he couldn't fix exactly what. A picture from his book of atrocities, perhaps.

"I could kill you," he observed with some detachment.

The thought had not escaped Swallows. He closed his eyes, and waited. But no blow came. The man simply said, "Thank you," and walked away.

Kneeling in the doorway, Swallows began to pray. He quite surprised himself with this show of godliness, reciting by rote the prayers he and Hosanna, his half-sister, had said together before and after they'd sinned.

He was still praying ten minutes later, when the rain started to come on in earnest.

65

It took Breer several minutes of searching along Bright Street before he found the yellow house. Once he'd located it, he stood outside for several minutes, preparing himself. She was here: his salvation. He wanted their reunion to be as perfect as he could make it.

The front door was open. Children were playing on the threshold, having been driven from their hopscotch and skipping games by the onset of the rain. He edged past them with caution, anxious that his lumpen feet shouldn't crush a tiny hand. One particularly fetching child earned a smile from him: she did not return it, however. He stood in the hallway, trying to remember where the European had told him Carys was hiding. Second floor, wasn't it?

———————

Carys heard somebody moving about on the landing outside the room, but that passage of shabby wood and peeling wallpaper lay across unbridgeable straits, far from her Island. She was quite safe where she was.

Then somebody outside knocked on the door: a tentative, gentlemanly knock. She didn't answer at first, but when the knocking came again she said, "Go away."

After several seconds' hesitation, the handle of the door was lightly jiggled.

"Please . . ." she said, as politely as possible, "*go* away. Marty isn't here."

The handle was rattled again, this time more strongly. She heard soft fingers working at the wood; or was that the slosh of waves on the shore of the Island? She couldn't find it in her to be frightened or even concerned. It was good H Marty had brought. Not the best—she'd only had that from Papa—but it took away every fiber of fear.

"You can't come in," she told the would-be intruder. "You'll have to go away and come back later."

"It's me," the Razor-Eater tried to say. Even through the haze of sunshine she knew the voice. How could Breer be whispering at the door like this? Her mind was playing unwelcome tricks.

She sat up on the bed, while the noise of his pressure on the door increased. Suddenly, tiring of subtlety, he pushed. Once, twice. The lock succumbed too easily, and he stumbled into the room. It wasn't mind-play after all, he was here in all his glory.

"Found you," he said, the perfect prince.

He carefully closed the door behind him and presented himself to her. She looked disbelievingly at him: his broken neck supported by some homemade contraption of wood and bandages, his shabby clothes. He worked at one of his leather gloves to take it off, but it wouldn't come.

"I came to see you," he said, the words fractured.

"Yes."

He pulled at the glove. There was a soft, sickly noise. She looked at his hand. Much of the skin had come off with the glove. He extended this seeping patchwork to her.

"You have to help me," he told her.

"Are you alone?" she asked him.

"Yes."

That was something at least. Perhaps the European didn't even know he was here. He'd come courting, to judge by this pathetic attempt at civility. His dalliance went back to that first encounter in the steam room. She hadn't screamed or puked, and that had won his undying loyalty.

"Help me," he moaned.

"I can't help you. I don't know how to."

"Let me touch you."

"You're ill."

The hand was still extended. He took a step forward. Did he think she was an icon of some kind, a talisman that—once touched—cured all sickness?

"Pretty," he said.

The smell of him was overpowering, but her drugged mind idled. She knew it was important to escape, but how? The door perhaps; the window? Or just ask him to leave: come again tomorrow?

"Will you go, please?"

"Just touch."

The hand was within inches of her face. Revulsion overcame her, bypassing the lethargy the Island had induced. She swatted the arm away, appalled by even the briefest contact with his flesh. He looked offended.

"You tried to harm me," he reminded her. "So many times. I never harmed you once."

"You wanted to."

"*Him*; never me. I want you to be with all my other friends; where nothing can hurt you."

The hand, which had returned to his side, suddenly darted up and took her by the neck.

"You'll never leave me," he said.

"You're hurting me, Anthony."

He drew her closer, and bent his head toward her as best he could, given the condition of his neck. In a patch of skin beneath his right eye she could see movement. The closer he came the more she saw the fat, white grubs that had been laid as eggs in his face, and were maturing there, awaiting wings. Did he know he was a home for maggots? Was it, perhaps, a point of pride to be flyblown? He was going to kiss her: she had no doubt of that. If he puts his tongue in my mouth, she half-thought, I'll bite it off. I won't let him do this. Gentle God, I'd rather die.

He put his lips on hers.

"You are unforgivable," said a thin voice.

The door was open.

"Let her go."

The Razor-Eater unhanded Carys, and drew away from her face. She spat to rinse the kiss off and looked up.

Mamoulian was in the doorway. Behind him stood two well-dressed young men, one with golden hair, both with winning smiles.

"Unforgivable," the European said again, and turned his vacant gaze to Carys. "You see what happens if you desert my custody?" he said. "What horrors come?"

She didn't respond.

"You're alone, Carys. Your erstwhile protector is dead."

"Marty? Dead?"

"At his house: going out for your heroin."

She was seconds ahead of him, realizing his error. Maybe it gave Marty an edge on them, if they thought him dead. But it wouldn't be wise to fake tears. She was no tragic actress. Best to feign disbelief; doubt, at least.

"No," she said. "I don't believe you."

"My own fair hands," said the blond Adonis at the European's back.

"No," she insisted.

"Take it from me," the European said, "he won't be coming back. Trust me in this at least."

"Trust you?" she murmured. It was almost funny.

"Haven't I just prevented your rape?"

"He's your creature."

"Yes; and he will be punished, depend upon it. Now I trust you will return my kindness in coming here, by finding your father for me. I will not brook delay of any kind, Carys. We will go back to Caliban Street and you will find him, or by God, I will turn you inside out. That is a promise. Saint Thomas will escort you down to the car."

The brown-haired smile stepped past his blond companion and offered a hand to Carys.

"I have very little time to waste, girl," Mamoulian said, and the changed tone of his voice confirmed that claim. "So please: let's be done with this wretched business."

Tom led Carys down the stairs. When she'd gone the European turned his attention to the Razor-Eater.

Breer was not afraid of him; he was afraid of no one any longer. The poky room they faced each other in was hot; he could tell it was hot by the sweat on Mamoulian's cheeks and upper lip. He, on the other hand, was cool; he was the coolest man in creation. Nothing would bring fear to him. Mamoulian surely saw that.

"Close the door," the European told the blond boy. "And find something to bind this man with."

Breer grinned.

"You disobeyed me," the European said. "I left you to finish the work at Caliban Street."

"I wanted to see her."

"She's not yours to see. I made a bargain with you, and like all the others, you break my trust."

"A little game," Breer said.

"No game is *little*, Anthony. Have you been with me all this time and not understood that? Every act carries some weight of significance. Especially play."

"I don't care what you say. All words; just words."

"You are despicable," the European said. Breer's smudged face looked back at him without a trace of anxiety or contrition. Though the European knew he had supremacy here, something about Breer's look made him uneasy. In his time Mamoulian had been served by far viler creatures. Poor Konstantin, for example, whose postmortem appetites had run to more than kisses. Why then did Breer distress him?

Saint Chad had torn up a selection of clothes; these, with a belt and a tie, were sufficient for Mamoulian's purposes.

"Tie him to the bed."

Chad could barely bring himself to touch Breer, though at least the man didn't struggle. He acceded to this punishment game with the same idiot grin still creasing his face. His skin—beneath Chad's hand—felt insolid, as though under its taut, glossy surface the muscle had turned to jelly and pus. The saint worked as efficiently as he could to get the duty done while the prisoner amused himself watching the flies orbiting his head.

Within three or four minutes Breer was secured hand and foot. Mamoulian nodded his satisfaction. "That's fine. You may go and join Tom in the car. I'll be down in a few moments."

Respectfully, Chad withdrew, wiping his hands on his handkerchief as he went. Breer still watched the flies.

"I have to leave you now," said the European.

"When will you come back?" the Razor-Eater asked.

"Never."

Breer smiled. "I'm free, then," he said.

"You are dead, Anthony," Mamoulian replied.

"What?" Breer's smile began to decay.

"You've been dead since the day I found you hanging from the ceiling. I think perhaps somehow you knew I was coming, and you killed yourself to escape me. But I needed you. So I gave you a little of my life, to keep you in my employ."

Breer's smile had disappeared altogether.

"That's why you're so impervious to pain; you are a walking corpse. The deterioration your body should have suffered in these hot months has been held at bay. Not entirely prevented, I'm afraid, but slowed considerably."

Breer shook his head. Was this the miracle of redemption?

"Now I no longer need you. So I withdraw my gift . . ."

"No!"

He tried to make a small pleading gesture, but his wrists were bound together, and the bindings bit into the muscle, causing it to buckle and furrow like soft clay.

"Tell me how to make amends," he offered. "Anything."

"There is no way."

"Anything you ask. *Please.*"

"I ask you to suffer," the European replied.

"Why?"

"For treachery. For being, in the end, like the others."

". . . no . . . just a little game . . ."

"Then let this be a game too, if it amuses you. Six months of deterioration pressed into as many hours."

Mamoulian crossed to the bed, and put his hand on Breer's sobbing mouth, making something very like a snatching gesture.

"It's over, Anthony," he said.

Breer felt a motion in his lower belly, as though some jittering thing had suddenly twitched and perished in there. He followed the European's exit with upturned eyes. Matter, not tears, gathered at their rims.

"Forgive me," he begged his savior. "Please forgive me." But the European had gone, quietly, closing the door behind him.

There was a brawling on the windowsill. Breer looked from door to window. Two pigeons had squabbled over some morsel, and were now flying off. Small white feathers settled on the sill, like midsummer snow.

66

I t *is* Mr. Halifax, isn't it?"

The man inspecting the boxes of fruit in the breezeless, wasp-woven yard at the back of the shop turned to Marty.

"Yes. What can I do for you?"

Mr. Halifax had been out sunbathing, and injudiciously. His face was peeling in places, and looked tender. He was hot and uncomfortable and, Marty guessed, thin of temper. Tact was the order of the day, if he hoped to win the man's confidence.

"Business OK?" Marty asked.

Halifax shrugged. "It'll do," he said, unwilling to be drawn on the subject. "Lot of my regular customers are on holiday at this time of year." He peered at Marty. "Do I know you?"

"Yes. I've been here several times," Marty lied. "For Mr. Whitehead's strawberries. That's what I came for. The usual order."

Halifax registered nothing; he put down the tray of peaches he was holding. "I'm sorry. I don't supply any Mr. Whitehead."

"Strawberries," Marty prompted.

"I heard what you said," Halifax replied testily, "but I don't know anyone of that name. You must be mistaken."

"You *do* remember me?"

"No, I don't. Now if you'd like to make a purchase, Theresa will serve you." He nodded back in the direction of the shop itself. "I'd like to finish here before I cook in this bloody heat."

"But I'm supposed to be picking up strawberries."

"You can have as many as you like," Halifax said, spreading his arms. "There's a glut. Just ask Theresa."

Marty could see failure looming. The man wasn't about to

give an inch. He tried one final tack. "You don't have any fruit set aside for Mr. Whitehead? You normally have them packed, ready for him."

This significant detail seemed to mellow the dismissal on Halifax's face. Doubt dawned.

"Look . . ." he said, ". . . I don't think you quite understand . . ." His voice dropped in volume, though there was nobody else in the yard to hear. "Joe Whitehead is dead. Don't you read the newspapers?"

A large wasp alighted on Halifax's arm, navigating the ginger hairs with difficulty. He let it crawl there, undisturbed.

"I don't believe everything I read in the newspapers," Marty replied, quietly. "Do you?"

"I don't know what you're talking about," the other man returned.

"His strawberries," Marty said. "That's all I'm after."

"Mr. Whitehead is *dead.*"

"No, Mr. Halifax; Joe is not dead. You and I both know that."

The wasp rose from Halifax's arm and careered in the air between them. Marty swatted it away; it came back, its buzz louder.

"Who are you?" Halifax said.

"Mr. Whitehead's bodyguard. I've told you, I've been here before."

Halifax bent back to the tray of peaches; more wasps congregated at a bruise on one of them. "I'm sorry, I can't help you," he said.

"You took them already, did you?" Marty laid a hand on Halifax's shoulder. "*Did you?*"

"I'm not at liberty to tell you anything."

"I'm a friend."

Halifax glanced round at Marty. "I've sworn," he said, with the finality of a practiced bargainer. Marty had thought the scenario through as far as this impasse: Halifax confessing that he knew something, but refusing to provide the details. What now? Did he lay hands on the man; beat it out of him?

"Joe is in great danger."

"Oh, yes," Halifax murmured. "You think I don't realize that?"

"I can help him."

Halifax shook his head. "Mr. Whitehead has been a valued customer for a good many years," he explained. "He's always had his strawberries from me. I never knew a man love strawberries the way he does."

"Present tense," Marty commented.

Halifax went on as though he hadn't been interrupted. "He used to come in here personally, before his lady wife died. Then he stopped coming. He still bought the fruit. Had somebody come and pick it up for him. And at Christmas, there was always a check for the kiddies. There still is, come to that. Still sends money for them."

The wasp had alighted on the back of his hand, where the sweet juice of one fruit or another had dried. Halifax let it have its fill. Marty liked him. If Halifax wasn't willing to volunteer the information Marty wouldn't be able to bully it out of the man.

"Now you come here and tell me you're a friend of his," Halifax said. "How do I know you're telling the truth? People have friends who'd cut their throats."

"His more than most."

"True. So much money, so few people who care about him." Halifax had a sad look. "Seems to me I should keep his hideaway secret, don't you? Or else who can he trust in all the world?"

"Yes," Marty conceded. What Halifax said made perfect and compassionate sense, and there was nothing he was prepared to do to make him rescind it.

"Thank you," he said, cowed by the lesson. "I'm sorry to have kept you from your work." He made his way back toward the shop. He'd gone a few paces when Halifax said: "You *were* the one."

Marty pivoted on his heel.

"What?"

"You were the one who came for the strawberries. I remember you. Only you looked different then."

Marty ran his hand across several days' growth of beard; shaving was a forgotten craft these mornings.

"Not the hair," Halifax said. "You were harder. I didn't take to you."

Marty waited somewhat impatiently for Halifax to finish this farewell homily. His mind was already turning over other possibilities. It was only when he turned back into Halifax's words that he realized the man had changed his mind. He was going to tell. He beckoned Marty back across the yard.

"You think you can help him?"

"Maybe."

"I hope somebody can."

"You've seen him?"

"I'll tell you. He rang the shop, asked for me. Funny, I recognized the voice immediately, even after all these years. He asked me to bring him some strawberries. He said he couldn't come himself. It was terrible."

"Why?"

"He's so frightened." Halifax hesitated, looking for the right words. "I remember him as being big, you know? Impressive. He'd come in the shop and everyone would part for him. Now? Shrunk to nothing. Fear did that to him. I've seen it happen. My sister-in-law, same thing happened to her. She had cancer. Fear killed her months before the tumor."

"Where is he?"

"I tell you, I went back home and I didn't say a word to anyone. I just drank half a bottle of Scotch, straight off. Never done that in my life. I just wanted to get the way he'd looked out of my head. It really turned my stomach, hearing him and seeing him that way. I mean—if the likes of him's scared, what chance have the rest of us got?"

"You're safe," Marty said, hoping to God the European's revenge wouldn't stretch as far as the old man's strawberry supplier. Halifax was a good man. Marty found himself holding on to this realization while staring at the round, red face. Here is goodness. Flaws too, no doubt: sins by the armful perhaps. But the good was worth celebrating, however many stains the man had. Marty wanted to tattoo the date of this recognition on the palm of his hand.

"There's a hotel," Halifax was saying. "It used to be called the Orpheus, apparently. It's up the Edgware Road; Staple Corner. Terrible, run-down place. Waiting for the demolition squad, I shouldn't be surprised."

"He's there alone?"

"Yes." Halifax sighed, thinking of how the mighty had fallen. "Perhaps," he suggested after a moment, "you might take him some peaches too?"

H e went into the shop and came back with a tattered copy of the *London A to Z Street Atlas*. He flicked through the age-creamed pages looking for the appropriate map, all the while sounding his dismay at this turn of events, and his hope that things might still turn out well. "Lot of streets been leveled around the hotel," he explained. "These maps are well out of date, I'm afraid."

Marty peered at the page Halifax had selected. A cloud, bearing the rain that had already dampened Kilburn and points northwest, covered the sun as Halifax's stained index finger traced a route across the map from the thoroughfares of Holborn to the Hotel Pandemonium.

XIII. AT THE HOTEL PANDEMONIUM

67

Hell is reimagined by each generation. Its terrain is surveyed for absurdities and remade in a fresher mold; its terrors are scrutinized and, if necessary, reinvented to suit the current climate of atrocity; its architecture is redesigned to appall the eye of the modern damned. In an earlier age Pandemonium—the first city of Hell—stood on a lava mountain while lightning tore the clouds above it and beacons burned on its walls to summon the fallen angels. Now, such spectacle belongs to Hollywood. Hell stands transposed. No lightning, no pits of fire.

In a wasteland a few hundred yards from a highway overpass it finds a new incarnation: shabby, degenerate, forsaken. But here, where fumes thicken the atmosphere, minor terrors take on a new brutality. Heaven, by night, would have all the configurations of Hell. No less the Orpheus—hereafter called Pandemonium—Hotel.

It had once been an impressive building, and could have been again if its owners had been willing to invest in it. But the task of rebuilding and refurbishing such a large and old-fashioned hotel was probably financially unsound. Sometime in its past a fire had raged through the place, gutting the first, second and third floors before being extinguished. The fourth floor, and those above, were smoke-spoiled, leaving only the vaguest signs of the hotel's former glamor intact.

The vagaries of the city planning department had taken a further toll on the building's chances of restoration. As Halifax had described, the land to either side of the hotel had been cleared for some projected redevelopment. None had been undertaken, however. The hotel stood in splendid isolation, mazed about with feed roads to and from the M1, no more than three hundred yards from one of the busiest stretches of concrete and tarmac in the south of England. Thousands of drivers glanced its way every day, but its shabby grandeur was by now so familiar they probably scarcely registered its existence. Clever, Marty thought, to hide in such plain sight.

He parked the car as close to the hotel as he could, then slipped in through a hole in the corrugated iron fencing around the plot, and picked his way across the wasteland. The instructions on the fence—"No Trespassing" and "No Dumping"—had been conspicuously ignored. Black plastic bags, bulging with rubbish, were piled in heaps among the rubble and the old bonfires. Many of the bags had been torn open by children or dogs. Domestic and manufacturing trash spilled out: hundreds of scraps of cloth—sweatshop off-cuts—were scattered underfoot; rotting food, the ubiquitous tin can, cushions, lampshades and car engines—all abandoned on a bed of rubble dust and gray grass.

Some of the dogs—wild, Marty guessed—looked up from their scavenging as he advanced, their pale flanks dirty, their eyes yellow in the twilight. He thought of Bella and her gleaming family: these curs hardly seemed of the same species. When he looked their way they hung their heads and watched him indirectly, like inept spies.

He went up to the main entrance of the hotel: the word ORPHEUS was still clearly carved above the door; there were mock-Doric columns to either side of the steps, and fancy tilework on the threshold. But the door itself had boards nailed across it, and notices warned of swift prosecution if anyone trespassed. There seemed little chance of that. The second-, third- and fourth-story windows were boarded up with the same thoroughness as the door; those on the first floor had been bricked up entirely. There was a door at the back of the building that was not boarded up, but it was bolted from the inside. This was probably where

Halifax had entered the building: but Whitehead must have given him access. Without breaking and entering, there was no way in.

It was only on his second orbit of the hotel that he gave some serious consideration to the fire escape. It zigzagged up the east side of the building, an impressive piece of wrought-iron work that was now rusting badly. Further mutilation had been done to it by some enterprising salvage firm that, seeing profit in the scrap metal, had started to cut the escape away from the wall, only to give up on the job when it had reached the second floor. This left the bottom flight missing, the escape's truncated tail hanging ten or eleven feet from the ground. Marty studied the problem. The fire-exit doors on most of the stories had been nailed up; but one, on the fourth story, showed signs of tampering. Was this how the old man had gained entrance? He would have needed help, presumably: Luther, perhaps.

Marty scanned the wall beneath the fire escape. It was graffiti-strewn, but smooth. There was no chance of a handhold or foothold to get him up the first few feet and onto the steps themselves. He turned to the wasteland, looking for inspiration, and a few minutes' search in the deepening dusk revealed a pile of discarded furniture, among it a table, three-legged, but serviceable. He hauled it back to the fire escape and then wedged a collection of refuse bags beneath it in lieu of its missing limb. It made an unsteady perch when he climbed up onto it, and even then his fingers missed the bottom of the escape. He was obliged to jump for a handhold, and on the fourth attempt he achieved one, leaving him swinging at arm's length from the bottom step. A drizzle of rust scales hit his face and hair. The escape creaked. He mustered his will and hauled himself up a vital few inches, then struck out with his left hand for a hold on a higher stair. His shoulder joints complained, but he pulled on upward, hand over hand, until he could lift his leg high enough to hoist his whole body onto the steps.

The first stage achieved, he stood on the escape and caught his breath, then started up. The structure was by no means stable; the salvage crew had obviously been at work loosening it from the wall. Every step he took, a grating squeal seemed to presage its capitulation.

"Hold on," he whispered to it, mounting the steps with as light a tread as he could. His efforts were rewarded on the fourth story. As he guessed, the door had been opened quite recently, and with no small sense of relief he stepped from the dubious safety of the fire escape and into the hotel itself.

It still stank of the conflagration that had defeated it: the bitter smell of burned wood and charred carpeting. Below him he could see—by the meager light through the open fire door—the gutted floors. The walls were scorched, the paint on the banisters diseased with blisters. But just a few steps up from here the fire's progress had been arrested.

Marty started up the stairs to the fifth story. A long corridor presented itself to him, with rooms to right and left. He wandered down the passageway taking a perfunctory look into each of the suites as he passed. The numbered doors let onto empty spaces: all the furniture and fittings that were salvageable had been removed years ago.

Perhaps because of its isolated position, and the difficulty of entering, the building had not been squatted or vandalized. The rooms were almost absurdly clean, their deep-pile beige carpets—too bothersome to remove, apparently—springy as cliff turf beneath his feet. He checked every suite on the fifth floor before retracing his path to the stairs and going up another flight. The scene was the same here, although the suites—which had perhaps once commanded a salable view—were larger and fewer on this floor, the carpets, if anything, lusher. It was bizarre, ascending from the charred depths of the hotel to this pristine, breathless place. People had perhaps died in the blindfold corridors below, asphyxiated or baked to death in their dressing gowns. But up here no trace of the tragedy had intruded.

There was one floor left to investigate. As he climbed the final flight of stairs the illumination suddenly strengthened until it was almost as bright as day. The source was highway light, finding its

way through the skylights and ineptly sealed windows. He explored
the labyrinthine system of rooms as quickly as possible, pausing
only to glance out of the window. Far below, he could see the car
parked beyond the fence; the dogs engaged in a mass rape. In the
second suite he suddenly caught sight of somebody watching him
across the vast reception room only to realize that the haggard face
was his own, reflected in a wall-sized mirror.

The door of the third suite, on this final floor, was locked, the
first locked suite Marty had encountered. Proof positive, if any
were needed, that it had an occupant.

Jubilant, Marty rapped on the door. "Hello? Mr. Whitehead?"
There was no answering movement from within. He rapped
again, harder, casing the door as he did so to see if a break-in was
plausible, but it looked too solid to be easily shouldered down. If
necessary, he'd have to go back to the car and get some tools.

"It's Strauss, Mr. Whitehead. It's Marty Strauss. I know you're
in there. Answer me." He listened. When there was no reply, he
beat on the door a third time, this time with fist instead of
knuckles. And suddenly the reply came, shockingly close. The old
man was standing just the other side of the door; had been all
along probably.

"Go to Hell," the voice said. It was a little slurred, but
unmistakably that of Whitehead.

"I have to speak to you," Marty replied. "Let me in."

"How the fuck did you find me?" Whitehead demanded. "You
bastard."

"I made some inquiries, that's all. If I can find you, anybody
can."

"Not if you keep your wretched mouth shut. You want money,
is that it? Come here for money, have you?"

"No."

"You can have it. I'll get it to you, however much you want."

"I don't want money."

"Then you're a damn fool," Whitehead said, and he laughed
to himself; a witless, ragged titter. The man was drunk.

"Mamoulian's on to you," Marty said. "He knows you're alive."

The laughing stopped.

"How?"

"Carys."

"You've seen her?"

"Yes. She's safe."

"Well . . . I underestimated you." He paused; there was a soft sound, as if he was leaning against the door. After a while he spoke again. He sounded exhausted.

"What did you come for, if not for money? She's got some expensive habits, you know."

"No thanks to you."

"I'm sure you'll find it as convenient as I did, given time. She'll bend over backward for a fix."

"You're filth, you know that?"

"But you came to warn me anyway." The old man leaped on the paradox with lightning speed, quick as ever to open a hole in a man's flank. "Poor Marty . . ." the slurred voice trailed away, smothered by mock pity. Then, razor-sharp: "How *did* you find me?"

"The strawberries."

What sounded like muffled choking came from within the suite, but it was Whitehead laughing again, this time at himself. It took several moments for him to regain his composure. "Strawberries . . ." he murmured. "My! You must be persuasive. Did you break his arms?"

"No. He volunteered the information. He didn't want to see you curl up and die."

"I'm not going to die!" the old man snapped. "Mamoulian's the one who'll die. You'll see. He's running out of time. All I have to do is wait. Here's as good a place as any. I'm very comfortable. Except for Carys. I miss her. Why don't you send her to me, Marty? Now that would be most welcome."

"You'll never see her again."

Whitehead sighed. "Oh, yes," he said, "she'll be back when she's tired of you. When she needs someone who really appreciates her stony heart. You'll see. Well . . . thank you for calling. Goodnight, Marty."

"Wait."

"I said goodnight."

". . . I've got questions . . ." Marty began.

"Questions, questions . . ." the voice was already receding. Marty pressed closer to the door to offer his final sliver of bait. "We found out who the European is; what he is!" But there was no reply. He'd lost Whitehead's attention. It was fruitless anyway, he knew. There was no wisdom to be got here; just a drunken old man replaying his old power games. Somewhere deep inside the penthouse suite a door closed. All contact between the two men was summarily severed.

Marty descended the two flights of stairs back to the open fire door, and left the building by the route he'd entered. After the smell of dead fire inside, even the highway-tainted air smelled light and new.

He stood for several minutes on the escape and watched the traffic passing along the highway, his attention pleasantly diverted by the spectacle of lane-hopping commuters. Below, two dogs fought among the refuse, bored with rape. None of them cared, drivers or dogs, about the fall of potentates: why should *he*? Whitehead, like the hotel, was a lost cause. He'd done his best to salvage the old man and failed. Now he and Carys would slip away into a new life, and let Whitehead make whatever arrangements for cessation he chose. Let him slit his wrists in a stupor of remorse, or choke on vomit in his sleep: Marty was past caring.

He climbed down the escape and scrambled onto the table, then crossed the wasteland to the car, glancing back only once to see if Whitehead was watching. Needless to say, the upper windows were blank.

68

When they got to Caliban Street the girl was still so high on her delayed fix it was difficult to communicate through her chemically elated senses. The European left the evangelists to do the cleaning up and burning he'd instructed Breer to do, and escorted Carys to the room on the top floor. There he set about persuading her to find her father, and quickly. At first the drug in her just smiled at him. His frustration began to curdle into anger. When she started to laugh at his threats—that slow, rootless laughter that was so like the pilgrim's laugh, as if she knew some joke about him that she wasn't telling—his control snapped and he unleashed a nightmare of such unrestrained viciousness upon her its crudity disgusted him almost as much as it terrorized her. She watched in disbelief as the same tide of muck that he'd conjured in the bathroom dribbled and then gushed from her own body. "Take it away," she told him, but he only increased the pitch of the illusion, until her lap squirmed with monstrosities. Abruptly, her drug bubble burst. A gleam of insanity crept into her eyes as she cowered in the corner of the room, while the things came from her every orifice, struggling to work their way out, then clinging to her with whatever limbs his invention had supplied. She was within a hairbreadth of madness, but he'd gone too far to withdraw the assault now, repelled though he was by its depravity.

"Find the pilgrim," he told her, "and all this vanishes."

"Yes, yes, yes," she pleaded, "whatever you want."

He stood and watched while she obeyed his demands, flinging herself into that same fugue state she'd achieved when pursuing

Toy. It took her longer to find the pilgrim, however, so long that the European began to suspect she'd canceled all link with her body, and left it to his devices rather than reenter it. But she finally returned. She had found him at a hotel no less than half an hour's drive from Caliban Street. Mamoulian was not surprised. It was not in the nature of foxes to travel far from their natural habitat; Whitehead had simply gone to ground.

Wrung out by the journey and the fear that had propelled her, Carys was half-carried down the stairs by Chad and Tom and out to the waiting car. The European made one farewell circuit of the house, to see that any sign of his presence there had been removed. The girl in the cellar, and Breer's detritus, could not be cleared at such short notice, but that was a nicety. Let those who came after construe what they liked from the atrocity photographs on the wall and the bottles of perfume so lovingly arranged. All that mattered was that evidence of his, the European's, existence here—or indeed *anywhere*—be thoroughly effaced. Soon he would be rumor again; gossip among the haunted people.

"Time to go," he said as he locked the door. "The Deluge is almost upon us."

Now, as they drove, Carys was beginning to find some strength. Balmy air through the front window caressed her face. She opened her eyes fractionally, and cast them in the direction of the European. He was not looking her way; he was staring out of the window, that aristocratic profile of his made blander than ever by fatigue.

She wondered how her father would fare in the approaching endgame. He was old, but Mamoulian was vastly older; was age, in this confrontation, an advantage or a disadvantage? Suppose—the thought occurred to her for the first time—they were equally matched? Suppose the game they were playing ended without defeat or victory on either side? Just a twentieth-century conclusion—all ambiguities. She didn't want that: she wanted finality.

Whichever way it went she knew there was small chance of *her* survival in the coming Deluge. Only Marty could tip the balance in her favor, and where was he now? If he returned to Kilburn and found it deserted, mightn't he assume she'd left him of her own accord? She couldn't predict the way he'd jump; that he was capable of the blackmail with the heroin had come as a shock. One desperate maneuver remained a possibility: to *think* her way to him and tell him where she was, and why. There were risks in such a gambit. Catching stray thoughts from him was one thing— it was no more than a parlor trick—but attempting to push her way into his head and communicate with him consciously, mind to mind, would require more mental muscle. Even assuming she had the strength to do it, what would the consequences of such an intrusion be for Marty? She pondered the dilemma in a daze of anxiety, knowing the minutes were ticking by, and soon it would be too late for any escape attempt, however desperate.

M arty was driving south toward Cricklewood when a pain began at the nape of his neck. It spread rapidly up and over his skull, escalating within two minutes to a headache of unparalleled proportions. His instinct was to pick up speed and get back to Kilburn as quickly as possible, but the Finchley Road was heavily trafficked, and all he could do was edge along with the flow, the pain worsening every ten yards. His consciousness— increasingly preoccupied with the upward spiral of pain—focused on smaller and yet smaller bits of information, his perception narrowing to a pinprick. Ahead of the Citroën the road was a blur. He was almost blinded, and a collision with a refrigerated meat truck was only prevented by the skill of the other driver. He realized that driving any further could be fatal, so he edged out of the traffic as best he could—horns blaring front and behind—and parked, inelegantly, at the side of the road, then stumbled out of the car to get some air. Completely disoriented, he stepped straight into the middle of the traffic. The lights of the oncoming vehicles were a wall of strobing colors. He felt his knees about to buckle and only prevented himself from collapsing in front of the traffic by hanging on to the open car door and hauling himself around the front of the Citroën to the comparative safety of the pavement.

A single drop of rain fell on his hand. He peered at it, concentrating to bring it into focus. It was bright red. Blood, he thought dimly. Not rain, blood. He put his hand up to his face. His nose was bleeding copiously. The heat ran down his arm and into the rolled sleeve of his shirt. Digging into his pocket he pulled out a handkerchief and clamped it under his nose, then staggered across the pavement to a shopfront. In the window, he caught his reflection. Fish swam behind his eyes. He fought the illusion, but it persisted: brilliantly colored exotica, blowing bubbles inside his skull. He stood away from the glass, and took in the words painted on it: Cricklewood Aquarium Supplies. He turned his back on the guppies and the ornamental carp and sat on the narrow sill. He had begun to shake. This was Mamoulian's doing, was all he could think. If I give into it, I'll die. I must fight. At all costs, *fight*.

C arys spoke, the word escaping her lips before she could prevent it.

"Marty."

The European looked at her. Was she dreaming? There was sweat on her swollen lips; yes, she was. Of congress with Strauss, no doubt. That was why she spoke his name with such demand in her tone.

"Marty."

Yes, for certain, she was dreaming the arrow and the wound. Look how she trembled. Look how her hands ran between her legs: a shameful display.

"How far now?" he asked Saint Tom, who was consulting the map.

"Five minutes," the youth replied.

"Fine night for it," Chad said.

Marty?

He looked up, narrowing his eyes to improve his vision of the street, but he could not see his interrogator. The voice was in his head.

Marty?

It was Carys' voice, horribly distorted. When it spoke his skull seemed to creak, his brain blowing up to the size of a melon. The pain was unbearable.

Marty?

Shut up, he wanted to say, but she wasn't there to tell. Besides, it wasn't her, it was him, *it,* the European. The voice was now replaced by the sound of somebody's breath, not his own. His was a sickening pant, this was a sleepy rhythm. The blur of the street was darkening; the ache in his head had become heaven and earth. He knew if he didn't get help, he'd die.

He stood up, blind. A hissing had filled his ears now, which all but blocked the din of traffic mere yards from him. He stumbled forward. More blood streamed from his nose.

"Somebody help me . . ."

An anonymous voice filtered through the chaos in his head. The words it spoke were incomprehensible to him, but at least he was not alone. A hand was touching his chest; another was holding his arm. The voice he'd heard was raised in panic. He wasn't sure if he made any reply to it. He wasn't even sure if he was standing up or falling down. What did it matter anyway?

Blind and deaf, he waited for some kind person to tell him he could die.

They drew up in the street a short way from the Orpheus Hotel. Mamoulian got out and left the evangelists to bring Carys. She'd begun to smell, he'd noted; that ripe smell he associated with menstruation. He strode on ahead, stepping through the rent fence and onto the no-man's-land that surrounded the hotel. Desolation pleased him. The heaps of rubble, the piles of abandoned furniture: by the sickly light of the highway the place had a glamor about it. If last rites were to be performed, what better place than here? The pilgrim had chosen well.

"This is it?" said Saint Chad, following on.

"It is. Will you find a point of access for us?"

"My pleasure."

"Only do it quietly, if you will."

The young man skipped off across the pit-fraught ground, stopping only to select a piece of twisted metal from among the rubble to force an entry. So resourceful, these Americans, Mamoulian mused as he picked his way after Chad: no wonder they ruled the world. Resourceful, but not subtle. At the front door Chad was tearing the planks away without much regard for surprise attacks. Can you hear? he thought to the pilgrim. Do you know I'm down here, so close to you at last?

He turned his cold eyes up to the top of the hotel. His belly was acid with anticipation; a film of sweat glossed his forehead and palms. I'm like a nervous lover, he thought. So strange that the romance should end this way, without a sane observer to witness the final acts. Who would know, once it was all over; who would tell? Not the Americans. They would not survive the next few hours with the tatters of their sanity intact. Not Carys; she would not survive at all. There would be nobody to report the story, which—for some buried reason—he regretted. Was that what made him a European? To want to have his story told once more, passed down the line to another eager listener who would, in his time, disregard its lesson and repeat his own suffering? Ah, how he loved tradition.

The front door had been beaten open. Saint Chad stood, grinning at his achievement, sweating in his tie and suit.

"Lead the way," Mamoulian invited him.

The eager youth went inside; the European followed. Carys and Saint Tom brought up the rear.

Within, the smell was tantalizing. Associations were one of the curses of age. In this case the perfume of carbonized wood, and the sprawl of wreckage underfoot, evoked a dozen cities he'd wandered in; but one, of course, in particular. Was that why Joseph had come to this spot: because the scent of smoke and the climb up the creaking stairs woke memories of that room off Muranowski Square? The thief's skills had been the equal of his own that night, hadn't they? There'd been something blessed about the young man with the glittering eyes; the fox who'd shown so little awe; just sat down at the table willing to risk his life in order to play. Mamoulian believed the pilgrim had forgotten Warsaw as he'd grown from fortune to fortune; but this ascent up burned stairs was proof positive that he had not.

They climbed in the dark, Saint Chad going ahead to scout the way, and calling behind him that the banister was gone in this place and a stair in that. Between the fourth and fifth stories, where the fire stopped, Mamoulian called a halt, and waited until Carys and Tom caught up. When they had he instructed that the girl be brought to him. It was lighter up here. Mamoulian could see a look of loss on the girl's tender face. He touched her, not liking the contact but feeling it appropriate.

"Your father is here," he told her. She didn't reply; nor did her features relinquish the look of grief. "Carys . . . are you listening?"

She blinked. He assumed he was making some contact with her, if primitive.

"I want you to speak to Papa. Do you understand? I want you to tell him to open the door for me."

Gently, she shook her head.

"Carys," he chided. "You know better than to refuse me."

"He's dead," she said.

"No," the European replied flatly, "he's up there; a few flights above us."

"I killed him."

What delusion was this? "Who?" he asked sharply. "Killed who?"

"Marty. He doesn't answer. I killed him."

"Shush . . . shush . . ." The cold fingers stroked her cheek. "Is he dead, then? So: he's dead. That's all that can be said."

". . . I did it . . ."

"No, Carys. It wasn't you. It was something that had to be done; don't concern yourself."

He took her wan face in both hands. Often he had cradled her head when she was a child, proud that she was the pilgrim's fruit. In those embraces he had nurtured the powers she had grown up with, sensing that a time might come when he would need her.

"Just open the door, Carys. Tell him you're here, and he'll open it for you."

"I don't want . . . to see him."

"But *I* do. You'll be doing me a great service. And once it's over, there'll be nothing to be afraid of ever again. I promise you that."

She seemed to see some sense in this.

"The door . . ." he prompted.

"Yes."

He loosed her face, and she turned away from him to climb the stairs.

In the deep-pile comfort of his suite, his jazz playing on the portable hi-fi he had personally lugged up six flights, Whitehead had heard nothing. He had all that he needed. Drink, books, records, strawberries. A man might sit out the Apocalypse up here and be none the worse for it. He had even brought some pictures: the early Matisse from the study, *Reclining Nude, Quai St. Michel*; a Miró and a Francis Bacon. The last was a mistake. It was too morbidly suggestive, with its hints of flayed flesh; he'd turned it to the wall. But the Matisse was a joy, even by candlelight. He was staring at it, never less than enchanted by its casual facility, when the knocking came.

He stood up. It was many hours—he'd lost track of time—

since Strauss had been here; had he come again? Somewhat groggy with vodka, Whitehead lurched along the hall of the suite, and listened at the door.

"Papa . . ."

It was Carys. He didn't answer her. It was suspicious, her being here.

"It's me, Papa, it's me. Are you there?"

Her voice was so tentative; she sounded like a child again. Was it possible Strauss had taken him at his word, and sent the girl to him, or had she simply come back of her own accord, the way Evangeline had after cross words? Yes, that was it. She'd come because, like her mother, she couldn't help but come. He began to unlock the door, fingers awkward in anticipation.

"Papa . . ."

At last he got the best of the key and the handle and opened the door. She wasn't there. Nobody was there: or so he thought at first. But even as he stepped back into the hall of the suite the door was thrown wide and he was flung against the wall by a youth whose hands seized him at neck and groin and pinned him flat. He dropped the vodka bottle he was carrying and threw up his hands to signify his surrender. When he'd shaken the assault from his head he looked over the youth's shoulder and his bleary eyes came to rest on the man who had followed the youth in.

Quietly, and quite without warning, he began to cry.

They left Carys in the dressing room beside the master bedroom of the suite. It was empty but for a fitted wardrobe and a pile of curtains, which had been removed from the windows and then forgotten. She made a nest in their musty folds and lay down. A single thought circled in her head: *I killed him*. She had felt his resistance to her investigation; felt the tension building in him. And then, nothing.

The suite, which occupied a quarter of the top story, boasted

two views. One was of the highway: a garish ribbon of headlights.
The other, that let on to the east side of the hotel, was gloomier.
The small dressing-room window faced this second view: a stretch
of wasteland, then the fence and the city beyond it. But from her
position lying on the floor, all of that was out of sight. All she
could see was a sky field, across which the blinking lights of a jet
crept.

She watched its circling descent, thinking Marty's name.

M*arty."*
They were lifting him into an ambulance. He still felt sick
to the pit of his stomach with the roller coaster he'd been on. He
didn't want consciousness, because with it came the nausea. The
hissing had gone from his ears however; and his sight was intact.

"What happened? Hit-and-run?" somebody asked him.

"He just fell down," a witness replied. "I saw him. Fell down
in the middle of the pavement. I was just coming out of the
newsagents when I—"

"Marty."

"—and there he was—"

"Marty."

His name was sounding in his head, clear as a spring-morning
bell. There was a renewed trickle of blood from his nose, but no
pain this time. He raised his hand to his face to stem the flow but
a hand was already there, stanching and wiping.

"You'll be all right," a man's voice said. Somehow Marty felt
this to be indisputably true, though it was nothing to do with this
man's ministrations. The pain had gone, and the fear had gone
with it. It was *Carys* speaking in his head. It had been all along.
Now some wall in him had been breached—forcibly perhaps, and
painfully, but the worst was over—and she was thinking his name
in her head and he was catching her thought like a lobbed tennis
ball. His previous doubts seemed naive. It was a simple act, this
thought catching, once you had the knack of it.

S he felt him wake to her.

For several seconds she lay on her curtain bed while the jet winked across the window, not quite daring to believe what her instincts were telling her—that he was hearing her, that he was alive.

Marty? she thought. This time, instead of the word getting lost in the dark between his mind and hers, it went unerringly home, welcomed into his cortex. He didn't have the skill to frame an answer, but that was academic at this point. As long as he could hear and understand, he could come.

The hotel, she thought. Do you understand, Marty? I'm with the European at a hotel. She tried to remember the name she'd glimpsed over the door. *Orpheus*; that was it. She had no address, but she did her best to picture the building for him, in the hope that he could make sense of her impressionist directions.

H e sat up in the ambulance.

"Don't worry. The car'll be taken care of," the attendant said, pressing a hand on his shoulder to get him to lie back down. They'd wrapped a scarlet blanket across him. Red so the blood doesn't show, he registered as he threw it off.

"You can't get up," the attendant told him. "You're in bad shape."

"I'm fine," Marty insisted, pushing the solicitous hand away. "You've been wonderful. But I've got a prior engagement."

The driver was closing the double doors at the back of the ambulance. Through the narrowing gap Marty could see a ring of professional bystanders straining to catch a final look at the spectacle. He made a dive for the doors.

The spectators were disgruntled to see Lazarus risen, and worse, to see him smiling like a loon as he emerged, apologizing, from the back of the vehicle. Didn't the man have any sense of occasion?

"I'm fine," he told the driver as he backed off through the crowd. "Must have been something I ate." The driver stared at him, uncomprehending.

"You're bloody," he managed to mutter.

"Never felt better," Marty replied, and in a way, despite the exhaustion in his bones, it was true. She was *here*, in his head, and there was still time to make things right, if he hurried.

The Citroën was a few yards down the road; splashes of his blood painted the pavement beside it. The keys were still in the ignition.

"*Wait for me, babe,*" he said, and started back toward the Pandemonium Hotel.

69

It was not the first time Sharon had been locked out of her house while her mother entertained a man the young girl had never seen before, and would, on past form, never see again; but tonight the expulsion was particularly unwelcome. She felt a summer cold coming on, and she wanted to be in the house in front of the television instead of out in the street after dark vainly trying to devise new skipping games for herself. She wandered down the street, beginning a solitary game of hopscotch, then abandoning it on the fifth square. She was just outside Number Eighty-two. It was a house her mother had warned her to keep clear of. A family of Asians lived on the ground floor—sleeping twelve to a bed, or so Mrs. Lennox had told Sharon's mother—in conditions of criminal squalor. But despite its reputation, Number Eighty-two had been a disappointment all summer: until today. Today Sharon had seen peculiar comings and goings at the house. Some people had arrived in a big car and taken a sick-looking woman away with them. And now, as she idled at the hopscotch game, there was somebody at one of the middle floor windows, a big, shadowy figure, and he was beckoning to her.

Sharon was ten. It would be a year before her first period, and though she had an inkling of the matter between men and women from her half-sister, she thought it ridiculous palaver. The boys who played football in the street were foulmouthed, grubby creatures; she could scarcely imagine ever pining for their affections.

But the alluring figure at the window was a male, and it found something in Sharon; it turned over a rock. Beneath were the first stirrings of lives that weren't quite ready for the sun. They wriggled; they made her thin legs itch. It was to stop that itch that she disobeyed every prohibition on Number Eighty-two and slipped into the house when next the front door was opened, and up to where she knew the stranger to be.

"Hello?" she said, standing on the landing outside the room.

"You can come in," the man said.

Sharon had never smelled death before, but she knew it instinctively: introductions were superfluous. She stood in the doorway and peered at the man. She could still run if she wanted to, she knew that too. She was made yet safer by the fact that he was tied to the bed. This she could see, though the room was dark. Her inquisitive mind found nothing odd in this; adults played games, the way children did.

"Put on the light," the man suggested. She reached up for the switch beside the door and turned it on. The weak bulb lit the prisoner strangely; by it he looked sicker than anybody Sharon had ever set eyes on. He had obviously dragged the bed across the room to the window, and in so doing the ropes that tied him had bitten into his gray skin, so that shiny brown fluids—not quite like blood—covered his hands and trousers, and spattered the floor at his feet. Black blotches made his face, which was also shiny, piebald.

"Hello," he said. His voice was warped, as though he were speaking out of a cheap radio. Its weirdness amused her.

"Hello," she said back.

He gave her a lopsided grin, and the bulb caught the wetness of his eyes, which were so deep in his head she could scarcely make them out. But when they moved, as they did now, the skin around them fluttered.

"I'm sorry to call you away from your games," he said.

She dawdled in the door, not quite certain whether to go or stay. "I shouldn't really be here," she teased.

"Oh . . ." he said, rolling his eyes up until all the whites showed. "Please don't go."

She thought he looked comical with his jacket all stained and his eyes rolling. "If Marilyn found out I'd been here—"

"Your sister, is that?"

"My mother. She'd hit me."

The man looked doleful. "She shouldn't do that," he said.

"Well, she does."

"That's shameful," he replied mournfully.

"Oh, she won't find out," Sharon reassured him. The man was more distressed by her talk of a beating than she'd intended. "Nobody knows I'm here."

"Good," he said. "I wouldn't want any harm to come to you on my account."

"Why are you all tied up?" she inquired. "Is it a game?"

"Yes. That's all it is. Tell me, what's your name?"

"Sharon."

"You're quite right, Sharon; it's a game. Only I don't want to play anymore. It's started to hurt me. You can see."

He raised his hands as far as he could, to show how the bindings bit. A diet of flies, disrupted from their laying, buzzed about his head.

"Are you any good at untying knots?" he asked her.

"Not very."

"Could you try. For me?"

"Suppose so," she said.

"Only I'm feeling very tired. Come in, Sharon. Close the door."

She did as she was told. There was no threat here. Just a mystery (or two maybe: death and men) and she wanted to know more. Besides, the man was ill: he could do her no harm in his present condition. The closer she got to him the worse he looked. His skin was blistering, and there were beads of something like black oil dotting his face. Beneath the smell of his perfume, which was strong, there was something bitter. She didn't want to touch him, sorry as she felt for him.

"Please . . ." he said, proffering his bound hands. The flies roved around, irritated. There were lots of them, and they were all interested in him; in his eyes, in his ears.

"I should get a doctor," she said. "You're not well."

"No time for that," he insisted. "Just untie me, then I'll find a doctor myself, and nobody need know you've been up here."

She nodded, seeing the logic of this, and approached him through the cloud of flies to untie the restraints. Her fingers were not strong, her nails bitten to the quick, but she worked at the knots with determination, a charming frown flawing the perfect plane of her brow as she labored. Her efforts were hampered by the flow of yolky fluid from his broken flesh, which gummed everything up. Once in a while she'd turn her hazel eyes up to him; he wondered whether she could see degeneration occurring in front of her. If she could, she was too engrossed in the challenge of the knots to leave; either that, or she was willingly unleashing him, aware of the power she wielded in so doing.

Only once did she show any sign of anxiety, when something in his chest seemed to fail, a piece of internal machinery slipping into a lake around his bowels. He coughed and exhaled a breath that made sewerage smell like primroses. She turned her head away and pulled a face. He apologized politely and she asked him not to do it again, then went back to the problem at hand. He waited patiently, knowing that any attempt to hurry her along would only spoil her concentration. But in time she got the measure of the riddle, and the binding began to loosen. His flesh, which was now the consistency of softened soap, skidded off the bone of his wrists as he pulled his hands free.

"Thank you," he said. "Thank you. You've been very kind."

He bent to untie the ropes at his feet, his breath, or what passed for it, a gritty rattle in his chest.

"I'll go now," she said.

"Not yet, Sharon," he replied; speaking was drudgery now. "Please don't go yet."

"But I have to be home."

The Razor-Eater looked at her creamy face: she looked so fragile, standing under the light. She had withdrawn from his immediate vicinity once the knots were untied, as though the initial trepidation had begun again. He tried to smile, to reassure her that all was well, but his face wouldn't obey. The fat and muscle just drooped on his skull; his lips felt inept. Words, he knew, were close to failing him. It would have to be signs from now on. He was moving into a purer world—one of symbols, of ritual—a world where Razor-Eaters truly belonged.

His feet were free. In a matter of moments he could be across the room to where she stood. Even if she turned and ran he could catch her. No one to see or hear; and even if there were what could they punish him with? He was a dead man.

He crossed the room toward her. The little living thing stood in his shadow and made not the least effort to escape him. Had she too calculated her chances and seen the futility of a chase? No; she was simply trusting.

He put out a sordid hand to stroke her head. She blinked, and held her breath at his proximity, but made no attempt to evade the contact. He longed for touch in his fingers, so as to feel her gloss. She was so perfect: what a blessing it would be to put a piece of her in him, to show as proof of love at the gates of paradise.

But her look was enough. He would take that with him, and

count himself content; just the somber sweetness of her as a token, like coins in his eyes to pay his passage with.

"Goodbye," he said, and walked, his gait uneven, to the door. She went ahead of him and opened the door, then led him down the stairs. A child was crying in one of the adjacent rooms, the whooping wail of a baby that knows no one will come. On the front step Breer thanked Sharon again, and they parted. He watched her run off home.

For his part, he was not certain—at least not consciously—of where he was going to go now, or why. But once down the steps and onto the pavement his legs took him in a direction he had never been before, and he didn't become lost, though he soon made his way into unfamiliar territory. Somebody called him. Him, and his machete and his blurred, gray face. He went as quickly as anatomy allowed, like a man summoned by history.

70

Whitehead was not afraid to die; he was only afraid that in dying he might discover that he had not lived enough. That had been his concern as he faced Mamoulian in the hallway of the penthouse suite, and it still tormented him as they sat in the lounge, with the buzz of the highway at their backs.

"No more running, Joe," Mamoulian said.

Whitehead said nothing. He collected a large bowl of Halifax's prime strawberries from the corner of the room, then returned to his chair. Running his expert fingers across the fruit in the bowl, he selected a particularly appetizing strawberry and began to nibble at it.

The European watched him, betraying no clue to his thoughts.

The chase was done with; now, before the end, he hoped they'd be able to talk over old times for a while. But he didn't know where to begin.

"Tell me," Whitehead said, seeking the meat of the fruit right up to the hull, "did you bring a pack with you?" Mamoulian stared at him. "Cards, not dogs," the old man quipped.

"Of course," the European answered, "always."

"And do these fine boys play?" He gestured to Chad and Tom, who stood by the window.

"We came for the Deluge," Chad said.

A frown nicked the old man's brow. "What have you been telling them?" he asked the European.

"It's all their own doing," Mamoulian replied.

"The world's coming to an end," Chad said, combing his hair with obsessive care and staring out at the highway, his back to the two old men. "Didn't you know?"

"Is that so?" said Whitehead.

"The unrighteous will be swept away."

The old man put down his bowl of strawberries. "And who will judge?" he asked.

Chad let his coiffure be. "God in Heaven," he said.

"Can't we play for it?" Whitehead responded. Chad turned to look at the questioner, puzzled; but the inquiry was not for him, but for the European.

"No," Mamoulian replied.

"For old times' sake," Whitehead pressed. "Just a game."

"Your gamesmanship would impress me, Pilgrim, if it weren't so obviously a delaying tactic."

"You won't play, then?"

Mamoulian's eyes flickered. He almost smiled as he said: "Yes. Of course I'll play."

"There's a table next door, in the bedroom. Do you want to send one of your bum-boys through to fetch it?"

"Not bum-boys."

"Too old for that, are you?"

"God-fearing men, both of them. Which is more than can be said of you."

"That was always my problem," Whitehead said, conceding the barb with a grin. This was like the old days: the exchange of ironies, the sweet-sour repartee, the knowledge, shared every moment they were together, that the words disguised a depth of feeling that would shame a poet.

"Would you fetch the table?" Mamoulian asked Chad. He didn't move. He had become too interested in the struggle of wills between these two men. Much of its significance was lost on him, but the tension in the room was unmistakable. Something awesome was on the horizon. Maybe a wave; maybe not.

"*You go*," he told Tom; he was unwilling to take his eyes off the combatants for a single instant. Tom, happy to have something to take his mind off his doubts, obliged.

Chad loosened the knot of his tie, which was for him tantamount to nakedness. He grinned flawlessly at Mamoulian.

"You're going to kill him, right?" he said.

"What do you think?" the European replied.

"What is he? The Antichrist?"

Whitehead gurgled with pleasure at the absurdity of this idea. "You've been telling . . ." he chided the European.

"Is that what he is?" Chad urged, "Tell me. I can take the truth."

"I'm worse than that, boy," Whitehead said.

"Worse?"

"Want a strawberry?" Whitehead picked up the bowl and proffered the fruit. Chad cast a sideways glance at Mamoulian.

"He hasn't poisoned them," the European reassured him.

"They're fresh. Take them. Go next door and leave us in peace."

Tom had returned with a small bedside table. He set it down in the middle of the room.

"If you go into the bathroom," Whitehead said, "you'll find a plentiful supply of spirits. Mostly vodka. A little cognac too, I think."

"We don't drink," Tom said.

"Make an exception," Whitehead replied.

"Why not?" said Chad, his mouth bulging with strawberries; there was juice on his chin. "Why the fuck not? It's the end of the world, right?"

"Right," said Whitehead, nodding. "Now you go away and eat and drink and play with each other."

Tom stared at Whitehead, who returned a mock-contrite look. "I'm sorry, aren't you allowed to masturbate either?"

Tom made a noise of disgust and left the room.

"Your colleague's unhappy," Whitehead said to Chad. "Go on, take the rest of the fruit. Tempt him."

Chad wasn't certain if he was being mocked or not, but he took the bowl and followed Tom to the door. "You're going to die," he said to Whitehead as a parting shot. Then he closed the door on the two men.

Mamoulian had laid a pack of cards on the table. This wasn't the pornographic pack: he'd had that destroyed at Caliban Street, along with his few books. The cards on the table were older than the other pack by many centuries. Their faces were hand-colored, the illustrations for the court cards crudely rendered.

"Must I?" Whitehead asked, picking up on Chad's closing remark.

"Must you what?"

"Die."

"Please, Pilgrim—"

"Joseph. Call me Joseph, the way you used to."

"—spare us both."

"I want to live."

"Of course you do."

"What happened between us—it didn't harm you, did it?"

Mamoulian offered the cards for Whitehead to shuffle and cut: when the offer was ignored he did the job himself, manipulating the cards with his one good hand.

"Well. Did it?"

"No," the European replied. "No; not really."

"Well then. Why harm *me*?"

"You misunderstand my motives, Pilgrim. I haven't come here for revenge."

"Why then?"

Mamoulian started to deal the cards for chemin de fer.

"To finish our bargain, of course. Is that so difficult to grasp?"

"I made no bargain."

"You cheated me, Joseph, of a lot of living. You threw me away when I was no longer of any use to you, and let me rot. I forgive you all that. It's in the past. But death, Joseph"—he finished the shuffling—"that's in the future. The near future. And I will not be alone when I go into it."

"I've made my apologies. If you want acts of contrition, name them."

"Nothing."

"You want my balls? My eyes? Take them!"

"Play the game, Pilgrim."

Whitehead stood up. "I don't want to play!"

"But you asked."

Whitehead stared down at the cards laid out on the inlaid table.

"That's how you got me here," he said quietly. "That fucking game."

"Sit down, Pilgrim."

"Made me suffer the torments of the damned."

"Have I?" Mamoulian said, concern lacing his voice. "Have you *really* suffered? If you have, I'm truly sorry. The point of temptation is surely that some of the goods be worth the price."

"Are you the Devil?"

"You know I'm not," Mamoulian said, pained by this new melodrama. "Every man is his own Mephistopheles, don't you think? If I hadn't come along you'd have made a bargain with some other power. And you would have had your fortune, and your women, and your strawberries. All those torments I've made you suffer."

Whitehead listened to the fluting voice lay these ironies out. Of course, he *hadn't* suffered: he'd lived a life of delights. Mamoulian read the thought off his face.

"If I'd *really* wanted you to suffer," he said, snail-slow, "I could have had that dubious satisfaction many years ago. And you know it."

Whitehead nodded. The candle, which the European now lifted onto the table beside the dealt cards, guttered.

"What I want from you is something far more permanent than suffering," Mamoulian said. "Now play. My fingers are itching."

71

Marty got out of the car and stood for several seconds looking up at the looming bulk of the Hotel Pandemonium. It was not completely in darkness. A light, albeit frail, glimmered in one of the penthouse windows. He began, for a second time today, to make his way across the wasteland, his body shaking. Carys had made no contact with him since he had started on his journey here. He didn't question her silence: there were too many plausible reasons for it, none of them pleasant.

As he approached he could see that the front door of the hotel had been forced. At least he'd be able to enter by a direct route instead of clambering up the fire escape. He stepped over the litter of planks, and through the grandiose doorway into the foyer, halting to accustom his eyes to the darkness before he began a cautious ascent of the burned stairs. In the gloom every sound he made was like gunfire at a funeral, shockingly loud. Try as he might to hush his tread, the stairway hid too many obstacles for complete silence; every step he took he was certain the European was hearing, was readying himself to breathe a killing emptiness onto him.

Once he reached the spot he'd entered from the fire escape, the going got easier. It was only as he advanced into the carpeted regions he realized—the thought brought a smile to his lips—that he'd come without either a weapon or a plan, however primitive, of how he was to snatch Carys. All he could hope was that she was no longer an important item on the European's agenda: that she might be overlooked for a few vital moments. As he stepped onto the final staircase he caught sight of himself in one of the hall mirrors: thin, unshaven, his face still bearing traces of bloodstains, his shirt dark with blood—he looked like a lunatic. The image, reflecting so accurately the way he'd pictured himself—desperate, barbarous—gave him courage. He and his reflection agreed: he was out of his mind.

For only the second time in their long association they sat facing each other over the tiny table, and played chemin de fer. The game was uneventful; they were, it seemed, more evenly matched than they'd been in Muranowski Square, forty-odd years before. And as they played, they talked. The talk too was calm and undramatic: of Evangeline, of how the market had fallen of late, of America, even, as the game progressed, of Warsaw.

"Have you ever been back?" Whitehead asked.

The European shook his head.

"It's terrible, what they did."

"The Germans?"

"The city planners."

They played on. The cards were shuffled and dealt again, shuffled and dealt. The breeze of their motions made the candle flame flicker. The game went one way, then the other. The conversation faltered, and began again: chatty, almost banal. It was as though in these last minutes together—when they had so much to say—they could say nothing of the least significance, for fear it open the floodgates. Only once did the chat show its true colors—escalating from a simple remark to metaphysics in mere seconds:

"I think you're cheating," the European observed lightly.

"You'd know if I was. All the tricks I use are yours."

"Oh, come now."

"It's true. Everything I learned about cheating, I learned from you."

The European looked almost flattered.

"Even now," Whitehead said.

"Even now what?"

"You're still cheating, aren't you? You shouldn't be alive, not at your age."

"It's true."

"You look the way you did in Warsaw, give or take a scar. What age are you? A hundred? Hundred and fifty?"

"Older."

"And what's it done for you? You're more afraid than I am. You need someone to hold your hand while you die, and you chose me."

"Together, we might *never* have died."

"Oh?"

"We might have founded worlds."

"I doubt it."

Mamoulian sighed. "It was all appetite then? From the beginning."

"Most of it."

"You never cared to make sense of it all?"

"Sense? There's no sense to be made. You told me that: the first lesson. *It's all chance.*"

The European threw down his cards, having lost the hand. ". . . Yes," he said.

"Another game?" Whitehead offered.

"Just one more. Then we really must be going."

At the head of the stairs Marty halted. The door of Whitehead's suite was slightly ajar. He had no idea of the geography of the rooms beyond—the two suites he'd investigated on this floor had been totally different, and he could not predict the layout of this one from theirs. He thought back to his earlier conversation with Whitehead. When it was over he'd had the distinct impression that the old man had walked quite a distance before an interior door had closed to bring an end to the exchange. A long hallway then, possibly offering some hiding places.

It was no use hesitating; standing there juggling his odds only worsened the nervous anticipation he felt. He must act.

At the door itself he halted again. There was a murmur of voices from inside, but muffled, as if the speakers were beyond closed doors. He put his fingers on the door of the suite and pushed gently. It swung open a few more inches and he peered inside. There was, as he'd guessed, an empty corridor leading into the suite itself; off it, four doors. Three were closed, one ajar. From behind one of the closed doors came the voices he'd heard. He concentrated, trying to pick some sense from the murmur, but he failed to catch more than an odd word. He recognized the speakers, however: one was Whitehead, the other Mamoulian. And the tone of the exchange was apparent too; gentlemanly, civilized.

Not for the first time he longed to possess the ability to go to Carys the way that she had come to him; to seek out her location with mind alone, and to debate the best means of escape. As it was, all—as ever—was chance.

He advanced along the hallway to the first closed door, and surreptitiously opened it. Though the lock made some noise the voices in the far room murmured on, unalerted to his presence. The room he peered into was a cloakroom, no more. He closed the door and advanced a few more yards down the carpeted corridor. Through the open door he could hear movement, then the clink of glass. A candle shadow, thrown by someone inside, flitted across the wall. He stood absolutely still, reluctant to retreat a foot now that he'd got so far. Voices drifted from the adjacent room.

"Shit, Chad," the speaker sounded almost fearful. "What the fuck are we doing here? I can't think properly."

The objection was met with laughter. "You don't need to think. We're on God's work here, Tommy. Drink up."

"Something terrible's going to happen," Tom said.

"Sure as shit," Chad replied. "Why'd you think we're here. Now *drink*."

Marty had rapidly worked out the identity of this pair. They were here on God's work: including murder. He had seen them buying ice creams in the afternoon sun, with their bloody knives safely pocketed. Fear overrode the urge to revenge, however. He had little enough chance of getting out of here alive as it was.

There was one last door to be investigated, directly opposite the room occupied by the young Americans. In order to check it, he would have to cross in front of the open door.

The lazy voice began again.

"You look like you want to puke."

"Why don't you let me alone?" the other replied. He seemed— or was this just wishful thinking?—to be moving away. Then came the unmistakable sound of retching. Marty held his breath. Would the other youth go to his companion's aid? He prayed so.

"You OK, Tommy?" The voice changed timbre as the speaker moved. Yes, he was walking away from the door. Taking chance by the throat, Marty stepped smartly off from the wall, opened the final door, closing it behind him.

The room he had entered was not large, but it was dark. By the little light there was he could see a figure lying curled up on the floor. It was Carys. She was sleeping; her even exhalations marked a gentle rhythm.

He went to where she lay. How to wake her: that was the problem. Next door, one wall away, was the European. If she made the slightest sound as he roused her, he would surely hear. And if *he* didn't, the Americans would.

He went down on his haunches and gently laid his hand over her mouth, then shook her shoulder. She seemed resistant to waking. She frowned in her sleep and muttered some complaint. He bent closer to her and risked hissing her name urgently into her ear. That did the trick. Her eyes sprang open, wide as an astonished child's; her mouth formed a cry against his palm. Recognition came the instant before she gave voice.

He removed his hand. There was no welcoming smile; her face was pallid and grim, but she touched his lips with her fingertips in welcome. He stood up, offering her a hand.

Next door, a row had suddenly erupted. The mellow voices were raised in mutual accusation; furniture was being overturned. Mamoulian shouted for Chad. In answer there came the thud of feet from the bathroom.

"Damn." There was no time for tactical thinking. They'd have to make a break for it and take what the moment offered, good or bad. He pulled Carys to her feet and crossed to the door. As he turned the handle he glanced over his shoulder to check that Carys was still following him, but disaster had registered on her face. He turned back to the door and the reason—Saint Thomas, his chin shiny with vomit—was standing directly outside the door. He was apparently as startled to see Marty as the other way around. Using his hesitation, Marty stepped into the hallway and pushed Tom in the chest. The American fell back, the word "Chad!" escaping his lips as he stumbled through the open door opposite, knocking over a bowl of strawberries as he did so. The fruit rolled underfoot.

Marty ducked around the dressing-room door and out into the hall, but the American recovered his balance with speed, and reached out to snatch the back of his shirt. The attempt was sufficient to slow Marty down, and as he turned to beat the arresting hand away he saw the second American emerging from the room the old men were in. There was a frightening serenity in the youth's eyes as he closed in on Marty.

"Run!" was all he could shout to Carys, but the blond god stopped her as she slipped out into the corridor, pushing her back the way she'd come with a breathed "No," before continuing on his way toward Marty. "Hold her," he told his companion as he took over the hold on Marty. Tom stepped out of sight after Carys, and there was a noise of struggle, but Marty had little time to analyze it, as Chad doubled him up with a blow to the stomach. Marty, too confused by the sudden rush of action to prepare for the pain, groaned and fell back against the front door of the suite, slamming it. The blond boy followed him down the corridor, and through tear-bleared eyes Marty just caught sight of the next blow before it landed. He didn't see the third or fourth. There was no time between the punches and kicks to stand upright or catch a breath. The corn-fed body pummeling him was lithe and strong, more than Marty's equal. Vainly, he flailed against the tattoo. He was so damn tired and sick. His nose began to bleed again, and still the serene eyes fixed him as the fists beat his body black. So calm, those eyes, they could have been at prayer. But it was Marty who was falling to his knees; Marty whose head was dragged back in enforced adulation as the blond boy spat on him; Marty who said, "Help me"—or some bruised corruption of those words—as he collapsed.

Mamoulian stepped out of the gaming room, leaving the pilgrim to his tears. He'd done as the old man had asked—they'd played a game or two for old times' sake. But now the indulgence was over. And what was this chaos in the hall; the tangle of limbs at the front door, blood spattered on the wall? Ah, it was Strauss. Somehow the European had expected a late arrival at the celebrations; who it was to be, he hadn't foreseen. He stalked the corridor to see what damage had been done, looking down at the disfigured, spittle-laced face with a sigh. Saint Chad, his fists bloody, was sweating a little: the scent off the young lion was sweet.

"He was almost away," the Saint said.

"Indeed," the European replied, gesturing for the youth to give him room.

From his collapsed position on the hall floor Marty gazed up at the Last European. The air between them seemed to be itching. Marty waited. Surely the killing stroke would follow quickly. But there was nothing, except the gaze from those noncommittal eyes. Even in his broken state Marty could see the tragedy written in the mask of Mamoulian's face. It no longer terrified him: simply fascinated. This man was the source of the nullity he had barely survived in Caliban Street. Was there not a ghost of that gray air lurking in his sockets now, seeping from his nostrils and mouth as though a fire smoldered in his cranium?

In the room where he and the European had played cards Whitehead moved stealthily across to the pillow of his makeshift bed. Events in the hall had shifted the focus for a useful moment. He slipped his hand beneath the pillow and drew out the gun hidden there, then crept through into the adjoining dressing room, and slipped out of sight behind the wardrobe. From that position he could see Saint Tom and Carys standing in the hallway, watching events at the front door. Both were too intent on the gladiators to notice in the darkened room.

"Is he dead . . . ?" Tom asked, from a distance.

"Who knows?" Whitehead heard Mamoulian reply. "Put him in the bathroom, out of the way."

Whitehead watched as Strauss' inert bulk was hauled past the door and into the room opposite, to be dumped in the bathroom. Mamoulian approached Carys.

"You brought him here," he said simply.

She didn't reply. Whitehead's gun hand itched. From where he was standing Mamoulian made an easy target, except that Carys stood in the way. Would a bullet, fired at her back, pass through her and into the European? The thought, though appalling, had to be contemplated: survival was at issue here. But the moment's hesitation had snatched his chance. The European was escorting Carys toward the gaming room, and out of shot. No matter; it left the coast clear.

He slipped out of hiding and darted to the dressing-room door. As he stepped into the corridor he heard Mamoulian say: "Joseph?" Whitehead ran the few yards to the front door, knowing the chance of escape without violence was gossamer-thin. He grabbed the handle and turned it.

"*Joseph*," said the voice behind him.

Whitehead's hand froze as he felt invisible fingers plucking at the nape of his neck. He ignored the pressure and forced the handle around. It slid in his sweaty palm. The thought that breathed at his neck pressed around his axis vertebra, the threat unmistakable. Well then, he thought, the choice is out of my hands. He released the door handle and turned fully around to face the card-player. He was standing at the end of the corridor, which seemed to be darkening, becoming a tunnel extruded from Mamoulian's eyes. Such potent illusions. But simply that: *illusions*. He could resist them long enough to bring their forger down. Whitehead raised the gun and pointed it at the European. Without giving the card-player another moment to confound him, he fired. The first shot hit Mamoulian's chest; the second his stomach. Perplexity crossed the European's face. Blood spread from the wounds across his shirt. He did not fall, however. Instead, in a voice so even it was as if the shots had not been fired, he said: "Do you want to go outside, Pilgrim?"

Behind Whitehead, the door handle had started to rattle.

"*Is that what you want?*" Mamoulian demanded. "*To go outside?*"

"Yes."

"Then go."

Whitehead stepped away from the door as it was flung open with such venom the handle impaled itself in the corridor wall. The old man turned away from Mamoulian to make good his escape, but before he could take a step the light in the corridor was sucked away into the pitch darkness beyond the door, and to his horror Whitehead realized that the hotel had disappeared from beyond the threshold. There were no carpets and mirrors out there; no stairs winding down to the outside world. Only a wilderness he'd walked in half a life ago: a square, a sky shot with trembling stars.

"Go out," the European invited him. "It's been waiting for you all these years. Go on! *Go!*"

The floor beneath Whitehead's feet seemed to have become slick; he felt himself sliding toward the past. His face was washed by the open air as it glided into the hallway to meet him. It smelled of spring, of the Vistula, which roared to the sea ten minutes' walk from here; it smelled of blossom too. Of course it smelled of blossom. What he'd mistaken for stars were petals, white petals lifted by the breeze and gusted toward him. The sight of the petals was too persuasive to be ignored; he let them lead him back into this glorious night, when for a few shimmering hours the whole world had promised to be his for the taking. Even as he conceded his senses to the night the tree appeared, as phenomenal as he had so often dreamed it, its white head shaking slightly. Somebody lurked in the shade beneath its laden branches; their smallest movement caused a new cascade. His entranced reason made one final snatch at the reality of the hotel, and he reached to touch the door of the suite, but his hand missed it in the darkness. There was no time to look again. The obscured watcher was emerging from the cover of the branches. *Déjà vu* suffused Whitehead; except that the first time he'd been here there had only been a glimpse of the man beneath the tree. This time the reluctant sentinel broke cover. Smiling a welcome, Lieutenant Konstantin Vasiliev showed his burned face to the man who'd come visiting from the future. Tonight the lieutenant would not shamble off for a rendezvous with a dead woman; tonight he would embrace the thief, who had grown furrowed and bearded, but whose presence here he'd awaited a lifetime.

"We thought you'd never come," Vasiliev said. He pushed a branch aside and stepped fully into the dead light of this fantastical night. He was proud to show himself, though his hair was entirely burned off, his face black and red, his body full of holes. His trousers were open; his member erect. Perhaps, later, they would go to his mistress together, he and the thief. Drink vodka like old friends. He grinned at Whitehead. "I told them you'd come eventually. I knew you would. To see us again."

Whitehead raised the gun he still had in his hand, and fired at the lieutenant. The illusion was not interrupted by this violence, however, merely reinforced. Shouts—in Russian—echoed from beyond the square.

"Now look what you've done," Vasiliev said. "Now the soldiers will come."

The thief recognized his error. He had never used a gun after a curfew: it was an invitation to arrest. He heard booted feet running, close by.

"We must hurry," the lieutenant insisted, casually spitting out the bullet, which he had caught between his teeth.

"I'm not going with you," Whitehead said.

"But we've waited so long," Vasiliev replied, and shook the branch to cue the next act. The tree raised its limbs like a bride, shrugging off its trousseau of blossom. Within moments the air was thick with a blizzard of petals. As they settled, spilling their radiance onto the ground, the thief began to pick out the familiar faces that waited beneath the branches. People who, down the years, had come to this wasteland, to this tree, and gathered under it with Vasiliev, to rot and weep. Evangeline was among them, the wounds that had been so tastefully concealed as she'd lain in her coffin now freely displayed. She did not smile, but she stretched her arms out to embrace him, her mouth forming his name—"Jojo"—as she stepped forward. Bill Toy was behind her, in evening dress, as if for the Academy. His ears bled. Beside him, her face opened from lip to brow, was a woman in a nightgown. There were others too, some of whom he recognized, many of whom he didn't. The woman who'd led him to the card-player was there, bare-breasted, as he remembered her. Her smile was as distressing as ever. There were soldiers too, others who'd lost to Mamoulian like Vasiliev. One wore a skirt in addition to his bullet-holes. From under its folds a snout appeared. Saul—his carcass ravaged—sniffed his old master, and growled.

"See how long we've waited?" Vasiliev said.

The lost faces were all looking at Whitehead, their mouths open. No sound emerged.

"I can't help you."

"We want to cease," the lieutenant said.

"Go, then."

"Not without you. He won't die without you."

Finally the thief understood. This place, which he'd glimpsed in the sauna at the Sanctuary, existed within the European. These ghosts were creatures he'd devoured. Evangeline! Even she. They waited, the tattered remains of them, in this no-man's-land between flesh and death, until Mamoulian sickened of existence and lay down and perished. Then they too, presumably, would have their liberty. Until then their faces would make that soundless O at him, a melancholy appeal.

The thief shook his head.

"No," he said.

He would not give up his breath. Not for an *orchard* of trees, not for a *nation* of despairing faces. He turned his back on Muranowski Square and its plaintive ghosts. The soldiers were shouting nearby: soon they would arrive. He looked back toward the hotel. The penthouse corridor was still there, across the doorstep of a bombed house: a surreal juxtaposition of ruin and luxury. He crossed the rubble toward it, ignoring the soldiers' orders for him to halt. Vasiliev's cries were loudest, however. "Bastard!" he screeched. The thief blocked his curses and stepped out of the square and back into the heat of the hallway, raising his gun as he did so.

"Old news," he said, "you don't scare me with it." Mamoulian was still standing at the other end of the corridor; the minutes the thief had spent in the square had not elapsed here. "I'm not afraid!" Whitehead shouted. "You hear me, you soulless bastard? *I'm not afraid!*" He fired again, this time at the European's head. The shot hit his cheek. Blood came. Before Whitehead could fire again, Mamoulian retaliated.

"There are no limits," he said, his voice trembling, "to what I shall do!"

His thought caught the thief by the throat, and twisted. The old man's limbs convulsed; the gun flew out of his hand; his bladder and bowels failed him. Behind him, in the square, the ghosts began to applaud. The tree shook itself with such vehemence that the few blossoms it still carried were swept into the air. Some of them flew toward the door, melting on the threshold of past and present, like snowflakes. Whitehead fell against the wall. Out of the corner of his eye he caught sight of

Evangeline, spitting blood at him. He began to slide down the
wall, his body jangled as if in the throes of a grand mal. He let
out one word through his rattling jaws. He said:

"No!"

On the bathroom floor Marty heard the denial howled out. He
tried to stir himself, but his consciousness was sluggish, and his
beaten body ached from scalp to skin. Taking hold of the bath, he
hoisted himself to his knees. He'd clearly been forgotten: his part
in the proceedings was purely comic relief. He tried to stand, but
his lower limbs were traitorous; they buckled beneath him, and
he fell again, feeling every bruise on impact.

In the hallway Whitehead had sunk down onto his haunches,
mouth gaga. The European moved in for the *coup de grâce*, but
Carys interrupted.

"Leave him," she said.

Distracted, Mamoulian turned toward her. The blood on his
cheek had traced a single line to his jaw. "You too," he murmured.
"No limits." Carys backed off into the gaming room. The candle
on the table had begun to flare. Energy was loose in the suite, and
the spitting flame was fat and white on it. The European looked
at Carys with hunger in his eyes. There was an appetite on him—
an instinctive response to his blood loss—and all he could see
in her was nourishment. Like the thief: hungry for another
strawberry though his belly was full enough.

"I know what you are," Carys said, deflecting his gaze.

From the bathroom, Marty heard her ploy. Stupid, he thought,
to tell him that.

"I know what you did."

The European's eyes widened, smoky.

"You're nobody," the girl started to say. "You're just a soldier
who met a monk, and strangled him in his sleep. What have you
got to be so proud of?" Her fury beat against his face. "You're
nobody! Nobody and *nothing!*"

He reached to catch hold of her. She dodged him around the
card table once, but he threw it over, the pack scattering, and

caught her. His hold felt like a vast leech on her arm, taking blood from her and giving only the void, only purposeless dark. He was the Architect of her dreams again.

"God help me," she breathed. Her senses crumbled and grayness streamed in to take their place. He pulled her out of her body with one insolent wrench and took her into him, dropping her husk to the floor beside the overturned table. He wiped his mouth with the back of his hand and looked up at the evangelists. They were standing in the doorway staring at him. He felt sick with his greed. She was in him—all of her at once—and it was too much. And the Saints were making it worse, looking at him as though he were something loathsome, the dark one shaking his head. "You killed her," he said. "You killed her."

The European turned away from the accusations, his system boiling over, and leaned elbow and forearm on the wall like a drunk about to vomit. Her presence in him was a torment. It wouldn't be still, it raged and raged. And her turbulence unlocked so much more: Strauss piercing his bowels; the dogs at his heels, unleashing blood and smoke; and then back, back beyond these few terrible months to other ordeals: yards and snow and starlight and women and hunger, always hunger. And still at his back he felt the stare of the Christians.

One of them spoke; the blond boy whom once he might have lusted after. He, and she, and all.

"Is this all there is?" he demanded to know. "Is this all, you fucking liar? You promised us the Deluge."

The European pressed his hand over his mouth to stem the escaping smoke and pictured a wave curling over the hotel, over the city, descending to sweep Europe away.

"Don't tempt me," he said.

In the hallway Whitehead, his neck broken, became vaguely aware of a perfume in the air. He could see the landing outside the suite from where he was lying. Muranowski Square, with its fatal tree, had long since faded, leaving only the mirrors and the carpets. Now, as he sprawled beside the door, he heard somebody come up the stairs. He glimpsed a figure moving in the shadows; *this* was the perfumed one. The newcomer approached slowly, but doggedly; hesitating for only a moment at the threshold before stepping over Whitehead's crumpled form and making his way toward the room where the two men had played cards. There had been a while, as they'd chatted over the game, that the old man had fancied he might yet make a fresh covenant with the European; might escape for a few more years the inevitable catastrophe. But it had all gone wrong. They had rowed over some trivia, the way lovers do, and by some incomprehensible mathematic it had escalated to this: death.

He rolled himself over so that he could look the other way, down the corridor toward the gaming room. Carys was lying on the floor among the spilled cards. He could see her corpse through the open door. The European had devoured her.

Now the newcomer interrupted his view as he lurched to the door. From where he lay Whitehead hadn't been able to see the man's face. But he saw the shine on the machete at his side.

Tom caught sight of the Razor-Eater before Chad. His unruly stomach rebelled at the mingled stench of sandalwood and putrefaction, and he threw up on the old man's bed as Breer stepped into the room. He'd come a long way, and the miles had not been kind, but he was here.

Mamoulian stood upright from the wall and faced Breer.

He was not entirely surprised to see that rotted face, though he wasn't sure why. Was it that his mind had not quite relinquished its hold on the Razor-Eater, and that Breer was somehow here at his behest? Breer stared at Mamoulian through the bright air, as if awaiting a new instruction before he acted again. The muscles of his face were so deteriorated that each flicker of his eyeball threatened to tear the skin of its orbit. He looked, thought Chad—

his mind high on cognac—like a man full to bursting with butterflies. Their wings beat against the confines of his anatomy; they powdered his bones in their fervor. Soon their relentless motion would split him open and the air would be full of them.

The European looked down at the machete Breer was carrying. "Why did you come?" he wanted to know.

The Razor-Eater tried to reply, but his tongue rebelled against the duty. There was just a soft palate word that could have been "good," or "got" or "God," but was none of them.

"Have you come to be killed? Is that it?"

Breer shook his head. He had no such intention, and Mamoulian knew it. Death was the least of his problems. He raised the blade at his side to signal his intentions.

"I can wipe you out," Mamoulian said.

Again, Breer shook his head. "Egg," he said, which Mamoulian interpreted, and repeated as "Dead."

"Dead . . ." Chad mused. "God in Heaven. The man's dead."

The European murmured the affirmative.

Chad smiled. Maybe they were going to be cheated of the destroying wave. Perhaps the Reverend's calculations had been wrong, and the Deluge wouldn't be on them for a few more months. What did it matter? He had stories to tell—such stories. Even Bliss, with all his talk of the demons in the soul of the hemisphere, hadn't known about scenes like this. The Saint watched, licking his lips with anticipation.

In the hallway, Whitehead had managed to drag himself three or four yards away from the front door, and he could see Marty, who had managed to stand. Leaning on the lintel of the bathroom door, Marty felt the old man's eyes on him. Whitehead raised a beckoning hand. Groggily, Marty lurched into the hallway, his presence ignored by the actors in the gaming room. It was dark out here; the light in the gaming room, that livid candlelight, was all but sealed off by the partially closed door.

Marty knelt at Whitehead's side. The old man took hold of his shirt.

"You've got to fetch her," he said, the voice almost faded. His eyes bulged, there was blood in his beard, and more coming with each word, but his hold was strong. "Fetch her, Marty," he hissed.

"What are you talking about?"

"He *has* her," Whitehead said. "In him. Fetch her, for Christ's sake, or she'll be there forever, like the others." His eyes flicked in the direction of the landing, remembering the scourge of Muranowski Square. Was she there already? A prisoner under the tree, with Vasiliev's eager hands on her? The old man's lips began to tremble. "Can't . . . let him have her, boy," he said. "You hear me. *Won't* let him have her."

Marty had difficulty sewing the sense of this together. Was Whitehead suggesting that he should find his way into Mamoulian and retrieve Carys? It wasn't possible.

"I can't," he said.

The old man registered disgust, and let go of Marty as though he'd discovered he had hold of excrement. Painfully, he turned his head away.

Marty looked toward the gaming room. Through the gap in the door he could see Mamoulian moving toward the unmistakable figure of the Razor-Eater. There was frailty on the European's face. Marty studied it for a moment, and then looked down at the European's feet. Carys lay there, her face startled by cessation, her skin bright. He could do nothing; why didn't Papa leave him be to run away into the night and heal his bruises? He could do *nothing*.

And if he ran; if he found a place to hide, to heal, would he ever wash away the smell of his cowardice? Would this moment— the roads dividing, and dividing again—not be burned into his dreams forever? He looked back at Papa. But for the feeble movement of his lips he could have already been dead. "Fetch her," he was still saying, a catechism to be repeated until his breath failed. "Fetch her. Fetch her."

Marty had asked something similar of Carys—to go into the lunatic's lair and come back with a story to tell. How could he now not return the favor? *Fetch her. Fetch her.* Papa's words were fading with every beat of his failing heart. Maybe she *was* retrievable, Marty thought, somewhere in the flux of Mamoulian's body. And if not, if not, would it be so hard to die trying to fetch her, and have an end to roads dividing, and choices turning to ash?

But how? He tried to recall how she'd done it, but the procedures were too elaborate—the washing, the silence—and surely he had scant opportunity to make his voyage before circumstances changed. His only source of hope lay in the fact of his bloody shirt—the way he'd felt, on his way here, that Carys had snapped some barrier in his head, and that the damage, once done, was permanent. Perhaps his mind could go to her through the wound she'd opened, tracing her scent as relentlessly as she'd pursued his.

He closed his eyes, shutting off the hallway and Whitehead and the body lying at the European's feet. Sight was a trap; she'd said that once. Effort too. He must let go. Let instinct and imagination take him where sense and intellect could not.

He conjured her, effortlessly, putting the bleak fact of her corpse out of his head and evoking instead her living smile. In his mind he spoke her name and she came to him in a dozen moments: laughing, naked, puzzled, contrite. But he let the particulars go, leaving only her essential presence in his aching head.

He was dreaming her. The wound was open, and it pained him to touch it again. Blood was running into his open mouth, but the sensation was a distant phenomenon. It had little to do with his present condition, which was increasingly dislocated. He felt as though he was slipping his body off. It was redundant: waste matter. The ease of the procedure astonished him; his only anxiety was that he'd become too eager; he had to control his exhilaration for fear he throw caution to the wind and be discovered.

He could see nothing; hear nothing. The state he moved in— did he even move?—was not susceptible to the senses. Now, though he had no proof of the perception, he was sure he was abstracted from his body. It was behind, below him: an untenanted shell. Ahead of him, Carys. He would dream his way to her.

And then, just as he thought he could take pleasure in this extraordinary journey, Hell opened in front of him—

Mamoulian, too intent on the Razor-Eater, felt nothing as Marty breached him. Breer made a half-run forward, lifting the machete and aiming a blow at the European. He sidestepped to avoid it with perfect economy but Breer pivoted around for a second strike with startling speed, and this time, more by chance than direction, the machete glanced down Mamoulian's arm, slicing into the cloth of his dark gray suit.

"Chad," the European said, not taking his eyes off Breer.

"Yes?" the blond boy replied. He was still leaning on the wall beside the door, posed there like an indolent hero; he had found Whitehead's cache of cigars, pocketing several and lighting one. He blew a cloud of dusty blue smoke, and watched the gladiators through a blur of drink. "What do you want?"

"Find the pilgrim's gun."

"Why?"

"For our visitor."

"Kill him yourself," Chad replied nonchalantly, "you can do it."

Mamoulian's mind revolted at the thought of laying his flesh on such decay; better a bullet. At close range it would lay the Razor-Eater to waste. Without a head even the dead couldn't walk.

"Fetch the gun!" he demanded.

"No," Chad replied. The Reverend had said plain speaking was best.

"This is no time for games," Mamoulian said, taking his attention off Breer for a moment to glance across at Chad. It was an error. The dead man swung the machete again, and this time the blow found Mamoulian's shoulder, lodging in the muscle close to his neck. The European made no sound but a grunt as the blow fell, and a second as Breer pulled the blade out of its niche.

"Stop," he told his assailant.

Breer shook his head. This was what he had come for, wasn't it? This was the prelude to an act he'd waited so long to perform.

Mamoulian put his hand up to the wound at his shoulder. Bullets he could take and survive; but a more traumatic attack, one that compromised the integrity of his flesh—that was dangerous. He had to finish Breer off, and if the Saint wouldn't fetch the gun then he'd have to kill the Razor-Eater with his bare hands.

Breer seemed to sense his intention. "You can't hurt me," he tried to say, the words coming out in a jumble. "I'm dead."

Mamoulian shook his head. "Limb from limb," he murmured. "If I must. Limb from limb."

Chad grinned, hearing the European's promise. Sweet Jesus, he thought, this was the way the world would end. A warren of rooms, cars on the freeway winding their last way home, the dead and almost dead exchanging blows by candlelight. The Reverend had been wrong. The Deluge wasn't a wave, was it? It was blind men with axes; it was the great on their knees begging not to die at the hands of idiots; it was the itch of the irrational grown to an epidemic. He watched, and thought of how he would describe this scene to the Reverend, and for the first time in his nineteen years his pretty head felt a spasm of pure joy.

Marty hadn't realized how pleasurable the experience of travel had been—a passenger of pure thought—until he plunged into Mamoulian's body. He felt like a skinned man immersed in boiling oil. He thrashed, his essence screeching for an end to this Hell of another man's physicality. But Carys was here. He had to keep that thought uppermost, a touchstone.

In this maelstrom his feelings for her had the purity of mathematics. Its equations—complex, but elegant in their proofs—offered a nicety that was like truth. He had to hold on to this recognition. If he once relinquished it he was lost.

Though without senses, he felt this new state struggling to impinge a vision of itself upon him. At the corners of his blind eyes lights flared—perspective opened up and closed again in an instant—suns threatened to ignite overhead and were snuffed out before they could shed warmth or illumination. Some irritation possessed him: an itch of lunacy. Scratch me, it said, and you needn't sweat anymore. He countered the seduction with thoughts of Carys.

Gone, the itch said, deeper than you'd dare to go. So much deeper.

What it claimed was perhaps true. He'd swallowed her whole, taken her down to wherever he kept his favorite things. To the place where the zero he'd tampered with at Caliban Street was sourced. Face-to-face with such a vacuum he would shrivel: there would be no reprieve this time. Such a place, the itch said, such a terrible place. You want to see?

No.

Come on, look! Look and tremble! Look and cease! You wanted to know what he *was*, well you're about to get a worm's-eye view.

I'm not listening, Marty thought. He pressed on, and though—like Caliban Street—there was no up or down, no forward or back in this place, he had a sense of descent. Was it just the metaphors he carried with him, that he pictured Hell as a pit? Or was he crawling through the European's innards to the bowel where Carys was hidden?

Of course you'll never get out, the itch said with a smile. Not once you get down there. There's no way back. He'll never shit you out. You'll stay locked up in there, once and for all.

Carys got out, he reasoned.

She was in his head, the itch reminded him. She was flipping through his library. You're buried in the dung-heap; and *deep*, oh, yes, my man, so *deep*.

No!

For certain.

No!

Mamoulian shook his head. It was full of strange aches; voices too. Or was that just the past chattering to him? Yes, the past. It had buzzed and gossiped in his ear more loudly in these recent weeks than ever in the preceding decades. Whenever his mind had idled, the gravity of history had claimed it, and he had been back in the monastery yard with the snow falling and the drummer-boy at his right-hand side quaking, and the parasites leaving the bodies as they cooled. Two hundred years of life had sprung from that conspiracy of moments. Had the shot that killed the executioner been delayed by mere seconds the sword would have fallen, his head would have rolled, and the centuries he'd lived would not have contained him; nor he they.

And why did this cycle of thoughts return now, as he looked at Anthony across the room? They were a thousand miles and seventeen decades from that event. I'm not in danger, he chided himself, so why quake? Breer was teetering on the edge of total collapse; dispatching him was a simple, if distasteful, task.

He moved suddenly, his good hand snatching at Breer's throat before the other had a chance to retaliate. The European's slender fingers dug through the mush and closed around Breer's esophagus. Then he pulled, hard. A goodly portion of Breer's neck came away in a splutter of grease and fluids. There was a sound like escaping steam.

Chad applauded, cigar in mouth. In the corner where he'd collapsed Tom had stopped whimpering and was also watching the mutilation. One man fighting for his life, the other for his death. Hallelujah! Saints and sinners all together.

Mamoulian flung the fistful of muck away. Despite his formidable injury, the Razor-Eater was still standing.

"Must I tear you apart?" Mamoulian said. Even as he spoke, something scrabbled inside him. Was the girl still fighting her confinement?

"Who's there?" he asked softly.

Carys answered. Not to Mamoulian, but to Marty. Here, she said. He heard her. No, not heard: *felt*. She summoned him, and he followed.

The itch in Marty was in seventh heaven. Too late to help her, it said: too late for *anything* now.

But she was close by, he knew it, her presence choking back his panic. I'm with you, she said. Two of us now.

The itch was unimpressed. It smirked at the thought of escape. You're sealed up forever, it said, better concede it. If *she* can't get out, why should you be able to?

Two, Carys said. *Two of us now.* For the frailest of moments he caught the intention in her words. They were together, and together they were more than a sum of their parts. He thought of their locking anatomies—the physical act that was metaphor for this other unity. He'd never understood until now. His mind jubilated. She was with him: he with her. They were one indivisible thought, imagining each other.

Go!

And Hell divided; it had no choice. The province fragmented as they delivered themselves out of the European's grasp. They experienced a few exquisite moments as one mind, and then gravity—or whatever law pertained in this state—demanded its lot. Division came—a rude expulsion from this momentary Eden—and they were plummeting now toward their own bodies, the conjunction over.

Mamoulian felt their escape as a wounding more traumatic than any Breer had so far delivered. He put his finger up to his mouth, a look of pitiful loss on his face. Tears came freely, diluting the blood on his face. Breer seemed to sense a cue in this: his moment had come. An image had spontaneously appeared in his liquefying brain—like one of the grainy photographs in his book of atrocities—except that this image moved. Snow fell; the flames of a brazier danced.

The machete in his hand felt heavier by the second: more like a sword. He raised it; its shadow fell across the European's face.

Mamoulian looked at Breer's ruined features and recognized them; saw how it had all come to this moment. Bowed under a weight of years, he fell to his knees.

As he was doing so, Carys opened her eyes. There had been a vile, grinding return; more terrible for Marty than for herself, who was used to the sensation. But it was never entirely pleasant to feel muscle and fat congeal around the spirit.

Marty's eyes had opened too, and he was looking down at the body he occupied. It was heavy, and stale. So much of it—the layers of skin, the hair, the nails—was dead matter. Its very substance revolted him. Being in this state was a parody of the freedom he'd just tasted. He started up from his slumped position with a small cry of disgust, as if he'd woken to find his body crawling with insects.

He looked across to Carys for reassurance, but her attention had been claimed by a sight concealed from Marty by the partially closed door.

She was watching a spectacle she knew from somewhere. But the point of view was different, and it took a while for her to place the scene: the man on his knees, his neck exposed, his arms spread a little from his body, fingers splayed in the universal gesture of submission; the executioner, face blurred, raising the blade to decapitate his willing victim; somebody laughing somewhere nearby.

The last time she'd seen this tableau she'd been behind Mamoulian's eyes, a soldier in a snow-spattered yard, awaiting the blow that would cancel his young life. A blow that had never come; or rather had been deferred until now. Had the executioner waited so long, living in one body only to discard it for another, trailing Mamoulian through decade upon decade until at last fate assembled the pieces of a reunion? Or was this all the European's doing? Had his will summoned Breer to finish a story accidentally interrupted generations before?

She would never know. The act, begun a second time, was not

to be postponed again. The weapon sliced down, almost dividing head from neck in one blow. A few tenacious sinews kept it rocking—nose to chest—from the trunk for two succeeding blows before it departed, rolling down between the European's legs and coming to rest at Tom's feet. The boy kicked it away.

Mamoulian had made no sound; but now, headless, his torso gave vent. Noise came from the wound with the blood; complaints sounded, it seemed, from every pore. And with the sound came smoky ghosts of unmade pictures, rising from him like steam. Bitter things appeared and fled; dreams, perhaps, or fragments of the past. It was all one now. Always had been, in fact. He had come from rumor; he the legendary, he the unfixable, he whose very name was a lie. Could it matter if now his biography, fleeing into nothingness, was taken as fiction?

Breer, unassuaged, began to berate the open wound of the corpse's neck with the machete, slicing first down then sideways in an effort to cleave the enemy into smaller and yet smaller pieces. An arm was summarily lopped off; he picked it up to sever hand from wrist, forearm from upper arm. In moments the room, which had been almost serene as the execution took place, became an abattoir.

Marty stumbled to the door in time to see Breer strike off Mamoulian's other arm.

"Look at him go!" said the American boy, toasting the bloodbath with Whitehead's vodka.

Marty watched the carnage, unblenched. It was all over. The European was a dead man. His head lay on its side under the window; it looked small; vestigial.

Carys, flattened against the wall beside the door, caught Marty's hand.

"Papa?" she said. "What about Papa?"

As she spoke Mamoulian's corpse pitched forward from its kneeling position. The ghosts and the din it had spilled had stopped. Now there was only dark blood splashing from it. Breer bent to further butchery, opening the abdomen with two slashes. Urine fountained from the punctured bladder.

Carys, revolted by the attacks, slipped out of the room. Marty lingered awhile longer. The last sight he caught as he followed Carys was the Razor-Eater picking up the head by the hair, like some exotic fruit, and delivering a lateral cut to it.

In the hallway Carys was crouching at her father's side; Marty joined her. She stroked the old man's cheek. "Papa?" she said. He wasn't dead, but neither was he truly alive. There was a flicker in his pulse, no more. His eyes were closed.

"No use . . ." Marty said as she shook the old man's shoulder, "he's as good as gone."

In the gaming room Chad had begun to shriek with laughter. Apparently the slaughterhouse scenes were reaching new heights of absurdist brio.

"I don't want to be here when he gets bored," Marty said. Carys made no move. "There's nothing we can do for the old man," he said.

She looked at him, bewildered by the dilemma.

"He's gone, Carys. And we should go too."

A silence had started in the abattoir. It was worse, in its way, than the laughter, or the sound of Breer's labors.

"We can't wait around," Marty said. He roughly pulled Carys to her feet and propelled her toward the front door of the penthouse. She made only faint objection.

As they slipped away downstairs, somewhere up above them the blond American began to applaud again.

72

The dead man worked at his work for a good time. Long after the domestic traffic on the highway had dwindled to a trickle, leaving only the long-distance freight drivers to roar their way north. Breer heard none of it. His ears had long since given out, and his eyesight, once so sharp, could barely make sense of the carnage that now lay on every side of him. But when his sight failed completely, he still had the rudiments of touch. This he used to finish his commission, dividing and subdividing the flesh of the European until it was impossible to tell apart the piece that spoke and the piece that pissed.

Chad tired of the entertainment long before that point was reached. Grinding out his second cigar with his heel he sauntered through to see how things were progressing elsewhere. The girl had gone; the hero too. God loves them, he thought. The old man was still lying in the hallway, however, clutching the gun, which he'd retrieved at some point in the proceedings. His fingers spasmed once in a while, nothing more. Chad went back into the bloody chamber, where Breer was on his knees among the meat and the cards, still chopping, and raised Tom off the floor. He was in a languid state, his lips almost blue, and it took a good deal of cajoling to get any action out of him. But Chad was a born proselytizer, and a short talk got some enthusiasm back into him. "Nothin' we can't do now, you know?" Chad told him. "We're baptized men. I mean we've seen *everything*, haven't we? There ain't nothing in this whole wide world the Devil can fight us with, because we've been there. Ain't we been there?"

Chad was high on his new-found freedom. He wanted to prove the point, and he had this fine idea—"You'll like this, Tommy"— of doing a dump on the old man's chest. Tom didn't seem to care either way, and he just watched while Chad dropped his trousers to do the dirty work. His bowels would not oblige. As he started to stand upright, however, Whitehead's eyes snapped open, and the gun fired. The bullet missed plowing into Chad's testicles by a hairbreadth but scored a fine red mark on the inside of his milk-white thigh, and whistled past his face to slam into the ceiling. Chad's bowels gave then, but the old man was dead; he'd died with the shot that came so close to blowing off Chad's manhood.

"Near thing," Tom said, his catatonia broken by Chad's near-mutiliation.

"Guess I'm just lucky," the blond boy replied. Then they took their revenges as best they could, and went their way.

I'm the last of the tribe, thought Breer. When I'm gone the Razor-Eaters will be a thing of the past.

He hauled himself from the Pandemonium Hotel knowing that what coherence his body had was fast diminishing. His fingers could barely grip the petrol can he'd stolen from the boot of a car before he'd come to the hotel, and had left, awaiting these last rites, in the foyer. It was as difficult to grasp with his mind as it was with his fingers, but he did the best he could. He couldn't name the things that sniffed at his carcass as he squatted among the rubbish; couldn't even remember who he was, except that he had seen, once, some fine and wonderful sights.

He twisted the cap off the petrol can and spilled the contents over him as efficiently as he could. Most of the fluid simply pooled around him. Then he dropped the can and ferreted, blind, for the matches. The first and second didn't catch. The third did. Flames instantly engulfed him. In the conflagration his body curled up, taking on that pugilistic attitude common to the victims of immolation, the joints shortening as they cooked, drawing arms and legs up into a posture of defense.

When, at last, the flames went out, the dogs came to scavenge what they could. More than one of them went away yelping, however, their palates slit by a mouthful of meat in which, secreted like pearls in an oyster, were the razor blades Breer had downed like a gourmet.

XIV. AFTER THE WAVE

73

Wind had the world.

It blew exactly east-west that evening, carrying the clouds, buoyant after a day of rain, in the direction of the setting sun, as if they were hurrying to some Apocalypse just over the horizon. Or perhaps—this thought was worse—they were rushing to persuade the sun to back up from oblivion for another hour, another minute—anything to delay the night. And of course it wouldn't come, and instead the sun was taking advantage of their fleecy-headed panic to steal them over the edge of the world.

Carys had tried to persuade Marty that all was well, but she hadn't succeeded. Now, as he hurried toward the Orpheus Hotel once more, with the clouds suicidal and the night coming down, he sensed the rightness of his suspicions. The whole visible world carried evidence of conspiracy.

Besides, Carys still spoke in her sleep. Not with Mamoulian's voice perhaps, that cautious, looping, ironic voice that he'd come to know and hate. She didn't even make words as such. Just scraps of sound: the noise of crabs, of birds trapped in an attic. Whirrs and scratchings, as though she, or something in her, was laboring to reinvent a forgotten vocabulary. There was nothing human in it as yet, but he was certain the European was in hiding there. The more he listened the more he seemed to hear order in the muttering; the more the noise her sleeping tongue made sounded like a palate seeking after speech. The thought made him sweat.

And then, the night before this night of rushing clouds, he'd been startled awake at four in the morning. There were dreadful dreams, of course, and would, he supposed, be dreams for many years to come. But tonight they were not confined to his head. They were here. They were now.

Carys was not lying beside him in the narrow bed. She was standing in the middle of the room, her eyes closed, her face infested with tiny, inexpliable tics. She was talking again, or at least attempting to, and this time he *knew*, knew without a shadow of a doubt that somehow Mamoulian was still with her.

He said her name, but she made no sign of waking. Getting up out of bed he crossed the room toward her, but as he made his move the air around them seemed to bleed darkness. Her chattering took on a more urgent pitch, and he sensed the darkness solidifying. His face and chest began to itch; his eyes stung.

Again he called her name, shouting now. There was no response. Shadows had begun to flit across her, though there was no light in the room that could have cast them. He stared at her gabbling face: the shadows resembled those cast by light through blossom-laden boughs, as though she were standing in the shade of a tree.

Above him, something sighed. He looked up. The ceiling had disappeared. In its place a spreading tracery of branches, growing even as he watched. Her words were at its root, he had no doubt of it, and it grew stronger and more intricate with every syllable she spoke. The boughs rippled as they swelled, sprouting twigs that in seconds grew heavy with foliage. But despite its health, the tree was corrupted in every bud. Its leaves were black, and shone not with sap but with the sweat of putrescence. Vermin scuttled up and down the branches; fetid blossoms fell like snow, leaving the fruit exposed.

Such terrible fruit! A sheaf of knives, tied up in a ribbon like a gift for an assassin. A child's head hung up by its plaited hair. One branch was looped with human intestine; from another a cage depended, in which a bird was burning alive. Mementos all; keepsakes of past atrocities. And was the collector here, among his souvenirs?

Something moved in the turbulent darkness above Marty, and

it was no rat. He could hear whispers exchanged. There were human beings up there, resting in the rot. And they were climbing down to have him join them.

He reached through the boiling air and took hold of Carys' arm. It felt mushy, as though the flesh was about to come away in his hand. Beneath her lids, she rolled her eyes like a stage lunatic; her mouth still shaping the words that conjured the tree.

"*Stop*," he said, but she only chattered on.

He took hold of her with both hands and shouted for her to shut up, shaking her as he did so. Above them, the boughs creaked; a litter of twigs fell down on him.

"Wake up, damn you," he told her. "Carys! This is Marty; *me, Marty!* Wake up, for Christ's sake."

He felt something in his hair, and glanced up to see a woman spitting a pearl-thread of saliva down upon him. It spattered on his face, ice-cold. Panic mounting, he started to yell at Carys to make her stop, and when that failed he slapped her hard across the face. For an instant the flow of conjuring was interrupted. The tree and its inhabitants complained with growls. He slapped her again, harder. The fever behind her lids had begun to abate, he saw. He called to her again, and shook her. Her mouth lolled open; the tics and terrible intentionality left her face. The tree trembled.

"Please . . ." he begged her, "wake up."

The black leaves shrank upon themselves; the fevered limbs lost their ambition.

She opened her eyes.

Murmuring its chagrin, the rot rotted and went away into nothingness.

The mark of his hand was still ripening on her cheek, but she was apparently unaware of his blows. Her voice was blurred by sleep as she said:

"What's wrong?"

He held her tight, not having any answer he felt brave enough to voice. He only said:

"You were dreaming."

She looked at him, puzzled. "I don't remember," she said; and then, becoming aware of his trembling hands: "What's happened?"

"A nightmare," he said.

"Why am I out of bed?"

"I was trying to wake you."

She stared at him. "I don't want to be woken," she said. "I'm tired enough as it is." She disengaged herself. "I want to go back to bed."

He let her return to the crumpled sheets and lie down. She was asleep again before he had crossed to her. He did not join her, but sat up until dawn, watching her sleep, and trying to keep the memories at bay.

'm going back to the hotel," he told her in the middle of the next day; this very day. He'd hoped she might have some explanation for the events of the previous night—frail hope!—that she might tell him it was some stray illusion that she had managed at last to spit out. But she had no such reassurances to offer. When he asked her if she remembered anything of the preceding night she replied that she dreamed nothing these nights, and was glad of it. *Nothing*. He repeated the word like a death sentence, thinking of the empty room in Caliban Street; of how *nothing* was the essence of his fear.

Seeing his distress, she reached across to him and touched his face. His skin was hot. It was raining outside, but the room was clammy.

"The European's dead," she told him.

"I have to see for myself."

"There's no need, babe."

"If he's dead and gone, why do you talk in your sleep?"

"Do I?"

"Talk; and make illusions."

"Maybe I'm writing a book," she said. The attempt at levity

was stillborn. "We've got plenty of problems without going back there."

That was true; there was much to decide. How to tell this story, for one; and how to be believed for another. How to give themselves into the hands of the law and not be accused of murders known and unknown. There was a fortune waiting for Carys somewhere; she was her father's sole beneficiary. That too was a reality that had to be faced.

"Mamoulian's dead," she told him. "Can't we forget about him for a while? When they find the bodies we'll tell the whole story. But not yet. I want to rest for a few days."

"You made something appear last night. Here, in this room. I saw it."

"Why are you so certain it's me?" she retorted. "Why should *I* be the one who's still obsessed? Are you sure it isn't *you* who's keeping this alive?"

"Me?"

"Not able to let it go."

"Nothing would make me happier!"

"Then forget it, damn you! Let it be, Marty! He's gone. Dead and gone! And that's the end of it!"

She left him to turn the accusation over in his head. Maybe it *was* him; maybe he'd just dreamed the tree, and was blaming her for his own paranoia. But in her absence his doubts conspired. How could he trust her? If the European *was* alive—somehow, somewhere—couldn't he put those arguments into her mouth, to keep Marty from interfering? He spent the time she was out in an agony of indecision, not knowing a way forward that wasn't tainted with suspicion, but lacking the strength to face the hotel again, and so prove the matter one way or the other.

Then, in the late afternoon, she'd returned. They'd said nothing, or very little, and after a while she'd gone back to bed, complaining of an aching head. After half an hour sharing the room with her sleeping presence, hearing only her even breath (no chatter this time), he'd gone out for whisky and a paper, scanning it for news of discovery or pursuit. There was nothing. World events dominated; where there were not cyclones or wars there were cartoons and racing results. He headed back to the flat prepared to forget his doubts, to tell her that she'd been right all along, only to find the bedroom locked and from the inside her voice—softened by sleep—stumbling toward a new coherence.

He broke in and tried to wake her, but this time neither shaking nor slaps made any impression upon her possessed slumber.

74

And he was almost there now. He wasn't dressed for the cold that was creeping on, and he shivered as he crossed the desolation to the Hotel Pandemonium. Autumn was making its presence felt early this year, not even waiting for the beginning of September to chill the air. In the weeks since he'd last stood on this spot the summer had given in to rain and wind. He was not unhappy with its desertion. Summer heat in small rooms would never have benign associations for him again.

He looked up at the hotel. It was coral-colored in the sliding light—the details of scorch marks and graffiti looked almost too real. A portrait by an obsessive, each detail in absolute focus. He watched the façade awhile, to see if something signaled to him. Perhaps a window might wink, a door grimace; anything to prepare him for what he might discover inside. But it remained politic. Just a solid building, face staled with age and flame, catching the last light of the day.

The front door had been closed by the last visitor to leave the hotel, but no attempt had been made to replace the boards. Marty pushed, and the door opened, grinding across the plaster and dirt on the floor. Inside, nothing had changed. The chandelier tinkled as a gust from outside trespassed into the sanctum; a dry rain of dust flitted down.

As he climbed the first two flights, a smell began to infiltrate; something riper than damp or ash. Presumably the bodies would still be where they'd been left. Substantial decay would have set in. He didn't know how long such processes took, but after the experiences of recent weeks he was prepared for the worst; even the strengthening smell as he ascended scarcely touched him.

He halted halfway up and took out the bottle of Scotch he'd bought, unscrewed the top, and, still eyeing the remaining flights of stairs, put the bottle to his lips. The mouthful of spirits sluiced his gums and throat, and scorched its way down into his belly. He resisted the temptation to take a second swig. Instead, he resealed the bottle and pocketed it before continuing up.

Memories began to besiege him. He'd hoped to keep them at bay, but they came unbidden, and he wasn't strong enough to resist them. There were no pictures, just voices. They echoed around his skull as if it were empty, as if he were simply some mindless brute answering the call of a superior mind. The urge to turn tail and run came over him, but he knew that if he capitulated now, and went back to her, the qualms would only deepen. Soon he'd be suspecting every twitch of her arm, wondering if the European was preparing her for murder. It would be another kind of prison: its walls suspicion, its bars doubt, and he'd be sentenced to it for the rest of his life. Even if Carys left, wouldn't he still be glancing over his shoulder as the years passed, watching for a someone to appear who had a face behind his face, and the European's unforgiving eyes?

And still, with every step taken, his fears multiplied. He gripped the filthy banister, and forced himself onward and upward. I don't want to go, the child in him complained. Don't make me go, please. Easy enough to turn around, easy enough to delay the whole thing. Look! Your feet will do it, just say the word. Go back! She'll wake eventually; just be patient. Go back!

And if she doesn't wake? the voice of reason replied. And that made him go on.

As he took another step, something moved on the landing ahead of him. A flea-jump noise, no more; so soft he could barely hear it. A rat, perhaps? Probably. All manner of scavengers would come here, wouldn't they, in the expectation of a feast. He'd preempted that horror too, and was hardened to the thought.

He reached the landing. No rats scurried away from his footfall, at least he saw none. But there was something here. At the head of the stairs a small brown maggot rolled around on the carpet, twisting upon itself in its enthusiasm to get somewhere. Down the stairs probably: into the dark. He didn't look at it too closely. Whatever it was, it was harmless. Let it find a niche to grow fat in, and become a fly in time, if that was its ambition.

He crossed the penultimate landing and started up the final flight of stairs. A few steps up, the smell abruptly worsened. The stench of fetid meat assaulted him, and now, despite the Scotch and all the mental preparation, his innards turned over and over; like the maggot on the carpet, twisting and turning.

He stopped two or three steps up the flight, pulled out his whisky, and took two solid throatfuls, swallowing it so quickly it made his eyes water. Then he continued his ascent. Something soft slid beneath his heel. He looked down. Another maggot, the larger brother of the one below, had been arrested in its descent by his foot: it was squashed to a fatty pulp. He glanced at it for only a second before hurrying on, aware that the sole of his shoe was slimy; either that or he was pressing other such grubs underfoot as he went.

The gulps of liquor had made his head sing; he took the last two dozen steps almost at a run, eager to have the worst over with. By the time he'd reached the top of the stairs, he was breathless. He had an absurd image of himself, a drunkard's fancy, as a messenger coming with news—lost battles, murdered children—to the palace of some fabulous king. Except that the king too was murdered, his battles lost.

He started toward the penthouse; the smell had become so dense it was almost edible. As he had once before, he caught sight of himself in the mirror; he looked down, ashamed, from the frightened face and—God!—the carpet crawled. Not two or three but a dozen or more fat, ragged maggots were laboring, blindly it seemed, to find their way across the carpet, which was stained by their travels. They were like no insect he'd ever seen before, lacking any decipherable anatomy, and all different sizes: some finger-thin, others the size of a baby's fist, their shapeless forms purple, but streaked with yellow. They left trails of slime and blood like wounded slugs. He stepped around them. They'd got fat on meat he'd once debated with. He didn't want to examine them too closely.

But as he pushed open the door of the suite, and stepped, cautiously, into the corridor, an appalling possibility crept into his head and sat there, whispering obscenities. The creatures were everywhere in the suite. The more ambitious of them were scaling the pastel walls, gluing the slivers of their bodies to the wallpaper with seeped fluids, edging up like caterpillars, a peristalsis moving through their lengths. Their direction was arbitrary; some, to judge by their trails, were circling on themselves.

In the dim light of the corridor his worst suspicions merely simmered; but they began to boil when he edged past Whitehead's sprawled body and stepped into the slaughterhouse room, where the light from the highway made a sodium day. Here the creatures were in yet greater abundance. The whole room swarmed with them, from flea-sized fragments to slabs the size of a man's heart, throwing out tattered filaments like tentacles to haul themselves about. Worms, fleas, maggots—a whole new entymology congregated at the place of execution.

Except that these weren't insects, or the larvae of insects: he could see that plainly now. They were pieces of the European's flesh. He was still alive. In pieces, in a thousand senseless pieces, but *alive*.

Breer had been unrelentingly thorough in his destruction, eradicating the European as best his machete and failing hands would allow. But it had not been enough. There was too much stolen life buzzing in Mamoulian's cells; it roared on, in contravention of any sane law, unquenchable. For all his vehemence the Razor-Eater had not finished the European's life, merely subdivided it, leaving it to describe these futile circles. And somewhere in this lunatic's menagerie was a beast with a will, a fragment that still possessed sufficient sense to think itself—albeit stutteringly—into Carys' mind. Perhaps not one piece, perhaps many—a sum of these wandering parts. Marty wasn't interested in its biology. How this obscenity survived was a matter for a madhouse debating society.

He backed out of the room and stood, shivering in the hall. Wind gusted against the window; the glass complained. He listened to the gusts while he worked out what to do next. Down the corridor a piece of filth fell from the wall. He watched it struggle to turn itself over, and then begin the slow ascent again. Just beyond the spot where it labored lay Whitehead. Marty went back to the body.

Charmaine's killers had enjoyed themselves mightily before they left: Whitehead's trousers and underwear had been pulled down, and his groin scrawled on with a knife. His eyes were open; his false teeth had been removed. He stared at Marty, jaw sagging like a delinquent child's. Flies crawled on him; there were patches of decay on his face. But he was dead: which in this world was something. The boys had, as a final insult, defecated on his chest. Flies gathered there too.

In his time Marty had hated this man; loved him too, if only for a day; called him Papa, called him bastard; made love to his daughter and thought himself King of Creation. He'd seen the man in power: a lord. Seen him afraid too: scrabbling for escape like a rat in a fire. He'd seen the old man's odd species of integrity in practice, and found it workable. As fruitful, perhaps, as the affections of more loving men.

He reached across to seal off the stare, but in their zeal the evangelists had cut off Whitehead's lids, and Marty's fingers instead touched the slick of his eyeball. Not tears that wetted it, but rot. He grimaced; withdrew his hand, sickened.

Just to shut off the look on Papa's face he thrust his fingers under the corpse to heave it onto its belly. The body fluids had settled, and his underside was damp and sticky. Gritting his teeth he rolled the man's bulk onto its side, and let gravity pull it over. Now at least the old man didn't have to watch what followed.

Marty stood up. His hands stank. He baptized them liberally with the rest of the Scotch, to cancel the smell. The libation served another purpose: it removed the temptation of the drink. It would be too easy to become muzzy and lose focus on the problem. The enemy was here. It had to be dealt with; put away forever.

He began where he was, in the hall, digging his heels into the pieces of flesh that crawled around Whitehead's body, squashing their stolen life out as best he could. They made no sound, of course, which made the task simpler. They were just worms, he told himself, dumb slivers of mindless life. And it became yet easier as he went up and down the corridor grinding the meat into smears of yellow fat and brown muscle. The beasts succumbed without argument. He began to sweat, working out his revulsion on this human refuse, eyes darting everywhere to make sure he caught each wretched scrap. He felt a smile twitch at the corners of his mouth—now a low laugh, quite without humor, escaped. It was an easy decimation. He was a boy again, killing ants with his thumbs. One! Two! Three! Only these things were slower than the most laden ant, and he could stamp them down at a leisurely pace. All the power and wisdom of the European had come to this muck, and he—Marty Strauss—had been elected to play the God-game, and wipe it away. He had gained, at the last, a terrible authority.

Nothing is essential. The words he'd heard—and spoken—in

Caliban Street at last made absolute sense. Here was the European, proving the bitter syllogism with his own flesh and bone.

When he'd finished his work in the hallway he returned to the main room and began his labors there, his initial revulsion at touching the flesh dwindling, until with time he was snatching pieces from their perches on the wall and flinging them down to be ground out. When he'd done in the gaming room he went to scour the landing and stairs. Finally, when all was still, he returned to the suite and made a bonfire of the curtains from the dressing room, fueled by the table the old man had played cards on, and tindered by the cards themselves, and then went around the room kicking the larger pieces of flesh into the fire, where they spat and curled and were presently consumed. The smaller pieces he scraped up, the laugh still coming intermittently as he flung little rains of meat into the middle of the conflagration. The room rapidly filled with smoke and heat, neither having any escape route. His heart began to pound loudly in his ears; his arms shone with sweat. It was a long job, and he had to be meticulous, didn't he? He mustn't leave a living speck, not a fragment, for fear it live on, become mythical—grow perhaps—and find him.

When the fire died down he fed it the pillows, the records and the paperback books until there was nothing left to burn but himself. There were moments, as he gazed entranced into the flames, that the thought of stepping into the fire was not unattractive. But he resisted. It was only exhaustion tempting him. Instead he crouched in a corner, watching the play of flame-light on the wall. The patterns made him cry; or at least something did.

When, some time before dawn, Carys came up the stairs to claim him from his reverie, he neither heard nor saw her. The fire had long since died down. Only the bones, shattered by Breer's dismembering, and blackened and cracked in the fire, were still recognizable. Shards of thighbone, of vertebrae; the saucer of the European's skull.

She crept in as if fearful of waking a sleeping child. Maybe he *had* been sleeping. There were feathery images in his head that could only have been dreams: life was not that terrible.

"I woke," she said. "I knew you'd be here."

He could barely see her through the grimy air; she was a chalk drawing on black paper: so vulnerable to smudging. The tears came again when he thought of that.

"We must go," she said, not wishing to press him for explanations. Perhaps she would ask him in time, when the plaintive look had left his eyes; perhaps she would never ask. After several minutes of her coaxing him and pressing close to him, he slid up from his knee-hugging meditation and conceded to her care.

When they stepped out of the hotel the wind buffeted them, as antagonistic as ever. Marty looked up to see if the gusts had blown the stars off course, but they were steadfast. Everything was in its place, despite the insanity that had mauled their lives of late, and though she hurried him on, he dawdled, his head back, squinting at the stars. There were no revelations to be had there. Just pinpricks of light in a plain heaven. But he saw for the first time how fine that was. That in a world too full of loss and rage they be remote: the minimum of glory. As she led him across the lightless ground, time and again he could not prevent his gaze from straying skyward.

David Armstrong

Born in Liverpool in 1952, **Clive Barker** has written and produced a number of plays, including *The History of the Devil* and *Frankenstein in Love*, which are as diverse in style and subject as the fiction he has written since. His volumes of short fiction, *Books of Blood*, earned him immediate praise from horror fans and literary critics alike. He won both the British and World Fantasy awards, and was nominated for the coveted Booker Prize, Britain's highest literary award. His bestselling novels include *The Damnation Game*, *Imajica*, *Coldheart Canyon*, *The Thief of Always*, *The Great and Secret Show*, *Everville*, the Abarat series, and *The Scarlet Gospels*. He is also the creator of the now-classic Hellraiser films as well as *Nightbreed* and *Lord of Illusions*.

Ready to find
your next great read?

Let us help.

Visit prh.com/nextread

Penguin
Random
House